LAVISH ACCLAIM FOR
A FIRE IN THE BLOOD

"Fast paced, sizzling, adventurous. A true Western with a strong-spirited heroine and a provocative, hot-blooded hero who will set you on fire. I'm in love with Jess Robbins!"

—Roseanne Bittner

AND FOR SHIRL HENKE'S OTHER HISTORICAL ROMANCES

"White Apache's Woman is a fascinating book, rich in history, wonderful. I enjoyed it thoroughly."

—Heather Graham

Terms of Surrender is "a romantic romp of a Western. I loved it!"

—Georgina Gentry

"Terms of Love is a sexy, sensual romp. Without a doubt, Shirl Henke at her best!"

—Katherine Sutcliffe

"Strong characters, exotic settings, and a wealth of historical detail....*Return to Paradise* swept me away!"

—Virginia Henley

"A riveting story about a fascinating period. I highly recommend *Paradise & More.*"

—Karen Robards

CRITICAL PRAISE FOR SHIRL HENKE'S HISTORICAL ROMANCES!

A FIRE IN THE BLOOD

"You've got every man in the territory jumping through hoops for you."

"Every man but you." Lissa sighed. "I guess that's why I'm interested in you. It surely isn't because of your charming personality."

"So that's it, is it? I'm a challenge?" Jess cocked one eyebrow cynically and looked down at her. "I don't think so, lady. You're a ripe little virgin, all ready for the plucking—curious as hell to find out if the man-woman business is more than just hand holding and moonlight. And here comes the mysterious, forbidden stranger. The last man on earth your daddy'd ever approve of. You want me to do a lot more than just scrape and bow over you like the rest of your legions of admirers, princess."

A FIRE IN THE BLOOD

SHIRL HENKE

LEISURE BOOKS NEW YORK CITY

A LEISURE BOOK®

January 2000

Published by

Dorchester Publishing Co., Inc.
276 Fifth Avenue
New York, NY 10001

Copyright © 1994 by Shirl Henke

ISBN 0-8439-4672-5

Printed in the United States of America.

For my sister, Dorothy Nehrt Jaeger, who handed me my first Frank Yerby novel when I was fourteen years old.

And for my brother-in-law, Kenneth Jaeger, who gave up his elk tag to attend my wedding.

Acknowledgment

This tale of ruthless cattle barons and half-breed gunmen could only have been set on the high plains. Having visited the awesome vastness of Wyoming with its jagged mountain horizon and endless grassy basin lands, I knew it was the place where Lissa and Jess were fated to meet. Having read Owen Wister's classic *The Virginian* at least a dozen times before I was past puberty also encouraged me to select Wyoming.

My associate, Carol J. Reynard, and I had already done several traditional Western romances revolving around the cattle industry, but this one presented particular challenges; chief among them was researching the capital city of Cheyenne.

For assistance, I approached Mrs. Hildegard Schnuttgen, Head of Reference at the Maag Library. As always, she came through for us, locating a rare 1883 directory of the city that contained detailed information about streets, businesses, social and political organizations, even drawings and descriptions of the fabled Cheyenne Club. We wish to express our sincere gratitude to her, especially because she secured the materials for us while preparing for her richly earned retirement from the position she has filled so ably with Youngstown State University for over two decades. We shall miss her, but are grateful that she had the marvelous foresight to train an exceptional staff to carry on her standard of excellence.

As always, Carol read my descriptions of horses, their tack and handling. As always, she laughed and then corrected my errors. My husband Jim did the same while rechoreographing my fight sequences in the book. For once again making a house call to treat an ailing computer/printer in an emergency, we owe special thanks to Dr. Walt McGee.

Wyoming Territory was a dangerous land, and Jesse Robbins was a professional gunman. For researching his weapons and those of the rest of the cast, we again owe our special thanks to the expertise of Dr. Carmine V. DelliQuadri, Jr., D.O., weapons expert.

Prologue

Cheyenne, Wyoming—Autumn, 1881

"Good-bye, Lissa." His voice was bleak, final. He did not touch her, only stood on the railroad platform with his hands at his sides, his gray eyes as cold as winter storm clouds.

Lissa remembered when those same gray eyes had been silvery with warmth and his voice had been husky with words of passion. "Please, Jess. It isn't too late. Take me with you. We can start over again."

Her hands reached out to clutch his soft leather vest and pull him closer to her, but he grasped her wrists firmly and pushed her back. "There's no place to go, Lissa. Any yahoo could put a bullet in me tomorrow. Then where would you be—alone and penniless in some dusty cow town."

"You could quit—become a stockman like Papa."

13

A thin, bitter smile etched his lips fleetingly. "And inherit your papa's ranch? I don't think so, Lissa. Even if he'd offer, I wouldn't take it. I hire out my gun, but I don't sell myself."

The Union Pacific train belched a cloud of steam onto the platform as if punctuating his cruel words. "And you think gaining the J Bar through marrying me is selling yourself?" She felt the hope being squeezed from her body just like steam escaped from the train engine.

"Your father adores you, Lissa. He can take care of you. I can't," he replied stubbornly, ignoring the accusation in her voice. "That's the last train west today. I wired ahead to the Squaw Creek water stop. Your pa will be waiting for you."

"Don't do this, Jess." She hated the desperation in her voice. *I won't beg.* But Lissa knew she would if she believed it would change his mind.

"Everything's already been done, Lissa," he replied raggedly. He took her arm and walked the few brief steps to where the conductor stood waiting to assist her aboard.

The old man's wizened face was avid with curiosity. By that morning, all of southeast Wyoming had heard that Jesse Robbins had married Melissa Jacobson. Now he was sending her packing back to her father at J Bar Ranch. Jesse watched her turn away with the ingrained pride that he had come to recognize so well. Willful, spoiled, tenacious, that was old Marcus Jacobson's only child. She climbed up the steep stairs and disappeared into the railway car. *Lissa, what have we done?*

Not wanting her to see him waiting on the platform like some lovesick fool, Jess turned and strode toward the street before she could find her seat.

A Fire in the Blood

He retrieved his horse from the livery and rode away from the busy cattle town, ignoring the whispers and the stares that always followed him. The train was picking up speed now, moving across the flat open plain, headed toward the Medicine Bow Range, whose jagged peaks were outlined against the blazing summer sky. Jess reined in Blaze and sat hunched atop the big black, watching the train grow smaller in the distance.

Horse and rider remained silhouetted on the rise until the train had vanished and the hot breath of a high plains wind enveloped them. At last he turned the stallion about and kneed him into a slow, steady canter. He rode south and he did not look back.

Lissa felt the rhythmic swaying of the train as she stared out the window at the brown grama grass. Jess had not even waited until the train departed. He simply walked away. *Well, little fool, what did you expect? That he'd change his mind and come riding hell-bent to take you back?*

Jess would never do that, of course. But she could not help but wish that he would at least regret their parting and think of her once in a while—but not when he was working. He did not exaggerate the dangers of his profession. Lissa had come to accept that after all that had transpired over the past summer.

Suddenly the thought of him lying facedown in a pool of his own blood flashed into her mind. More than likely he was right. He would die just that way. *No, Jess, no . . .* She bit down on her fist and tried to banish the horrible image. The waste of it rushed over her like prairie wind.

Feeling another surge of tears gathering, she closed her eyes tightly and leaned her head back against the velvet seat cushion. First-class accommodations. Nothing but the best for old Marcus's daughter. Jess had probably spent his last cash money on the ticket. Her father owed him a lot more, but she knew he would never collect it. His infernal sense of pride, not her father's enmity, would prevent him from demanding what he had earned.

Damn his pride! Pride more than anything had driven them apart. But that same sizzling arrogance had been what first attracted her. Not wanting to face the bleakness of a future without Jesse Robbins, Lissa kept her eyes closed and remembered how it had all begun early last spring when the hard-looking stranger had ridden into Cheyenne and caught the romantic fancy of a foolish young woman. . . .

Chapter One

Cheyenne—Spring, 1881

Miss Charlene Durbin's dressmaking shop was doing a land-office business on Wednesday morning. The weather had finally broken at the end of May and the lashing spring rains abated, allowing the wealthy ranchers' wives to flock to the capital city and gird themselves for the season of galas that always took place in cattle country after the spring roundup. Louella Wattson and her daughter Emmaline were cooing over a bolt of puce velvet, while Sissy Markham and her sister Kaddie searched pattern books with the avid interest of prospectors just handed the map for a motherlode.

"Does it fit comfortably, Miss Jacobson?" Charlene's assistant Clare asked timidly as she stood back to inspect her handiwork, made of

17

yards and yards of bronze satin edged in cream lace. The colors were unusual, but so was Melissa Jacobson. Her pale ivory skin and fiery dark red hair were set off perfectly by the gown.

Lissa turned and inspected herself in the oval mirror standing in the middle of the large, crowded shop. She adjusted the rich lace gathered at the low-cut neckline and nodded to Clare.

"Ooh, look at *him!*" Julia Creed hissed, looking out the front window. "Bold as if he owned the capital—governor and all. I've never seen such insolence." As she had intended, a crowd of curious women quickly clustered around her and peered at the street below.

"He's a breed right enough," Lucy Moorhead said with the contempt only a woman raised in Sioux country could muster.

Louella Wattson shooed two of the younger women aside and squinted at the new arrival in town. "Why, it's a disgrace. Where is the marshal at a time like this?"

"Cowering in Professor McDaniel's saloon, or I miss my guess," Lucy replied.

"What's all the fuss about?" Lissa asked. Raising the satin skirts of her unfinished ball gown, she walked to the window and peered out. Her eyes fastened on him at once in spite of the noonday crowd on the street. Surrounded by crude cowboys and officious merchants, the rider on the big black stallion stood out like a mountain lion in a flock of woollybacks.

Lissa's eyes were riveted to the stranger as he rode slowly past, holding his reins carelessly in one hand with a negligent ease that belied the watchful expression on his hard, chiseled features.

◇ TROY-BILT®

102nd Street and 9th Avenue
Troy, New York 12179-0014

My Garden Size Is:

1. ☐ SMALL (under 30' x 30')
2. ☐ AVERAGE (up to 50' x 60')
3. ☐ LARGE (over 50' x 60')

Dept. C556

Name _____

Address _____

City _____ State _____ Zip _____

⟨⟩**TROY-BILT**®

An American Legend Caring For The Land.™

Mid-sized
ECONO-HORSE
Model

Small-garden
JUNIOR Model

Half the price
of our largest
Model!

© 1992 Garden Way Inc.

His other hand rested casually on the handle of the fancy Colt revolver strapped to his thigh. Although his wide black hat with a silver concho headband shaded his face from the sun, she could see that his features were exotically handsome in a bronzed, hawkish way. His nose was straight and prominent, his eyebrows thick and dark, and his mouth wide with sensuously shaped lips. She studied his firm jawline with the faint stubble of a dark beard growing on it. How would it feel to run her fingers across its scratchy surface, to touch those magnificent lips and stare into those slitted eyes? *What color are they, I wonder.*

She felt powerless to look away as he swung down from his horse at a hitching post across the street. His body was long and lean, with wide shoulders and narrow hips. He moved with the sinuous grace of a stalking puma. Pulling his hat from his head as he stepped into the shade, he ran his fingers through a shaggy head of night-black hair that lightly brushed his shirt collar.

Lissa continued to stare transfixed at the stranger, who affected her in a way no other man ever had. "That is the most sinfully dangerous man I've ever seen," she murmured breathlessly. *What possessed me to say that!*

Sissy Markham snorted disgustedly. "Yer pa'd be real pleased to see you makin' eyes at a dirty Injun."

"He looks neither dirty nor like any Indian I ever saw," Lissa replied dismissively. Sissy and her sister were vicious-tongued old maids.

"You'd best watch yourself, young lady," Louella chimed in, her voice stern. "We all realize you've spent the past years back east in school, but you were born here. You should know what it means when a man has mixed blood. That odious stranger is not only a half-breed lowlife, but a hired killer as well. He's got a fearful reputation. Name's Jesse Robbins, and he hires out to wealthy stock growers who want to rid the range of squatters and rustlers. Why, he's little better than an outlaw himself."

Lissa arched her eyebrows as she glanced fleetingly at the fat old matron. "And how do you happen to know so much about this Mr. Robbins?"

"I overheard my Horace talking to Mr. Mathis just yesterday. Why, he was aghast at the sort of riffraff the Association was bringing in."

"Then Lemuel has hired him for the Association?" Lissa asked. Lemuel Mathis was president of the Wyoming Stock Growers Association and a suitor of hers, although she did not encourage him.

Louella looked a bit flustered. "Well, I'm not completely certain which one of the members is hiring him."

"But we all know he's no good—and so should you," Emmaline Wattson added in the patronizing, nasal voice that had grated on Lissa since they were children.

"I wonder who he's working for," Lissa said pensively.

Suddenly, the women's attention was again drawn to the street when one of the cowhands lounging against the wall of the saloon hauled himself up and stepped off the wooden walkway. He was young, slightly built, and looked purely mean. Spoiling for a fight, he spoke loudly so his voice carried the length of the muddy street.

"We don't cotton to no Injuns drinkin' our whiskey in Wyoming," he said in a heavy Texas drawl.

Robbins finished tying his horse to the hitching rail, then turned slowly and faced the youth.

"You yeller, gut-eater?" the half-drunk kid prodded as the other men around the saloon scooted out of the line of fire.

Robbins betrayed no emotion at the racial slur or the questioning of his courage. He just walked slowly around the young cowhand.

"You *are* yeller. A damned yeller gut-eating redskin." The boy moved in the tall stranger's path again.

"I never shoot a man for free, but I might make an exception because I'm trail weary and thirsty," Robbins said as he brushed the slight figure out of his way.

That was all the encouragement the boy needed to reach for the Navy Colt on his hip. Before he had it halfway out of the holster, the barrel of Robbins's double-action revolver came crashing down on his forehead.

"Would yew lookit thet," one tall, skinny Texas cowhand said with awe in his voice.

"Never even seen him pull it," another man added as the group watched the stranger step over the crumpled body of their companion.

At the dressmaker's across the street, the cluster of women watched Jesse Robbins disappear into the dark interior of the saloon. "Well, I do declare, a lady isn't safe on the streets of the territorial capital anymore. You really must move from this dreadful location, Charlene, or I shall just have to find another modiste," Louella pronounced to the chorused agreement of the others.

All but Lissa, who ignored the badgering of poor Charlene Durbin and glided across the cluttered shop to her dressing room. As she stripped off the satin gown, her thoughts were not of dresses or dances, but of the dark, dangerous stranger who worked for the Wyoming Stock Growers Association. She was dying to know who had hired Mr. Jesse Robbins.

Jess walked into the Metropolitan Hotel and stopped to look around. Classy place all right, with big, ugly, overstuffed chairs covered in maroon velvet sitting in clusters around the lobby, flanked by potted palms that were as big and showy as any he had seen in Algiers or Tunis. Maroon and dark-blue carpeting swallowed up the sound of his footfalls as he strolled to the big walnut counter beside the steep stairs.

He leaned his leather weapon case against the wall, then swung his saddlebags from his shoulder and laid them on the wide countertop. "I'd like a room and a hot bath."

The hotel clerk drew back as if his nostrils had just been assailed with scrapings from a livery stable floor. His thin lips puckered up, causing his chin to retreat even further into his neck. "I don't think you got the right place, cowboy. Rawlins's place on Eddy Street might give you a room."

"I want a room here . . . now," Jess said in a low, silky voice.

"We don't take in no breeds—hotel policy," the clerk added quickly, half-indignant, half-wary as he watched the stranger's cold gray eyes lighten to the color of boiling mercury.

"I'm making an adjustment in hotel policy," Jess said, reaching for the register and the pen lying beside it. Before the sputtering clerk could stop him, he signed his name and shoved the book across the counter.

"The owners'll fire me," the clerk whined, as Jess tossed a gold piece on the counter and picked up his bags. He walked around the counter and pulled a key from one of the small wooden compartments on the wall, then turned toward the stairs.

"You can't just . . . just . . ."

"Don't get your shirt full of fleas, Noah," a calm, stentorian voice interrupted. "The stranger works for me," a tall, elegant man with iron-gray hair and a thin, austere face informed the clerk.

"Mr. Jacobson. I didn't . . . I mean, I didn't know—"

"It's all right, Noah. Go see that Chris fetches up some bathwater for Mr. Robbins. And put Lissa's things in her room as well," Jacobson commanded as he bypassed the desk and approached Jess.

Jess set down his bags and sized up Marcus Jacobson. He was dressed in the plain rough clothes of a stockman who worked his own range. His hand, when he extended it, was callused from hard work, and his ice blue eyes were keen and incisive. Jess returned the handshake. "I'm a day early. Didn't think you'd be in town yet."

"Just arrived this afternoon. I'm going to the club to clean up before dinner."

Jess had heard of the famous Cheyenne Club, a private and very exclusive men's organization whose membership was restricted to the wealthiest of Wyoming cattlemen. He knew that no invitation would be extended to him to join Jacobson at that establishment. They did not even allow cowhands, much less Indians. "I look forward to a long, hot soak myself," he replied noncommittally.

"Good. I'll be back here around seven. We can have dinner in the hotel dining room and discuss the job I need to have done."

Within half an hour, Jess was luxuriating in a steamy tub. The boy who had filled it seemed as nervous as a half-broken mustang, but had said nothing, merely done his job, then stuttered his thanks for the coins Jess had tossed him. He dismissed the memory and laid his head back against the rim of the fancy copper tub. A half-breed gunman always made folks nervous, whether it was in Texas or Wyoming.

Looking around the small bathing room, Jess admitted his surprise about the accommodations, which were modern and elegant. A water closet sat in one corner, and on the other side of the partially closed door was a suite with a parlor and a large, well-appointed bedroom. Purely by chance, he had helped himself to the fanciest setup in the place!

With almost ten thousand inhabitants, Cheyenne was more than a territorial capital. It was the main hub for the high plains cattle industry. The powerful Wyoming Stock Growers Association had its headquarters here, and the Union Pacific railroad shipped over one hundred thousand head of beef east every fall. Smiling to himself, Jess wondered how rich old Marcus Jacobson really was. He would soon find out. Jesse Robbins planned to charge a fearfully high fee for his services.

He had always spent his money as soon as he earned it, buying up more land and good breeding stock for his own small ranch in western Texas.

The Double R would never be as big and fancy as the spreads of cattle barons like Jacobson, but it was home for Jess and his younger brother, Jonah. A home they had earned with blood and tears.

Pushing thoughts of the tragic past from his mind, Jess considered the terms of his deal with Jacobson and began to lather up.

Lissa tired of the gossiping women at the dressmaker's shop and left to meet her father at the hotel. By now he should have arranged for Chris to unload her baggage in her usual rooms and draw her a steamy bath.

When she entered the hotel, Noah was not at the front desk. Knowing the nasty-tempered little man's predilection for a late afternoon nip at the bottle, she considered herself fortunate. She would be able to slip upstairs without having to deal with him. Hoping her bath was ready, she reached behind the desk for her key. The pocket marked #12 was empty.

"Chris must have taken it so he could fill my tub," she murmured to herself as she climbed the stairs. The door to suite 12 was indeed unlocked. She swept into the parlor.

Now where the devil are my bags? Nothing had been brought up yet. She muttered a small, unladylike oath about Noah Boswick, then stopped as she heard the sound of splashing water from the adjacent bathing room.

"Chris, put orange blossom bath salts in—ooh!" Lissa stood frozen in the doorway. *He* was in *her* bathtub! Naked! His bronzed shoulders rippled with muscles, and one long-fingered hand rested against the pelt of black hair on his chest, holding a

25

bar of soap. His hair was wet and he shook his head to clear the water from his eyes. She could see the faint outline of his body beneath the water—but not too clearly, thank God. Then he opened those mysterious eyes that she had wondered about earlier. They made her heart stop beating. Fringed by long black lashes, they were pure silver. His sensuous mouth curved in an intimate smile that heated her blood. Then he spoke and her heart raced wildly.

"Orange blossom isn't exactly my fragrance," he said drily. "You don't look like the hotel maid. Might I hope you're a present from my employer?"

Lissa was unable to tear her eyes from his gleaming wet skin. The tantalizing patterns of soap bubbles foaming on his shoulders fairly beckoned her hands to glide over the lean, hard muscles.

"What are you doing in my suite?" she finally managed to choke out.

"Your suite? I have the key." His voice was laced with laughter.

"Well, you certainly didn't use it!" she said indignantly as a flush scalded her cheeks. "The door was unlocked. This is the suite my father always reserves for me. I naturally assumed—"

"You naturally walked right in and opened the bathroom door when you heard me splashing," he interrupted ungraciously, still smiling. "Do you often spy on men in their baths?" Before she could sputter an answer, he started to rise out of the water, saying, "Sweetheart, hand me one of those towels as long as you're here."

She whirled and fled to the echoing sound of rich male laughter.

What a breathtaking little cat, he thought as he rinsed off and rubbed himself dry. Since it was unlikely that any other uninvited guest would be so lovely, Jess strolled into the lavishly appointed parlor, slipped the lock on the outer door, then returned to the steamy bathing room with his razor to complete his toilette. The uncharacteristic carelessness of the unlocked door niggled at the back of his mind.

As he pulled a clean shirt and pants from the armoire where the bellboy had hung them, Jess turned his thoughts to his fire-haired intruder. For certain no hotel maid. He had known that at a glance. Her tan linen traveling suit was far too expensively cut for her to be a mere servant, and her hands were too pale and soft to have endured any kind of manual labor. She might have been a very expensive whore, but he doubted it. The way she blushed gave away her lack of experience, but there was the matter of those hungry gold eyes. He chuckled. A she-wolf never eyed up a young maverick with any keener interest than the little redhead had shown while she studied him in that bathtub. She was ripe for the taking all right.

But before he accepted her unconscious invitation, he wanted to know who she was. A man of his background could get in a mountain of trouble over a rich white lady, even if she was the one who initiated the whole affair. Maybe after dinner he would head to the biggest saloon in town and ask around. A beauty with her unusual coloring would certainly be well-known in a territory with as few females as Wyoming.

He inspected his appearance in the mirror. The black homespun suit made him look like a preacher—or a politician. He considered wearing his .41-caliber double-action Colt Lightning, but decided

27

against it. After all, this was the classiest hotel in Cheyenne and he was having dinner with one of the wealthiest cattlemen. There was an unwritten law on the plains about rich men. Seldom did anyone try any fireworks around them. They were too powerful, and the retribution for any disgruntled cowhand or outlaw was swift and terrible.

"Just in case the unlikely occurs," he muttered grimly and pulled open his gun case. He selected a single-action Colt pocket revolver and its specially-made shoulder holster. He strapped it on and shrugged into his suit coat, then glanced in the mirror one last time. He needed a haircut, but what the hell. It was not likely that Jacobson would bring his wife along, and even if he did, Jess was not interested in impressing Lissa Jacobson.

Lissa inspected her appearance in the mirror. Her hair had turned out rather well. How heavenly to have a hairdresser here in Cheyenne! The woman had fashioned it in an elegant bouffant style with a heavy chignon at the crown and soft wispy curls framing her face. "Now all I need do is select a gown," she murmured, moving to her wardrobe, which overflowed with neatly pressed dresses in a rainbow of colors.

Dinner in a civilized dining room was quite an occasion after the endless winter months spent snowbound at the J Bar Ranch. The isolation had nearly driven her mad, with only her father and that hateful housekeeper for company. In desperation, she had often gone down to the bunkhouse to talk with Vinegar Joe, the crotchety old cook, and Moss, the ranch foreman. The young hands were not much company since they mostly tended to stare gape jawed at Marcus's beautiful daughter and shuffle around trying to please her. All the poor, homely illiterates did was add to her sense of frustration.

Marcus had sent his only daughter East for an education when her mother died. Her Aunt Edith and Uncle Phineas had taken in the frightened girl and lavished everything on her that a childless couple could give. She had spent brief summer vacations at J Bar, but her life had been in St. Louis.

When she was eighteen, Lissa had made her debut at the Veiled Prophet Ball, the most elegant social event of the aristocratic old city's season. Handsome, wealthy young men from all the best families had courted her. She had adored their attention, thinking that she would eventually marry one of them and settle down to be one of the social arbiters of the city, like Aunt Edith.

Then Marcus had swooped down and snatched her back here to this beastly wilderness the summer before last. His plans for his sole heir were quite different from hers. She was to marry an influential stockman who could run his empire. Together they would provide heirs to inherit the kingdom Marcus Jacobson had spent his life building.

As if that had not been bad enough, his first choice for the position was Lemuel Mathis, a well-to-do attorney in town and president of the Wyoming Stock Growers Association. Lemuel was, she supposed in all fairness, a fine-looking man for one approaching the advanced age of forty. Unfortunately, he was a crashing bore.

All Lemuel was interested in was the cattle industry. Of course, Marcus and all the rest of their friends shared the same singleminded interest. At least Lemuel did attempt to court her in his own punctilious way.

But Lemuel Mathis was the farthest thing from her mind as she prepared for dinner. All she could think about was the possibility of encountering the gunman again. Just thinking of that swarthy, hawkish face with the mocking silver eyes made her heart pound. He was an arrogant beast, no doubt of that, a mixed blood, forbidden to all decent women. Her mouth went dry, and she felt queerly faint and flushed just thinking about him naked in that tub. She could still envision the soap bubbles coating his dark skin, the cunning patterns of hair on his chest and forearms, the lean, sinuous rippling of his muscles. How would it feel to touch that hard body and run her fingertips along the contours of his heated flesh?

Lissa gave herself a mental shake and turned her attention to the gowns. They were cramped in this smaller room, which had fewer armoires and chests for her extensive wardrobe. Damn his insolence for taking *her* suite! She had to settle for a smaller room at the end of the hall.

She could not keep her wayward thoughts from trespassing to Jesse Robbins. There had been a great deal of trouble here lately with cattle and horses being stolen. She knew that her father and several of the other big ranchers like Cyrus Evers had been conferring about how to solve the problem. *Could Papa be the one who hired Robbins?*

Just thinking about it made her smile wickedly. If so, the presumptuous devil was in for quite a rude awakening. He would be Marcus's employee, and she would be the boss's daughter. Now that might just make him a bit more polite!

Just then a rap sounded at the door, and her father's voice called out, "Are you there, Princess?"

"Come in, Papa. I was just deciding which gown to wear for dinner tonight. I thought the aqua, but perhaps the gold . . ."

Marcus turned his hat in his hands, fingering the leather headband nervously. "Princess, I know how you've been looking forward to dinner here in Cheyenne, but something has come up—"

"You promised, Papa! What could be more important? I'll wait if you have to have some boring old meeting over at the Association."

"I'm afraid that won't be possible, Lissa," he said placatingly.

"But I just had my hair done, and the hotel maid pressed all my gowns in a special rush. . . ." she wheedled.

His jaw was set in that stubborn way that she knew meant he would not be moved. Lissa recognized it because she too clenched her jaw the same way on frequent occasions.

"I'm sorry, Princess. I'm going to have to have a business dinner. A man I just hired has arrived a day early, and Lemuel and I need to discuss vital J Bar affairs with him."

Her heart skipped a beat. *Jesse Robbins!* "I don't see why I can't sit in. I promise to keep quiet and let you talk."

His blue eyes were glacial as he replied, "This man is not the sort that a lady would ever be seen socially with. He's a half-breed stock detective from Texas."

31

So it *was* he. "Oh, poo! What difference does that make to me? I only want to dress up and have an elegant meal in a civilized place." She knew Marcus shared the Westerner's prejudices about good women associating with Indians or gunmen—and stock detectives were by definition gunmen. But the whole thing was narrow-minded and silly. She had half a mind to say so, but he gave her no opportunity.

"I know you've spent your formative years away from here, and for that reason I'll ignore that foolish remark," he said sternly. "I promise to take you to dinner tomorrow night. Now be a good girl and order whatever you want sent up from the hotel dining room for tonight." He walked over to her and placed a kiss on her forehead, then started for the door. He paused midway and said, with a twinkle softening his cold blue eyes, "Oh, Princess, your hair does look grand. Have the hairdresser come again tomorrow—and wear the gold dress."

After her father left, Lissa began to pace and scheme. If Lemuel was going to be present, too, then she could say she was so eager to see him that she just couldn't wait. Papa would be furious, but since he had been pushing Mathis at her for over a year, he could not stay mad. And he would never guess that her real motive for coming to the dining room was the silver-eyed gunman.

Lissa could not wait to see Jesse Robbins's face when she made her grand entrance and was introduced as Marcus Jacobson's daughter. "I bet he swallows his tongue!"

Chapter Two

Jess waited in the lobby of the hotel, which was adjacent to the fancy dining room. The aroma of rich coffee and fresh-baked bread perfumed the air. His stomach let out a low grumble, and he realized that he had not eaten since a hasty breakfast of bacon and beans on the trail at daybreak.

Marcus Jacobson and three companions strolled into the hotel, laughing and talking jovially. *They must've had a drink at their club.* He imagined them inviting him to enter that hallowed sanctuary. *Hell would freeze over first.*

As they approached, he studied the men with Jacobson. One of them wore expensive boots with a dress suit that was stiff and ill-fitting. He had a weathered face, creased as old buckskin and blasted by the elements. The second fellow was better dressed, with well-barbered hair and Celtic features. He, too, wore boots. The two of them were like old Marcus, no mistaking their hard-eyed toughness.

The third fellow had the look of a townsman. His clothes were well-tailored and he moved as if at ease in a fancy shirt and buttoned suit coat. He wore highly polished shoes and gold jewelry. Jess studied his face, which was flat and broad, with pale colorless eyes beneath sandy eyebrows. Quick eyes, missing nothing. He was younger than the others but no kid by any means. His thick sandy hair was liberally thatched with gray, and his hairline receded slightly.

"Good evening, Mr. Robbins," Marcus said, as jovial as one of his saturnine disposition could be.

Yeah, they had a drink or two. Aloud, Jesse returned the greetings when Jacobson introduced his companions.

"This is Cyrus Evers. Jamie MacFerson. Lemuel Mathis. Gentlemen, Jesse Robbins." Both of the older cattlemen returned Jess's keen inspection, measuring him with the shrewd gaze of men whose survival skills were hard won in this harsh wilderness.

As Jess shook hands with Mathis, he felt the soft skin of a man unused to physical labor. "You aren't a stockman, Mr. Mathis."

Lemuel Mathis's eyes narrowed for an instant as he withdrew his hand. Then he smiled. "No, but I'm president of the Stock Growers Association and vitally interested in protecting and promoting the cattle industry in our territory."

"Lemuel is modest. He'll be one of the biggest ranchers in Wyoming in a year or two when he marries my daughter," Jacobson replied.

"Now, Marcus, the lady hasn't done me the honor of saying yes yet," Mathis protested.

"Just a matter of time. She'll come around," Marcus said with self-assurance.

As they walked into the dining room, Jess could feel curious eyes on him, hear speculative whispers. He had grown used to it over the years. *How many men has he killed? Does he notch his gun? How much is he paid to shoot a man?* People were vultures, feeding their own prurient curiosity through him.

A prim, punctilious waiter, probably a first cousin to the desk clerk, showed them to a table in the rear of the room. It was situated privately so no one would overhear their conversation. No doubt Jacobson reserved it regularly.

Just as they were pulling out chairs to be seated, a familiar voice called out. "There you are, Papa! I declare, I almost couldn't find you all hidden away in that corner."

The beautiful redhead, fetchingly dressed in a topaz silk gown, wended her way across the crowded dining room toward them. She did not see Jess, who was standing behind the latticed partition wall. Jacobson stiffened but said nothing as she fluttered up to them, wreathed in smiles. So Lissa was old Marcus's daughter, not his wife! Jess cursed his luck. Just what he needed, some spoiled little chit getting her dander up because of the incident in his room. Still he could not help but wonder how she would react when she saw him. He knew her pa was furious that she had interrupted their dinner, but the old man said nothing as she effusively greeted the other ranchers and Mathis.

"Why, Cy Evers, Cridellia said you looked splendid in that new suit and she didn't exaggerate one bit. Mr. MacFerson, I've missed you since round-up last fall."

"How good it is to see you again, Lissa," Mathis said, gallantly bowing over her proffered hand.

"Why, thank you . . ." Her voice faltered as Jess stepped out of the shadows and his eyes met hers. She felt her heart accelerate like a runaway train when his smile mocked her.

"Lissa, this is Jesse Robbins. He's a stock detective," her father said tightly, his eyes promising retribution.

Her smile was dazzling as she inclined her head, quickly recovering her poise. What was it about the man that wrecked her composure every time he smiled at her? "A pleasure, Mr. Robbins. I trust the hotel accommodations are to your liking?" she asked innocently.

"Yes, ma'am. The rooms are very luxurious," he replied. The little flirt was playing with him!

"I especially enjoy the luxury of the bathing facilities." She smiled as his face darkened.

"Lissa, I don't think—"

"Are you gentlemen going to stand around and let a lady perish of hunger?" she said, interrupting her father's careful remonstrance.

Mathis rushed to pull out a chair. "Please, do have a seat, Lissa," he said in a stiffly formal voice, ushering her pointedly away from the gunman and placing her at his side.

Cy Evers cleared his throat nervously and took the chair on her other side. "And how have you been these past months?"

"Now that winter is finally over, I'm splendid, thank you."

Jess watched Lissa work her wiles. She was obviously used to getting her way. Surrounded by her little court of admirers, she quickly recovered her courage and delighted in baiting him. Obviously, she would never tell her father about barging in on him mother-naked in a bathtub. He smiled grimly to himself as he listened to them discuss the long northern winters and the coming of spring.

"I've been so anxious for the snow to melt," Lissa said, sipping from her glass of sherry daintily.

"Eager for the smell of orange blossoms?" Jess asked in a low voice.

She choked on her wine, then quickly recovered and replied, "Why no, Mr. Robbins. There are no orange blossoms in Wyoming, but I carry the fragrance with me all year long." Her big gold eyes were fathomless as she met his gaze with an innocent expression on her face.

Marcus watched the exchange between his daughter and the half-breed with growing unease. What the devil was going on? Then he glanced at Lemuel, and a slow smile spread across his face. The spunky little filly was making him jealous! Lissa always wanted Lem to be more exciting and attentive. Well, this was certainly putting a burr under his blanket. The idea that she would find the half-breed attractive never occurred to him.

"The winters in Cheyenne are much more hospitable than out in the basin. I think you would find life in the city much to your liking, Lissa," Mathis put in smoothly.

Lissa rewarded him with a wide smile. "Perhaps I would, Lemuel."

"I've certainly missed you. It's been a long time since your birthday celebration," Mathis said.

"That was a princely affair," MacFerson added,

rolling his r's in a thick Scots burr.

Lissa turned to Jess. "My father throws a big party every spring in honor of my birthday. He's a very generous man who gives wonderful presents. Don't you, Papa?" She turned to Marcus but watched Jess scowl from the corner of her eye.

"Only what you deserve, my dear," Jacobson said indulgently.

Jess coughed.

The waiter appeared to take their orders before she could make a riposte.

As their food was served, Lissa sipped her sherry and flirted with Mathis, who fairly fawned over her, basking in the unexpected attention.

Jess realized that riding a sunfishing bronc would be safer than continuing these parlor games with Lissa Jacobson. Best to get down to business. "Before you tell me about the situation at your ranch, Mr. Jacobson, there is one thing I have to make clear. I'm not Tom Horn. I don't shoot nesters and I don't dynamite sheep. You have any problems with sheepmen or squatters, you'll have to settle them some other way."

Cy Evers chortled and slapped his thigh. "Blanton said you was plain-speaking with lots of nerve."

"We have rustler troubles, Robbins, nothing else that we can't handle ourselves," Marcus said levelly.

Jess nodded. "Good. Horses or cattle?"

"Mostly beeves. Last month I lost nearly five hundred head. Cy here lost two hundred."

"And I lost one hundred fifty," MacFerson said, chomping on his piece of apple pie as if it were going to get away from him.

Jess whistled low. "Seems as if you're the main

38

target, Jacobson. Any idea why?" Jess studied the tough old man's unyielding expression as he sipped his coffee.

"I've posted as many men as either Cy or Jamie, but my herds are more spread out."

"And there is more of 'em," Evers interjected.

Jacobson shrugged. "I'm the biggest stockman in southeastern Wyoming. But I can't sustain these losses. If rustlers took five hundred head when the snow wasn't even off the ground, by the time spring roundup is done I can't even imagine how many head I could lose."

"For such large-scale losses, the thieves must be doing more than separating calves from their mothers and slapping a running iron on them," Jess said.

"Last week they ran off a whole herd on Fork Creek." Jacobson's eyes blazed with anger.

"I had some calves taken, too. That always goes on in spring when the cows drop 'em," Cy said philosophically, then added, "But what Marcus is havin', why it's real bad. They're cutting out whole herds."

"Papa, you never told me it was this serious." Lissa leaned forward and tilted her head at her father.

The men had almost forgotten her presence during their discussion. Now Marcus wiped his mouth with a snowy linen napkin and rose, then walked over to his daughter's chair. "Lissa, you shouldn't worry about such things. Let the menfolk handle it. Now, young lady, we have to talk lots of boring stock business. I'm certain the gentlemen will forgive you if you excuse yourself and go up to your room." His eyes narrowed on her sternly, indicating that she had pushed him as far as he was willing to allow.

Sighing, Lissa recognized that hard expression. Much as she would have liked to continue the sparring with Jesse Robbins and learn exactly how a range detective went about his job, she knew her father would not permit it. She stood up when Marcus pulled back her chair and bade the men good night, then kissed her father on the cheek.

As she turned to leave she said, "It was really a pleasure to make your acquaintance, Mr. Robbins." Her eyes danced with devilment.

Jess watched Lissa swish away, leaving behind the subtle hint of her perfume. *That woman is going to be nothing but trouble.*

Once Jacobson returned to his seat, the men broke out expensive cigars. The waiter poured fine aged bourbon and set the bottle on the table, then quickly cleared the dishes, leaving them alone to conduct business.

"You wired me, Mr. Jacobson. Are you an agent for the Association?"

"No. I'm hiring you myself, but since these men's spreads adjoin mine—and since Lem here is almost a part of the family as well as president of the Association, I felt they had a stake in what we do."

"Fair enough. I get three hundred a month and keep while I'm working. If I stop the rustling I get a bonus. Five thousand for the whole job."

Evers whistled low, the Scot grunted, and Mathis coughed. All three looked at Jacobson expectantly.

"Hell, you get rid of those damned cow thieves. I'll pay it."

Jess nodded, then continued his questioning. "Any chance these rustlers are helped by someone working for you?" His eyes moved from Jacobson to Evers to MacFerson.

Cy Evers was adamant. "I know ever one of my boys and they's good loyal hands. Worked for me for years."

"I hire a lot of grub-line drifters every year, but I doubt they're in with cattle thieves," the Scot replied. His face and voice betrayed a faint grimace, as if he were perpetually sucking on a persimmon.

Marcus considered the problem. "I'd hate to think it. Known most of my hands since they were slick ears, but I run such a big operation. There are always new men signing on. Since I'm the main target . . . could be."

"Have your ramrod assign any men you aren't sure of to chores close in. That way I can watch them easier." Jess scraped back his chair and rose. "I think that about takes care of things for now. I'll ride to your ranch as soon as you're ready."

The others also stood up. "I'll need several days in town, but I can get a couple of my boys to ride back with you, say day after tomorrow," Jacobson replied.

"Good. I'll be waiting."

As Jess turned away, Mathis added, "Oh, Robbins, you'd better be good. Damn good. Five thousand is what Horn charges."

Jess locked stares with the shorter man. "You lobbying for Tom Horn, why not hire him? He's available, so I heard."

"Because I heard you were better," Marcus interjected. "Don't disappoint me."

*   *   *

Dreams haunted Lissa's twilight world between wakefulness and oblivion. Dreams of a darkly handsome face with a blinding white smile and wicked silver eyes that mocked her. She heard his voice, rough and gravelly, whispering low, taunting her. He laughed huskily.

Lissa bolted upright. That was no dream. The voices were coming from the alley below her room. She threw off the quilt and slid into her velvet wrapper as she quickly crossed the thick carpet to the open window. She drew up the shade and peered through the lace curtains.

Jesse Robbins's voice drifted up to her, mingled with the higher yet sensuous chuckle of a woman.

"Hell, it's been too long, Cammie."

"I couldn't believe my eyes, *querido*, when you walked into the music hall. You never change, Jess—only grow more wicked." More low, husky laughter floated up on the still night air.

Lissa strained her eyes, looking through the darkness to where the two figures were entwined in the shadows below. The woman was small and dark-haired, wearing a fantastical costume made of some glittering red material, perhaps sequins. It was cut low, revealing an ample bosom and milky shoulders, barely swathed in a fluffy feather wrap.

She ought to freeze wearing no more than that on a Wyoming night!

But the woman called Cammie was far from freezing as she pressed her breasts against Robbins's chest. "You're still a furnace, *querido*, no matter this thin air."

42

"It's not warm like El Paso was," he said drily as he nibbled at her neck.

She buried her fingers in his shaggy hair and pulled him closer. "Ah, so you remember El Paso, eh?"

Lissa could see the gleam reflected in her big dark eyes as Cammie turned her face into the moonlight, dropping her head back to allow Jess access to her throat and breasts. The feather wrap floated to the ground as she held him tightly. Her eyes closed in bliss as he cupped a breast, then reached inside the low gown and fondled it.

A low, feral growl escaped him as he claimed her mouth in a rapacious kiss. Lissa could see their lips open and then meld together. *Why their tongues must be . . . !* A strange hot flush stole over her, radiating from her face in a relentlessly lowering path, swelling her breasts, tightening the nipples, then clenching her stomach and washing through her belly until it pooled thickly between her legs.

Her throat was dry. She darted her tongue out to lick her lips as she watched the lovers kiss. He seemed to be hurting the woman, but not hurting her, as his mouth ground down over hers and he bent her backward over one arm. Cammie kissed him back with relish, moaning deep in her throat and clawing at his shirt until she had it unfastened and could reach inside.

Lissa's fingers came up unconsciously and touched her lips, rimming them as she watched Jess do the same to Cammie with his tongue. Her breath came in unsteady gasps as she stared down into the alley, mesmerized. They were behaving like lust-crazed animals. In spite of her father's attempts to shield her, Lissa had seen bulls and

43

stallions service cows and mares. This avid tearing at each other was not all that different. It should repel, not excite her. What was wrong with her?

Suddenly, Jesse broke off the rough kiss and held Cammie at arm's length. "You had better come to my room, *querida*, before I take you right here in the mud."

Cammie laughed. "It would not be the first time. Are you certain I won't cause you to be evicted from the hotel?"

"No one will evict me," he said raggedly. She reached down and scooped up the feather wrap just before he swept her up into his arms. He carried her toward the side entrance to the hotel, the feathers floating behind them as they vanished with an echo of soft laughter.

Lissa stared into the moonlit alley, her eyes wide, unseeing. Her mind pictured what Jesse Robbins was doing to the painted actress, undressing her, running his dark hands over her flesh, caressing her breasts. Kissing her deeply with his lips and tongue. But what came after that?

Her eyes closed and heat scorched her face as she tried to imagine him standing before her naked, but she could only envision his face and upper body, not the rest that had been covered in the water of the bathtub. She had seen the great ugly staffs of the stud bulls and stallions. Surely a man was not built like that! A shiver of excitement raced along her spine as she pulled down the shade and turned toward her big lonely bed.

Sinking down onto it, she imagined Jesse laying a woman across it and covering her with his body. But it was not the dark-haired music hall doxy. The woman was her, lying beneath him, clasping him to her and feeling the rasp of his whiskers against the soft skin of her face and neck. She reached up to touch the hard expanse of his chest . . . only to find cold, empty air.

With a sob, she rolled over and pounded the pillows. "What is wrong with me? I've never thought such a vulgar thing before in my life." Her whisper hung in the still, empty room. Tears clogged her throat and spilled from beneath her lashes. Lissa wiped them away, mortified by her emotional response almost as much as she had been by her fantasy.

"I won't let that arrogant beast affect me this way. I simply won't," she vowed resolutely. If she had half of St. Louis worshipping at her feet, surely she could get the better of one half-breed gunman.

Jesse Robbins would probably be eager to earn his pay and start chasing rustlers as soon as possible. Her father planned to remain in town for a couple of days, attending to Association business. How could she contrive to ride home with the gunman? Smiling, she relaxed and leaned back against the pillows to lay her plans.

Chapter Three

Lissa surveyed the open country rising before them in rolling waves of thick, newly greened grama grass. In the west, the Medicine Bow Mountains rose jagged against the skyline. The warm breeze was redolent with the scent of damp, fecund earth. Spring had come to the high plains. But her mind was not on the spectacular scenery or the promise of a beautiful day. She stared at Jesse Robbins's back, fuming.

Here I've given up a week in Cheyenne and for what! Getting her father to allow her to return to the ranch with Robbins and several of the other hands had been easy. She had packed up one of her new dresses and explained to Marcus that it was a gown Cridellia Evers was considering for the spring roundup party. Mrs. Durbin had asked that she bring it to the valley so Cridellia could ride from the nearby spread and try it on.

When she had shown up at the livery stable that morning, Robbins had been ready to leave, mounted on his blaze-faced black. He wore a pair of snug-fitting soft denims and a dark red shirt with a leather vest over it, and of course the low-slung Colt. With the broad-brimmed hat shadowing his face, he looked almost satanic as his eyes blazed silver and narrowed on her. He had not been pleased to have her returning to the ranch with their small party and made the fact quite plain, issuing only a curt good morning and the admonition that she had better be prepared to ride hard.

Over an hour had passed as they pushed west. Jess seemed intent on ignoring her while they rode. She retreated into a pouting silence—which affected him not at all. He turned and rode past her to talk with the hand in charge of the pack animals at the rear of their group. As the sun beat down warmly on her back, Lissa turned over various ideas in her mind to get his attention.

Rob Ostler, one of the young hands, pulled up beside her and engaged her in shy conversation. He was a homely youth from Texas with carrot-red hair and a gap-toothed grin that was quite engaging. "We'll be stoppin' fer a spell by the Little Sandy, Miz Lissa. I expect you'll be wantin' ta rest a mite by then."

"We are riding like the devil's chasing us, Rob," she said as she turned back to stare balefully at Robbins.

"If'n yer tired, we cud stop now, Miz Lissa," the youth volunteered earnestly. "I'll jest go 'n tell thet fancy range detective they's a lady present." His Adam's apple bobbed up and down like a windmill pump in a gale.

Shirl Henke

"That's not necessary, Rob. I can keep up. If I take a fancy to stop later on, we will," she added with bravado she did not feel. The hands would stop with her, but that mule-headed savage would ride right on without a backward glance.

Two other hands, one young and the other a grizzled trail veteran, rode with her, offering to draw her fresh water from the packhorse and pointing out various sights and sounds of spring on the high plains. Finally, when she could stand Robbins's icy aloofness no more, Lissa excused herself from her father's men and rode ahead to catch up with him.

When she pulled abreast of him and reined in, he did not spare her a glance. "Get tired of holding court, Princess?" he asked in a bored voice.

"Are you always this rude or have you made a special effort just for me?" Her tone was dulcet.

A small cynical smile barely curved his mouth. "You're used to men making special efforts for you, aren't you?"

"You really are trying to get my back up. Why, Jesse Robbins?" Her eyes gleamed with challenge. No man was this insufferable to the boss's daughter unless he felt something.

He finally turned and looked her in the eye. "You've really gone out of your way to attract my attention. I might ask you the same question, but I won't. I already know the answer." His direct silvery glare brought a flush to her cheeks. He cursed beneath his breath and turned away before his eyes trespassed lower, following the course of that flush down her neck to the open collar of her shirt, where softly rounded breasts strained against the silky fabric.

"You have a very high opinion of yourself," she retorted. "As to that encounter in the hotel—what happened was simply a mistake. You were in *my* suite."

"So you walked right in and decided to stay and see what you could see." One eyebrow arched as he gave her a sidelong glance.

"You really are insufferable, but you needn't think you're so special." Lissa decided that two could play the game of brazen insults. "Yes, I was curious. I've never seen a naked man before. It was a bit disappointing," she added with a forced sigh.

"That's only because you can't make comparisons that would lead you to appreciate my—ah, imposing stature," he said drily, grudgingly admiring her grit. The little devil was persistent and cheeky—and altogether too beautiful.

"You were only my first naked man. Who says I won't make comparisons?" she replied with a flip of her reins as she pulled her gelding away to hide her chagrin at having been bested in the ribald exchange. Riding back to Rob and Butch, she complained, "I'm ready to break for some food and rest. At this rate, we'll ride the horses lame."

Jess watched her confer with the men, then pull in and dismount. He debated hauling her back up on her horse and making them all ride another hour but decided against it. That kind of physical attention was just what she was trying to get him to give her. He was damned if he would play her game.

They built a fire and made some beans and coffee. Jess watched the men all vying with each other to wait on her. The young pups he could understand, but even the crusty old cowpunchers treated her like royalty. Of course, out here, any woman, young or old, pretty or plain, was prized. To be the only child and heir of a cattle baron like Marcus Jacobson, not to mention startlingly beautiful, was to be full-fledged royalty in Wyoming.

He sat nursing a cup of scalding black coffee and studied her covertly. She had made a special point of ignoring him since they stopped to eat. What was that devious little mind of hers up to?

Lissa waited until Jess finally went to check on his stallion. Then she walked quickly to her horse. She looked about to be certain no one was watching, then began to saw on the cinch strap with her small pocketknife until it was almost cut through. "That should do it," she said with a smile.

Shortly thereafter they broke camp and mounted up. Lissa rode very carefully until she could catch up to Jess, who, as usual, was riding point. "You act like you expect rustlers to come sweeping down on us, shooting."

"That's a possibility." He kept his eyes fixed on the horizon.

"Do you believe we're really in danger?" she asked, edging closer as she felt the saddle begin to slide.

Before Jess could reply, Lissa let out a cry and reached out to him. He turned just in time to see her saddle sliding around the gelding's side. Her hands clawed at his arm and he quickly slid his hands around her waist and lifted her against him as she kicked free of her horse. The gelding bucked a few times as the slipped saddle hung at an uncomfortable angle on his side, then began to graze, ignoring the commotion as the men raced up to Jess and Lissa.

She held tightly to him with her arms twined around his neck. His body was hard and lean, just as it had been in her fantasy. And his fingers felt like steel bands, holding her tightly against him. She pressed her breasts against his chest and felt him stiffen. He smelled of shaving soap with a faint hint of tobacco and some other unidentifiable scent.

She ran her fingers across his beard-stubbled jaw. "Your beard is awfully heavy. I thought men with Indian blood didn't have beards."

He reined in with an oath while she clung to him tight as a tick. His pants were getting tight, too, and the last thing on earth he wanted was to let her know how she really affected him. Jess peeled her away from his body and dropped her on the ground.

"You could've broken your neck with that damn fool stunt!" he said as he dismounted and stalked back to where her horse stood in the waving grass.

"Stunt! You say I could've been killed and still call it a stunt!"

He picked up the cut cinch strap and held it out, glaring at her. "Stunt," he echoed flatly.

"Well, since you have the biggest horse—and since you bathe regularly—I guess you'll have to carry me to the J Bar," she said cheerfully, ignoring his scowl and her own pounding heart.

The other men came tearing up and leaped from their horses.

"Miz Lissa, you all right?" Rob asked breathlessly.

"Gal, you scared more years off'n me than the blizzard of '76!" Luke Deevers said in his sharp Tennessee twang.

"I'm all right. One of the cinches just broke. Nothing to get excited about. Mr. Robbins saved me from taking a spill."

"Oh, you might just take a spill yet, Princess," Jess said in a silky voice that only she could hear.

"A durn good thing yer daddy believes in good old Denver saddles with double rigging, else yew cudda been throwed," Deevers said, noticing the cut leather but saying nothing.

"Can you repair it?" Jess asked the old man.

Deevers spit a shot of tobacco juice like a Union Pacific engine expelling steam, then replied, "Reckon I kin sew 'er up good 'nough fer a leetle bitty gal like Miz Lissa to ride it home."

"Coward," she whispered to Jess, then turned and stalked away.

Repairing the saddle took little time and they were soon on their way again. Lissa rode with Rob Ostler and Matt Helmer, forcing laughter at their outrageous cowboy humor while she stole furtive glances at Jess, still the solitary point rider.

"'N this here English feller starts talkin 'bout goin' ta Paree. Then old Deevers, he says, 'I been ta Paree.' 'You been to Paree, France?' the English dude asks. 'How'd you get to Paree?' 'Went with a herd of beeves,' old Deevers says. 'How in hell'— beggin' yer pardon, Miz Lissa, but old Deevers, he's powerful profane," he added as an aside to her. She nodded with a smile and he reddened, then continued. "Wal, the English feller he kindy gets his back up 'n asks, 'How'd you git across the ocean with a herd of beeves?' 'Didn't cross no ocean,' says Luke, 'trailed them critters around the Divide!'"

Everyone around them burst into laughter, even Pappy Deevers, who had heard the story told on him for years.

"Tell us about the time you tangled with that lantern-jawed bronc at the Triple E," Matt urged Rob.

With a shy look at Lissa, Rob warmed to his subject with the zeal of a natural-born storyteller. "Wal, I climbed aboard thet critter with a belly full of butterflies, I wanna tell yew." Lissa grew restive, and was only half listening to the young wrangler's tale of the high-bucking bronc. She was glad when he concluded, "I ain't never goin ta ride no broncs agin."

As everyone laughed, Ostler continued to pledge that his bronc-busting days were over forever. Then an impulse born of boredom and frustration seized Lissa and she asked, "You don't bust horses, but how about racing yours? Seems to me I recall beating you last summer. Bet I can do it again."

"Aw, Miz Lissa, I let you win that time."

A chorus of guffaws drowned out the young cowhand's protests until he threw up his hands. "All right, I'll race. Where do you want to—"

"Right here! I'll race you to that big rock up ahead," Lissa said as she dug her heels into her gelding. The startled horse took off at a gallop with a whooping Ostler close behind her, his hat waving wildly up and down as he urged his rangy buckskin in pursuit of her big gray.

From his vantage point on the rise, Jess watched the two young fools head toward the sharply jutting promontory in the center of the valley floor. Then his eyes swept across the terrain in front of them. Winter snows had been heavy, followed by spring rains. The creeks in the valley had overflowed their banks. In marshy, low-lying areas, the ground was treacherous. Lissa, pulling well ahead of Rob Ostler, was heading for a brushy, overgrown area that could be dangerous.

Cursing, Jess kicked Blaze into a gallop and headed after the reckless girl. By the time he came within fifty yards of her, Ostler was calling out for her to stop as he reined in his mount and turned it away from the creek. Ignoring him, she jumped the shallow, swiftly running stream and plunged ahead until the gray's legs sank quickly into the treacherous mire, throwing her. She, too, began to sink.

"Quicksand!" Ostler yelled as he began to uncoil his lariat, sliding the loop wide.

Jess, too, reached for his ketch rope as Lissa flailed in the quagmire, sinking deeper with every desperate move she made. "You have a stronger reata than I do—pull out the gray. I'll get the girl," Jess commanded.

The young hand tossed his heavy grass rope around the gray's neck and proceeded to haul him out of the quicksand. Jess, with his lighter Mexican reata of braided rawhide, quickly dropped the loop around Lissa.

"Put it under your arms and hold on to it," he shouted.

She obeyed him and he pulled her free. When he dismounted, she was sprawled on all fours on the stream bank, gasping for breath and covered with slimy sand.

Lissa saw his fancy black boots stop in front of her. She sat back on her haunches and looked up at him. "You know how to do anything but scowl?"

she asked, raising one grimy hand to him.

He pulled her up roughly. "You haven't given me any reason not to scowl. That was the dumbest damned thing I've seen since my commander tried to negotiate with the Tuareg chieftain."

She began to brush off the excess debris with her hands. "What's a Tuareg? An Indian? Were you in the army?"

Jess ignored the questions as his eyes swept over her soaked body. Damnation, even covered with muck she was beautiful. Every curve of her breasts and hips was revealed by the ooze-plastered clothes. "You're a mess and you reek like a dead cow rotting in the sun."

"I have clean clothes in my pack," she muttered. "Just give me a few minutes to scrub off in the creek and change."

"Ten minutes or I'll tie you to one of the pack-horses," Jess threatened as the rest of the men rode up with the pack animals.

Luke, Matt, and Festus were a great deal more concerned over her safety than was the hateful gunman. She fought the childish urge to stick out her tongue at his retreating back. Why was it that everything she did around Jesse Robbins seemed to backfire on her, making her look like a spoiled child? Couldn't anything go right? She stomped over to her luggage.

As she was unfastening the straps of her port-manteau, a thought occurred to her. *We'll just see, Jesse Robbins, what you do about this!* A slow smile spread across her face as she seized a carefully chosen change of clothes from the pack and head-ed for a copse of cottonwoods that sheltered the creek.

Barely within the time allotted, she emerged from the trees, dressed in a frilly white blouse and green silk skirt, which was cut with narrow paneled gores, completely unsuitable for riding. She walked briskly up to where Jess was talking to Luke Deevers. "I'm ready," she said sweetly.

He turned and his eyes narrowed as they swept down her figure. "How in the hell do you plan to ride in that regalia?"

She shrugged ingenuously and grinned at him. "This is the only thing I brought—other than two low-cut evening gowns." That was not strictly the truth, but the small oversight suited her purpose. "I guess I'll just have to ride on the front of your saddle . . ." She watched his whole body stiffen. He looked as if he were going to shake her until her teeth rattled.

"You brassy little bitch," he muttered low beneath his breath. Jess turned and gave the command to mount up. Then he swung onto his big stallion and reached down for her, lifting her across the saddle. She put her arms around his waist and her breasts pressed intimately against his chest. Her hips wriggled against his inner thighs until he reached down with steely fingers and held her still.

"Ouch, that hurts. You're pinching me."

"Lady, that's nothing compared to what you're doing to me," he said darkly. "Is that what you've been wanting to hear? Well, now you've heard it, so shut up and sit still. I'm in no mood for conversation."

After they had ridden for a few minutes, she said, "You never did tell me what a Tuareg was."

He ignored her and fixed his eyes on the horizon.

She studied his profile as they rode in silence. His beard was a heavy black stubble that made him look piratical and fierce. Again, she wondered about his family. She could see the thick black curls of his chest hair peeking out above the open collar of his shirt. Half-breeds normally had little body hair. His face did not have the flat contours or curved roman nose of an Indian even though his complexion was as swarthy as any savage's. The straight blade of a nose and cleanly chiseled brow and jawline looked almost Latin.

"You're Mexican, not Indian."

He looked down at her, startled. "No, I'm Indian, too."

"Then you *are* Mexican," she said with satisfaction. "You might as well talk to me, Jess. It's a long boring ride to J Bar. Tell me about your family," she wheedled. When he did not answer she said, "All right. I'll tell you about mine. My mother was a St. Louis belle, a Busch. She died in a cholera epidemic when I was very young, so all I remember of her is what Papa's told me. Papa must've loved her very much because he never remarried all these years. He built J Bar up from nothing— started with a fifty-dollar grubstake and worked it into the largest ranch in southeast Wyoming. He insisted I have a proper education the way my mother would've wanted, so he sent me to live with my Aunt Edith and Uncle Phineas when I was eight years old."

He laughed as she babbled on. "As an old partner of mine used to say, 'You sure was first in line when tongues was give out'." He could feel

57

her bristling and looked down into her blazing gold eyes. "Have you ever had a thought in that beautiful empty little head of yours besides what you were going to wear or who was going to amuse you today?"

"You make me sound incredibly shallow," she said softly. "I should be furious—I *was* furious, but . . . maybe you're right. I do usually get my way." She gave him a wistful smile.

He snorted in derision. "You've got every man in the territory jumping through hoops for you."

"Every man but you." She sighed. "I guess that's why I'm interested in you. It surely isn't because of your charming personality."

"So that's it, is it. I'm a challenge?" He cocked one eyebrow cynically and looked down at her. "I don't think so, lady. You're a ripe little virgin, all ready for the plucking—curious as hell to find out if the man-woman business is more than just hand-holding and moonlight. And here comes the mysterious, forbidden stranger. The last man on earth your daddy'd ever approve of. You want me to do a lot more than just scrape and bow over you like the rest of your legions of admirers, Princess."

She reached up with a squeal of outrage to slap his face but he caught her wrist and held it fast. She struggled, kicking and squirming, trying to raise her other hand. The big black sidestepped nervously and Jess swore, seizing her other hand and subduing her roughly.

Between gritted teeth he rasped out, "You're causing a scene for your daddy's men. If you don't want them tattling back to him, you'd better straighten up and at least try to act like a lady, even if it puts a real strain on your liver."

She subsided with a glare and leaned as far away from him as she could, mortified by the accuracy of his assessment, but too honest to deny it to herself even though she wanted to do so. "You're an insufferable cad," she said with as much dignity as she could muster.

He laughed mirthlessly.

As the day wore on, the horizon billowed up with fat, fluffy gray clouds that moved toward them. The wind gusted up to gale force, stinging their eyes with dust and sand. Then the rains came pouring down.

"Damn, not so much as a sapling for shelter," Jess muttered, scanning the horizon through the driving rain. "We'll have to keep pushing on and hope we can find some shelter before the lightning starts up," he shouted to Deevers. The old man nodded, and they rode silently while the forces of nature erupted around them.

Jess could feel Lissa shivering as the cold rain soaked through their clothes. "Surely a bold adventuress like you isn't afraid of a little storm?" he teased as he reached back to unfasten his saddle roll.

"I've hated storms ever since I was a little girl," she admitted.

"You're taking a chill. That frilly thing is pretty but not very practical out here on the high plains." He could nearly see through the sheer batiste blouse. It melted against her skin with a translucent whitish gleam, revealing the outlines of her low-cut lace camisole. Only the row of ruffles down the front kept him from seeing the color of her nipples through the thin, soaked cloth!

Their impudent pebbly outline protruded sharply against the fabric. Damn, before he knew it he was dreaming about touching them, feeling them arch up against his mouth when he suckled the delicate points. He growled in frustration as she snuggled closer against him.

Jess unrolled his poncho with a sharp flick of his wrist, and pulled it over his head, covering them both at the same time. Her arms circled his waist tightly, and she laid her head against his chest. Soon a layer of warm body heat cocooned them inside the heavy woven rain gear. He could smell her orange blossom fragrance mixed with the subtle scent of woman, and he knew he was growing hard.

Lissa felt the pressure of his erection against her thigh. So, she was just a spoiled little virgin? Well, he was just as interested in her as she was in him. In spite of her misery a small burble of laughter welled up inside her.

"Does it put a real strain on your liver riding next to me this way?" she whispered.

He swore, muttering, "It isn't my liver that's strained, lady."

A few bolts of lightning zigzagged across the horizon. Then one struck just in front of Deevers's horse. He snarled an oath and raised his fist at the sky, yelling, "All right, yew ole bald-headed son of a bitch up there! Yew want ta kill me, git it done er quit foolin'!"

"Jeehosaphat! Deevers, don't say thet!" Rob gulped and pulled his horse away from the crotchety old man.

Matt Helmes laughed. "He always does that. Ain't never got him killed yet."

"Just the same, I ain't hankerin' after a belly full of lightnin' bolts. I'll jest ride clear of him for a spell."

Another jagged shaft of lightning hit the ground about twenty yards from them. Lissa jumped, then burrowed down beneath the warm poncho, still holding Jess tightly.

The rain finally broke and the sun came out, hanging low on the western horizon like a great molten ball of orange fire. The sky around it was streaked with gold and fuchsia. They caught their first sight of the J Bar ranch against this glorious backdrop. It sat majestically, as if such a natural spectacle was the only appropriate setting for the vast cattle kingdom's headquarters.

And a kingdom it was, spread out across the wide floor of a shallow basin at the foot of the Medicine Bow Mountains. A winding stream curled around the valley, and a natural windbreak of tall cottonwoods and evergreens grew by the edge of the water. Several long, low buildings and bunkhouses and a mess hall sprawled beside a series of high corrals where horses and stud bulls were kept. A dairy and an icehouse were situated beside a large dugout for storing root vegetables. The little village of outbuildings was completed by a large stable adjacent to the corrals, a henhouse, and a blacksmith shop.

The real focal point of the place was the big house, old Marcus Jacobson's elegant home. It was made of dressed lumber shipped in from Denver and whitewashed a blinding white with red shutters and trim on the gables along the second-story roof. The windows were in big double pairs, the panes shining in the evening light, revealing lace curtains within. A wide veranda circled the rectangular house on three sides, and clusters of tall sycamores and oaks shaded the shingled roof from sun and wind.

Jess let out a low whistle. Lissa, who had dozed while snuggled comfortably beneath the poncho, sat up as Jess peeled it off and stuffed it partially back into his saddlebag.

"It is rather imposing the first time you see it, I suppose," she said quietly.

He looked down at her, surprised. "You don't like your castle, Princess?"

"I've never felt it was really home, I guess. I've been away at school for the past twelve years. I only spent a month or so, summers, on the ranch. Papa's been gone a lot of the time on business. Germaine is always here, though," she added bitterly.

Jess could see a tall, solitary figure standing on the porch, peering out at the approaching riders. This must be Germaine. She had dark hair pulled high atop her head in a severe coil of thick braids. Her body was lank and thin, and her face was composed of harsh angular planes. A prominent nose with a small knobby tip was framed by sunken cheeks. Her eyes dominated her face—small, piercing black eyes that moved like malevolent raisins from side to side beneath thin, flat eyebrows. The Wyoming wind and sun had not been kind to that face.

As they rode up, Jess could see her purse her lips when she saw Lissa seated in front of him. She stepped onto the first riser of the porch stairs and glared at them.

A Fire in the Blood

Germaine inspected Jess briefly, then turned her burning eyes on Lissa. "What will your father say to see you riding with his kind, looking as if you slept with him, *hein?*" she said in a heavy French accent.

Chapter Four

"And just what kind is that, ma'am?" Jess asked in a low, silky voice.

Germaine Channault peered at him, meeting his steely gray eyes for a moment, then shifting her gaze nervously to Lissa. "Your father will hear about this escapade," she hissed. Backing up a step, she gave Jess a swift glance and quickly retreated into the house.

Lissa chuckled darkly as she dismounted from the big black horse, holding fast to Jess's arm and sliding along his leg until her feet touched the ground. "You're the first man since Vinegar Joe Riland to buffalo Germaine."

"She any kin?" He could see no resemblance.

"Scarcely. She's French Canadian. She came here with my mother from St. Louis. After Mama died, Papa kept her on as cook and housekeeper. We detest each other."

"And your father won't get rid of her?" He found it difficult to believe that Marcus would deny his princess anything.

As if reading his thoughts she said, "There are some things Papa won't do even for me."

Jess studied her enigmatic expression and wondered what was between the Frenchwoman and Jacobson to so upset his daughter. She returned his perusal with a slow smile spreading across her lips. Realizing the direction of her thoughts, he touched the brim of his hat in a mocking salute and turned Blaze toward the bunkhouse. "Evening, Princess."

"See you in the morning, Jess."

He rode slowly to the cluster of long, low buildings situated around the corrals, all the while thinking about Melissa Jacobson. *She's trouble with a capital T and I have to avoid her.*

But avoiding a spoiled, willful female like Lissa was going to be easier said than done. She had led the sheltered life of an Eastern belle. A man who lived by his guns, a man of mixed blood with a fearful reputation, was a novelty. After being cooped up on an isolated ranch all winter, she was bored; he could furnish excitement and amusement for her.

"Her spring juices would have to start flowing right at the time I arrived," he muttered to himself, vexed by his own response to the girl. She was a beauty, no doubt of that, with her dark red hair and those big honey-colored eyes. But she was forbidden, a white woman from a respectable family. Besides, she was his employer's daughter. One of Jess's strictest rules was that he never mixed business and pleasure.

Putting the disturbing female from his mind, he swung down in front of the stable door, where Rob Ostler stood holding Lissa's gray.

"I'll take care of yore horse, Mr. Robbins," the younger man offered.

"Obliged," Jess said. He handed the reins to Ostler and unfastened his gear from the saddle. The young hand led Blaze and the gray into the musty interior of the big barn.

Jess slung his saddlebags over his right shoulder and carried his weapon case in his left hand. The sounds of coarse male laughter drifted from the long log structure directly across the corral as he approached. He stood in the open doorway and took in the scene, typical of bunkhouses across the plains from Texas to the Canadian border.

The first thing that assaulted his senses was the smell, a composite of coal-oil lamp smoke and sweaty men, liberally mixed with old work boots encrusted by cow manure and the sickly sweet aroma of licorice in chewing tobacco. Because J Bar was such a big spread, the room was spacious as such edifices went, nearly one hundred and fifty feet long. It was large but spartan, with pages from mail order catalogues, newspapers, and dog-eared photographs covering the tightly chinked log walls. Pictures of musical performers and faraway sweethearts were nailed up side by side with advertisements for Dr. Dennigan's Most Marvelous Elixir for Lumbago, Croup, Catarrh, and the Piles. The floor was made of rough wooden planks and littered with boots, saddlebags, and various articles of clothing that had been put there so they would not fall down and get lost.

A Fire in the Blood

The men, relaxing after a long, hard day, were the usual lot, mostly young with painfully vulnerable faces and poorly barbered hair. Here and there grizzled veterans sat among them with gnarled hands and weather-blasted faces.

At the moment, all attention was turned to the confrontation between a tall, thin young man and a wizened veteran who lobbed a mouthful of tobacco into the well-worn spittoon and said, "Gawd dammit, Sly, that's the third time this week I seen you throwin' a grayback on the floor without killin' it first." The old-timer's voice was high and raspy, as if his chaw had coated his vocal cords.

"I didn't neither," the young cowboy protested.

"Did so."

"There it goes," a third man yelled and proceeded to stomp a rapidly moving louse into the rough pine plank.

"I got witnesses now, don't I?" the toothless veteran asked. Several of the men nodded and murmured their agreement with varying degrees of vehemence.

"You gotta pay up, Sly. The fine's ten cents," one said to a chorus of yeahs.

The old-timer held out his hand as the red-faced Sly scratched his belly through a greasy flannel shirt and rummaged in his vest pockets until he produced the required revenue.

"It goes to the readin' fund. Pretty soon we got enough to buy us that new women's catalogue."

The babble of agreement quickly died down as Jess stepped into the bunkhouse. Nearly eighty pairs of eyes fastened on the stranger, quickly sizing him up by the expensive Colt Lightning on his hip and the cold look in his eyes, gray as

Shirl Henke

a winter sky. "I'm looking for the ramrod, Moss Symington."

"I'm Symington," a big, barrel-chested man with slouched shoulders and a bulbous, red-veined nose said, stepping through the crowd of men. His expression was guarded as he combed a thick pawlike hand through the few dozen strands of gray hair remaining on top of his head. "You must be Robbins. Boss said you'd be along in a few days. They's a free bunk at the end of the wall down there. Stow your gear and then meet me in my cabin." He jerked one hamlike hand toward a small log building directly across the corral. "We got some things to talk out." He headed toward the cabin, walking with the rolling, bowlegged gait of a man who had spent his life on horseback.

As Jess walked down the long rows of bunks, the hands stepped back, some insolently appraising him with hard eyes, most backing out of his way with nervous nods. He glanced curiously over them as he passed until he neared the end of the long aisle and one tall, rangy figure stepped into his path.

"Jess, it *is* you! Damnation, I knew it. I'd recognize you in hell with your hide burned off, even after ten years." His coal-black face split in a wide grin as he extended his hand.

Jess seized the older man by the shoulders and inspected him fondly. "Tate, you leather-legged son of a bitch. Last time we parted company, you were heading to Arizona to work for the Hash Knife outfit."

"This ole boy had him purely enough of hot country. Shit, Jess, after a year in Arizona, when a feller goes to hell, he has to wire home for his overcoat.

68

I quit. Drifted some after that." His liquid brown eyes were haunted.

"Tabitha?" Jess asked, already knowing the answer.

"She up 'n died, Jess. That winter while I was workin' Hash Knife. After that, I lost interest in savin' to buy that little spread. Seemed kinda pointless."

"I'm real sorry about Tabitha, Tate," Jess said.

"I reckon I was a lucky cuss to have a gal like her, even for a few years. You still buildin' that place of yorn in the Big Bend Country?"

"Yes. Jonah takes care of it for me." He noticed the worn denims and scuffed boots the black man wore. Even more, what he did not wear. Tate Shannon was unarmed.

Seeing the direction of Robbins's gaze, Shannon said softly, "I give up guns, Jess. Got too old. Too old and too tired of dodgin' bullets. Don't need the money anymore since Tabby's gone. Got no reason to hire out. You oughta give it up yourself. Find a good gal and settle down. Raise a passel o' kids."

Jess chuckled. "Someday, maybe, but not just now." He stepped over to the empty bunk next to Shannon and piled his gear on it.

"You here to stop this rustlin'?"

"If I can. I have to palaver with the ramrod right now, but I'll be back in a bit. Then you and I have some catching up to do."

"Right enough, Jess, right enough."

While the two men talked, other hands studied them furtively, some curious about the allusion to Tate Shannon's hanging up his gun. The rest just figured blacks and breeds naturally belonged together and went back to getting ready for supper.

Jess left the bunkhouse and walked quickly to Symington's cabin. The big ramrod was waiting for him outside the front door. He nodded curtly and did not invite Jess inside. "I know Mr. Jacobson hired you, Robbins, and he's the boss, but I want to speak my piece. These here is good boys, but they ain't gunhands. Hell, half of 'em'd shoot their own feet off if'n they had to strap on a fancy Colt like you wear. I know we got us a problem with thievin', but I don't hanker ta see any of my boys shot up." He hung his thumbs belligerently on the big brass buckle attached to a fancy braided leather belt and leaned back against the cabin wall.

"I fight my own battles, Symington. The last thing I want is a bunch of greenhorn kids and crippled old men riding out like a pack of vigilantes. If I need backup, I'll call in professional help."

"'N Marcus Jacobson'll foot the bill?"

"Yeah. Jacobson'll foot the bill," Jess echoed softly. "You say these are all good hands. You hire anyone new since the trouble started?"

Symington pushed off the wall angrily.

"You mean you think one of my boys is in with them vultures?"

Jess shrugged indifferently. "It's always possible. Jacobson told me the rustling started last summer. Who's signed on since then?"

The ramrod's eyes narrowed, but he sighed, then said grudgingly, "A couple of them come last year. Ralph Sligo. Billy Argee. Nate Blum. Oh, yeah, 'n that nigger, Tate Shannon."

Jess did not move, but his eyes turned to silver ice. "Shannon's a friend of mine. He's no thief. I'll see about the others. Don't send them on round-up. Assign them jobs around the ranch so I can keep an eye on them easier." The foreman nodded stiffly. Jess started to leave, then turned back to Symington and said, "I'll try not to get crossways of you, Symington. Try not to get crossways of me."

While Jess had ridden to the bunkhouse, Lissa followed Germaine inside. "You had no reason to insult Mr. Robbins."

The Frenchwoman snorted as she poured a glass of sherry from the decanter sitting on the parlor credenza. "No reason, *hein?* He is mixed blood, one of your father's hired men, and you ride up on his horse as if he were courting you. Look at yourself—damp and disheveled. I can see through that blouse."

Her hard little eyes burned through the sheer batiste as Lissa stiffened angrily and walked past the cook with her back rigidly straight. "We were caught in the rain this afternoon. It was scarcely my fault—unless you plan to blame me for the weather, too."

"You're wearing clothes fit for a drawing room, not a day's ride on these desolate high plains," Germaine said scornfully.

"I had an accident and was thrown into some quicksand. Of course I had to change out of the ruined riding skirts."

"Of course," Germaine echoed snidely, her eyes following Lissa up the wide stairs. "I must, of course, tell your father how you have consorted with this gunman," she called out, then quickly swallowed the amber liquid in her glass.

When she reached for the decanter and began to pour another drink, Lissa leaned over the railing at the landing and said, "Tell him anything you want—if you can stay sober enough to remember it."

The stench of burning hair and the hoarse bawls of steers carried on the cool morning air. Men cursed and spit as they subdued the thrashing cattle they had roped, dragging them by their bound feet to the fire. There the iron men held glowing, cherry-red running irons ready to change the J Bar brand to the Diamond T by the judicious addition of two straight lines.

Tom Conyers stood back from the frenetic activity surrounding him, smoking a cigarette and watching the sun climb over the eastern horizon. His men had begun work as the first faint rays of dawn tinged the horizon. The J Bar herd had been stolen from an isolated stretch of northern range last night and driven to their hidden camp in a brushy basin off Lodgepole Creek.

"Your information about the roundup helped us decide on this range. Should be at least five hundred head we can take down before their crew and wagon reach this basin." He tossed his cigarette in the fire.

"I told you I could do good working for Jacobson this way," Billy Argee said.

"Yeah, but it's getting dangerous. You could be followed to our camp or even missed, riding out this far," Conyers said as he rolled another cigarette and licked the coarse brown paper to seal it. Wilt reached over with a stick from the fire and the rustler boss leaned down to get a light.

Conyers's angular face was creased like crumpled parchment. He closed his pale, heavy-lidded eyes and took a drag from the cigarette, letting the smoke expel slowly through long thin nostrils. Then he walked over to Billy Argee and Wilt Mason and squatted down. In a low, melodic voice, oddly at variance with his harsh appearance, he said, "I think we ought to set up a meeting site."

"Like we did in Idaho, boss?" Wilt asked.

"Yeah. We need us an isolated line shack, somewhere off the well-traveled trails. A dry place where Billy and Sligo can drop messages and I can pick them up." He looked at the curly-haired boy, then continued, "There's a deserted line shack I seen once a few months back during the winter. Hands built a new one further down Squaw Creek. The old one's clean in the end of a little box canyon near the start of the creek."

"I seen the place last month, boss," Billy said, warming to the idea.

"From now on you ride over there whenever you got news for us of somethin' worth hitting," Conyers said. "Have Sligo write a note saying what needs to be said and one of you put it under the floorboard next to the door. I'll check the shack every few days."

"What if something big comes up—something that can't wait?" Billy asked.

Conyers considered for a moment. "Be damn sure it can't wait. Then ride here."

"You nervous about that breed range detective Jacobson hired?" Argee asked.

The rustler boss made a dismissive gesture with his hand and took another deep drag on his cigarette.

73

Argee persisted, saying, "This is the biggest haul yet, Tom. You reckon we ought ta take all this time to run them brands?"

"Too far trailin' a herd this size all the way to the Nebraska railhead with a brand as well known as J Bar. We'd need papers—bills of sale—to do that," Conyers said.

Billy scratched his curly hair and shifted his weight nervously. He was a wiry little banty rooster, twenty years old and full of himself. "Moss takes care of that for old Jacobson. Maybe I could steal some of them papers."

A sharp bark of laughter cut him off. Conyers looked at Argee with complete disgust. "You couldn't teach a settin' hen to cluck, Argee. You can't read—how in hell you gonna know what you're stealing?"

Argee's face turned beet red and he stiffened in outrage. "Just 'cause I can't read don't mean nothing, Conyers. I'm real handy with this here gun. I ain't afraid of that breed range detective neither. I could take him."

Another man working an iron spat a lob of tobacco into the branding fire and laughed. "Yew oughta be afeered o' Jesse Robbins. He'd squirt enough lead in yew ta make it a payin' job meltin' yew down."

"Finishing off Robbins'd be about as easy as tying down a bobcat with bootlaces," Conyers said, looking at Argee speculatively. The kid had shot several men back in Nevada before moving into Wyoming and joining his band of rustlers. Word was he was good. "You say you could take him. I'll give you the chance."

Conyers turned to a squat, thickset man with a neck like a bull buffalo. "Ace, you and Wilt ride with Argee as soon as we finish this branding. Head to J Bar land and lay for that breed. Be real careful. Get him alone first—then let Argee here do the shooting." Conyers smiled, revealing square yellow teeth with one front incisor missing.

Ace ran a callused palm across the back of his thick neck. "Thought you said the boss was goin' to take care of everythin'. Warn't no need to worry 'bout the breed."

"He pays us good and ships the stock we steal, but when Jacobson brought in Robbins . . ." Conyers shrugged expressively. "It complicates things. Best we take care of it before the breed starts to figure things out. When I get to Nebraska with the herd, I'll talk to him. He might just be real grateful and give us a bonus this time."

Several of the men listening to the conversation chorused their agreement and the rest nodded. Everyone had been nervous since getting word about Jacobson's hired troubleshooter. Conyers planned to solve two problems. He would get rid of Robbins, and in so doing eliminate the possibility that Billy Argee's connection to their operation would be discovered.

I give it about one more year until old man Jacobson's cleaned out. Tom Conyers smiled. When the boss took over the ranch, he would earn a hefty bonus and retire to California. *I'll never smell the stink of another branding fire as long as I live.*

Jess slowly retraced his path to the ranch, deep in thought. He had ridden out at dawn this morning and spent the day checking on the ranges from which steers and horses had been taken over the past months. Every trail he had cut had gone cold.

75

Finally he gave up for the day, figuring he would go to the big spring roundup camp at dawn tomorrow. Perhaps someone there could tell him something useful. Over sixty of the J Bar men would participate in the branding of all the new calves dropped this spring and those yearlings missed last fall and the preceding spring. In addition, representatives from all the neighboring ranches, large and small, would be present to put a brand on their calves and then herd the strayed cows and calves back onto their home ranges.

"Someone has to have seen some sign. A band of rustlers taking this much stock has to be a pretty big bunch. They need a base camp somewhere in this area," he said to Blaze. The big black shook his head as if agreeing.

Jess often talked to the horse about his work. It was a way to think things through in his mind. The western and southern ranges had yielded nothing, but the northeast was closer to the railhead, near the territorial line. It was the likeliest area for the rustlers to be using.

He scanned the horizon, noting the way the low serviceberry bushes had leafed out in the past weeks. Soon it would be full summer, a season that followed hard on the long, bitter chill of winter's blizzards. Just ahead of him by about fifty feet lay an outcrop of shale fringed with scrub pines. By long habit his eyes traveled across the formation. He was about to look away when the glint of sunlight on something metallic bounced from the copse of pines to the south.

Jess leaned to the left side of Blaze and slid his 44-40 Winchester from its scabbard just as the first shot whizzed over the stallion's head with a high-pitched whine. He urged the horse into the small swale by the east side of the road and rolled from the saddle as another barrage of rifle shots shattered the high plains stillness.

Before he reached cover, one shot found its mark, tearing a long wicked slash across his right side. He gritted his teeth and levered the rifle, then searched the pines along the rim of the outcrop.

Amateurs. He had the sun behind him, obscuring their vision while it reflected off their guns. Seeing a flash of metal, he aimed his Winchester and squeezed off a shot. Jess was rewarded by a low guttural cry and the sound of a body rolling back into the brush. He scanned their cover. There were two of them left—unless he had counted the rifle reports wrong or someone had held his fire. Pulling a bandana from his pocket, he stuffed it against the seeping wound in his side and hoped the blood flow would slow down soon.

Rather than wait and risk growing light-headed or having his attackers come after him, Jess began to crawl along the ravine, gaining higher ground. After a few more desultory shots which he did not return, he heard the two bushwhackers calling to each other.

"You think we got 'im, Wilt?"

"Don't use my name, you dumb son of a bitch!"

The latter gravel-voiced command came from a cluster of greasewood about thirty feet from him. Jess tossed a fistful of pebbles near the bushes and waited a beat. A shot zinged out, revealing Wilt's location. Jess fired so closely after it that the two reports almost blended. His blind shot hit its mark. Wilt tumbled backward and landed with a thud, followed by more questioning from his youthful-sounding companion.

Billy Argee was sweating in the cool evening air. This was not going according to plan. First he had missed what should have been an easy shot when that damned breed dived off his horse for no reason—no reason at all. Then Ace took a slug and now Wilt was dead enough to skin. That just left him and the breed. Indians could creep up on a man and shoot him before he even knew one was there. He swallowed the brackish metallic taste of fear and began to move. Maybe he could circle around the breed. After all, he had hit the bastard after he rolled off his horse.

Probably gutshot and bleeding, he reassured himself.

Jess watched the curly-headed young bushwhacker clumsily thrash through the underbrush. Then Argee turned his head, and Jess got a close look at his face. One of the J Bar hands! He stepped out from behind a hawthorn tree and leveled his rifle.

"Drop the weapon, boy. Right now." He watched for any sign the kid would try to make a break, but Argee threw the rifle to the ground.

"Damn you, you gut-eatin' greaser," Argee screamed as he whirled around and grabbed the Army Colt on his hip.

Jess shot him before he cleared leather. As the youth lay sprawled on the hard, rocky ground, Jess muttered, "Second dumb thing you did today." He shook his head. "Stupid way to die, especially considering I didn't want to kill you."

He walked over to the still form, knelt, and began to search the dead man, hoping for some clue to the rustlers. He found a couple of dollars, a photo of some saloon girl, and makings for cigarettes. He studied the dog-eared picture, then put it in his pocket. "Maybe if I can find her, she'll be able to tell me something about the man you worked for."

A search of the other two men and their gear yielded nothing of any use. By this time, Jess was growing decidedly light-headed. He leaned against the nervous bay and whistled for Blaze. When the stallion trotted up dutifully, Jess held on to the saddle horn for a moment to steady himself before attempting to mount. He was several hours from the ranch and not at all optimistic about his chances of staying conscious long enough to get there. As he rode, he wrapped his soogan around his waist, letting the excess of bedroll fall over his leg. Bulky and hot, it at least staunched the blood. He gritted his teeth and kept his eyes on the horizon.

Chapter Five

Lissa dashed across the grass at the side of the house, darting between two birch saplings. The huge gray dog loped effortlessly at her heels, emitting low rumbling woofs as he followed his mistress in the familiar game.

"You awful fellow, Cormac. You know you're not supposed to catch me. Wait until I throw the ball," she said, laughing as she leaned against his rough-coated side and let the dog nuzzle her. Standing on four feet, he could reach her face. His shaggy chin whiskers tickled her as he slurped her, making halfhearted attempts to seize the small leather ball she held aloft in her right hand.

The sound of a rider approaching caused the hound and his mistress to cease their roughhousing. Glancing toward the western horizon, where the sun was setting in a glorious ball of orange fire, Lissa saw the man leaning over the neck of his blaze-faced horse.

"Jess!" She dropped the ball and raced toward him. Cormac loped past her in long, ground-eating strides.

Jess saw the specter galloping across the yard, too small to be a horse but too large to be any kind of dog he had ever seen. A timber wolf? He shook his head, which was spinning from loss of blood. Was he seeing things? He reached for his gun, aware that his hand was moving horrifyingly slow. Then he heard Lissa's cry as she ran up behind the brute.

"Don't shoot, Jess. He's only a dog—an Irish Wolfhound. You're hurt. What's happened?"

She reached up as he started to dismount. When he stumbled against her, the dog interposed his considerable bulk between Robbins and his mistress. Shooing him away, she placed Jess's left arm on her shoulder and began helping him toward the house. When her right hand touched his side and came away wet with blood, she gasped.

"You're bleeding!"

"Sometimes that happens when I get shot," he said through clenched teeth.

"But who? Where?"

"Three rustlers—one of them worked for your father. Don't recall catching their names."

"Worked . . ." she said with dawning horror.

"Yeah. I tried to bring in their horses but couldn't pull the reins. Had to turn them loose about an hour ago."

Swallowing her bile, she said nothing.

They were approaching the ranch house porch before Jess realized where she was headed. "Not here. I need to get to the bunkhouse."

"Don't be foolish. You'll never make it that far."

"I need patching up. That's usually the cook's job."

"Not at J Bar. I'm the nurse. Come on." She tugged him toward the steps.

Jess considered resisting but knew he would pass out soon and opted not to do it in the yard. A grim-faced Germaine came charging down the hall to head them off at the front door.

"He can't come in here," she hissed at Lissa.

"We always treat injured hands at the big house."

"He's no cowhand," Germaine replied.

"Get out of my way or I'll turn Cormac loose on you."

Germaine gasped in indignation but backed stiffly aside as Lissa and Jess entered the front door.

"He'll bleed on my carpets," the housekeeper said tightly.

"Thoughtless of me, ma'am," Jess said with a grin that ended in a grimace.

Lissa ignored the woman's hateful remarks and headed down the long hall to the kitchen. "Make yourself useful, Germaine, and boil me some water."

They made it into the kitchen and she eased him onto a high-backed chair, then set to work gathering bandages and disinfectant while Madame Channault, moving as stiffly as if she were moribund, boiled a kettle of water on her fancy new cast-iron stove.

"Let me help you take off that shirt," Lissa said with a briskness she was far from feeling. "You've lost a lot of blood. You're soaked all the way down your pant leg!" Beneath his swarthy skin, his face was deathly pale.

"You should've seen the soogan I wrapped around me. It took the worst of it," he said as he fumbled with the buttons of his shirt. "You got something to drink around this place? I need reviving."

"Germaine, fetch a glass of brandy from Papa's stock."

"I do not think your father—"

"Considering how much of his liquor you consume, I'm sure he won't mind Jess having a small draught for medicinal purposes." Her eyes met the housekeeper's in a steely glare which convinced the older woman to capitulate.

Lissa finished unbuttoning Jess's shirt and peeled it off, trying not to cause him any further pain.

Germaine returned with the brandy and handed it to Jess, then attended to the water now boiling on the stove. He raised the delicate crystal glass in a mock salute, then downed its contents in a quick gulp and shook his head. "Better," he pronounced.

Kneeling, Lissa inspected the deep gash. "I've never treated a gunshot wound before," she said, chewing her lip as she wrung out a cloth soaked in the hot water and began to cleanse the affected area.

He cocked an eyebrow. "You've treated injuries before though?"

She forced a gamine grin. "You afraid of my skills, Robbins? I was a hospital volunteer in St. Louis." She did not add that she had only been allowed to tend women and children in the hospital. Here at J Bar her duties had never been more serious than to bind up blistered feet or rope-burned fingers.

She felt the housekeeper's eyes burning into her back as she worked. "Hold that pot of water closer, Germaine."

Casting a half fearful look at Jess, the housekeeper spoke in rapid French. "You have never tended a half-naked man before. You should have had the hands carry him to the mess kitchen for treatment. You are only doing this because you desire him. 'Tis a foolish schoolgirl's fancy."

"Somehow I suspect Miss Lissa's touch is a lot gentler than the mess cook's, whatever her motive," Jess replied in smooth, idiomatic French.

Germaine Channault almost dropped the pot she was so reluctantly holding. Her face took on a hue even darker than the rosy color of the bloody water inside the pot. She sputtered but said nothing.

Lissa jerked the cloth away from his wounded side, her cheeks, too, scalded with a blush. "Where on earth did you learn to speak French?"

His voice was amused. "Not in the same place you did."

"Certainly not likely, since I learned in a girls' school—Miss Jefferson's Academy in St. Louis. Every lady must possess the social graces of French conversation," she parroted in that language. "Where did you study?"

He shrugged, then winced as she resumed her ministrations. "North Africa. I was in the French Legion."

"The French Foreign Legion?" Her eyes were round as Mexican gold pieces.

"It's not as romantic as they'd like you to believe," he said drily, then changed the subject. "You ever sew up flesh before?"

She blanched but met his eyes. "I've embroidered hundreds of samplers." She swallowed. "It can't be all that different. The gash is clean now." She stood up and began to search through the medical supplies for a needle and thread.

Jess watched her work, noticing the faint trembling in her hands. For all that, she had been amazingly calm and levelheaded at the sight of so much blood. "Most women I know would have a fit of vapors and leave me to tend myself. I've sewn up more than a few of my own wounds."

"I think you'd better let me handle this one," she said as she pressed a clean towel to his side. "This will slow the bleeding," she added. Covertly Lissa studied his bronzed, muscular arms and chest. His skin was marred in several places by small white scars. *What a pity such a beautiful body has to be disfigured.* Heat flamed her cheeks again as she tore her eyes from the sleek muscles and patterns of crisp black hair. On second thought, the scars were not very discernible and only added to his exotic virility. She fought the urge to run her hands over his skin. "I see you've led every bit as dangerous a life as your reputation would lead me to imagine."

"A debauched and disreputable life, too." He smiled cynically, as if reading her mind, and watched her blush again.

She eyed the needle and thread. "You're the one who'll pay for making me nervous. Her tone was acerbic.

"I make you nervous because I'm forbidden, Lissa. You're just intrigued because you're defying convention." He turned his gaze to Germaine.

The housekeeper's lips thinned, but she said, "He

is telling the truth, Lissa. You should leave him alone."

"Is that what you really want, Jess? For me to leave you alone?" she teased as she reached for the needle she had laid out on the table beside them.

Ignoring her taunt, he removed the cold towel and said, "What a man wants usually has little to do with what he gets. Just sew me up and be done with it."

"First I have to put this carbolic solution on the wound." He held still as she poured the fiery liquid into the gaping slash. "You're amazingly stoic. Is it because of your Indian blood?"

"No. My Spanish blood. My mother was half Mexican, remember? They're a cussed tough lot."

Taking a deep breath, she punctured the skin and pulled the needle through, then connected the lower side to the upper. Puncture. Pull. Tighten. She repeated the methodical stitching, drawing the ragged edges of flesh closed. He held perfectly still, the only indication of his pain a fine sheen of sweat dotting his forehead.

"You're not going to pass out and ruin my stitches, are you?"

"No. The brandy had remarkable restorative powers," he replied through clenched teeth as she tied off the last stitch.

"That wasn't too hard, considering it's the first time I've done it," Lissa said speculatively.

"Easy for you to say," he countered, raising his arm and flexing his side experimentally. "What did you use—a braided reata and a Tuareg scimitar to draw it through?"

"Number seven embroidery thread," she replied waspishly.

As she tore off clean linen strips to bandage his wound, she looked at his ruined shirt and then turned to the housekeeper. "Germaine, go to the washroom and get one of Papa's old shirts. Mr. Robbins's is beyond repair."

Madame Channault threw up her hands in disgust. With a few choice remarks in French, she swished out the kitchen door to do as she was ordered.

Lissa knelt beside him, bandages in hand. "Raise your arms." He complied. Beneath his dark skin, sinuous muscles flexed in marvelous symmetry. Her mouth went dry. She licked her lips and reached around him with the bandages.

Jess could see the tip of her pink tongue flick across her lips as she concentrated. Then, as she reached around him, her breasts pressed against his chest. Against his will he felt the blood rushing to his groin and cursed silently. *I shouldn't have that much blood left!*

Lissa could smell the faint scent of horse and male sweat combined with that undefined essence that she now thought of as his own. A deep, pervasive heat stole into her limbs and pooled low in her belly, causing her pulse to race. She knew she was trembling as she wound the bandage repeatedly around his slim waist. Her blood thrummed through her veins. Every fiber of her being felt sensitized yet oddly lethargic at the same time. *No man has ever made me feel this way!*

She tied off the bandage, but did not pull away from him. Instead she raised her face to his and their eyes met. Her hands fell to rest against his chest, her fingertips burying themselves in the springy black hair. He lowered his arms but sat

87

very still, making no move to touch her.

"Lissa, this is dangerous."

"I know," she said in a small choked voice.

Finally, hearing Germaine at the back porch, he brushed her hands away, then stood up on very shaky legs. His unsteadiness was caused by a great deal more than the injury he had sustained, and they both knew it.

"Much obliged for the doctoring," he said hoarsely and turned away, reaching for the shirt the housekeeper thrust at him. With a grimace of pain he slipped it on and began to button it. It was a soft pale gray that emphasized his eyes and contrasted with his swarthy skin. Germaine had selected it because it was old and faded, but the effect was the opposite of what she intended.

"You really should get some rest," Lissa said. Her voice cracked.

He cut off her train of thought by saying, "I will—at the bunkhouse." Picking up his hat, he walked very carefully toward the back door. With one hand on the sash, he asked, "That great brute of a dog still around? I don't think I'm up to a tussle just now."

"I'll keep Cormac from licking you to death," she replied, struggling to regain her composure. "Consider yourself lucky; he normally eats strangers. For some peculiar reason, he's taken a considerable liking to you." Lissa called the dog, who bounded up, tail wagging and tongue lolling as if he were a sheepdog instead of a yard-high behemoth.

She held her arms around the great brute's neck while Jess whistled for Blaze. When the stallion trotted around the corner of the house and stopped next to him, he very carefully mounted and rode toward the corrals. She watched his retreating back, mesmerized.

Germaine Channault studied the troublesome younger woman through slitted eyes. Marcus would not be pleased with Lissa's fascination for that savage. She considered how she could use the situation to her own advantage as she turned back to the kitchen.

Late the following morning, Germaine watched from the kitchen window as Lissa slipped quietly from the side door carrying her medicine basket. The smitten girl was going down to the bunkhouse to tend Robbins's injury.

If only Marcus would ride home in time to see his precious daughter acting like a common trollop, treating that half-naked mongrel alone in his quarters!

Jess lay stretched out on his bunk, enjoying the blissful quiet now that the last of the hands had finished their chores around the corral and headed out for their day's assignments on the range. Normal rising time was four a.m., when the bunkhouse cook yelled, "Grab it now or I'll spit in the skillet!"

Cowpunchers had stumbled from their beds cussing and rubbing their eyes as they threw on their clothes and made halfhearted attempts at washing their faces in ice-cold water before lining up at the mess hall for their morning meal of bacon, beans, and sourdough biscuits.

The food had smelled passable, but Jess decided to rest his injured side. When he rolled over and pulled a blanket over his head, no one disturbed him.

Tate had brought him a plate of food last night and they talked about what happened. Once he located the rustlers' home base, he knew he would need backup to deal with them. Tate knew it, too. But the older man had lost the will to use his gun. In fact, he'd lost his will to do much of anything but drift, it seemed to Jess. All over losing a woman.

Jess tried to imagine ever loving a woman so much that her loss would destroy him. He could not do so. The only female he had ever loved was his mother, and she had died when he was in North Africa. There had been a procession of women moving in and out of his bed since he was fifteen, but none of them ever troubled his heart. Once he had saved enough money to complete his plans for the ranch, he thought he would marry some chaste young Mexican girl who would not object to his Indian blood, someone who would be content with the simple life of a small rancher's wife. But he never expected to have any great *tendresse* for her, just the comfortable affection of shared work and children.

That had always been his plan, but this time when he closed his eyes and thought of the future, no raven-haired, sloe-eyed Mexicana appeared. Rather, an amber-eyed, fair-skinned woman with hair like the cherry glow of live coals filled his dreams. *Lissa.* He could feel the soft pressure of her breasts and thighs as she rubbed her body provocatively against his, and smell the sweet spicy scent of orange blossoms that clung to her.

She's a spoiled little tease. Forget her. He rolled

over and cursed as the tight stitches in his side pulled. That she was such a levelheaded nurse had surprised him. A society belle like Lissa Jacobson should have fainted at the sight of blood. But Marcus Jacobson's daughter should have had the vapors at the sight of a half-breed gunman, too, and she did just the opposite.

The more he thought about the fire-haired witch, the more restless he became. Finally, he threw off his blankets and sat up. Just as he slid on his denims and began to button them, the bunkhouse door opened with a loud creak. He had his Colt cocked and leveled before she stepped inside.

"I surrender. Don't shoot," Lissa said, walking toward him with her basket.

He uncocked his weapon and slid it into the oiled holster lying on his bed. "That's a damn-fool dangerous thing to do. Never creep up on a man, Princess. You could get shot." He scowled as she neared him. She wore an apple-green cotton dress with a rounded neckline that was filled with frilly white lace ruffles. Her hair tumbled down her back in a riot of soft curls, held back from her face by a matching green ribbon. The picture was one of girlish innocence combined with sensuous beauty. She was enchanting—and she knew it!

Lissa drank in the sight of him, his dark, splendid chest bare except for the snowy bandage. Her eyes followed the patterns of black hair that vanished into his denims, which were only half-buttoned. Her pulse hammered and her breath caught. She licked her lips and tried to speak. "I figured you wouldn't come to the house for me to change your dressing, so . . ."

"Lady, you're plain crazy, you know that? You

have no business alone here with any man, much less me. Your father would skin you if he knew."

"But he isn't here," she said breathlessly. "And you do need to have that wound tended." Steeling her courage, she approached. When there was only a foot separating them, she could smell his scent. He stood stock-still, not retreating, but not accommodating her either, as if waiting to see what she would do.

"Raise your arms so I can untie the wrap." The command came out like a squeak.

Slowly he did as she asked. All those familiar muscles flexed as she reached around him to unwrap the linen. His chest hairs brushed the tip of her nose and she flinched, wanting to bury her head against the crisp mat but knowing that to do so would be a tactical error just now. Her hands fumbled with the knot for a moment, then it gave and she unrolled the stripping and inspected the angry red gash.

"It'll leave a rather large scar, I'm afraid."

He lowered his arms as she fussed with the carbolic. "It'll have lots of company, so it won't matter."

She looked up, the question stamped plainly on her face. He grinned raffishly. "The other ones are below my waist."

"Oh," was all she could think to say, hating the breathy squeak in her voice. *I sound like a ten-year-old!* His low chuckle almost caused her to drop the medicine bottle. He was laughing at her. Angrily, she ran the carbolic-soaked rag along the stitches and was rewarded by a guttural oath as he stiffened and drew back.

"Easy with that stuff," he said between clenched teeth.

A small grin touched her lips and danced impishly in her eyes, turning them to deep gold. "What about your stoic Spanish blood?"

"I'd as soon not lose any more of it if you don't mind."

Smugly, she finished cleaning the sutures and replaced the cork on the carbolic bottle. "I should remove the stitches in a couple of days. Think you're up to it?" she dared, holding out clean wrappings.

"Oh, I'm up to it, Princess, but I don't think you are. . . ." His voice trailed away, gravelly and suggestive.

He had made some sort of sexual reference, she knew, but did not understand. Still, she could see that her presence disturbed him. His eyes were smoldering like molten silver and his body was taut. Then, as she reached around him with the bandages, she glanced down and saw the bulge in his denims. Her face flamed anew and she faltered.

Sensing her thoughts and furious at his own body's reaction to her, Jess lashed out. "You see the effect you have on a man like me, Princess. You'd better scamper back to that big fancy house and lock all the doors."

She tied off the bandage but was strangely unable to back away from him. Head bowed, she whispered, "What if I don't want to run away?"

"Then this is what happens," he said savagely as one arm wrapped around her waist, pulling her tightly against his half-naked body, while the other hand tangled in her fiery curls, tilting her face up to his. His mouth descended with deliberate roughness, pressing against hers as he held her immobile. When she gasped for breath, his tongue plundered inside, dancing across her small, smooth teeth and twining with her tongue.

He seemed to consume her, tasting, stroking, taking as his lips ground against hers and his hot, bare skin fused with her cool starched cotton dress until it was rucked up and wrinkled, filled with the scent of the male.

At first Lissa was frightened, but only for an instant. She had wondered what his kiss would feel like when she watched him meld his body with the music hall woman's. Now he was showing her. And it was glorious. Her arms crept around his narrow waist, and she raised herself into the kiss, opening to it, to him, emulating his every movement with the untutored hunger of the curious young virgin he had named her.

Jess could feel her return the embrace, fusing her body to his in blind acquiescence. His blood boiled in his veins as it had not since he was a callow boy on fire during his first sexual encounter. One hand cupped her breast while the other raised her buttocks, grinding her hips in rhythm with his.

Almost. He almost threw her onto the bunk and ripped her clothes off, but the sound of horses' hooves pounding up to the corral and the old cook's greeting broke through his haze of lust.

"Howdy, Mr. Jacobson. Figgered you'd be here afore roundup started."

Jess pushed her away from him and she stumbled back, nearly falling against his bunk. Her delicate skin was abraded by whisker burns, and her eyes were dilated. One small hand touched finger-tips to lips. Her breath, like his, was ragged.

Seizing a shirt, he pulled it on, then threw her supplies into the basket and thrust it at her. "Here, take this and get the hell out of here before I end up having to shoot your pa!"

When she took the basket and numbly began to walk to the side door, he grabbed her arm and pointed her to the opposite end of the long build-ing. "That way. He's heading into the stable. Don't let him catch you, or there'll be hell to pay."

Clutching the basket to her breasts, Lissa fled down the creaky wooden planks and out the door. She was up the road and inside the house before Marcus emerged from the stable.

Chapter Six

Germaine set the platter of sausages down beside the tall, fluffy stack of pancakes, then bustled stiffly from the room, leaving Lissa and Marcus alone to eat their breakfast.

He served himself, cut a neat square of golden pancake dripping with sticky syrup and ate it, then wiped his mouth with the snowy napkin. "Germaine tells me you rode up to the front door on Jesse Robbins's horse, making quite a spectacle of yourself."

I wondered how long it would take her to spill her venom. "I was forced to ride with him. My horse fell into quicksand, and I had to change into city clothes. I couldn't ride astride that way or I'd have really created a spectacle."

"You were soaked to the skin."

"That's what usually happens when I get caught in a thunderstorm. The storm came up so suddenly I was already drenched before he could give me his poncho." She did not add that he had been inside the rain gear with her.

"She also said you tended the half-breed's gunshot wound." His pale blue eyes studied her.

Lissa shrugged carelessly. "Germaine didn't approve, I realize, but you know I'm a capable nurse."

"I was never happy about you volunteering in that St. Louis hospital, but at least you only treated females and children. I don't want you mixing with common cowhands, Princess."

"For all you're paying this fellow, it scarce seemed sensible to leave him to Vinegar's home remedies."

He took a sip of coffee, then stared at her over the rim of the cup. "I'm paying the fellow so much because he has a fearful reputation. He's a hired killer. Not at all the sort any decent woman should associate with."

"Sewing up his gashed side is scarcely the same as letting him escort me to the roundup dance," she said with asperity. "I thought you wanted me to take an interest in J Bar."

"I do, Princess. But your role is to preside over the household, not work with the men."

"Preside over the household—*humph*," she said pettishly. "With Germaine in charge, I can scarcely walk through the parlor, much less preside over anything."

His expression grew stony as he carefully set his cup down. "We've had this discussion about Germaine before, Lissa. The matter is closed. She has been an excellent and invaluable employee, and I will not dismiss her."

"Why not? What is it about her—what hold does she have over you?"

"That will be quite enough, Lissa. Germaine stays." His eyes were as cold as a Wyoming blue norther. "You'll have to make your peace with her."

"How can I? Every time I so much as set foot outside my room, she tattles to you about my supposed indiscretions. She hates me, Papa."

"Nonsense. You're just too headstrong for your own good. You don't use common sense. I attribute part of the blame to your being raised in St. Louis."

She threw down her napkin. "I never asked to be sent away. You decided I had to go."

"You needed a woman's touch after your mother died, Lissa. Don't tell me you didn't enjoy going to school in St. Louis."

"You know I did, but—"

"No buts, young lady. I've worked and slaved to build a fine life for you, but you have to understand how things are done in Wyoming. All Germaine has done is to point out your unsuitable behavior. Take the matter of Jesse Robbins. He has Indian and Mexican blood, Lissa."

"I did nothing wrong, Papa. I've treated the injuries of the other hands ever since I came home last year. Germaine has made this into something . . . sordid."

"He was shot in the side, and you had him strip off his shirt to work on the wound."

"I could scarcely tend it if he kept his shirt *on,*" she countered stubbornly.

"That's just the point—he was unclothed in front of you and you're an unmarried young lady."

Her cheeks heated as she remembered seeing far more of Jesse Robbins when he was naked in his bath. "So, we're back to marriage again," she said with a frustrated sigh.

"Lemuel Mathis is a fine man, eminently suitable for you, Lissa. I have tried to be patient, as has he, but you're trying us both sorely."

"I know how you feel, Papa . . . but I'm not certain how I feel. What if I chose someone else?"

He looked up sharply. "You've always said there was no one else."

She made a dismissive gesture with her hand. "There is Yancy Brewster. He asked me to the spring roundup dance."

His eyes narrowed. "Brewster's only a foreman. It'll be years before he can afford to build his own spread."

"But he knows cattle. He'd be as good a choice as Lemuel to run J Bar. That is your main concern, after all."

"You know that's not true, Princess. I want you to be happy."

"Then give me some time to look around, please, Papa."

"You really fancy Brewster?" He cocked one eyebrow and stroked his chin consideringly.

In fact, she thought Yancy a mean-spirited bully, but he had been courting her and right now she grasped for any straw just to keep her father from foisting Lemuel Mathis on her. And to keep him from discovering her fascination with the forbidden Jesse Robbins. "I don't know that I really fancy him. Why not wait and see how things develop? He'll be at the dance and so will Lemuel. . . ." She smiled impishly and let the matter drop.

Marcus resumed eating his breakfast. Neither father nor daughter saw the venomous look Germaine gave Lissa from the kitchen doorway.

Jess rode up to the big canvas-covered wagon. Its tailgate was pulled out to form a worktable where the J Bar cook, Vinegar Joe Riland, was busy beating biscuits for the noon meal. The wiry little man spat tobacco without missing a beat with his big wooden spoon. Vinegar Joe wore a perpetual scowl on his wizened face, which was covered by a grizzled salt-and-pepper beard with a peculiar reddish cast—whether the color was a freak of nature or the result of stains from his chaw was conjectural.

One lantern-jawed older hand tossed the silty remains from his tin cup and said, "Now I ain't kickin', Vinegar, but I had to chaw on thet coffee afore I cud swaller it."

Vinegar spat again, then fixed the offender with one baleful brown eye while its mate wandered vaguely off to stare in Jess's general direction. "They ain't no such thing as coffee too strong—only men too weak."

Several men guffawed as they nodded greetings to Jess. He dismounted and tied Blaze to a wagon wheel.

"Morning, Vinegar," he said as he reached for a cup and poured himself some of the inky brew.

"Yew come ta bitch about my java, too?" the old cook snorted, still beating the sticky grayish batter in the big crockery bowl.

Jess took a swallow and raised the cup. "Coffee's Texas strong."

What was almost a smile creased the old man's

face. "It takes a real Texan to know what's good," he said, casting a disparaging glance toward the hand who had complained.

The sounds of roundup sent up a cacophony in the swirling dust. Calves bawled, and cowboys cursed and sweated in the noon heat. They roped and dragged the critters up to the fires, where others wrestled the thrashing animals down, bound them by three legs, and held them fast. Then the cattle were branded with the appropriate iron. Simultaneously, other hands wielding sharp knives notched their ears. With the smell of their own burning hair and hide in their nostrils, the calves were then released to scamper back to their mothers.

The work was grueling and endless, from predawn to full dark, up to six weeks in the larger districts set up by the Association. When all the spring stock had been branded and cattle returned to their home ranges, soon it would be time for the fall roundups to commence. Then the four-year-old beeves were trailed to the railhead in Cheyenne for sale.

Jess watched the men work around one of the fires as he sipped his coffee. He sauntered over to where the old cook was working, away from the rest of the men.

Vinegar chomped on his plug as he studied Jess with that unnerving single-focused eye. "Whut kin I do fer ya?"

Jess nodded, then asked, "Billy Argee have any special friends on the J Bar crew?"

Vinegar rolled out a slab of biscuit dough with a few hard, practiced strokes of his big wooden rolling pin. "Heerd yew up 'n sent him on fer harp lessons."

Jess smiled grimly. "Where he went, I reckon I more likely was fitted for coal shoveling."

"Kid was a loner. Always on the prod, kindy like a rained-on rooster."

"That's what Tate said," Jess echoed noncommittally.

"The kid in with them rustlers? Guess it don't surprise me none. Yew figger they's more J Bar hands in on this, don't yew?" He scratched his head and considered for a moment, then began cutting biscuits and tossing them into a heavy tin pan.

"Could be. I'd be obliged if you pass along anything suspicious you see or hear." The cook nodded briskly and continued his task as Jess ambled toward the branding fire. Where in the hell was old Marcus? Jacobson had agreed to meet him at the roundup site and show him the location from which the last herd had been stolen. He had slept later in deference to his injured side, fully expecting the old man to be in the thick of the roundup when he arrived. Perhaps something could be gleaned around the fire. He stood off to the side and listened to the men exchange banter while he waited.

Lissa saw him standing alone as she and her father approached the camp. A small shiver of anticipation danced along her spine, but she maintained a carefully neutral expression on her face. When Cormac bounded ahead, she did not call him back. He loved Vinegar's biscuits. But the dog surprised her, heading directly toward Jess, who had his back turned. Her first impulse was to yell out a warning, but she glanced quickly at Marcus and decided against it. If Cormac took a shine to the gunman, all the better—as long as her father did not think she had done anything to encourage it.

The big wolfhound loped toward the branding fire and Jess. When he came within a dozen yards, he let out a resounding "woof" and charged. Jess spun around, gun drawn, sighting on the huge shaggy hound. Recognizing the dog, he slid his Colt back into its holster and braced himself as the beast's front legs came to rest on his shoulders. Yards of dripping pink tongue laved his face, knocking his hat to the ground.

"If'n thet don't beat all. Never seed thet hound take to a new man like thet," one of the hands said.

Lissa galloped into the camp and jumped from her horse, laughing and calling to her pet. "Get down, Cormac, you great oaf!"

Standing on his hind legs, the dog towered over the tall man by nearly a foot. When Lissa walked up and seized his collar, he backed down, tail still furiously wagging, then looked at her with wounded eyes.

"You've caused me to spoil his fun, you know," she said, amused at the look of consternation on the man's face.

Jess regarded the hundred-and-seventy pounds of hound warily. "So he wasn't something I hallucinated when I was shot. You'd better keep a tighter leash on him. I might have shot him."

"You'd better keep a tighter leash on your guns, Mr. Robbins. Cormac is a very valuable hunter."

"So am I, Miss Jacobson," he said as he dusted off his hat and replaced it on his head. He inspected her trim figure. A soft green blouse of silk clung seductively to the curves of her breasts. Images of the way they had showed through the wet camisole flashed in his mind before he let his eyes travel to the buff twill riding skirt, tailored to fit her tiny waist and rounded derriere perfectly. He could still feel those delectable buttocks pressed against his inner thighs.

In such thoughts lurked madness. He looked up and studied her face. She had braided that dark, burnished hair into a single fat plait which hung down her back, leaving her face austerely adorned only by a few wispy curls. She blushed under his bold perusal, obviously pleased at the attention.

"You seem to be mending remarkably quickly," she said, returning his inspection. "How's the side?"

He shrugged. "It aches like hell."

"I need to take out the stitches soon."

"I can do that myself. I've done it before—in harder-to-reach places," he added with a grin.

Lissa's expression grew smug. "Why, Jesse Robbins, you aren't afraid of one little woman with a scissors and tweezers, are you? I have a real steady hand."

He did not respond to her taunt but watched her father rein in his big roan. "Time to say good-bye, Miss Jacobson." He tipped his hat and walked over to Marcus.

"Morning, Mr. Jacobson. I'm ready to ride to the place where that last herd was taken."

"Can I come along, Papa?" Lissa interjected.

Marcus frowned. "Stay here, Princess, and keep out of harm's way, else I'll not let you come to the roundup camp again." His eyes sent a deeper message to her.

Stay away from Jesse Robbins.

Knowing it would do no good to argue with him, she acquiesced. "I'll help Vinegar with the midday meal."

"There's my girl," Jacobson said with a steely smile. "When you're ready to ride home, have Moss send one of the hands with you. I have to ride over to the Evers roundup when I finish with Robbins. I'll see you at home tonight, Lissa."

The two men rode away from the noise and dust of the camp. Neither spoke for quite a while. Then Jacobson broke the silence. "My daughter is a very beautiful young woman, used to getting her own way. I'm afraid I've indulged her more than I should have, but she's all the family I have left in the world. I mean to see her marry well." He paused and turned to Jess with his ice-blue eyes glowing. "You take my meaning, Robbins?"

"I take your meaning, Mr. Jacobson," Jess replied levelly. He held the older man's imperious stare until Jacobson broke it off, pointing to the shale outcropping directly ahead of them.

"We'll circle around those low bluffs until we reach a shallow basin. Used to be filled with J Bar beeves."

They rode into the basin, and Jess told Marcus to wait by the ashes of the long-dead campfire. He moved in widening circles, away from the central location, studying the soft, muddy ground. The old man took a drink from his canteen and wiped his mouth with the back of his hand as he observed Robbins's careful inspection.

"He cuts sign just like a savage. Blood always tells." Marcus considered how highly recommended Jesse Robbins had come. In all likelihood, the breed could finish this rustler business in a few weeks and be on his way back to Texas—or wherever the hell he drifted next.

Germaine had been certain Lissa was infatuated with the handsome gunman. But Germaine and Lissa had always been oil and water, ever since Lissa was a child. He knew she was restless and bored at the ranch, but that was just natural high spirits after a long winter of confinement. What she needed was a passel of new dresses and some fancy social events at which to wear them. That would distract her from the gunman quickly enough. Then, too, a man like Robbins had not survived by being a fool. He knew better than to touch a white lady. Having settled things in his own mind, Marcus dismissed Germaine's dire warnings as Jess rode up to where he was sitting.

"Find anything?" Marcus asked as he remounted.

"There are about twenty of them, I'd guess. Very fast and careful. No distinctive markings on the shoes. This is a big, professional operation, not some bunch of hungry nesters or grub-line riders swinging a wide loop."

Marcus cursed. "Any idea which direction they went?"

"East, toward the Nebraska line. But an outfit this large has to have a base camp, someplace to hole up between raids. I need to get the lay of the land before I start searching. Also, I have a lead I need to check out in Cheyenne. I may not be back to the ranch for a couple of days."

Jacobson studied Robbins intently. "You still think more of my hands are involved?"

"Argee sure as hell was, and he's not the only new man hired on last fall. That's one of the things

I mean to follow up in town," Jess said, thinking of the dog-eared old photograph in his vest pocket. He said nothing more to Jacobson.

"You'll be needing some help with a bunch this size."

Jess grinned. "True. I'm good, Jacobson, but I'm sure not figuring to take on twenty armed men alone. While I'm in town, I'll wire for the men I need."

"Good enough. I'll see you back at the J Bar in a few days." Marcus turned his horse south and rode off while Jess studied the far horizon to the east before kneeing Blaze in that direction.

Lissa helped Vinegar dish up a hearty meal of beef, beans, and biscuits with "spotted pup" —rice pudding with raisins— for dessert. As he scrubbed the mountain of tinware, she stayed to talk with the crotchety old cook, who had carried her around on his shoulders when she was a little girl.

"This here's gonna be the biggest roundup yet, gal," Vinegar said as he dipped his arms up to their knobby elbows in a big pan of suds and seized a fistful of clattering plates. " 'N me havin' ta feed all them leather-legged galoots with gullets as empty as a banker's heart. I'll be cookin' twenty-five hours a day till snow flies."

"There are a lot of new men," Lissa said, blowing on a cup of Vinegar's "horseshoe floater." "What do you know about the stock detective, Robbins?" she asked casually.

Vinegar spat with gusto. "Humph. A cold one. Got him a rep from the Pecos to the Canady border." He paused and looked at her. "Gal, you ain't fixin' any fool notions on thet breed, are yew? I know he's fine lookin', kindy smooth talkin' too, the way the women like, but he's pure poison. Yer pa'd be mad 'nough ta kick a hawg barefoot if'n he caught yew makin' eyes at Robbins."

She huffed. "I'm *not* making eyes at him!"

He scratched his scruffy beard. "I seen yew 'n him talkin' real cozy when yew come ridin' in with thet hellhound yew call a dawg."

"I was just asking him about his stitches," she replied primly.

Snorting, Vinegar asked, "He take up sewin'?"

"No, I did—on him. I sewed up a bullet wound in his side."

"Wal, cain't say I'm sorry to pass on thet job o' work."

Regarding Vinegar's large gnarled hands and the fast, rough way he used them, she imagined Jess had been just as happy to have him pass on the first-aid job, too. "It's a long ride back to the house. I'd better be going. Cormac and I did enjoy lunch," she added, dimpling.

The grizzled little man cast a baleful eye to where the big dog lay sleeping beneath the wagon. "He oughta have! Et two pans of biscuits all by his lonesome."

"Well, since he's enjoying your cooking so much, I know you won't mind my leaving him here for a few days. Moss wants to get rid of some coyotes who've been killing calves."

"Now, jist a minnit, Miz Lissa. Thet lummox is purely more trouble than a box a skunks at a prayer meetin'. I ain't foolin' with him. Next time he gits in the biscuits, I'm takin' my ten-gauge to the damn-blasted critter!"

"I don't know who dislikes you more, Germaine

or Vinegar," she said as the dog rose and walked over to nuzzle her neck with an affectionate lick.

"You ready to ride, Miss Lissa?" Rob Ostler asked. He walked up leading her favorite horse, Little Bit, a small, fleet pinto.

"Take good care of Vinegar, Cormac," she called out as they rode away.

After they had cleared the basin and crossed Lodgepole Creek, Lissa reined in and pointed to the west. "If we cut through the scrub pines here we can be home an hour earlier."

"I don't rightly know, Miz Lissa. Thet's pretty rough country," the young Texan objected.

"Oh, stuff. It isn't that rough. I've crossed it several times on Little Bit. I promise, no race," she said, raising her hand in a pledge.

"I reckon it couldn't hurt," Ostler said dubiously, already won over by Lissa's cajoling.

They set out to cross a narrow band of scrubby pines and juniper that ran like a divider between the open cattle ranges to the north and the ranch to the south. The terrain was rough and they rode slowly, sparing their horses until they had reached a second fork of the Lodgepole. As they dismounted to allow the horses to drink, a piteous bawling cry came from across the stream.

"Thet's a calf in big trouble," Rob said, swinging up on his piebald and splashing across the shallow water.

Lissa did likewise, but before she could reach the thicket where Rob was freeing a thrashing calf, he called out, "Don't come nearer, Miz Lissa. This here ain't nothin' fer a lady to see."

But she had already seen. The calf's mother lay on the ground behind some serviceberry bushes along with half a dozen other beeves, all with their throats cut. Flies droned noisily around the gory carcasses, feasting on congealed blood. She put her handkerchief to her mouth. "Who would do this?"

"Squatters most likely. By the look of it, they drove off a bunch o' calves. This here lil' feller got hisself tangled up and went lame, so they up 'n left 'im. Butchered the best cuts from the steers and cows. Somewhere they's gonna be a real fancy feast tonight or I miss my guess," Rob said grimly.

"Is it too late for Moss to send some hands after them?"

Rob scratched his head. "I cud ride hell-bent fer the camp and bring back some men, but I can't do it carryin' this here little feller."

"Give him to me. I'll ride behind you, carrying him, while you fetch help," she said, reaching down to take the catch rope Ostler had looped around the calf's neck.

"Now, Miz Lissa, I can't leave yew all alone. Mister Jacobson'd peel the hide clean off me."

"You're wasting time, Rob. The thieves are getting away while we argue." She seized the rope and began to walk the injured calf toward her horse. Rob followed, protesting, even though it would do no good.

She swung up on Little Bit and waited. "Lift him up onto my saddle, Rob," she commanded.

Sighing raggedly, he did as she asked, then jumped on his big gelding and took off as she yelled, "I'll be right behind you."

But she could not ride with any speed weighed down with the calf, who proved to be a very restive passenger. After twenty minutes or so, she reined in near a small swale, where a hawthorn offered some welcome shade.

"We'll just take a little rest and wait until Rob comes back with the men," she said, dismounting carefully. The problem of getting her unhappy passenger down was solved when he squirmed over the opposite side of the saddle. He nearly choked himself before she was able to loosen the rope, but was otherwise none the worse for wear.

"You're dumber than a herd of woollybacks," she said crossly. "And everybody knows a sheep's brain cavity wouldn't make a drinking cup for a hummingbird."

While the calf regarded her with liquid brown eyes, she took a drink from her canteen, then soaked her handkerchief and bathed her sweaty face and neck. "Aah, that's better," she said softly.

"Yeah. Be even better, little lady, if'n you was to undo a few more of them buttons and let us see your teats," a raspy nasal voice said.

Lissa dropped the canteen and turned to where a pair of scruffy-looking drifters had stepped from behind the hawthorn.

Chapter Seven

"Lookee here, Mace. Some soft-hearted female come to rescue that orphaned calf," the shorter, skinny one said.

His tall, thickset companion licked his lips and wiped his grimy hands on equally filthy denims, a gesture of nervous habit. His watery pale eyes squinted at her. He just grinned, saying nothing as he advanced.

"How do you know this calf is an orphan?" *Unless you killed its mother!* Lissa forced herself to stand her ground in spite of their stalking. These down-at-the-heels hard cases had to be part of the bunch who had butchered the cattle. *Rob, Moss, where are you?* Maybe she could face them down if she didn't show the least sign of fear. "I'm Melissa Jacobson. My father owns J Bar Ranch. You're trespassing, and my foreman will be here to evict you any moment."

"E-vict? Whut's thet mean, Pike?" the big fellow said in the nasal twang of the Ozarks. His fleshy face was rent by a long scar that curved around the side of his temple down to his jaw, oddly distorting his coarse features.

"Seems real peculiar, you bein' here all alone," Pike said, ignoring his companion's question. "You're a real fancy piece, awright."

"I told you, I won't be alone long. My foreman will be riding down here any minute," she replied with more bravado than certainty.

The pair were closing in on her like two timber wolves. If only she had Cormac with her. The thin one put out a bony hand with blackened, broken nails and ran them over the soft fabric of her blouse, snagging the delicate silk. She jerked away, but the heavyset man had moved behind her. He seized her by both arms and pulled her against his body.

The smell of stale tobacco and rotted teeth blended with the acrid odor of unwashed skin. She gagged, kicking and screaming as he continued to pinion her, but it was difficult to inflict much damage kicking backward. He only laughed at her feeble efforts. Then Pike tried to grab her braid. She jerked her head back and rewarded him with a hard bite on his finger. The taste was foul. Lissa spat in disgust as he howled an oath and jerked back his hand, then raised it and struck her full across the mouth.

"Damn hellcat. I reckon we can break you good." He scanned the horizon, looking for her supposed rescuers. "But this here ain't the time or place—hold her while I get a rope," he instructed Mace.

Lissa screamed louder and thrashed, to no avail. Pike quickly returned with a length of rope and tied her hands securely, then stuffed a filthy blue bandana in her mouth and secured it. Mace put her up on her horse and led her to where their horses were hidden in a swale behind a copse of pines. The two men mounted and rode east at a hard gallop with Mace leading the pinto.

Jess had circled east, trying to pick up a trail that might give him some clue as to where the rustlers had their base camp.

If only he knew the lay of this land, he might be able to figure a likely place . . . Tate had been working J Bar for a couple years. Deciding it was time for the former stock detective to come out of retirement, he turned Blaze to the southwest. First he would ride to Cheyenne and show the picture of Argee's lady friend around. Maybe Cammie could help. A slow smile creased his face. There was one particular problem he knew she could solve. But as soon as the thought of a lusty romp in bed crossed his mind, it was not Camella Alvarez's sloe-eyed beauty he envisioned. The image of burnished cherry hair and big gold eyes filled his imagination.

He cursed the damnable little tease, recalling old Marcus's threat. *You take my meaning.* He had taken it right well enough. Marcus Jacobson was not a man to make idle threats and Jess was too cynical and experienced to ever become involved with a spoiled virginal temptress like Lissa, no matter how desirable she was. Her kind was always trouble. He scowled, remembering the last time an innocent-looking beautiful white woman had seduced him. The bitter betrayal of Monique still stung, even after all these years.

His thoughts were interrupted by the sound of a woman's scream echoing over the next rise. He kneed Blaze into a canter and slipped his rifle from its scabbard.

When Pike and Mace finally stopped to water their horses, Lissa was hauled off her mount and stood roughly on her feet. With her bound wrists secured to the pommel of her saddle, she had been unable to work the gag free during their flight. However, she now held her bound hands in front of her mouth and tugged the kerchief off.

"What in hell are you—"

Pike's question was cut short by her piercing scream. When he reached to grab her, she twisted away, struggling to breathe after so long with the vile, suffocating bandana in her mouth.

"Pike! Someone's a comin'," Mace yelled as he pulled his gun and aimed at the horseman barreling over the rise at them. He fired his Army Colt rapidly, missing the target.

Pike reached for the rifle on his saddle and yanked it free, but just as he sighted on Jess, Lissa lowered her head and lunged into his midsection, causing him to fire into the air. He snarled an oath and swung at her with the rifle barrel, but she dropped to the ground before he could hit her.

Jess fired and struck Mace squarely in the chest while Pike and Lissa were struggling. Afraid to risk a shot from a bouncing horse while she was so near the other target, Jess kicked free of his stirrups as Blaze galloped up, then jumped at the ugly-looking little outlaw and sent him crashing to the ground.

Pike was surprisingly strong for a small man and thrashed free, attempting to draw his pistol and fire it as Jess grabbed his wrist and pointed the weapon away. They rolled over, fighting for control of the gun while Lissa crouched on the ground near the horses, frantically attempting to untie her hands by tugging at the ropes with her teeth.

Jess rolled atop Pike and slammed his right fist into the outlaw's face. Pike's head rolled to the side and his body went suddenly limp. Jess leaned back, straddling the unconscious man, and carefully massaged his knuckles. Ever so gingerly, he flexed his fist. In spite of the pain, there were no broken bones. Then he looked over to where Lissa sat working on the ropes that bound her hands.

She watched him turn his steely gaze on her as he approached. Slipping a knife from his belt, he slashed the rope from her wrists, then yanked her to her feet by pulling none too gently on her arm. Caught off balance, she stumbled, clutching him to keep from falling.

"Oh, Jess, I can't—"

"Jesus! Are you a complete idiot, lady?" He grabbed her wrists and held her angrily away from him.

"You're hurting me," she gasped as her abraded wrists burned from his rough grip. He released her with an oath and turned to the outlaw at his feet, tying him up as she watched. "You saved my life, Jess."

"It wasn't intentional," he replied savagely.

"Why are you acting this way?"

He looked up at her, fury blazing in his face. "You spoiled, brainless little bitch! What the hell were you doing—going out for a ride to view the scenery, all alone so a pair of hard cases like this could carry you off and rape you?"

She stiffened. "You can't call me vile names like that!"

"I just did and they fit you custom-made." He stood up, glaring at her, fighting the urge to shake her. "I'd paddle you good if I weren't afraid of busting up my gun hand even worse than I already have."

"Germaine was right. You're nothing but a half-breed killer—a savage!"

The instant she flung the words at him she wanted to call them back. He stood very still, with eyes turned to molten silver. His face could have been carved from granite as he said, "There's your horse. Mount up." He turned to the outlaw he had bound and began to hoist him up.

"Jess, I'm—"

"Just ride, Lissa," he said raggedly. He tossed Pike over the saddle of his horse and tied him securely to it, then mounted Blaze and kicked the stallion into a canter, pulling Pike's horse behind him.

Chastened, Lissa mounted Little Bit and followed. They rode to the roundup camp in silence.

Jess turned the mean little rustler over to Moss Symington after questioning him at length about any involvement with the big outfit preying on J Bar herds. Satisfied that he and his partner Mace were simply drifters who had thrown in with a small wagon train to make money by increasing their meat supply, Jess left the pleading and desperate Pike to the tender mercies of the J Bar hands. He envied neither the pale, sweaty little drifter nor that train of settlers. The old-timers were very protective of their herds—not to mention Marcus's daughter.

His business now was in Cheyenne. He rode into town a few hours after dark and headed straight up Eddy Street to the Royale Theater where Cammie worked. "The show should just be beginning, Blaze," he said to the stallion as he reined in outside the big frame building with its elaborate false front, painted in garish shades of red and blue.

The billboards outside proclaimed, "Miss Camella Alvarez, the Spanish Songbird." Jess grinned as he purchased his ticket. Cammie had never even been in Spain. She was born in Matamoros and raised in south Texas. The music hall boasted polished plank floors covered with clean sawdust. The stage was elevated four feet above the crowded room and surrounded by a tier of boxes. The main floor was filled with oak chairs and tables to accomodate the overflowing crowd of music hall denizens. Most were townsmen, clerks, and tradesmen in stiff, storebought clothes of cheap cut and poor fit, but here and there sat wealthy businessmen smoking expensive cigars and displaying gold watch fobs on their ample midsections.

Jess pulled out a chair near the far left side of the stage, straddled it, and rested his arms across the splintery oak back. He knew Cammie always checked the house before curtain. She would be watching him about now. The lights dimmed, and a round of applause and raucous cheers went up as the curtain rose to reveal the Spanish Songbird, clad in a gown of scarlet sequins and feathers, slashed daringly up one side to reveal a lushly curved leg in a black fishnet stocking. She gave Jess a seductive wink before she began to sing.

When the performance was over, he bought another beer and waited. No one was allowed backstage without the lady's permission. Her note arrived at his table before the head was off his beer.

Camella's dressing room was a cramped cubicle, horrendously overcrowded and filled with rainbow hues of sparkling satin gowns, rhinestone tiaras, and feather wraps tossed carelessly over greasy benches or hung on pegs sagging from the rough pine walls. She sat at a tiny round table covered with faded pink shantung, looking in a mirror that leaned precariously against the back of a scarred-up set of steamer trunks.

"Great show, Cammie," he said, leaning in the open door.

She dropped her rouge pot and turned with her arms open wide. "Jess, *querido*, you have finished your work for Jacobson already?" She flew into his embrace, not waiting for an answer as she pulled his head down and kissed him passionately.

He kicked the door closed with one foot and moved into the kiss, bending her over his arm and nuzzling her throat. "Mmm, you smell good," he murmured as his hands tangled in a thick cloud of curling ebony hair. Her perfume was a heavy attar of roses. Nothing subtle about it. Unlike the delicate essence of orange blossoms. He shoved the unwanted thought away as she laughed and nibbled on his ear.

"You will stay the night, no?" Her tongue darted along his jawline, then rimmed his mouth teasingly.

"I'll stay the night, yes. If you've worked up a good appetite, I'll take you to dinner at Dyer's first."

Finally they broke off the playful embrace. Camella turned her back and raised her long mane of hair, saying, "Unfasten me, *querido*. I cannot go out in public in this torture rack of a dress."

He obliged, baring a creamy expanse of olive skin as the dozens of tiny hooks on the costume gave way. She let it slither to the floor, then stepped carelessly over it and shook down her hair. She stood before him clad only in a lace corset and underpants. She looked good and she knew it as she held up various dresses, deciding which to wear to dinner that night. Jess let her pose and play her games.

"How long can you stay?" she asked, inspecting an emerald taffeta dress.

"Just tonight. I'm still working for Jacobson." He pulled out the photograph he had taken from Argee's body. "Ever see this girl in town?"

She looked at the well-worn picture. "That is Pearl Soames. She left for Deadwood a month ago. What is she to you?" Camella asked with a pout on her full lips.

He chucked her beneath her chin. "Just a lead—found it on a dead rustler and thought she might know more about his friends."

"Who was the rustler?" She pulled the taffeta over her head with a loud rustling crackle, then turned for him to fasten her up.

"Who does this when I'm not around, Cammie?"

She turned with wide dark eyes and said, "Ah, Jess, someone is always around to button me up . . . and unbutton me, but I would always prefer you, *querido.*"

He let the comment go and replied to her earlier question, "The rustler's name was Billy Argee. Curly-haired young pup, thin, wiry build, medium height."

"Yes, I knew him. He fancied himself a dangerous gunman," she added scornfully. "You shot him."

He shrugged. "Yeah. Wanted the fool alive, but he wouldn't have it that way. Know any of his friends?"

"He usually rode in alone, but once I saw him and Pearl with another J Bar man—Sligo, I think, is his name. A big thickset hombre with yellow hair."

Jess rubbed his chin consideringly. "Sligo. I'll have to watch where he goes when he rides away from the ranch tomorrow."

She insinuated herself in his arms and said, "That is tomorrow, Jess. This is tonight. . . ."

On the ride back to J Bar, Jess turned the matter of Ralph Sligo over in his mind. He and Argee had been careful not to chum together around the other hands. Sligo was older, probably smarter than Argee. Getting him to lead Jess to the rustlers' base camp would not be easy. He considered facing the man down and threatening to kill him—or have some of Symington's boys beat it out of him. But there was always the chance Sligo would make the same violent choice Argee had. If he talked, he would stretch rope anyway. Better to follow him and see what developed.

Jess's thoughts strayed from Sligo and the rustling to the vicious-tongued little bitch at J Bar. He had saved her wretched life, and she had turned on him like a cornered wildcat. The insults he had grown used to hearing. Monique had called him a dirty, lying savage when her father caught the two of them.

Would Lissa disavow her attraction for him as easily if Marcus confronted her? Somehow he did not think so. There was an apparent honesty about Melissa Jacobson, a bold openness at odds with the usual female subterfuges. *Why am I even thinking of her?* She would only get him killed. Women like Cammie were his for the asking. The two of them had surely burned up the sheets last night. Still, in the height of passion, he had thought of Lissa's fiery tresses and wide gold eyes. He swore at the troubling turn of mind that continually drew him back to her.

Marcus Jacobson's vast cattle empire once more materialized before him as he crested the rise. Most of the men were out with the roundup. He had requested that the new hands be assigned to duties around the ranch. Sligo was lounging against the corral gate, talking with another hand when he rode up and dismounted.

Jess nodded to the pair, then led Blaze into the stable and gave him to Bob Abbot for a thorough rubdown. He turned toward the bunkhouse, figuring on getting some rest, but he had no sooner stretched out on his bunk when Tate walked in with a worried look on his face.

"Boss wants to see you at the big house."

"What for?" Jess asked, rolling off the bunk.

"Didn't feel it my place ta ask," Tate replied drily. "But I got a hunch it's about Miz Lissa gettin' in that scrape you pulled her out of."

Jess's expression darkened, but he said nothing about the matter. "Do me a favor, Tate. Keep an eye on Sligo while I'm gone. I want to know where he heads if he rides away."

Tate's expression grew intent. "You figure Sligo's workin' both sides?"

"Maybe," was all Jess would say. He walked up to the imposing white house, noting an expensive-looking rig with a handsome sorrel hitched to it standing at the side door. Marcus had company.

Germaine opened the door to his knock, her thin face frozen in a hostile glare. "Mr. Marcus will see you in the library." She gestured stiffly to the second door down the wide, carpeted hallway.

"*Merci,*" he said with a sardonic smile, then strolled to the door, which was slightly ajar. He could hear Jacobson speaking to the visitor. Lissa was nowhere in sight. Jess was grateful for that as he knocked on the door.

"Come in, Robbins. You remember Lemuel Mathis from Cheyenne?"

Mathis nodded his immaculately barbered head but did not offer to shake hands. Jess returned the nod while standing in the middle of the opulent room. The walls were covered with books, and a large walnut desk dominated the rich masculine surroundings. Against one wall a matching piece of dark furniture served as a bar. Although it was not near the dinner hour, Jacobson and Mathis were sharing a drink.

"You wanted to see me for some reason?"

"Several reasons. First, Lemuel and I are both grateful for your timely intervention that saved Lissa from those cutthroats. Moss has taken care of the one you brought back."

"I thought he would," Jess replied levelly. "You ought to keep a tighter rein on that girl, Mr. Jacobson. It was pure luck that I was coming back in that direction."

Marcus sighed and ran his hand through his thin silver hair. "I can't order my daughter around as if she were a cowpuncher. She was raised back East where things were safe. It's been a difficult adjustment, her coming home last year. She feels isolated here at the house with only Germaine for company."

Jess's eyebrows rose and a look of dry amusement touched his face. He could well appreciate how spending a week or two with Germaine Channault could make anyone get cabin fever. "What was the other reason you needed to talk to me?"

"We wanted a report about how your campaign with the rustlers is progressing," Mathis said with an arrogant wave of his hand.

Jess paused, studying the thickset man with his soft, citified airs. "The Association didn't hire me. Mr. Jacobson did." He looked to Marcus, who nodded, then replied, "There's not much to tell yet. Three men tried to ambush me, and I killed them. Two were from the gang. The third was an inside man."

"Yes. Billy Argee. I knew the lad. I can't believe he was a thief," Lemuel said stiffly.

"Believe it. That or he had some strong reason to dislike me. Considering I'd never even been introduced to him, that seems unlikely. I did some nosing around town after the shooting—to find out about his friends."

Marcus's eyes narrowed. "What did you learn?"

"Seems Argee and Sligo have been seen drinking together in town."

"You think Sligo's crooked, too?" Jacobson blanched. "Hell, have I got anyone on the payroll I *can* trust?"

"Surely you're seeing bugbears beneath every bed," Mathis said dismissively.

Jess shrugged. "Maybe. We'll see. Meanwhile, I'm going to keep an eye on Sligo."

"That doesn't seem like much to earn the kind of money Mr. Jacobson is paying you," Mathis said stiffly.

Jess's eyes flashed a silvery warning. Then he dismissed Mathis and turned to the old man. "I'll work this my way, Mr. Jacobson—if that's all right with you. If not . . ."

Marcus nodded. "For now, I'm satisfied." Sensing the tension between the two men, he changed the subject. "Next week we're going to the Evers spread. Between J Bar and Diamond E's parts of the roundup, all the hands from the neighboring ranches get together to blow off some steam. Have a bunch of riding and roping contests, what you Texans call a rodeo. Why not go to the shindig? It's a good chance to watch all those hands and nose around. You said Sligo's involved with the rustlers. Maybe you'll learn something more."

Shrugging, Jess agreed. "I'll go."

"Good, good," Marcus said, ushering Jess to the door. "Keep me posted if you learn anything else."

Ignoring Mathis, Jess nodded to Jacobson, then stepped out the door and closed it. He retraced his steps down the hall, but just as he passed the arched entry to the parlor, Lissa stepped out into his path. She was wearing a peach silk dress and a tremulous smile.

"You are going to the rodeo with us?" she asked uncertainly.

"You always get what you want. This time you might think twice before you ask for me—I might just be the biggest mistake you ever made."

He turned away and strode angrily through the front door, slamming it as he left.

"Sligo just rode out, Jess," Tate said when Robbins returned to the corral.

"You got a horse I can use? Blaze is ridden out."

"Yeah. Take your pick from my cavvy," Shannon said as they walked over to the corral.

In moments Jess had saddled a big buckskin and was trailing Ralph Sligo. He headed southeast for several miles. Then, just before crossing the boundary line of J Bar range, Jess saw Sligo's horse standing before a deserted line shack. Quickly pulling the buckskin behind a cluster of low-growing ash trees, he waited and watched.

Very shortly Sligo emerged from the shack, looked warily around the seemingly deserted horizon, then mounted up and rode back toward the ranch. Jess stayed hidden until the hoofbeats of the cowboy's horse grew silent. He cautiously rode up to the line shack with his gun drawn. The cabin had not been used in years from the look of the broken windows and sagging door frame. Cocking his gun, he shoved open the door, which creaked a feeble protest as he flattened himself against the inside wall. Empty. He holstered his gun. The interior smelled stale and musty, but a faint yet unmistakably fresh aroma of tobacco hung on the air. A burned-out butt lay on the edge of the crude log table.

Jess checked the butt. Cold. It had not been smoked by Sligo. He walked around the small dingy room. The ill-fitted floorboards groaned and squeaked with every step. A grimy layer of silty dust was disturbed by footprints all over the floor, but one board out of the traffic pattern beside the door had other smudges on it. Handprints.

He knelt down and used his knife to pry up the loose board. A note lay inside the small wooden frame beneath it. Whistling low, he unfolded it and read the crude pencil scrawl.

"Herd on S. fork of Logg Pol. Roundup will not git to beevs til Sun."

A crude map was drawn on the other side of the wrinkled sheet of paper indicating where the isolated herd was scattered, unattended. Jess smiled darkly. Sligo's assurance that the herd would not be rounded up until Sunday was about to be violated. He could do nothing more until he was able to hire extra guns from Texas and hoped Ringo Pardee would answer his wire soon. Pardee's men would be needed to set a trap for the rustlers.

He couldn't wait to shake Wyoming dust off his boots for good. But he knew a lot could happen between now and then. Getting together a dozen professionals could take a month or more. Jess swore to himself as he replaced the paper and left the shack.

Chapter Eight

"It's a beautiful day for a ride," Lissa said brightly to no one in particular as they approached the Diamond E.

"I expect the turnout will be real good." Moss Symington chuckled, recalling the previous rodeo. "Remember how it rained last year and old Deever's roan slid in the mud?"

"He wasn't the only one to take a mud bath." Lissa looked to where Jess rode just ahead of the others. He had been even more distant than usual since the small group met at the corrals early that morning. Marcus had spent several days in Cheyenne tending to business and would join them later in the day. She had carried on a spirited conversation, laughing and joking with the rest of the hands, but Jess held himself aloof.

She maneuvered her small pinto alongside his big stallion. "That white-faced devil of yours looks fast. Yancy Brewster's white won the past three years in a row, but this fellow could give him a run for his money. Are you going to race him?" She waited, but he didn't answer her.

"I won't go away, Jess, so you'll have to talk to me sooner or later," Lissa said in a low voice that only he could hear. "I'm sorry for what I said the other day. I didn't mean that I thought you were a savage. I . . . well, I have a sort of rotten temper at times."

His lips quirked unwillingly, and he looked at her with a sardonic expression on his face. "*Sort* of rotten temper?" he echoed.

Lissa blushed as she drew herself up, trying to appear affronted, yet pleased that she had finally succeeded in eliciting a response. "You were yelling perfectly awful things at me. Naturally I lost my temper, too."

"Naturally."

"Strange, I don't ever recall there being an echo out here on the open plains," she teased. "Are you going to race your black?"

He sighed. "You never give up. No, I'm not risking my neck or Blaze's in a fool race."

"Fool race!"

"Now who's an echo?"

"Surely you aren't afraid of taking a little tumble? All the boys join in the fun."

"I'm not one of the boys, in case you hadn't noticed," he said drily.

"No, you certainly aren't," she replied crossly. "Don't you ever have fun, Jess?"

Thoughts flashed into his mind of the preceding night, which he had spent with Cammie, and he coughed discreetly, hiding his smile behind his hand. "Yeah, every time I get a chance."

A rider on a showy white stallion appeared on the horizon. As he approached them, he doffed his expensive, high-crowned hat and waved it with a flourish at Lissa.

"It's Yancy!" Lissa waved excitedly, seeing a chance to make Jess jealous. Yancy Brewster was the foreman at Diamond E, a tall, rangy man with light brown hair and regular features. He was considered quite a charmer by the local females, and he had made no secret about courting Lissa at every opportunity. If forced to choose between Lemuel Mathis and Yancy, she would probably choose the older man, who was more amenable and indulgent. Yancy was full of himself and intent on running his women much as he ramroded Cy Evers's ranch hands.

For the moment, Lissa ignored that and bestowed on him a dazzling smile as he reined in beside her. "Good morning, Yancy. I was just telling Jess about the rodeo. Oh, forgive my bad manners. Jesse Robbins is the new stock detective Papa hired—from Texas. Jess, meet Yancy Brewster, ramrod of the Diamond E."

Brewster appraised Jess as he skillfully maneuvered his horse between Jess and Lissa. "Heard all about you, Robbins. The baddest fellow west of anyplace east," he said. His hazel eyes had a hard glint to them.

Jess only nodded and would have pulled away. Brewster's question brought him up short.

"You're a Texan. Secesh?"

"My father was Union Army during the war." Jess did not elaborate.

"I never heard of Federals from Texas," Lissa said curiously.

"There weren't very many of us," he replied grimly.

"It must have been hard on your family." She was dying to know more but did not want to seem overeager.

"That why you took up guns?" Brewster asked.

Jess stiffened but did not reply. Tension hung in the air as heavy as clouds before a thunderstorm until Lissa changed the subject back to the upcoming rodeo. "I was trying to get Jess to enter some of the contests. His black might just give you some competition, Yancy."

Brewster appraised Blaze dismissively, then patted his white's thickly muscled neck. "Thunderbolt's never been beat. Course, I never raced against an Indian. Hear you boys are good," Brewster said with a cool grin that dared Jess. "I might just make you a side bet—if you think you got a chance."

Jess sensed that the animosity from Brewster was because of Lissa. The foreman was the sort most white women thought handsome, and he was used to winning. How the hell was he going to defuse this mess? Jess cursed as he observed Brewster's smirk. No matter what he did, the bastard would be laying for him until they settled matters. He did not need the grief he would inherit if he killed the troublemaker.

Sighing, he looked Brewster in the eye and replied, "You want a race, ramrod. You got a race." Maybe it would be a way to observe the hands and listen to their casual banter without having any of them suspect he was there looking for rustlers.

"How much you want to bet, Robbins?"

Jess shrugged negligently. "Let's make it interesting. Say, a month's pay—two hundred fifty dollars." He knew even a top ramrod only made around a hundred and fifty a month.

Brewster blanched imperceptibly, then grinned at Lissa and replied, "Done. Miss Lissa, you hold our markers."

The Diamond E was a big spread. Not as big as J Bar, but impressive nonetheless, with a wide, low ranch house made of dressed lumber weathered to the color of rich tobacco. The bunkhouses were almost identical to J Bar's, but the corrals were not as well laid-out or numerous. The mid-roundup break was traditionally celebrated by a rodeo alternating between the two largest ranches in the southeast part of the territory.

As this year's host, old Cy Evers and his daughter Cridellia presided over the festivities, welcoming the cowboys from all the surrounding spreads. A festive air pervaded the gathering, and the spicy, mouth-watering aroma of several whole barbecued steers wafted on the warm summer breeze. Vinegar Joe worked with the Everses' cook, Sourdough Charlie, stirring a huge iron kettle of beans. The two cooks had drafted a number of the junior hands to assist, pitting cherries for pies and scrubbing the mountains of pots and pans dirtied in preparing for the feast.

Cy greeted the arrivals heartily, then ushered them to the cook's big tent set up between the mess hall and bunk house, where they drank scalding, inky coffee, talked, and joked as they waited for the contests to begin.

Cridellia Evers was a mousy little woman with prim lips that rarely smiled and slightly popping eyes. She blinked her pale lashes nervously as she watched the crude men assemble for their rough-and-tumble exhibitions. She was dressed in a paisley blouse and heavy twill skirt with a bustle. The dark purple shade did not flatter her sallow complexion and light brown hair.

Beside the fiery Lissa, clad in a butternut brown riding skirt and clear yellow blouse, poor Cridellia looked like a molting purple wren. The young women were the only daughters of the two wealthiest ranchers in the basin, and as such had been continually thrown together since early childhood. When Lissa had been sent East to school, Cy had kept Cridellia at home, where her mother Ethel had educated her as best she could before passing to her reward several years earlier. If Dellia and Lissa were not friends, they at least held their rivalry at bay in front of their doting fathers.

"The bustle on your skirt is all the rage back East, Dellia," Lissa said as they sat together on a small bench placed just in front of the big corral where the first contests would be held. Lissa forbore mentioning how uncomfortable and inappropriate the drawing room outfit looked at a dusty corral.

Dellia smoothed her skirts and wriggled her bottom discreetly, trying to seat herself more comfortably with the bustle shoved over the backside of the bench. "Papa almost had a seizure when he got Charlene Durbin's bill for making the skirt," she replied smugly. Her eyes rolled like a calf's at a branding fire when she talked, an unfortunate habit she had never been able to break. Searching the crowd, she fastened on Yancy Brewster, watching him exchange some bawdy joke with two other hands. "Yancy rode out to meet you," she observed. "I imagine he wanted to get a look at your pa's half-breed gunman," she added more casually.

"Jess and Yancy made a bet on the horse race. I think Yancy might lose this year."

"No, sir! Yancy always wins," Dellia declared. She looked over at the gleaming black stallion with the blaze face and his owner standing next to him. "Emmaline Wattson told me you were taken with the gunman." Her eyes protruded even further from her thin, sallow face as she studied Jesse Robbins.

"I'm not taken with him." Lissa smiled puckishly, then added, "But he is sinfully beautiful, isn't he?" She loved giving Dellia apoplexy.

Her companion almost swallowed her tongue. "I hope your pa doesn't hear you talking this way. He'd marry you off to Lemuel Mathis so fast everyone in Cheyenne would be counting on their fingers."

Lissa laughed to cover her revulsion at the thought of Lemuel's thick blunt hands touching her intimately. "I'm not going to marry Lemuel."

"If your pa takes a notion, you will. My pa's already talking about giving Diamond E to Yancy someday—when he marries me, of course," she added hastily. "Men decide those things. We don't."

"I'll choose my own husband. And it won't be a man who wants me just for my papa's ranch either."

Dellia stiffened at the implied insult, but before she could respond, Cy signaled one of his hands to bang on the cook's big wash pot. Everyone quieted when Evers began to speak.

"I'm happy as a spotted pup in a new red wagon to see all you boys here for some fun afore we head on back to finish up this here roundup. First event is calf ropin'. All you top hands, come on 'n bring yer best ketches with you."

The morning progressed through calf roping, wild bronc riding, even a contest between the intrepid hands and a very large ornery mule named Jake Ass, who unseated every rider. Dust billowed while the men cheered and bet openly, and cussed and sneaked liquor covertly so as not to offend the two females. By the time the midday meal was announced, Marcus had arrived. Lissa was relieved to see Lemuel had not returned with him.

Her eyes scanned the crowd of rumpled hands in their dusty denims, scuffed boots, and sweaty cotton shirts. Jess stood out among the sea of homely faces and unruly cowlicks. His elegant face was beginning to show just a hint of virile black whiskers, adding to his appeal. Straight thick hair fell against a snowy white shirt of soft lawn that fit across his muscular shoulders indecently well. Unlike the callused hands of the rest of the men with their blackened and broken nails, his were smooth, with long, tapered fingers and clean nails. Everything about him was graceful, quiet, and charged with a dangerous sort of sensuality that drew her like wind plucking rich pollen from the heart of a high plains wildflower.

"There you are, Lissa. I've been looking all over for you. I thought we could share our meal. I fetched you a plate." Yancy held aloft two heaping plates filled with slices of juicy brown beef, rich beans in spicy molasses, and high, fluffy sourdough biscuits.

Her first impulse, sensing the murderous look Dellia was casting at her, was to suggest they join their host and hostess and her father, but then she saw Jess watching her and changed her mind. With a blinding smile, she took the ramrod's arm and led them toward the shade of a big cotton-wood tree. "How gallant of you, Yancy." Eating with Dellia always gave her indigestion anyway.

Jess saw Lissa's bright curls bounce as she tossed back her head and laughed at some remark by the foreman. He also observed Marcus's scowl and the malevolent expression on the face of that plain little daughter of Cy Evers. "God save me from your scheming, Lissa," he muttered as he sipped some of the bitter black coffee. Too bad Mathis was not here.

The next event was the rooster ketch, a sport much loved by Mexicans and Californios, which had spread across the high plains. A large mean old rooster was buried up to his neck in soft sand near one side of the corral. The contestants all took turns riding a full circle around the hapless bird. As they approached, they bent down low, hanging precariously from their saddles, and attempted to pull the snapping, squawking rooster from the sand by his neck, while avoiding getting bitten. Some wore buckskin gloves to protect themselves, which handicapped them when they tried to pluck up the prize. Others went after it bare-handed and came away bloodied.

After over two dozen passes, the terrorized rooster was still embedded in the sand when Yancy Brewster prepared for his turn.

"Yancy will win," Dellia said smugly, now over her pique with Brewster, who had come solicitously to the family's table after Lissa insisted on sharing dessert with her father.

While she and Marcus had talked, the smooth-tongued foreman had quickly brought Dellia out of her sulk, plying her with compliments in a feckless attempt to make Lissa jealous and regain her wandering attention. Once Jess disappeared in the crowd, Lissa had lost interest in the vain, oily Brewster.

"Maybe Yancy will win." Lissa shrugged indifferently as the foreman mounted up on one of his cavvy, a small fleet gray with a steady gait.

"Yancy'll take that cock—I got me five dollars says so," one hand wagered.

"Done. I say he'll end up with his fingers bit jist like the rest," another hand countered.

All around the corral, men exchanged bets and cheered or harangued the ramrod. He spurred the sleek little filly into a canter and circled the track, increasing his speed until he drew a roar from the assembly. Just as he approached the prize, he swung one long arm down and seized the rooster, yanking the flapping, squawking bird cleanly from the wet sand, which went flying every direction as he reined in the gray.

The bird continued to flap and screech, twisting his thick neck and pecking with a sharp curved beak at the offending fingers choking him until

137

he succeeded in biting Brewster's thumb. With an oath, the foreman dropped the reins, seized the bird in both hands, and wrung its neck with a vicious twist. Grinning, he tossed the dead rooster to the ground and dismounted to the cheers of the crowd.

"Nice fellow," Jess said drily to Tate as they observed the uproar.

"Brewster is purely mean," Tate said, sucking on a toothpick. "Watch him when you race—and them Spanish rowels he wears. Ain't afraid to use 'em on any rider or horse who gets near."

"I'll remember that," Jess said as he headed toward the stable where Blaze waited for the race along with the favorite mounts of a dozen contestants. He had sized them all up earlier and decided that Moss's big sorrel, ridden by Rob Ostler, would be the only other competition besides Brewster's white.

Lissa, sickened by Yancy's cruelty and eager to escape the aromatic press of sweaty cowhands on a hot day, slipped through the crowd and followed Jess into the stable. The air was heavy with dust motes dancing in the rays of golden sunlight filtering through the thin cracks between the boards. The nose-tickling smell of hay blended with the sweet musk of horse droppings. She let her eyes grow accustomed to the indirect light, then walked silently toward Jess, who was replacing his tack on Blaze.

"Are you ready for the race?"

He turned toward her with a look of irritation on his face. The subtle, clean scent of orange blossoms floated over the baser smells of the livery. His senses were humming with it, and he resented her for it. "Thought I warned you about sneaking up on me," he said, even though he had been aware of her presence.

"I'll take my chances," she replied with a smile, drawing closer to pat the big black's nose. "If you win today, you'll make an enemy of Yancy. You bet him almost two months' pay."

"It's a month's pay to me." He shrugged indifferently. "I just saw what a gracious winner your champion is. Wouldn't hurt him to lose for a change."

"But it might hurt you. He rides rough, Jess," she said, placing one hand on his chest experimentally.

He closed his hand over hers, planning to lift it away, but somehow, once he made contact with her silky pale skin, he couldn't let go. When she smiled, he knew she'd felt his heartbeat accelerate. "I consider myself duly warned," he said as he slowly removed her hand, "against both of you."

She stuck out her lower lip in a mock pout and stepped closer. "For luck, Jess," she whispered, tiptoeing up to plant a kiss on his lips. She only meant it to be a swift, light peck, but when her breasts brushed against his chest and she felt the scrape of his whiskers on her fingertips, she sank forward, leaning into him.

His arms closed around her involuntarily, crushing her against his body. She melted with a small, whimpering moan that opened her lips. His tongue responded by plunging into her mouth to taste her forbidden sweetness yet again. She met his invasion, letting her tongue touch his, sleek and hot, as their lips molded together, brushing, pressing, devouring.

She traced the hard line of his jaw and touched his bearded cheek with the pads of her thumbs, then sank her fingers into the long shaggy hair touching the collar of his shirt. Jess lifted her up, pressing her hips firmly against his and rocking them slowly as reality faded and they lost themselves in each other.

Tate's discreet cough brought back sanity. Jess broke off the kiss. Dazed, Lissa did not even notice the big black cowhand standing embarrassed in the stable door.

"Brewster's a comin' for his horse," was all Shannon said. He touched the brim of his hat respectfully to Lissa, then cast his reproachful brown eyes on Jess before turning his back and walking out the door.

"Get out of here before they find you," Jess gritted between clenched teeth as he shoved Lissa toward the smaller door on the opposite end of the stable. Once she was gone, he seized the rough boards of an empty stall and held on to them until he felt the splinters biting into his fingers.

What the hell's wrong with me? I'm the one who's a complete idiot!

Lissa raced from the stable with her fingers touching her bruised lips, looking neither left nor right. As she circled the outside of the building, she collided with Yancy Brewster, who took her shoulders and held her for a narrow-eyed inspection. He had just seen Shannon come from the stable, now Lissa, with her hair mussed and her breathing erratic. Then Jesse Robbins led his stallion through the front door, and the foreman understood.

A look of furious incredulity flashed across Brewster's face. "You 'n that breed!" he gasped, his breath catching in his throat.

Lissa jerked free of his clawlike hands, but stood her ground. "Keep your crazy accusations to yourself, Yancy," she hissed. "You say anything like that to my father and he'll kill you. Or Robbins will." She flung her tangled hair over her shoulder and stalked away as rage-filled hazel eyes met cold, deadly gray ones.

"Don't push, Brewster," was all Jess said.

"Push? Breed, I'll ride you into the ground," Brewster whispered hoarsely.

A crowd of the other hands who were riding in the big race converged on the two tense figures, laughing and joking, oblivious of the impending conflict.

Brewster turned and stalked into the stable to get his horse, and several of the others followed. Tate Shannon fell in step beside Jess as he led Blaze toward the start of the two-mile race course.

"You're playin' with fire, Jess. Oh, I seen her a-comin' after you, battin' them big yeller eyes 'n smilin' like Eve with an apple, but Brewster always figgered on gettin' her. She's poison for you."

"If I remember my Bible, that first apple was poison, too," Jess replied grimly.

"I jes hope you ain't fixin' to take a bite," Tate said dolefully, then added, "Watch Brewster durin' the race. He'll sure try 'n cut you now."

Jess nodded grimly as he mounted up.

The eleven contestants lined up their horses while Cy Evers explained the rules to the assembled crowd. "Course is from here around the big stand of cottonwoods by the creek and back. First one who comes under my flag here wins. Get fixed to race when I fire my rifle."

Lissa stood behind the corral gate, steadying her trembling legs by holding on to the rough log poles of the fence. She could see the two tall riders at the starting line, could sense the crackling animosity between them. Would Yancy go to her father? Why had she done such a rash, reckless thing? *I haven't had a sensible thought since I first laid eyes on Jesse Robbins*. She was drawn to him like a moth to a flame, mesmerized by his dark, savage sensuality. Even now her unwilling gaze fastened on him as he bent low over Blaze's neck, crooning softly to the stallion.

Cy Evers's rifle cracked and the riders exploded from the starting line in a cloud of dust. Yancy dug his sharp Spanish rowels into Thunderbolt's side, drawing blood on the gleaming white coat, and the big white leaped ahead. One of the hands on a big dun and Rob on Moss's sorrel pulled close to Yancy. Jess seemed to be pacing his big black midway back. The dun quickly faded, but the white and the sorrel raced neck and neck for several lengths. Then, with a lightning flash, Yancy's quirt caught the sorrel on the neck, causing the horse to break stride and stumble.

Her heart in her throat, Lissa climbed on the corral fence to get a better view, but the riders were headed around the trees by the shallow creek. The last thing she saw was Jess pulling closer to Yancy as they went into the turn. She clung to the top rail of the corral, frantically searching the horizon for the riders, afraid to breathe until she saw Jess reappear.

Finally they emerged, thundering back toward the finish line with the white still in the lead, but Blaze was relentlessly gaining. Yancy heard the pounding of hooves growing nearer and turned to see the black closing the gap. As Jess pulled alongside, Yancy began slashing with his quirt, landing several blows. Jess fell back, then surged forward once more, this time ready for the onslaught. When Yancy struck out, Jess seized the foreman's quirt in his gloved hand, almost yanking Brewster from his saddle.

The spectators could partially see the struggle between the two men as Jess tossed away the quirt. Then Brewster kicked free of his right stirrup and slashed at Blaze's side with the wicked rowels on his spur, but Jess blocked him with his boot. Brewster tried again, but this time Jess's hard response jammed the foreman's leg backward. The boot with its sharp rowels slid past the sweat flap and raked hard into Thunderbolt's flank. The big stallion screamed and veered sharply to the left. Brewster was off balance and could not regain the stirrup. As the horse lunged in pain, the foreman pitched headfirst off the right side of the frenzied animal.

Jess crossed the finish line well ahead of the others. Everyone thundered by Brewster, who rose slowly, brushing dust and twigs from his clothes, apparently none the worse but for his pride.

Lissa sat frozen on the rail as Jess dismounted amid cheers from the J Bar men. His shirt was torn in several places, and small weals of blood seeped through the thin cotton. She wanted to run to him and tend his hurts, to hold him safe in her arms and whisper that she loved him. But to do so would seal his doom.

Chapter Nine

Jess accepted the good wishes of the J Bar men. A few had bet on him and were collecting their winnings, but the cheerful excitement died into a tense lull as the foreman rode in mounted behind the Diamond E man who had stopped to pick him up when the white bolted. Everyone grew silent as Brewster approached Robbins.

"I always heard greasers and gut-eaters were natural-born riders. You bein' both, I reckon a white man never stood a chance."

The silence was thick enough for Vinegar Joe to slice and fry for dinner. Everyone waited to see what the fearful gunman would do.

"You gonna shoot me, Robbins?" Brewster taunted. His face was coated with a thick gray film of dust. Rivulets of sweat ran down his temples and cheeks. He looked pale beneath the dirt, and a crazy light gleamed in his narrowed eyes.

"I hear you never shoot a man unless you're paid." Sneering, the foreman threw down a handful of silver dollars.

Lissa climbed off the fence, desperately searching the crowd to find her father and Cy Evers. They had to intervene before the two fools shot each other!

Jess smiled thinly and wiped the trickle of blood from his temple with the back of his hand. Then he pulled off his gloves and stuck them in his belt. "I'm paid real good, Brewster. Sometimes I can afford to indulge myself."

"Why don't you just do that?" Brewster said savagely. "You been indulgin' yourself real handy already from what I seen."

"There'll be no more of that on Diamond E, Yancy," Evers said then. "You slap leather 'n I'll send you packin'—ridin' if you win, feet first if you lose."

The crowd cleared as he and Marcus strode toward the two combatants, who stood facing each other. Brewster was tense as a bobcat on a wire. Jess stood indolently still, muscles loose, hands resting casually on the buckle of his gunbelt.

"I hired you to shoot rustlers, not the ramrod of Diamond E, Robbins," Marcus said coldly.

Jess shrugged, his deadly gaze never leaving Brewster. "He made the call, not me."

By this time Lissa had elbowed her way through the men and thrust herself, breathless, into the clearing. "Jess is telling the truth, Papa. Look at what Yancy did to him," she said, gesturing to the quirt marks on Jess's face and arms.

"You stay out of this, Lissa. It has nothing to do with you," Jacobson commanded.

Jess's eyes narrowed on Brewster, waiting for him to challenge the old man's last statement, but the foreman said nothing, just let his eyes rake Lissa contemptuously.

"The man owes me money. I'll just collect it and be on my way. Very peaceable," Jess said, relaxing now that Brewster had held his silence.

Jacobson said nothing, looking to Evers since this was his ranch. The old man pulled a well-worn cowhide purse from his belt. "How much you owe, Yancy?"

"Two hundred fifty. I'm good for it, boss."

"I reckon you will be." Evers peeled off a thick wad of bills and handed them to Jess. "That settle it for you?"

Jess shoved the money in his pocket, then touched his fingers to the brim of his hat and walked to his horse. He felt Lissa's eyes on him as he mounted up and rode off.

The promised heat arrived, leaving the July earth as scoured by blazing sun as it had been by May thunderstorms, whose moisture had long since been sucked up by thirsty vegetation. Lissa stood in her room, staring out the window at the merciless, pale blue sky. "Not a cloud in sight, much less a thunderhead," she murmured.

A trickle of perspiration ran between her breasts and she rubbed her sheer camisole to absorb it. Even stripped down to underwear, she was cooking. She watched two hands ride over the horizon, their horses kicking up big soft puffs of dust. The thick grama grass had turned from tender green shoots to tough brown stalks, thinning but still rich in nutrients.

Roundup was over, and plans for the big celebration dance were under way. It would be held at J Bar this year. Germaine worked all the servants at a killing pace. Not a crevice or cranny in the big house escaped her scrutiny. Every inch must be dusted, scrubbed, polished, or painted before the grand event.

Three girls were hired just to act as maids and to assist with the enormous number of kitchen chores. The ball would include a lavish buffet table. Marcus Jacobson stinted nothing when he entertained. Because there had always been such animosity between the housekeeper and Lissa, the younger woman refused to have anything to do with planning the menus or overseeing the beautiful house.

She could not cook. In fact, she possessed no domestic skills whatever. Would that make her a poor wife? Not if she married a rich townsman like Lemuel Mathis, who wanted nothing more than a beautiful ornament. What would Jesse Robbins want in a wife? He was not rich or socially prominent. Baking a good pie was probably worth more to him than being a graceful dancer.

He had kept his distance ever since the incident at Evers's rodeo, preferring to avoid her and the trouble that always sparked when they were together. She had overheard her father and Moss arguing about the extra gunmen Jess was bringing in from Texas and New Mexico. Some sort of a big showdown was brewing with the rustlers, but she did not know when or how it would come about. She only knew that once it was over, Jesse Robbins would ride out of her life forever. And she would never be the same again.

"I must escape this infernal heat! It's affecting my mind." An idea popped into her head. As a child, she had often sneaked away during the summer to a small swimming hole that she and Cridellia had discovered when they were children, still playing together before growing up and becoming spiteful rivals.

If only Lissa could remember where it was located. The more she thought of a long, cool swim, the more the idea cheered her flagging spirits. She quickly donned an old cotton blouse and riding skirt and gathered up a blanket, a thick towel, soap, and shampoo, determined to find that secluded pool. The hands all used a deep, wide spot out on the southern fork of Lodgepole Creek as their summer cooling-off place. No one would intrude on her blissful, forbidden fun.

Smuggling her gear from the house proved easy enough, since she took the bane of Germaine's existence—Cormac—with her. The last time he had bounded through the parlor to greet her, he had shattered two very expensive Royal Worcester vases with his thrashing tail and had frightened one of the extra maids so badly she had fainted.

Lissa told the housekeeper that she was going to take Cormac for a long walk, then spend some time with Vinegar down at the cook's shed. Always happy to have the girl out of her hair, Germaine scarcely noticed when she left. Sneaking into the stable and saddling Little Bit was easy. When Luke Deevers asked where she was riding without an escort, she assured the old man that she would go no farther than the creek. Since she had the big wolfhound with her, he accepted her story.

Before the sun was at its zenith in the blindingly bright sky, she was riding across the open plains with the hot summer wind blowing her hair like a fiery banner behind her. Her father always said thirsty cattle could smell water from ten miles away. So hot and desperate for its respite was she, she could smell the swimming hole from five.

"The place hasn't changed much," she said to Cormac as she dismounted and scanned the small pool bubbling up from deep in the earth. Much of J Bar land held underground water sources that erupted here and there into swift-running creeks and deep pools that were cold even on the hottest days. This one was especially well hidden in a narrow, rocky ravine only a few miles from the flat, fertile basins where the main herds were held. Since grass and water were abundant there, no one bothered to ride over the barren escarpment to disturb the circle of lush green trees and shrubs at the bottom of the steep little canyon.

Of course cattle wandered everywhere, and cowboys followed to reclaim them. She walked around the edge of the small pool after leaving her pinto to drink and graze. The soft mud at the bank bore no traces of recent visitors, except for deer and wolves. Although prairie wolves did not prowl during the day, Lissa was glad of Cormac's protection. The lacy rustling of a stand of birch drew her to undress beneath its canopy. She peeled off her skirt and blouse, boots and underwear, and stood with the sunlight softly dappling her pale ivory skin as it danced between the rustling leaves.

Cormac sat and watched her disrobe, curious at first, for he had never been allowed upstairs in her room. She stretched languorously, experimenting with the delicious freedom of being completely nude in the open air. The hound's big brown eyes studied her, then he turned his attention to the pond, as if daring her to race him into the icy water.

"What are you looking at? Do you think I'm beautiful, Cormac?" She studied her body uncertainly, wondering how it would compare to that voluptuous music hall entertainer's. "Her breasts are larger," she conceded grudgingly, "but I have more delicate hands." She ran her fingers over her hips and buttocks, remembering how Jess had cupped them, pulling her against his bulging erection. Her cheeks flamed.

"I came here to cool down, not heat up more," she whispered hoarsely, quickly dashing over to the large boulder that had served her and Cridellia as an elevated platform from which to plunge into the frigid water. They had quickly discovered that inching their way in from the bank was an exercise in self-torture.

Cormac had no such qualms. He galloped into the shallows, splashing and barking furiously, then began to paddle back and forth across the small, deep pool. Lissa teetered on the boulder for a moment, working up her nerve for the jump. What if she had forgotten how to swim? What if the cold water paralyzed her with cramps?

"I'll just have to rely on you to rescue me, old friend," she said, then jumped from the rock, landing with a big, ungraceful splash beside the frolicking dog.

A Fire in the Blood

*   *   *

Jess had ridden since dawn in the growing heat, checking Sligo's line shack rendezvous, which had received no recent visitors, then cutting sign but finding nothing. The rustlers must have been warned to lie low. He saw a deer break from some low juniper and vanish over the escarpment ahead of him. The thought of a savory venison stew as a break from the endless beef and beans appealed to him. Sliding the rifle from his scabbard, Jess kneed Blaze into a trot and followed the deer.

The rocky shelf left no trail, but Jess had spent a lifetime hunting in bleak West Texas terrain. In this heat, spooked deer would eventually head for water unless dogged too closely. After half an hour traversing the escarpment in the direction the deer had taken, Jess was rewarded when the ground dipped sharply, falling away to a small, narrow ravine. He reined in and peered down its steep side to the circle of green below.

"Even if the buck gets away, that looks mighty inviting, old hoss," he said to the stallion, who was nickering excitedly as he smelled water.

A quick search yielded a rough, zigzagging trail into the ravine. Once he hit level ground, Jess heard the racket. Loud woofs that fairly reverberated off the rocky walls mixed with peals of silvery laughter. He froze in disbelief. *Lissa!*

Swinging down from the black, he led him toward the pool, which was hidden by dense stands of birch, willows and serviceberry. When he cleared the bushes, the pool lay like a gleaming gemstone in front of him, its placid surface broken by the roughhouse playing of the woman and her huge hound. She had just finished working a thick suds through that magnificent mane of fiery hair and was trying to rinse it. Cormac jumped at her, knocking her backward. Laughing, she tumbled beneath the surface.

He held his breath when she emerged shaking her head and sending water flying in every direction as she waded into the shallows. Her milky flesh gleamed with silvery droplets that traced sensuous patterns, following the curves of small, perfectly upthrust breasts and slim, subtly rounded hips. Blood raced to his groin, pooling there in a deep, unrelieved ache that tore a primitive growl from him. He remembered the feel of her soft, yielding flesh when he had cupped that sleek little bottom, pulling her against him. And she had come so willingly, issuing the same invitation she had given him again and again until he was tormented beyond reason with it.

Avoiding her had not assuaged the need. Neither had his lusty romps with Cammie. Lissa had been a fire in his blood, singing her siren's song, luring him to his destruction. He walked into the clearing and let Blaze amble down to the water to drink.

The wind shifted and Cormac raised his head, sniffing, then turned toward where Jess was standing. He let out a joyous peal, barking his welcome.

"Cormac, what on earth—?" Lissa turned toward the bank where the dog's eyes were fastened. "Jess!" Her eyes widened and she stood knee-deep in the cold water, too surprised to cover herself. She watched him methodically strip off his clothes.

Her mouth went suddenly dry, and a low trembling began to radiate from deep inside her, filling her with a strange lethargy. Yet at the same time she had never felt so alive, so breathless and eager as she did at the moment. "What . . . what are you doing?" Her voice sounded far away, hoarse and raspy, as if she had just run for miles.

He paused, tossing his shirt onto the growing pile of his belongings at the edge of the pool. "What does it look like, Lissa? You're reckless. I might as well be reckless, too."

"I'm not reckless." Her eyes devoured the ripple of muscles across his shoulders and the patterns of hair on his chest.

"Playing mother-naked in a deserted water hole where any man could come on you—that's not reckless? Almost forcing me to kill Brewster— that's not reckless? Wandering off into the hands of a couple of randy rustlers—that's not reckless? Almost breaking your horse's legs in a quicksand bog—not reckless? Lady, I haven't seen a woman get herself into so much stupid trouble since the last time I saw a showboat melodrama." His fingers moved to unbutton his fly.

His accusations made her face burn, but she refused to acknowledge their validity. "I brought Cormac along. He's more than equal to any man."

His eyes blazed at her, filled with scorn. "For some things maybe, but not for all." He paused and then asked, "For instance, when's the last time you saw Cormac fire a Winchester?" He resumed unfastening his denims.

She backed up a step, looking uncertainly over to the dog, who was standing, puzzled, in the shallow water with his tail beating a steady tattoo on the rippling surface of the pond. "Some watchdog you are," she whispered as her gaze once more was drawn to Jess.

He kicked free of his denims and began to walk into the pool, slowly, deliberately, like a wild predator stalking his prey. Every hard, sinuous plane of his body was relentless, graceful, hungry. He was male, hot and hard and feverish to take her. She could see all of him this time as her eyes swept from his face down to that splendid chest, then over the faint reddish puckering where she had stitched the gunshot wound. When she looked below at the rampantly male part of him, standing stiffly, proudly erect, she stumbled backward another step, unwilling to protest, unable to run. *This is what you wanted.*

As if echoing her very thought, Jess said, "You've hounded me since the day I set foot in Wyoming, Lissa. You've teased and taunted, flaunted that beautiful, untried little body until I lay awake nights burning. I'm burning now, Lissa. I can strangle you, or I can love you."

As if to emphasize his words, he stepped deeper and deeper into the icy water, oblivious of the cold, until he stood directly in front of her. She could smell sweat and male musk, could feel the heat radiating from his flesh. Against her will, one hand reached out and touched his chest. His heart slammed against her palm so hard she tried to jerk away, but his hand came up and covered hers, pressing it back where it had been.

Neither of them felt the blazing sun or the icy water as they stood gazing into each other's eyes. "See what you do to me?" he asked raggedly as he held her palm against his racing heart. "And what I do to you." His other hand grazed the curve of her breast, then touched the pale pink tip, which had hardened into a nubby point. "You ache, don't you?" he whispered seductively.

Lissa gasped, feeling the tight, heavy throbbing gather in her breasts and pool low in her belly. Her other hand glided up his arm ever so softly, skittering over the curve of his shoulder, her fingers tangling in the long, straight hair at his nape. "Yes, Jess," she said simply.

With a feral growl, he scooped her into his arms and splashed through the water to the shore where she had earlier spread a blanket on the soft grass. She buried her face against his shoulder and held tightly to him as he knelt. Cormac, bored with the humans who were so roundly ignoring him, caught the scent of a squirrel scampering down the trunk of a tree. With two huge bounds, he cleared the pool and vanished down the ravine after it.

Jess laid Lissa down and covered her with his body, tangling his hand in her long, wet hair and tugging on it until she raised her face to his. His mouth came down, crushing hers, demanding entry. She acquiesced and his tongue met hers, gliding, twining, thrusting in sync with his hips as they rocked her rhythmically.

Lissa could feel his breathing grow harsher, faster, as his hands found all the soft, shadowed curves and hollows, the wet, silky secrets of her untried body. Her own breath came in fierce pants while she held him tightly, lost in his rough, savage sensuality.

Finally he broke off the kiss, leaving her dazed, and raised himself up on one elbow to look down at her flushed face and glistening white flesh. How dark his skin looked beside the milky pallor of hers. She was forbidden by every law and code of the west, and he would have her anyway.

Lissa shivered as he suddenly shifted from wild passion to soft wandering caresses, letting his hands stroke gently, exploring her responses as much as fueling his own lust. "You are incredibly lovely," he breathed as he brushed the hard points of her breasts. When the flat of his hand slid down her belly to rest at the mound of dark red curls, her hips arched involuntarily. She stared up into his harsh, beautiful face, meeting those blazing silver eyes, seeing the fierce need, the desperation that drove him.

He lowered his head, and his hair shadowed his face as he teased her aching, sensitive nipples. His tongue circled one nubby peak and drew it into his mouth. She cried out wildly, almost flying up off the blanket with the raw pleasure of his assault. He switched to the other breast, and she sobbed his name as her fingers dug into the hard muscles ridging his back, leaving the imprint of her nails. His hot mouth trailed searing kisses over her quivering flesh. She writhed under him, unknowingly opening when his knee slid between her legs.

Lissa could feel the insistent pressure of his erection as it pulsed against her belly, coming to rest at the juncture of her thighs. She had thought his staff was large and menacing when he strode into the water after her. Now the fear returned when he rocked his hips, prodding the portal to her body.

Jess felt her tense and gritted his teeth, drawing a long, ragged breath, cursing himself for being seven times a fool. She was a virgin, and he had always forsworn them. He reached for her hand and guided it between them. "Touch me, Lissa. Feel me," he said hoarsely as his hand closed hers around his phallus.

So hard yet so smooth, velvety, and hot. Her fingers tightened around the thick length. He showed her how to stroke him, then released her hand, growling deep in his throat as she pleasured him. The shuddering helplessness of his response thrilled her. He belonged to her from this moment on, this dark, dangerous stranger who had drawn her from the instant she first watched him ride into her life.

When she whispered his name, he expelled the breath he had been holding for so long, trying desperately not to spill his seed before he completed the act. He rose over her, his hand on her slim wrist, guiding her hand as he positioned himself to enter her.

Lissa felt the tip of his staff as he rubbed it over her wet, slick flesh. All this aching, throbbing want, the hot liquid craving that had invaded her dreams and tortured her since she met him centered now at the core of her body. It was unbearable. It was sweet heaven. "Please," she gasped brokenly, not fully knowing for what she begged, yet desperate to have it.

He pulled her hand away and thrust slowly into her, testing her readiness to receive him. He moved from side to side with just the tip of his staff inside her. Her hips moved, trying to envelop him deeper, and he was lost. Jess plunged downward, feeling the tight, tearing pressure of her maidenhead, driven far beyond the flimsy barrier, completely into the silky heat of her.

She let out a low moan, partly pain but more than pain. So very much more—fullness, wholeness and yet an unbearable pressure that naturally urged her to move. His lips sought hers, muffling her cries with a hungry kiss, moving over her mouth, thrusting his tongue in rhythm with his phallus as he began to move deep inside her, raising himself, then stroking down, slowly, experimentally at first.

In shuddering pleasure, he murmured against her mouth, "So tight, warm, beautiful," while his hips increased their tempo. "Come with me, Lissa. Ride with me," he commanded.

And she obeyed, letting her hips thrust and fall in rhythm with him, aching and hungry, yet at the same time pleasured and filled. A frenzied, animal hunger grew from a small ripple, swelling to waves of spiraling, breathless pleasure. Every stroke increased it, until she thought she would go mad with it.

Jess held on to sanity by a slim thread as he rode her savagely, thrilled by the pleasure of her sleek, virginal tightness, her splendid young body. Above all he was thrilled by the hot, eager way she responded to him, wanting this, wanting him. Then he felt her nails score his back and heard her whimpering cries of amazed pleasure. Her silken sheath tightened convulsively around him and he let go, pumping his life force deeply within her.

Lissa felt the slick, glorious heat consume her, building to a pinpoint of light at the end of a long tunnel. Then suddenly she burst through from hot darkness into hotter light, to the shattering, glorious end of the madness, appeasement of the hunger. When his wild thrusts increased until he stiffened and swelled within her, crying out, she held on tightly, knowing on some subliminal level that he had joined her in surfeit.

Sweaty and exhausted, he collapsed on top of her, burying his face in shining curls that smelled of orange blossoms. "Now you are mine," she sighed.

Chapter Ten

Jess stiffened as her softly whispered words registered, breaking through his lethargy of satiation. He rolled away from her and sat up, then turned his back and reached for his discarded denims. Without saying a word, he pulled them on.

Lissa, too, sat up when he turned away from her. Sensing his tense withdrawal, she felt confused and uncertain of what to say. "You're angry with me. Why, Jess?" she asked softly.

He gave his boot a fierce yank to force it on, then looked down at her. She sat huddled with her arms wrapped around her knees and all that glorious hair spilling in burnished curls around her shoulders. The blanket was stained with her virgin's blood. He felt guilty—and angry. "What do you want me to say, Lissa? That I love you? That I want to marry you? You know better."

His voice was low and tight. The words stung like

a slap. What had she expected? In truth, she had not thought through what would happen after they made love. She only knew that she was obsessed with him, could think of nothing but him. Was that love? Surely it must be, for the very thought of doing with Lemuel or Yancy what she had just done with Jess filled her with revulsion. But Jess obviously did not feel the same about her. "I didn't lure you here, Jess. You came after me," she stated matter-of-factly.

He laughed. "You are a piece of work, Princess, you know that? The bored little rich girl, wanting a dangerous new toy that everyone says she can't have. You've been throwing yourself at me since the day we met. I'm only a man, Lissa, with a man's needs. When I saw you alone and naked in that water, I did what any other man would've done."

She scrambled to her feet, wrapping the blanket about herself. "You vain, arrogant, crude . . ." Words failed her as she battled the acid burning of tears threatening to overflow.

She started to walk away with as much dignity as she could muster, but Jess stopped her. With a muttered imprecation, he had her in his arms, turning her to face him. "Lissa, I'm sorry. I didn't mean that to come out the way it sounded."

"What exactly did you mean, Jess? Do you think I'd do this with any man who happened along—just because I was bored?" She fought to keep her voice steady and would not meet his eyes.

He sighed but did not relinquish his hold on her. "No, you wouldn't. I know there's been something between us since the first time we met . . . but, dammit, it just won't work."

The anguish in his voice communicated itself to her, and she looked up into his face. "Why not?" She raised one hand and touched his cheek with a butterfly-soft, experimental caress.

"You know why not. What do you think your pa'd say if you told him you wanted to marry me?"

"He'd be furious. He wants me to marry Lemuel Mathis, but I could bring him around, Jess. We could—"

"No, Lissa. It's more than just Mathis. I'm a gunman and a breed. Either one by itself is enough to get me strung up for even looking at a woman like you."

"I don't care about any of that. And don't lie. You aren't afraid of a rope. You could hang up your guns and become a peaceful rancher."

"Marry the boss's daughter and inherit all of this." He gestured to the rich land surrounding them.

"That's really it, isn't it? No matter about your Indian blood or your reputation as a gunman— your pride wouldn't let you accept J Bar. You're really afraid of being accused of marrying for money."

"No one's offering J Bar," he said savagely, fighting the urge to shake her.

"Then forget the ranch. I'll go away with you. We don't need my father's money," she replied stubbornly.

"Lissa, Lissa. You live in luxury and think you could give it up, but you have no idea what your life would be like without money." He took one of her small, soft hands and turned it palm up. "Your hands would grow red and callused from scrubbing your own clothes. You'd never have another fancy ball gown—or any more of that incredible lacy underwear."

"I could live without ball gowns and lacy underwear." A blush heated her cheeks, but she met his eyes.

"No, you couldn't. You're not used to the kind of grinding hard work it would take to survive—and I'll never ask you to live that way."

Lissa sensed the finality in his voice, and panic welled up inside her. *He'll leave me. I'll never see him again. Never feel his touch again.* She smiled and forced a lightness into her voice that she did not feel. "All right, you won't ask me. So I'll just have to settle for the time we have together . . . now." She rose on her toes to place a light kiss on his lips, then tried to turn away before he could protest.

"We can't keep on this way. Brewster suspects. It won't be long before word gets back to your father."

She said solemnly, "Then we'll just have to be more careful." *Until I can convince you to give us a chance.*

"Dammit, Lissa, this isn't a fairy tale. Your reputation would be ruined if anyone knew about this. And that's real." He looked down at the blanket she clutched around her breasts. Several faint smears of blood were visible. "You're going to be sore tomorrow, and you can't let that housekeeper guess why."

She blushed furiously as she followed his eyes to the telltale stains. "I'll be all right. She won't notice."

"The man you marry will." She looked as if he had struck her. *Why did I say that?* "Look, I'm sorry, Lissa. I'm just no good for you. You have to stay

163

away from me. All I'll ever do is hurt you more."
He paused thoughtfully for a moment. "And all
you'll ever do is hurt me."

Suddenly she realized that he was taking a far
greater emotional risk than she. "I'll never hurt
you, Jess."

He ignored the rejoinder. "You'll feel better if
you go back in the water for a few moments before
you dress. I'll wait up on the rise, then follow you
and that hound back to the ranch."

As if summoned, Cormac trotted tardily up to
them and sat down to await his mistress's pleasure.

She gave Jess what she hoped was a teasing
smile. "As long as you're here, I'll be safe."

"Safe from everyone but me," he muttered.

Lissa dropped the blanket at the edge of the pool
and waded into the water with Cormac splashing
alongside her. She did not turn when she heard
Jess riding up the trail out of the ravine.

After a restless night, Jess saddled up to ride
into Cheyenne. Maybe Pardee had wired him back
about the job offer. The sooner the hired guns
arrived, the sooner he could deal with the J Bar
rustlers, collect his money, and shake the dust of
Wyoming off his boots.

"Yesterday couldn't be soon enough," he said
aloud to Blaze.

As he rode past the big house, Jacobson's French
housekeeper stopped pruning her rosebushes and
glared at him with her glittering dark eyes. He
wondered if he suspected anything. Lissa had
not exactly been subtle in front of the old crone.
"Bonjour, madame." He smiled evilly. She clutched

her rose shears and backed up a step.

Damn, but he had bought into a gallon jug of trouble. A man like Marcus Jacobson was a law unto himself in Wyoming Territory. If the old man even suspected that a half-breed gunman had touched his princess, Jess would have to kill the bastard or Jacobson would have him strung up to the nearest tree. If he had a lick of sense, he would ride south to Denver right now, the hell with the five thousand dollars.

But Jonah needed the money to buy those new stud bulls and prove up the ranch. Although Jess's reputation was well known, he had never gotten the kind of money Tom Horn did—until this time. If he handled it well, the money for future jobs would only get better. He simply had to stay clear of Lissa.

Easier said than done. When he had seen her naked in that water, he had been like a man possessed, beyond thought, beyond reason. She fancied herself in love with him. Avoiding her would be next to impossible since she had already demonstrated her persistence and ingenuity—and that was before he had lain with her.

Sweet lord, just thinking about her slender, delicate body made him hard all over again. He had never taken a virgin before. Her very innocence had fueled his passion. Lissa was not the only one thrilled by the forbidden. Jess could see them again, entwined, with his dark hands on her pale flesh.

Strange, he had made love to many white women over the years and felt no different about them than he had about those with Indian blood. All of them had been experienced. Some were plain whores who charged for their favors; the rest were faithless wives cheating on their husbands. He had always felt contempt for the double standard that made him at once an enticement and a pariah from civilized society. That would never change. His relationship with Lissa Jacobson was impossible. What did she really feel for him? He had accused her of the sins committed by so many of his women over the years, but now he had doubts.

The pain in her wide gold eyes had been real. The answering pain that tightened his chest was just as real. He would not call it love, but he feared that Lissa might.

"I should be thinking about how I'm going to finish the job, not about her." A man in his business could snag some lead if his mind was not focused on survival every minute. In more ways than one, Lissa was a luxury he could not afford.

Marcus looked up as Germaine entered his library with a tray in her hand. She placed it on the desk and handed him a cup of coffee, saying, "Black with extra sugar, just the way you like it, *Chéri*."

A frown creased his face. "I've told you, don't call me that. Someone might overhear."

"Someone! You mean Lissa," she replied angrily.

"Yes, Lissa, my daughter," he said levelly, his eyes the color of a frozen lake.

"You are a fool, Marcus. She is not the proper lady your wife was. She and that Indian—"

"That will be quite enough, Germaine," he interrupted sharply. "You've made these wildly inaccurate, insanely jealous accusations before. I refuse to listen to such errant nonsense again." He stood up, at six feet towering over her even though she was tall for a woman.

"You refuse everything! After all I have given you, you should know I would not lie—"

"All you've given me," he mocked with an ugly sneer. "You made your sexual favors available when I met you in St. Louis, then when I was alone and desperate for a woman after Mellisande died. You would lie, my dear. You would do anything to discredit my only child."

"She is not—"

"Silence! Don't say it again. I know where this conversation is leading, and I refuse to hear it one more time."

"You treat me badly, Marcus."

"I treat you admirably and you damn well know it," he snapped. "I've given you a hefty bequest in my will and a position here running my household for as long as I live."

"And made me swear an oath by the Blessed Virgin that I would never reveal our relationship on pain of losing everything!" she said in a scathingly bitter tone.

He smiled a cold, nasty smile. "The oath is bound only by your own papist superstitions. Break it," he dared.

She seemed to crumple in on herself for a moment, then straightened and faced him with that same old black fire in her eyes. "No, I will not break it as you well know. Unlike you, I keep to my loyalties. You and your daughter are alike— faithless. She will bring you low, Marcus. I will have to do nothing. Nothing at all but sit back and wait."

She turned and walked from the room, leaving Marcus Jacobson to ruminate on his own folly, ruing the day he had ever been desperate enough to take Germaine Channault as his mistress.

Their liaison had ended long before Lissa returned from St. Louis, of course. He would never have permitted his gently reared child to learn about his sordid arrangement with a common woman like Germaine.

No woman could ever replace his beloved Mellisande. He had never considered remarrying, and if he had, it would not be to an impoverished French Canadian who was homely and possessed of morals that would bear no close inspection.

In the early days there were so few women in Wyoming, he temporized for the hundredth time. Yet he cursed the fate that had ever kept him in Germaine's bed.

She was irrationally jealous of Lissa, which was understandable, and the two had been at odds ever since his daughter was a child. Since she returned home permanently last year, the feud had worsened. Now it had become so virulent as to include Germaine's ridiculous accusations about Lissa having an affair with that half-breed gunman. Of course Lissa had shown an interest in the exotic stranger, but he knew that Robbins was too smart to try and touch her. Even more important, Lissa's morals were of the same caliber as those of her mother.

"Damn Germaine, always stirring up trouble," he said aloud as he took a swallow of the coffee. There was a bitter edge to the thick, sweet liquid and it grated on his teeth as he set down the cup and resumed working on his books.

168

A Fire in the Blood

*   *   *

When he arrived in Cheyenne, Jess went straight to the telegraph office. Pardee's wire was waiting for him. The gunman would arrive on the Monday train along with a dozen well-chosen companions. As soon as he had the backup he needed, the trap could be sprung on the rustlers. He had watched Sligo's trips to the line shack and checked all the messages he had left. Rather than tip off the rustlers, he had let them take several small bunches of cattle on isolated ranges and merely doubled the hands who guarded the larger herds closer to the J Bar big house. That had held down losses, but it was not a long-term answer to the problem.

After the fall roundup, when the four-year-olds were shipped for sale, the remaining cattle would spread out across the vast rangelands. Winter snows would isolate them, and hands would be fewer since many quit after roundup, using their warm-weather earnings to live in town during the bitter blizzard season. By spring, before another roundup crew could be organized, the scattered cattle would again fall prey to the rustlers who only waited for the weather to break before swooping down.

But why did such a carefully coordinated bunch of thieves single out J Bar? Diamond E and Empire Land and Cattle were almost as big, yet Evers and MacFerson had barely been touched, and the beeves they did lose were taken from herds adjacent to J Bar. Someone was squeezing Marcus Jacobson. Who? Why?

Deep in thought, Jess folded the telegram, tucked it into his vest pocket, and strolled out of the Western Union office into the busy street. He nearly collided with Camella Alvarez. She was sporting a frothy concoction of ruffles and bows that was supposed to be a parasol.

"Watch that damn thing, Cammie. You almost put out my eye," he said, directing the point away from his face.

She turned from the distraction of the medicine show drawing a crowd in the center of the street. A rumpled man in a stovepipe hat proclaimed the miraculous curative powers of Dr. Hamlin's Wizard Oil, Blood Pills and Cough Balsam. "What are you doing in town, Jess?"

Her liquid black eyes danced mischievously as she twirled her parasol on her shoulder and studied him. She was a confection in a bright pink taffeta dress sporting a poufed bustle in the back. The color flattered her olive skin and ebony hair. A big white smile played across her generous mouth. "I've missed you, *querido*," she said, running her hand up his arm proprietarily.

For reasons he preferred not to examine, he felt uncomfortable with her, knowing where their conversations always led. The last place he wanted to be now was in Cammie's bed. "You're out early in the day. Some special reason?" he hedged.

She shrugged. "A woman gets bored rehearsing all day, performing for that pack of slavering drunks every night. I just wanted some air. What are your plans? I have the afternoon free."

"Sorry, Cammie. I don't. I just came to check on a wire I sent. I have to ride back to J Bar before nightfall."

"If you walk me back to the theater, I can tell you about Sligo . . . and some of his friends." She let the bait dangle.

He fell into step beside her. "So tell me about Sligo."

"He was in the audience three nights ago. Got mean drunk. Talked like he was planning to leave Wyoming soon."

He digested that. Things had not been going well for the thieves. "Maybe the rustlers are displeased with their inside man."

She shrugged. "The barmen were ready to evict him when a couple of Diamond E hands came over and quieted him down."

He stopped in midstride. "Who were they?"

"An older fellow—Kirk, I think is his name. And Yancy Brewster."

"I'll be damned. You ever see them together before?" he asked as he opened the back door to the music hall stage. They stepped into the gloomy silence. The place was deserted so early in the day.

"I heard both men rode together in Colorado before Brewster became the Diamond E foreman."

Jess whistled low. "Cammie, I owe you."

"Oh, I can think of lots of ways to make you pay, Jess," she said with dancing eyes. "Come upstairs with me now. You have plenty of time to ride back to J Bar before dark."

He shook his head. "Not today."

She studied him, feeling the tension coiled in him when she stroked his arm. "There is more than your job involved in this, isn't there, *querido?* I could tell when I first touched you. You *feel* different. Who is the woman?"

He muttered an oath beneath his breath. "Look, Cammie, I can't explain now. Maybe never."

Her expression was troubled. "Whoever she is, she has hurt you."

171

"More like I've hurt her," he replied grimly.

"Old Marcus's daughter! Yes, it must be." Now her eyes were wide with concern. "Jacobson will kill you if you so much as look at her—or did she do the looking first?"

He ignored the question. "I know it won't work, Cammie. As soon as this job is done, I'm leaving Wyoming." He gave her trembling lips a light kiss, then reached for the stage door. "If you hear anything more, leave a message at the telegraph office for me. And thanks, Cammie."

"I would say stay away from her, but I will bet my newest hat you will not listen. Just be careful, *querido*. And remember, I am always here."

"But Lissa, you must realize what a perfect opportunity the dance would present." Lemuel's smile was indulgent as he sat holding her hand in the ranch parlor. He and Marcus had just concluded some business transactions in the library. Her father then excused himself, leaving his associate and his daughter alone until dinner. Lemuel was staying the night.

"I've already explained that I need more time to consider your proposal, Lemuel. Announcing our engagement at the dance is simply out of the question." There, she had said it. She met Mathis's piercing gaze head-on.

His face was faintly flushed, as if he were at the end of his patience. "You know how dearly your father wishes us to be wed," he wheedled.

"Nothing could be clearer, believe me. And I don't want to hurt Papa. . . ." Her words trailed away as she compared the stodgy older businessman sitting next to her with Jesse Robbins.

As if reading her thoughts, Mathis asked, "Is there someone else, Lissa? That Brewster fellow, perhaps?"

"No," she answered almost too quickly, then realizing that Yancy's suit was perhaps the safest camouflage she could devise, she added, "That is, Yancy is one of the men who has courted me. I'm only nineteen, Lemuel. I just want some time for myself." *Some time with Jess.*

Mathis's broad forehead creased in a frown. "Nineteen is past the age when most women are married, Lissa. And marriage won't be the end of parties and gaiety if you marry me. Then you could live in Cheyenne. Preside over my splendid brick residence and attend all of the city's social events. Quite a bit different from what young Brewster could offer. He's nothing but a cowhand who's worked his way into Cy Evers's good graces," he added righteously.

Lemuel was insufferably pompous and stuffy. What would he think if she told him she fancied marrying a man like Jess? He would have a seizure, she was certain.

"A penny for your thoughts, my dear?" he said, leaning close to her, preparing to steal a clumsy kiss.

"Oh, nothing really, Lemuel," she said, as she quickly stood up and paced over to the big front window.

Mathis followed, irritated by her jumpiness. He stood behind her, letting his hands rest lightly on her shoulders. "I've been a patient man, Lissa. So has your father, but you're a woman grown now and you have serious responsibilities as Marcus's only heir."

His touch felt leaden to her. "I'm daily reminded of that, Lemuel," she said somberly.

Just as she was about to twist away from beneath his hands, Jess rode past, headed toward the bunkhouse. Her pulse raced, and her blood thrummed crazily through her whole body just watching the graceful way he swung his long leg over Blaze's back and dismounted. Would Lemuel notice?

"Well, I see that breed gunman made it back from Cheyenne after his little assignation," he said with annoyance.

"Assignation?" Her voice was too sharp.

Mathis colored and coughed discreetly. "I—er, I only meant that I saw the ruffian dallying with one of the scarlet poppies at the Royale Music Hall this afternoon as I left town to come here. For the handsome sum your father pays him, the least he could do is restrict his leisure activities to the time after he's dealt with these rustlers," he added.

For a hysterical instant Lissa almost blurted out that Jesse Robbins's leisure activity yesterday had been with her! "Who was the entertainer? Perhaps he was pursuing information about the rustling." Her words sounded hollow even to her ears.

"I doubt that pretty little Mexican tart Camella Alvarez has anything to do with the rustlers," he said drily.

"If you'll excuse me, Lemuel, I must see if Germaine needs any assistance in the kitchen." She did not wait for his reply but turned away from him before he could see the tears threatening to overflow. She walked with a stiff spine from the room, trying her damnedest to be sedate and regal, a lady, just as they had taught her at Miss Jefferson's Academy.

Dinner that evening was a wretched affair for Lissa, sitting between Lemuel and her father, listening to their conversation and making appropriate comments, attempting to hide her misery behind a facade of smiles. When they discussed Jesse Robbins and the rustling, she wanted to run from the room but knew she must sit and endure it.

"Tomorrow I'm riding to the roundup over on Evers's east range, Princess. Would you like to go with me?" Marcus asked as Germaine served him a flaky slice of freshly baked gooseberry pie.

Lissa shoved her pie about on her plate, forcing down a few bites lest her lack of appetite be further remarked upon. "Yes, Papa, that would be fine."

"Good. We'll set out early. Take that worthless hound with us. Let him eat Vinegar out of supplies. I'm afraid Germaine is out of patience with him."

Lissa survived the rest of the meal, then pleaded that her headache was growing worse and asked to be excused. A huffy, disappointed Lemuel Mathis bade her good night and reminded her rather pointedly that he would be her escort for the gala dance on Saturday, which would be held at J Bar.

After Lissa retired, she kept waking up with the sheets bunched around her legs where she had tangled them in her restless thrashing. The night was warm and sultry, with barely any breeze stirring. Visions of Jess with that Mexican harlot Camella filled her dreams—Jess's lean, dark body entwined with the raven-haired woman's, doing to Camella the same exquisite, breathtaking things he had done to her.

175

When morning came, she had dark circles beneath her eyes and felt exhausted. "Damn if I'll let him see me this way, grieving with jealousy over his philandering." She splashed cool water on her face, then soaked a towel and made a compress to take away the puffiness and discoloration. She brushed her hair and plaited it, then used the small cask of cosmetics she kept hidden from her father and Germaine. After a faint touch of powder beneath her eyes, a daub of rouge on her lips, and a hint of kohl on her eyelids, she looked considerably better. She selected a yellow silk blouse to go with her tan riding skirt.

When she walked down to the stables with Cormac loping at her side, Jess was there talking with Marcus. Hearing her and her companion approach, he turned and tipped his hat politely. His warm, silvery gaze sent sparks tingling through her as she walked regally past him with a curt, "Good morning."

Luke Deevers came up to Marcus with a question just as they were mounting up, leaving Jess to assist her. Much as she did not want his hands on her, there was nothing she could do without causing a scene.

"Allow me, Miss Jacobson," he offered, holding her pinto steady. His movements were cool and proper, but a current of raw sexual energy charged the air as he stood so near her.

Hurt and anger flared in her eyes before she could mask her reaction when his hands touched her waist. He lifted her up onto the saddle, and she cursed his effect on her. All she had wanted to do was show him that she did not care a fig for him. Instead she was trembling, on the verge of tears. Gritting her teeth, she regained control of her roiling emotions before speaking. "Thank you, Mr. Robbins," she said stiffly, shrugging off his touch.

"You're welcome, Princess," he replied in a soft, insolent voice that no one else could hear. So, now that she had time to reconsider, her highness had decided that he was beneath her after all. He should have been relieved. Wasn't that what he had wanted? But instead he felt hurt and anger, oddly mixed with chilling desolation, as if something bright and precious had been taken from him.

Damn, I should've accepted Cammie's offer yesterday.

The ride to the roundup camp was brief and accomplished with little conversation. Marcus made a few passing remarks to her about the dance, and he and Jess exchanged thoughts about the plans to entrap the rustlers. Lissa stared straight ahead, watching Cormac's antics as he ran effortlessly across the flat, open grasslands.

As soon as the hound saw Vinegar Joe's chuck wagon on the horizon, he headed straight for it at a run. Remembering his penchant for trouble around food, she decided that this was as good an excuse as any to escape the disturbing presence of the gunman.

"I'm going to catch up with Cormac before he gets a barrel full of buckshot from Vinegar," she yelled at her father as she kneed Little Bit into a gallop.

Chapter Eleven

Lissa was too late. By the time she approached the roundup camp, pandemonium had already erupted. Vinegar's arthritic little body moved with surprising alacrity as he chased Cormac and another, smaller black-and-white mutt through the camp, swinging a big straw broom in the dogs' wake. He was enraged enough to chew the sight off a sixgun.

"Yew come back here with my quail, yew thievin' sons of bitches, afore I draw 'nough blood from yew ta paint a house!" The smaller culprit was in the lead, with the big wolfhound right on his tail.

Cormac lunged away from a mighty swipe of the broom and almost caught up to Pepper, Moss's dog, who was dragging a frayed rope with several braces of quail attached to it.

"I been aging them birds special fer two weeks. They's jist 'bout tender, gawddammit!"

One dead bird stuck out of the smaller dog's mouth, which was smeared with reddish-brown feathers. Just as they both careened around the corner of the chuck wagon, Vinegar's broom connected with Cormac's rump, causing him to break stride. One huge paw stepped on the rope Pepper was dragging. The shaggy mut whipped his head around, which caused the rope of quail to fly into a wire basket filled with eggs. The rope caught on the basket and it overturned, leaving a trail of broken shells and glistening yolks smeared across the dusty ground. The big wolfhound churned through the mess, enjoying the chase.

Vinegar slid in the broken eggs and threw down his broom. Seizing an iron skillet, he hurled it at the culprits. The skillet missed its mark and instead shattered a large crock of sorghum sitting on a shelf at the opposite side of the tarpaulin that shaded the cook's table. The sticky syrup flew in all directions, almost coating Pepper, Cormac, and the stolen quail.

As the shrieking little cook seized a big iron ladle and brandished it, Pepper bounded from beneath the canvas and ran around Vinegar's bubbling pot of stew. Cormac headed him off by circling the cauldron from the opposite side. A crowd of hands had gathered by this time, hooting, cheering, and making bets on whether Pepper and Cormac would escape with the prize, or Vinegar Joe reclaim it.

"Vinegar's madder 'n a rained-on rooster," Rob Ostler said to Lissa as she dismounted.

Her eyes round with horror, she called to both dogs. Pepper obeyed no one but Moss, who was not in camp. The noise was so great that even Cormac, who normally heeded Lissa's commands, could not hear her over the din.

"Betcha five dollars he gets them birds back," another called out to Ostler.

Cormac almost collided with Pepper as he snapped at one of the dangling quail. His big teeth sank into the bird and the rope. A tug of war ensued until Vinegar, wielding the iron ladle and a long barbecue fork, alternately swung and poked at the larger target, the wolfhound.

Cormac let out a muffled woof as the fork pierced his shaggy brindled rump, then took off. Since Pepper was holding the other end of rope at the opposite side of the fire, the unfortunate result was that the huge pot overturned onto the ground, spilling meat and gravy in a giant puddle. The little cook did a yelping dance as boiling chunks of beef and sauce enveloped his boots and splashed onto the grimy white apron he wore. Jumping as high as a Pecos twister, he hopped out of the mess, still cursing the dogs and searching for another weapon.

By this time the men, realizing that their dinner had just been demolished, began to view the cook's plight in a somewhat more sympathetic light. When the pair of felons ran toward the nearby cavvy, a cry went up.

"Watch them horses!"

"Oh, shit!"

"Cormac! I'll put you on bread and water for a year!"

"Will ya lookit that!"

The cavvy was contained in a makeshift corral of flimsy posts with rope strung between them. Pepper dashed beneath the rope, but Cormac ran smack into it, toppling the posts. The two thrashing dogs sent the neighing, prancing horses into a mad stampede. Men on foot cursed and dodged flying hooves, then raced for their saddled horses while those already mounted seized their ketch ropes and gave chase in a vain attempt to head off the stampede.

By this time, Vinegar was digging through the chest strapped on the side of the wagon like a crazed chipmunk searching for acorns, screeching imprecations at the dogs. The objects of his wrath avoided the stampeding horses by turning back to the security of the wagon and its tent. Now Cormac had the rope of birds and Pepper was chasing him. As they ran beneath the canvas, Cormac bumped one of the support poles holding the tarpaulin up. Following hard on his heels, Pepper did likewise and the heavy canvas fell with a great whoosh that toppled over the two sets of open shelves filled with tin plates, cups, and heavy crockery.

Vinegar let out another volley of oaths that could be heard even over the clattering crash. Lissa held her hands over her ears as the scene unfolded before her horrified eyes. The cook yanked an ancient shotgun free from the tangled mess of tools in the chest and raised it in the general direction of the canvas. Two writhing lumps, one very large, one smaller, thrashed beneath the tarpaulin, trying to scratch their way to freedom.

"No, Vinegar, don't shoot!" Lissa yelled as she ran toward the cook, who was pulling back the hammer.

She grabbed the gun just as he fired, knocking his aim awry. The recoil of the gun sent both the skinny little cook and Lissa tumbling to the ground.

181

A strange, grayish-white cloud came billowing out from beneath the canvas with the force of a tornado wind.

The spectators began to cough and rub their eyes as a fine white dust settled on them. Lissa stumbled to the edge of the canvas and pulled it back, freeing the prisoners, who had at last relinquished their prize quail.

"Oh, Cormac, Pepper, look at you!" she gasped in dismay while another fit of coughing seized her.

"What the hell's going on here?" Marcus bellowed as two white dogs, severely chastened, with tails between their legs, cowered behind Lissa.

Jacobson dismounted while Jess sat astride Blaze, looking down on the wreckage with amusement. When his eyes swept over Lissa's flour-coated hair and sticky hands, she reddened in mortification and quickly looked away.

Blinking her lashes, she rubbed Cormac's head. Her fingers stuck in his fur. "It's flour," she said inanely, knowing she was blushing and hating herself for it. "Vinegar was trying to shoot them, and he hit the flour sack instead, underneath the canvas. It just sort of exploded all over them . . . and us," she added, looking sheepishly down at her ruined clothes and boots. So much for dressing up to impress that philandering gunman!

To add insult to her injury, Cormac shook himself, sending more flour, along with droplets of drool, spraying over her.

"Well, if thet don't put a hair in the butter," Vinegar shrieked. "Them thieves steal my quail 'n wreck my whole shebang 'n alls yew kin say is I shot my own bakin' flour like it wuz a stray coyote!" He threw down his greasy, battered hat, which miraculously had stayed on his head, and stomped on it with muddy, flour-coated boots. "I quit! I ain't playin' nursemaid ta no hellhound big 'nough ta saddle 'n ride. Ner any sniveling little sneak-thiefs neither," he said focusing his one good eye on Pepper.

Marcus ignored Vinegar's continuing tantrum. The crotchety old cook quit every few weeks over some infraction in his domain. He turned to Moss, who had just ridden up to behold the mess.

"Aw, Pepper. Shitfire, this is the last time," Symington said as he stared at the whimpering dog, who slunk over to him. The rest of the foreman's face was as red as his bulbous nose. "I'll get rid of him, boss. Ole Harley Freye's been pestering me to let him have Pepper to service his bitch."

"Just get him out of here before anything else happens," Marcus said with a sigh.

Jacobson turned to Cormac, who had recovered his aplomb and now sat, thoroughly unrepentant, by Lissa. The hound's tongue lolled out of the side of his mouth, and his tail thumped in the sticky muck that had earlier been hard-packed dirt. "If he gets near the house in that condition, Germaine will have a seizure. Get that mess off him at the creek," he commanded Lissa.

She touched his back experimentally. "It's molasses . . . and eggs underneath the flour." An idea was playing in the back of her mind as she looked at the expression of condescending amusement on Jesse Robbins's handsome face. "I'll need someone to hold him while I scrub. You know how he hates to have a bath." She emphasized the last word.

Cormac's tail stopped wagging, and a low growl emanated from his throat.

The men began to shuffle and back away, some finding tasks of immediate urgency that sent them flying after their horses. Rob Ostler even volunteered to help Vinegar clean up the muck around the chuck wagon. Moss Symington was the only one not afraid of the big wolfhound, and he had conveniently left camp with Pepper.

Lissa smiled up at Jess. "Cormac's taken a shine to Mr. Robbins here, Papa. I think he'd do better than any of the other hands."

"Thet's right, Mr. Jacobson. He's the onliest feller I ever seen thet critter let pet him 'cept for Miz Lissa 'n Moss," Butch said.

Several others chorused immediate agreement. Marcus nodded curtly at Jess. "Give her a hand, Robbins." He did not see the slyly beatific smile that spread across his daughter's face as he strode away.

Jess scowled at the girl and the dog. He did not even want to consider what was embedded beneath the white paste on the hound's shaggy fur. "You say he hates baths?" His voice was deadly.

Lissa smirked. "What's the matter? Surely the baddest man west of anyplace east can't be bothered by one molasses-covered dog," she said in a syrupy voice.

He eyed the dog, then moved his piercing gaze to her, raking her disheveled hair and clothing until the smile erased itself from her face. "The dog doesn't bother me," he replied stonily. "Let's get this done."

Her revenge did not seem at all the clever idea it had when she first contrived it. In fact, she could handle Cormac all by herself—and had on numerous occasions. "Forget it. I'll wash him without your help."

She turned away, but his whispered question stopped her. "What's the matter? Surely the Princess of J Bar can't be bothered by one half-breed gunman."

He was smiling, but it was not a nice smile. She refused to meet his eyes. "Like you said, let's get it done."

Jess watched her stiff-spined walk down to the creek, wondering what had set her off. After they made love, she had practically begged him to marry her, offered to give up everything for him. He reevaluated his first reaction to her rebuff this morning. She was not behaving like a woman who has realized a great gaffe and wants to pretend the whole incident never happened. Lissa was still trying to get his attention—almost in spite of herself.

He dismounted at the water's edge as she pulled off her boots and waded in, coaxing the huge dog to follow her. He bounded in, splashing wildly, much as he had cavorted with her in the pool, but when she produced the bar of soap she had taken from the chuck wagon, he backed away warily.

"Cormac, I'll nail your hide right alongside those wolf pelts on the bunkhouse wall if you give me any trouble," she said in a low, menacing voice, trying not to look at Jess as he stripped off his weapons and boots in much the same deliberate manner he had used before coming into the pool after her. *Don't think about that!*

He entered the water and approached the dog. "Cormac, old pal, you better listen to the lady," he said as he took a firm hold of the dog's leather collar.

Lissa concentrated on working up a stiff lather of suds from Vinegar's homemade lye soap and rubbing it through the dog's matted, filthy hair. He held amazingly still under Jess's stern, low voice but quivered in outrage at the soap. She worked furiously, trying to avoid touching Jess's hands or getting too near his body.

"You're acting like the women in Cheyenne who don't want to be contaminated by touching a breed," he said in a low voice.

She jumped and the soap slipped from her hand. He bent over and retrieved it. When he handed it to her, she hesitated, then snatched it angrily from him.

"Not *all* the women in Cheyenne avoid you, you music hall Romeo," she blurted out furiously, then dropped her eyes back to the dog.

His hands gripped hers on Cormac's sudsy coat, stilling them. "What the hell are you talking about?"

"Don't deny it, Jess. Lemuel came courting yesterday. He told me he saw you and that Camella Alvarez going into her place of business," she said scornfully.

A slow, incredulous smile spread across his face. "Oh, I won't deny I talked to Cammie. I was in town picking up a wire from the telegraph office when I ran into her—accidentally. She had some information about a J Bar hand who's involved with the rustlers. All we did was talk, Lissa."

"Like you talked that first night in town, out back of the Metropolitan Hotel?" His warm, firm hands holding hers were doing wild things to her heart, which pounded madly. She could not think straight.

Jess could feel the pulses racing in her delicate wrists. He caressed them sensuously. She was jealous of Cammie! "I've known Cammie since we were kids on the Texas border. It wasn't always so innocent between us, no. But I didn't make love to her yesterday, Lissa."

She pulled her hands away and resumed scrubbing the dog, who stood patiently, looking from Lissa to Jess and back as they talked so intensely. "Why should I believe you?"

Jess reached up and brushed a soap bubble from the tip of her nose. "Because I have no reason to lie," he answered flatly. "I'm not courting you like Lemuel Mathis. I don't want your ranch, and I can't offer you marriage. But I never lied to you about that or anything else, Lissa."

She studied his eyes, lost in their silvery depths. "I don't want the ranch either." Then grudgingly she added, "I believe you."

He sighed. "Hell, I should've let you stay angry with me. It would've made things easier."

She looked up. "Then why didn't you?"

Under her scrutiny, his swarthy face heated and he looked away uncomfortably. "Damned if I know."

Cormac chose that moment to give himself a mighty shake, flinging suds everywhere. Then he made a dash for freedom, still covered with soap. With a squeal of laughter, Lissa grabbed for his collar and stumbled in the shallow water. Jess, pulled off balance when the dog jumped free of his hold, fell forward, landing on Cormac's back. The dog slithered from beneath them and bounded into the deeper water while Jess and Lissa went down, arms and legs entangled as they splashed in the water on their hands and knees.

Vinegar Joe had come down to the creek with one of his pack mules to load up a barrel of water for cleaning the campsite. He paused at the top of the rise, partially hidden by a cottonwood tree, and watched Jess and Lissa earnestly holding hands over the big dog. He could not hear their exchange but knew they were not discussing Cormac. Then the dog broke free, and they fell into the creek, laughing and splashing each other like lovers.

A worried frown creased his face as he muttered, "Gawddamn, if this here really don't put a hair in the butter!"

Jess watched Ralph Sligo for the next couple of days, hoping he would not leave another message for the rustlers until Pardee and his guns arrived. So far Sligo had not ridden to the line shack. Jess needed backup before he could bait the trap. He estimated there were around twenty rustlers. There was no way he could know how many of them were any good with a gun, and he could not be certain about the men Pardee picked. Normally, a dozen professional gunmen would be more than enough to handle matters, but that was when he knew exactly who he was going up against.

Jess followed Sligo the next afternoon. When the rustler did nothing amiss, Jess returned to the ranch, all the while turning the matter of the impending confrontation over in his mind. Tate Shannon had been a damn reliable man. Jess decided to try enlisting him again. It was not good for a man like Shannon to give up on life, even over a woman like Tabby.

Such thoughts brought Lissa to mind again, a subject he tried to forget. Useless. What foolery had led him to confess the truth about his relationship with Cammie to her? She would have kept her distance if he had let her believe Mathis's accusations.

I can't stay away from her any more than she can stay away from me. She was a fire in his blood, racing along every nerve, scorching him with her sweet, wild heat. He lay awake each night in his bunk, hungering for her beautiful body, but more than that, for the sound of her voice, her laughter, the pleasure of her very presence. Lissa Jacobson was not a woman he could take and then walk away from. *I'll pay for loving her the rest of my life.*

Loving her! Had he actually thought those words? He cursed to himself and pushed the thought aside as he rode up to the stable where he had just seen Shannon enter.

"You got a few minutes, Tate?" he asked as he began to unsaddle Blaze.

The big black man shrugged as he applied a rub rag to his dun gelding. "Yeah, I got nothin' but time, Jess. Been meanin' to talk to you anyways. What you want?"

"Pardee's coming with twelve men."

A harsh smile that was really more of a grimace slashed Tate's face. "And you want me to make it a baker's dozen?"

"I don't know the men Pardee's bringing," Jess said as he swung the heavy saddle over the rail and began to rub down his stallion.

"Knowin' Pardee, they'll be snake-mean and armed to the teeth."

Shirl Henke

"I'd still like you to watch my back, Tate. Pay's fifty dollars a day from the time we ride after the rustlers."

"Just like the old days, huh, Jess?" Shannon pondered, then looked up at Robbins. "I might be interested. What're your plans when this is done?"

"I'll collect the biggest purse I've gotten yet. Probably ride home to see Jonah for a while. After that . . ." He shrugged. "I'll see what comes along."

"You ain't figgerin' on stayin' at J Bar?" Shannon's eyes were wary.

Jess caught the nuance of tension in his companion's voice and looked up. "Hell, no. What makes you ask that?"

Tate looked around the stable before answering. No one was close enough to overhear, but he lowered his voice just the same. "Vinegar mentioned something to me the other day. It really stuck in his craw."

Jess froze, staring straight ahead. "Go on."

"He started askin' me 'bout you. Heard we rode together down in Arizona. At first I thought it was just the usual, you know, curiosity about a fast gun. But he had something real particular in mind. He saw you 'n Miss Lissa together at the creek the other day when you helped her clean up that dog."

"We washed a dog, nothing more," Jess said levelly, cursing inwardly.

Shannon snorted. "Funny, he didn't see it that way. Vinegar Joe Riland's downright ornery, but he ain't no fool. You didn't have to drag her down and kiss her in front of him for him to pick up

190

on the idea somethin's goin' on. He's worked for the J Bar since that girl was born, and he's loyal to ole Marcus. Shit, Jess, you know what a man like Jacobson would do to you if he even suspects you're foolin' with his daughter!"

Jess let out a long slow breath. "Yeah, Tate. It's been on my mind here lately."

Shannon watched Jess methodically continue rubbing down Blaze, working with short, powerful strokes of the body brush. "Look, I know it ain't my place to try 'n tell you what to do—aw, hell, Jess, she's white. You know as well as me what that means."

"Let it rest, Tate. You're right. It isn't your place," he said tightly.

The big black man sighed and turned to his dun. Pulling on the hackamore, he started to lead the horse out to the corral where the cavvy was held.

Jess called out, "Wait, Tate. I appreciate your telling me about Vinegar."

"Just be careful," the black man admonished.

"You going to watch my back when I go after the rustlers?"

Shannon nodded with a resigned expression on his face. "Hell, reckon I got no choice, but you'd better be careful 'bout whose back you been watchin'."

Chapter Twelve

"You are the most beautiful woman west of the Mississippi, Princess. Lemuel will be enchanted." Marcus inspected Lissa as she descended the stairs at the front of the hallway.

It was not Lemuel she had dressed to please, although he would be her escort that night. She smiled her thanks to her father, but just as her eyes swept the decorations for the gala, she caught a look of unguarded murderous hatred on Germaine Channault's face. Only for an instant, then it was gone. With uneasiness, she remembered the other times she had caught the sour older woman glaring at her with malice. *Why does she hate me?*

"The house looks positively breathtaking, Germaine," she said as she touched a Sevres vase containing a huge spray of fresh wood lilies and larkspur.

"Germaine has outdone herself this year," Marcus said in a self-congratulating voice. The unsmiling housekeeper nodded curtly and stalked down the hall, ignoring Lissa entirely.

The whole entryway was filled with flowers. In the large front parlor, the furniture had been moved and the carpets rolled up. The hardwood floors were polished to a high luster, ready for dancing. The dining room table was arranged with snowy damask and high stacks of plates, while the kitchen staff worked overtime preparing the lavish buffet.

Heavenly aromas wafted from the rear of the big house.

Marcus took his daughter's hand as she reached the bottom of the stairs. "You look more like your mother every day, child." His ice-blue eyes grew warm, and a smile softened his austere features.

The full-length mirror across the hallway attested to the truth of his statement. She could see herself in comparison to the long-dead Mellisande. Her wide golden eyes and the dark fire of her hair were certainly inherited from her mother, but the straight nose and the determined line of her jaw were her father's features, cut in a delicate feminine version.

"I guess I don't want to know what that gown cost me, but whatever, it's worth it," he said as he looked at the bronze satin and yards of cream-colored lace. "Lemuel's eyes will pop out of their sockets," he added with a chuckle.

"The dress was extravagant," she replied, not wanting yet another lecture about accepting Mathis's proposal. Just the prospect of spending the night with him was dreary enough. How

193

she longed to dance with Jess instead of Lemuel Mathis. If only there were a way . . .

Her reverie was interrupted by the sound of horses' hooves on the dry, dusty ground out front. The first guests had arrived. From a distance she recognized Cridellia Evers's high-pitched giggle and old Cy's low answering chuckle.

Dellia came fluttering in, preening in a periwinkle-blue satin gown that made her pale complexion and mousy brown hair seem even more faded than normal. Her eyes flashed over Lissa with dismay, but she quickly smiled as her hostess approached.

"My, what an unusual color, Lissa. Whoever thought of wearing a brown ball gown," she cooed.

"Wal, it shore looks good ta me," Cy answered. "Both yew gals is pretty as a pair of puppies settin' in a new red wagon."

"Thank you, Cy," Lissa replied, noting the way Dellia was squinting out the open front door at the road. Always a bit nearsighted, she refused to wear glasses. Lissa knew Dellia was dying to see if Yancy Brewster was among the riders converging on the J Bar big house.

After all the social amenities had been dispensed with, Lissa whispered in Dellia's ear, "Yancy should be here." The arrogant ramrod had been invited, although Lissa certainly did not look forward to seeing him after the debacle at the horse race. "I'm surprised he didn't ride over with you and your father."

Dellia feigned indifference. "Oh, I suppose he'll be along. He and Pa have been on the outs since that silly ole bet Yancy lost to that nasty gunman of yours." Her eyes narrowed. "Do you still fancy him?"

Lissa laughed. "Who? Yancy or Jesse Robbins?"

The brunette stiffened angrily. "I've half a mind to tell your pa about the way you've been swishin' around a dirty Indian."

Lissa shrugged. "Germaine already has. He thinks the idea is ridiculous. He almost fired her for bringing it up." Her pulse was pounding as she turned away to greet more arriving guests. "If you'll excuse me, Dellia?"

Lemuel strode over to her and took her hand, standing far too close to her, as was his habit. His broad chest and thick, compactly built body seemed to fill the crowded entry hall. She could smell the expensive cologne he always wore and fought the urge to sneeze as he raised her hand and kissed it with a flourish.

"You're looking ravishing tonight, Lissa. That unusual color is striking on you, although I would have favored something a bit more conventional, say blue."

She withdrew her hand. "I'm an unconventional woman, Lemuel—or hasn't Papa mentioned that fact?"

He smiled indulgently. "Merely the fire of youthful high spirits, my dear. You need a more mature hand to guide you."

Yancy Brewster, Moss Symington, and several small ranchers chose that time to arrive. She turned her most blinding St. Louis belle smile on them and was quickly surrounded with admirers. Even Yancy seemed to have forgotten the incident between her and Jess at the stable. As he charmed her with compliments, she could feel Dellia's piercing glare from across the room. Before he could ask her for the first dance of the evening, Mathis was at her side, taking her arm possessively.

"Your father asked that you see when the buffet will be ready," he said smoothly, gliding her away from Brewster. As they crossed the rapidly crowding hall, he murmured low, "I don't understand why those barbarians are allowed to mix with polite society."

"Moss has ramroded J Bar for twenty years. Foremen are always invited," she said, then could not resist adding, "Yancy Brewster runs a few head of his own. One of these days he'll be a substantial rancher himself. That's how lots of the richest men in Wyoming started out—as barbarians."

"Some of them just married a rich rancher's daughter. Surely you aren't considering the ruffian, Lissa?"

She gave him an innocent look. "Why, he has paid me court, but then so have most of the single men in the area. If you'll excuse me, Lemuel, I must check with Germaine."

"The first dance, Lissa," he reminded her.

She nodded and vanished down the hall toward the kitchen, passing two serving girls with laden trays. What a dreadful evening it would be. Usually such an affair would have delighted her and she would have danced all night. But that was before Jesse Robbins had held her in his arms. Now the prospect of dancing and making small talk with a bevy of admirers filled her with distaste.

When she pushed open the kitchen door, Germaine was surreptitiously emptying the contents of a cordial glass in a swift, fortifying gulp.

"More medicine for your nerves?" she asked sweetly.

Madame Channault turned quickly, her posture defensive as she set the glass down behind her and advanced on Lissa like a war chief about to count coup. "What are you doing out here—spying on me?"

"Papa wanted to know if the food will be ready to serve shortly."

"Certainement," she replied in stiff affront. "The men are bringing in the roast pig right now."

"Good." Lissa spun around and left the kitchen, thinking how loudly the drunken old sot would snore tonight.

Lemuel was waiting for her when strains of the first dance wafted out on the warm evening air. All the doors and windows had been opened, and the sounds of fiddles and guitars carried down the hill to the bunkhouse. As she whirled around the room in Mathis's stiff embrace, her thoughts were of Jess.

Lots of the hands walked up to the edge of the gardens surrounding the big house to glimpse the grandeur within and listen to the music. Jess sat on his bunk while Tate and Vinegar played a desultory game of five-card draw. He tried to write a letter to his brother, but gave it up after a few sentences when he found himself describing Lissa to Jonah. With a muttered oath he wadded up the paper and threw it into the corner.

"Either of you have any whiskey?" he asked. Tate shoved the remnants of a bottle across the rickety plank table. Jess eyed the scant inch remaining inside and said, "I had in mind enough for at least half a swallow."

Vinegar, who had just been called, triumphantly displayed a pair of fours. Tate poured the last drop from the bottle and downed it as he laid out a pair of eights.

"I think this means I win," he said innocently.

"Damnation, beatin' yew's like tryin' ta scratch my ear with my elbow." The old cook threw down his cards and cussed a blue streak, then turned to Jess. "I got me a full bottle over in my kitchen. Helps my rheumatism, ya know. Think I'm feelin' an ache comin' on just 'bout now." He scooted back the rickety stool on which he had been sitting and stood up, affixing Shannon's guileless black face with his one good eye. "Keep them cards warm. I'll be right back."

As they walked across to the cook shack, Jess looked up at the bright lights shining down from the big house on the hill. The mellow cadence of a waltz drifted on the warm summer breeze.

Vinegar opened the door, then paused and studied Jess intently. "I like yew, Robbins, but I been on J Bar sincst thet leetle gal was birthed. She always wuz a handful, 'n I reckon I kin see how yew might take her fancy, but it ain't no good."

Jess sighed. "You think I don't know that? That I haven't told her that?"

Vinegar spat a lob of tobacco, which landed with a loud ping. Chuckling, he wiped his matted gray beard with the back of his hand and replied, "Miz Lissa ain't a female ta take no fer an answer." He sobered as he fished out a bottle of tangle-leg from a shelf by the door. Pulling the cork, he took a generous pull, then handed it to Jess. "She's young 'n full of fool female notions she got back East. Don't hurt her, Robbins. Hell, don't hurt yer-self neither," he added with a kindly sigh.

Jess took a long swallow from the whiskey bottle. It was cheap and strong and it burned going down, spreading fiery fingers deep into his gut. "Thanks," he said, handing the bottle back to the old man.

Vinegar took another drink, then handed the bottle back to Jess with a crooked grin that revealed an uneven row of brown teeth punctuated by half-a-dozen gaping spaces. "Keep it. I gotta stay sober. I'm fixin' ta win a week's pay from thet black son of a bitch. Way yer hurtin', yew kin use it more 'n me. Jist don't tell no one I gave whiskey ta an' Injun."

Jess saluted Vinegar's retreating back as the banty-legged little man hobbled to the bunkhouse. He strolled along the corral fence, then headed toward Jethro Bullis's blacksmith shop. A solitary place to get drunk held great appeal at the moment.

"If I had any brains, I'd ride into Cheyenne and screw Cammie until we both collapsed," he muttered beneath his breath, then took another swallow of the tangle-leg. It was beginning to taste better. He found a quiet spot against the rough plank wall of the shop and sat down, unable to keep his eyes from traveling up the hill, following the sounds of music and laughter.

She was surrounded by suitors, probably dancing with Lemuel Mathis. The idea of Mathis's big square hands touching her made his gut tighten. He took another drink and closed his eyes, willing the images of Lissa's fiery beauty to go away.

Yancy Brewster watched Lissa Jacobson with narrowed eyes as she stood serenely laughing and chatting with a gaggle of suitors. He sauntered through the crowd just as the musicians were preparing to resume playing. Mathis, the pompous old fool, was deep in conversation with several other members of the Association. He reached for Lissa's elbow with a proprietary gesture and made a courtly bow.

"You always give me the first waltz, Miss Lissa. I hope tonight's no exception." Without giving her an opportunity to refuse, he swept her into the dance just as the music started.

"This isn't a waltz, and I've never favored you with the first of anything," she said tartly.

"I lied," he answered glibly, the smile on his face predatory and mean. "As to being the first to receive your favors, well . . . I reckon we both know you favor dark meat, don't we?"

She tried to pull her hand free, intent on slapping the nasty sneer off his face, but he held it tight. "Let me go," she ground out, stopping at the edge of the dance floor.

"Now, Miss Lissa," he said with exaggerated oily charm. "Don't go getting mad. After all, you wouldn't want to ruin your pa's fancy shindig."

"Cy Evers will ruin your *life* if you don't release me this instant," she hissed, stomping on his foot with all her strength and grinding the pointed heel of her slipper into the toe of his dress boot. He released her. Lissa turned and walked from the floor, knowing several of the younger women had watched the altercation with avid curiosity, among them Cridellia Evers, whose narrowed eyes glittered with venom.

Lissa paused by Dellia long enough to whisper, "If you have half the sense of a sun-baked brick, you'll keep clear of that snake."

Dellia's pale lashes blinked rapidly and her pop eyes flew to Yancy's tall figure, glaring after Lissa. "I'll do as I please—just the same as you, Melissa Jacobson," she replied.

When Brewster stalked over to Dellia and asked her to dance, she blushed and bobbed her head. As she whirled by in his arms a few moments later, she gave Lissa a preening smirk.

The evening, off to such an inauspicious beginning, dragged on interminably. Lissa danced with old ranchers and young suitors, until she felt her tight smile was frozen onto her face. Her toes smarted from being stepped on by clumsy boots, and her head throbbed from a bit too much of the champagne Marcus had ordered specially from the Cheyenne Club's private stock for this gala. After the altercation with Yancy Brewster, she had felt in need of its restorative powers. Now she regretted it.

What exactly did Brewster know about her relationship with Jess? He had seen her coming from the back door of the stable before the horse race. But as far as she could tell, that was all he had seen. He had no proof of what she had done with the gunman. But he was mean and did not like to lose. He could cause trouble.

"I feel the most terrible headache, Lemuel," Lissa said, rubbing her temples as they walked from the dance floor.

"Perhaps a bit of fresh air?" Mathis said solicitously.

The very last thing Lissa wanted was to be alone outside with Lemuel.

"I think the roast pork didn't agree with me. Better if I put some cool compresses on my head

201

and lie down for a bit." She smiled weakly as she slipped her hands from his.

A worried frown creased his face. "I'll call your father."

"Nonsense. He'd only worry for nothing. Germaine has retired upstairs for the evening. She can help me. I'll return in a half hour or so. Please don't say anything to Papa."

Lissa could feel his hard hazel eyes on her as she made her escape from the press. Her story was only half a lie. She did feel dreadful, but the encounter with Yancy and Lemuel's oppressive protectiveness were the reasons, not what she had eaten for supper.

Lissa climbed the stairs and walked down the hall, pausing at Germaine's door long enough to hear the drunken snoring issuing from within. As soon as the buffet had been served, the housekeeper instructed the maids about cleaning up, then retired to her room, where she had secreted a bottle of Marcus's excellent brandy. Lissa continued on to her own room at the far end of the hall and entered.

Pouring some tepid water into the basin, she soaked a kerchief in it, wrung it out and dabbed at her forehead, then walked over to her window to stare out toward the bunkhouse and other outbuildings. Her room was stifling. She threw up her window sash and felt a faint breeze brush by. Out in the distance, the faint glow of a cigarette bobbed in the shadows beside the smithy's shed. Most of the hands were up by the orchard across from the big house watching the party. No one else stirred around the work area, but for that solitary smoker.

Lissa suddenly felt an acute need for more fresh air. She slipped from her room and opened the door to the back stairs. In moments she was clear of the house, halfway to the work sheds. No one would question her absence for another half hour. The music floated lazily on the soft breeze, and a coyote howled far in the distance beneath the big yellow moon. This was madness. Yet she felt her footsteps speeding up to match the racing of her pulse.

Jess sat with his back against the wall and one long leg sprawled out in front of him. The other was bent at the knee with his arm resting on it, a half-empty whiskey bottle dangling from one hand. He held a cigarette to his lips with the other.

She stood rooted to the ground, watching him sitting there in the moonlight, indolently blowing smoke that the breeze carried to her, spicy, masculine, alluring. Then he sensed her presence and cocked his head at her. He did not get up.

"You're drunk," she accused.

"You're right," he countered. "But you're crazy. What the hell are you doing here dressed like that? One of those men slavering after you will follow you—and I'll have to shoot him."

Her lips curved into a wistful smile. "Before you do, would you dance with me?"

The music seemed to reiterate her invitation, swelling in a sweet, old-fashioned ballad from the war.

He took another pull from the bottle, then threw it into the weeds and uncurled himself from the ground with surprising grace. "I'm crazy, too, but I'm really not drunk. Not that I haven't tried my damnedest." He flipped his cigarette after the bottle, then stood facing her, motionless.

"Well?" she coaxed, waiting.

"What if I don't know how to dance?"

"I'll risk my feet." She held up her satin skirt, revealing her matching bronze leather slippers and a bit of delicate ankle in the bargain. He smelled of whiskey and tobacco as he took her in his arms and began to move to the cadence of the music. He danced with the consummate grace of a stalking mountain lion.

They glided across the small clearing, whirling in lazy circles. Her hair, piled high in an elaborate coiffure entwined with rosebuds, gave off a delicate fragrance. His fingers gently slipped into the silky curls, cradling her head against his chest. She snuggled her face against the soft abrasion of crisp black hair, remembering the enticing male smell from that first day when they had ridden through a rainstorm bundled together.

"You never did tell me what a Tuareg is."

He threw back his head and chuckled. "Persistent little heifer, aren't you?"

"It has something to do with your being in the French Legion, doesn't it?"

"They're North African desert tribesmen. Murderously fierce fighters."

"Were they anything like your mother's people?" She could feel him stiffen, although he did not miss a beat in the dance.

"I don't know," he said flatly. "My grandmother was raped by some marauding tribe in Mexico. She bore my mother as a result. It's ironic. All my life I've been called a breed. I don't even know what tribe of Indians my blood comes from."

She reached up with one hand and stroked his cheek. "It must've been awful for your mother, too."

He shrugged. "Her family were *Kineños*. The Mexicans Richard King brought to Texas to work his Running W Ranch. He hired on the whole village. Gave them a new life. In return they became fanatically loyal to him. When she was just sixteen, my mother married my father."

"Robbins is an American name."

"John Jeremiah Robbins was a Boston Yankee who went west to make his fortune."

"And your mother's Indian blood didn't bother him at all, did it?"

Jess smiled grimly. "He was the only one in Texas it didn't bother."

He had never talked this much about his mysterious past. The liquor had not affected his reflexes, but it did seem to ease his closemouthed restraint. "Tell me about your father."

Just then the music ended. Jess stopped moving, but did not release her. She burrowed more tightly against his body, knowing he would tell her to go.

"You're going to smell of whiskey and cigarettes."

"I don't care."

"Your pa and Lemuel Mathis will care." He took her by her shoulders and held her at arm's length, letting his eyes rake up and down her body. "That is some creation," he said in a low, hoarse voice. One hand slipped down to touch the heavy lace dripping from the low-cut neckline. He ached to pull it off, baring her luscious breasts. His fin-

205

gers lightly traced the swell of bare silvery flesh above the bodice, then withdrew as if he had been burned. "Go back where you belong, Lissa."

She framed his face with her hands. "I belong with you, Jess."

"More fairy tales, Lissa?"

She choked back a sob of frustration and seized his hand, replacing it on her breast. "Feel me, Jess, feel my heart beat. It beats for you. Oh, please, please." She melted against him, raising her lips for his kiss.

He tried to put her aside again, but she would have none of it and held his hand until he found himself cupping her breast, reaching inside the frothy lace to tease her nipple into pebbly hardness. "Which of us is the craziest," he murmured as his lips savaged hers in a fierce, possessive kiss.

She returned it, letting her tongue duel with his, tasting the tang of liquor and the pungency of his cigarettes. Their lips brushed, pressed, reformed over each other with growing ardor. Then the sudden crunch of boots moving through the dry grass penetrated Jess's fevered brain. He broke away and pulled her behind him in one fluid motion, while pulling his gun from its holster.

They stood in silence, each fighting to still their ragged breathing. The music had stopped inside the big house, and the hum of voices was low. The intruder's cough came from somewhere across the other side of the corral, followed by the trickle of liquid hitting the earth as he urinated. Finally he retraced his steps toward the bunkhouse.

As soon as they were alone again, Jess whispered, "Go now before someone else comes along."

She could sense the determination in his voice and knew it was madness to remain out here in the open. She took a deep breath and swallowed. "I can only bear to let Lemuel and those other men touch me, to smile and dance and pretend I'm enjoying the party, if you'll be there when it's over."

Her big golden eyes glowed at him in the moonlight. "You can't come back here—"

"You can come to me. My room is at the far west end of the house. See the light?" She pointed to her window, overlooking the blacksmith shop where they stood. "Watch for the guests to leave. It should only be another hour or two. As soon as the house is asleep, come up the outside stairs. I'll be waiting by the door to let you inside."

He shook his head. "Will you understand? We can't be caught together! I might even have to shoot your pa—or let him kill me."

"Papa and Cy Evers have been drinking. He'll sleep long past sunup. Germaine is the one who spies on me, and she's already passed out. No one will see us."

"No, Lissa."

"If you don't come to me, I *will* come to the bunkhouse," she said desperately. "I know your bed is right by the door at the north end—"

"Jesus! You'd do it, wouldn't you?" he said raggedly.

"I'll do whatever I have to, Jess."

He swore beneath his breath, then whispered, "Go back and stay there."

"Only if you promise to come to me," she replied stubbornly.

"Wait. I'll come." He kissed her again, hard and fast, then shooed her roughly away from him, toward the glittering lights and raucous laughter at the big, elegant house on the hill.

Chapter Thirteen

All the guests departed with hearty farewells. The creaking of buggy springs and soft plodding of horses' hooves finally faded away. Down at the bunkhouse, the main topic of conversation among the cowboys was the fancy shindig.

"You see Yancy sparkin' that homely little filly of Cy Evers?" one hand asked.

"Yep. Always figgered he'd set his sights on Miz Lissa," another chimed in. "Cridellia Evers got a face built fer a hackamore. Wonder whut changed his mind?"

"Reckon he finally realized Miz Lissa's bound to marry ole Lemuel Mathis," Rob Ostler said.

"Funny, though. Brewster useta be sweet as honey on a hive fer Miz Lissa, but tonight them two got on like a pair o' bobcats in a gunnysack," Luke Deevers said speculatively.

"Best yew let off a jawin' bout the boss's daughter and let me git some shuteye," Vinegar said balefully, "'er I'll roust yew outta yer blankets at three-thirty when I gotta start fixin' breakfast."

Jess lay on his bunk, waiting for the last desultory conversations between the hands to die down. The bunkhouse finally grew quiet, and the varied cadences of loud and soft snores filled the still night air. Jess reclined motionlessly, yet the tension in his body belied all the whiskey he had drunk earlier. Yancy was already suspicious about Lissa's relationship with him. It was madness to risk sneaking into the big house. Yet the sweet allure of her perfume still haunted him, and the feel of her as she danced with him under the stars would not leave his mind.

She had been the stuff of dreams, with her hair piled high on her head, gleaming like dark fire in the moonlight, which made her skin appear even more milky. Hell, her dress doubtlessly cost more than he made in a month. What was he doing with a rich, spoiled white girl? If she had been older, married, more worldly, he would not have had any qualms, but Lissa was none of those. He could still feel the instant of raw male triumph when he had sundered her maidenhead. She belonged to him in a way no other man could ever claim.

Yet he knew that one day another man would claim her—a rich white man who would put his hands on her silken flesh. The thought of it made his gut clench with jealous fury. All of his life he had been an outsider, understanding his place even if he did not accept it meekly. He had drawn a shell of indifference around himself, scorning white society, white rules, white women. His life had been satisfactory until now. He lived by his own code and bowed to no man. Now he was willing to sneak around in the dark for a few stolen hours of pleasure with Lissa.

Lissa. Would she keep to her threat and seek him out here? He smiled grimly. She was just spoiled and reckless enough to do it. If he was caught in this tortuous coil, he was not alone. She seemed as powerless to break free as he.

With a silent oath, he swung his legs over the side of his bunk and started to rise. Sounds of snoring were all that broke the late-night stillness. He began to pull on his boots when Tate Shannon's low voice cut through the hum of the bunkhouse nocturne.

"Don't do it, Jess."

"Don't do what? Take a leak?"

"Cut the crap, Jess. You'll get caught sooner or later. Then there'll be hell to pay."

"Shit, Tate, there already is hell to pay," Jess whispered as he finished pulling on his boots and silently slipped from the bunkhouse.

The moon had set and the warm night air blew softly, sending the tall stands of sycamores and oak around the house to soughing. In the distance a coyote wailed—for its mate? He walked slowly, careful to stay in the shadows as he approached the narrow wooden stairs at the back of the mansion. When he looked up the steep steps, he could see the door was opened just a bit. He climbed them as if they were a gallows, his hand never moving from the butt of his revolver.

As soon as he reached the top step, Lissa swung the door wide and flung herself into his arms. He held her tightly, kissing her with fierce possessiveness, as if to erase the touch of all those men who had danced with her earlier in the night.

She pulled him into the dark, silent hallway as she returned his kiss with ardor.

Lissa was barefoot, clad only in the sheerest white batiste nightgown. She looked ethereal, shimmering in the darkness like some fairy vision bent on working mischief on a mere mortal such as he. Thick, soft carpet absorbed the sound of his boots while she pulled him the scant six feet to her room.

He could see little of the furnishings, for the light from the window was filtered out by a set of frilly curtains. A narrow bed with a canopy sat against the inside wall. As she pulled him toward it, he whispered hoarsely, "Someone will hear us, Lissa."

She shook her head as she unbuttoned his shirt. "The next room is a storage closet, and Papa is near the end of the hall. Germaine sleeps across from him, but she's dead drunk tonight."

By this time she was pulling his shirttail from his denims. He unbuckled his holster and let it slip onto the braided rug beside the bed. Lissa ran her hands hungrily over his shoulders and down the hard muscles of his chest, letting her fingers play in the dark patterns of hair that narrowed into a vee at the waistband of his pants. When her busy fingers began to unbutton the fly, he picked her up and laid her on the bed, whispering, "Boots first."

Sitting on the edge of her small bed, he quickly pulled the boots off, then turned to where she sat crouched on the mattress with her glorious hair tumbled about her shoulders, the soft folds of the gown rucked up about her hips. He reached out and tugged at the drawstring on the prim neckline. It gave way, baring the hollows of her collarbone and swell of her breasts. He reached out to touch the pale skin, his hand looking black as sin against her pristine flesh. His fingertips traced the rise of her breast. Then he took both hands and cupped the small, perfect spheres, gently massaging them until her breathing grew even more ragged.

His mouth descended on one hard, pebbly nipple, wetting the sheer cloth as he teased it with his tongue, then bit and suckled on it, leaving the fabric translucent so he could see the perfection of the pink rosette. He repeated the process with her other breast. Her fingers threaded through his long straight hair, tugging him closer, thrusting her aching breasts against his hot, questing mouth.

"Jess, Jess, oh, yes, yes." Her hands moved down his neck, over the bunched muscles in his back, then around his waist, sliding inside his denims. He knelt on the bed and ran his hands over the curve of her hips, bunching up the gauzy nightgown in his fists, shoving it out of the way.

His palms splayed across her lower back and he cupped her buttocks, pulling her against the growing shaft still imprisoned by his tight denims. She held tightly to him, kneeling in the center of her bed—the lovely virginal bed where she had fantasized about her swarthy lover for so many weeks. The fierceness of his desire burned her like a licking, consuming flame. She moaned low in her throat and unbuttoned his pants until they slid lower, freeing his sex.

"Touch me, Lissa," he whispered, willing her to obey his bold command. When her soft little hands slid between their bodies and took hold of him, he almost cried aloud in exultation, knowing that he must bury himself deeply within her now or he would spill his seed at once, so desperate was his need.

"Open for me." He spread her knees and felt between her legs for the pearly wetness that told him she was ready to receive him. His mouth absorbed her small, animal-like cries as he impaled himself inside the slick, tight walls of her sheath.

Bracing himself, he thrust deeper within her, then held her very still until he could regain control of his body. She wrapped her arms tightly around his neck, letting him support their weight as they knelt together on the bed. He held her quietly as she accommodated the length and fullness of his flesh within her, then lifted her legs and wrapped them around his hips.

Lissa could feel him slide deeper inside her as she clung to him, squeezing her thighs tightly around his waist and moving restlessly against the hardness of his body. She was desperate for him to quench the ache rippling deep in her belly. When his hips began to thrust slowly, he guided her movements in perfect counterpart to his own. Quickly she caught the rhythm, matching his building frenzy, until she rocked against him with such force that she felt herself falling backward onto the bed, pulling him down on top of her.

Without breaking their joining, Jess continued the fierce, frantic mating. The tip of his tongue tasted the curve inside her small ear, then his teeth sank softly into the lobe and his lips moved lower, brushing the racing pulse in her throat. Her nails scored his back as she urged him on, writhing like a demented thing beneath him until he could feel the delicate silky flesh that sheathed him begin to convulse in sweet release.

Lissa wanted it to go on forever, this hot wild ecstasy, but she ached for that perfect peace, that shattering fulfillment that she had experienced only once before, the first time Jesse Robbins had loved her. Yet when the first tiny waves began to build, she cried out in regret for how quickly the beauty of their joining would be over.

His mouth drank up her cries, as his body felt the delicious tremors rack her from head to toe. She was the most passionate, responsive woman he had ever taken—and the least experienced. The satiny squeezing of her hot flesh against his robbed him of breath. All too quickly he lost control and felt himself swelling and throbbing, releasing his seed in a white-hot wave of pleasure that left him so utterly spent that he could do nothing but lie atop her, holding her, with his face buried in her tangled, fiery hair.

Lissa felt his body stiffen and shudder as he pulsed his life force into her, melding it with her own, increasing and prolonging her ride into the realm of pleasure so intense that it was truly madness. And she knew she would do anything to hold this man. Anything at all.

Finally, when he could breathe freely, Jess pulled away from her, careful not to tumble off the small bed. He straddled her hips with his pants halfway down his thighs, while she lay beneath him, her filmy, virginal nightgown tangled about her waist and slipped off one shoulder. She looked as wanton and satiated as the most expensive harlots he had ever known, and he knew he would never again desire a woman as he did this one.

Lissa felt bereft by the loss of his body heat when he withdrew from her. She could feel his eyes, glittering in the dim predawn light as he stared down at her, his expression unreadable. She lay dazed and disoriented while he swung his legs over the side of the bed and stood, pulling his pants up and shrugging into his shirt.

I look like a whore, she thought miserably, pulling her bunched-up gown down to cover her legs. They had torn at each other and coupled with their clothes still on! Shame flooded her as she watched him methodically pull on his boots and turn to face her.

She looked so forlorn and small huddled on the rumpled sheets. No longer the wanton, now she appeared a woeful child who had been caught in some terrible transgression. His heart gave an unfamiliar lurch, and a wave of tenderness washed over him. Then he saw the thin, silvery trails of tears that trickled from the sides of her eyes, gliding silently over her cheekbones. "Lissa, Lissa," he whispered raggedly and drew her into his arms.

She came up off the bed with a strangled sob. "Don't hate me, Jess. Please, don't hate me." She buried her face against his chest and held on to him with trembling hands.

He tipped her chin up and touched her tear-thick lashes, drying the droplets with the pads of his thumbs. "Don't, Liss, don't cry. I don't hate you."

But you don't love me either.

He held her until her sobs quieted and her arms dropped away, falling lifelessly to her sides when he stepped back, releasing her. "I have to go, Lissa. Vinegar's probably already in his mess kitchen."

"Will you come back?" she whispered, amazed at the question that seemed to ask itself. *Have I no mind, no pride, no self-control left?*

He hesitated. "I shouldn't. We both know that." His voice turned bitter then. "All right, Lissa. I can't help myself, but not here. Your watchdogs won't be drunk every night. I'll ride to the pool by the escarpment any afternoon when I get the chance. Take Cormac with you when you slip off."

"I'll be careful, Jess."

He closed the door silently and disappeared into the predawn stillness while she stood hugging herself, alone in her room.

Yancy Brewster watched Cridellia Evers pick her way through high grass thick with dust that she was assiduously trying to avoid. It coated her pale yellow dress anyway. Strange, on Lissa Jacobson the color was vibrant, making her hair glow like live coals and her skin appear touched by sungold. On the plain little wren prissily mincing to the corral, the color had just the opposite effect. When she waved to him, her pop eyes strained as if trying to jump from their sockets. Old Luke Deevers's words flashed through his mind. "She ain't nothin' fer a drinkin' man ta look at."

Tipping his hat gallantly, he returned her smile. She was stick-thin and as homely as a Mexican sheep, but she possessed the qualities he prized above all others in a female—she was heiress to a big ranch and she had never cast a lustful eye on a dirty, gut-eating greaser.

His smile deepened, carving harsh grooves in his handsome face as he thought of the seeds of gossip he had gleaned the other night at Jacobson's fancy dance. Lissa's "dear friend" Dellia had been eager to divulge every juicy detail about Lissa's reaction to Jesse Robbins at the rodeo. His instincts had been right when he had caught her fleeing from the Diamond E stable before the horse race. Her lips had been swollen from that filthy breed's kisses and her expression breathless with desire. She was a beautiful slut, but he would never take the leavings of an Indian. Lissa Jacobson had rejected him, and for that she would pay.

He could never face old man Jacobson with the truth about his precious daughter. Marcus would have him whipped and gutshot if he even hinted at it. But if dear little Cridellia happened onto the two of them, well, the stubborn old coot would have to believe her.

But first he had to find out where they sneaked off to for their dirty rutting and then let the ice-blooded little Evers twit get an eyeful.

"Mornin', Miss Dellia. You sure look pretty as a buttercup in yellow," he said as she blushed and batted her pale lashes.

"Why, thank you, Yancy. I . . . I came down to the stable to see your new horse. Pa says it's even faster than Thunderbolt was." In fact, she was not in the least interested in horses, but any excuse to meet Yancy Brewster suited her purposes. Since he had paid her such court at the Jacobsons' dance, she had decided to act boldly.

"He really is a beauty. I haven't named him yet. Maybe you could help me with that?" He extended his arm with a gallant flourish, and she blushed beet-red and seized it like a hungry child would a shiny peppermint stick.

"It was too bad about Thunderbolt," she said as they entered the stable. The magnificent white had come up lame after the race against Robbins and had to be destroyed when a fracture had been discovered in his right foreleg.

"Yeah, well, that damn—pardon me for swearing in front of a lady—that breed ran into me apurpose. Good as put the bullet in Thunderbolt's brain."

Dellia shuddered. "I can't see how Lissa can be so . . ." she groped delicately for the words, then said, "so infatuated with that savage. Her poor pa would be beside himself if he ever knew."

"Mebbe he ought to be told—to save him from more disgrace, you know." He let her digest the idea.

"But we couldn't just repeat speculation. Even if she confessed a certain carnal fascination for him—well, Mr. Jacobson would refuse to believe it was anything more. He's always spoiled her," she added spitefully.

"I know, but I think she's meeting the breed somewhere."

"For illicit—" She stopped with a gasp of mortification.

"Biggest favor we could do for her and her pa is to put a stop to it. Have him kill the Injun and send her back East. You're her friend, Miss Dellia. You might be able to learn something when you visit the J Bar. Sort of keep your eyes open."

"Yes, then we might have evidence enough to open Mr. Jacobson's eyes."

She jumped at the idea of removing her beautiful rival, just as he'd thought she would. He showed her his new chestnut, and they discussed various schemes for spying on Lissa and Jesse Robbins. By the time he walked her back to the ranch house, his plan was in place.

*   *   *

Jess and Tate had taken turns watching Sligo to see when he would again leave a message in the line shack. This morning, he finally headed to it with Jess following carefully behind. Sligo was unwittingly baiting the trap that would lead to a final showdown. Jess watched him dismount and enter the line shack. Paydirt.

Jess was on edge as always just before a case broke, but this time he knew the impending violence had little to do with his agitation. Soon the reason for his being in Wyoming would be gone. And so would he. "I should feel relieved," he muttered to Blaze, but instead he felt a peculiar anguish that he had never before experienced. Somehow he knew it would follow him all the way back to Texas and never leave him.

For the past weeks they had been lovers, meeting at the pool where they had first been tempted to madness. As he waited for Sligo to emerge from the line shack after leaving his message, Jess ruminated over the disturbing conversation they had had after a passionate interlude in the water yesterday.

Lissa had lain on the blanket with the sun dappling her skin gold through the rustling leaves, watching him dress.

"That gunman is here from Texas, isn't he?" she asked. "Pardee."

He had paused, his shirt pulled over one shoulder. "Yeah, Pardee's here. His men are slipping into town a few at a time. I don't want them to raise any notice from the Association."

She cocked her head, puzzled. "You suspect

someone in the Association is involved with rustlers?"

He finished buttoning his shirt. "Could be. Or, more likely, someone working for an Association member who eavesdrops on his boss's conversations."

She had reached for her clothes and pulled on her sheer cotton underdrawers. "As soon as you have all those men ready, Papa says you'll attack the rustlers." He looked at her sharply. She smiled wistfully. "Your rustlers aren't the only ones who have ways of learning what my father's doing. All I have to do is ask."

"He wasn't supposed to talk to anyone about Pardee."

She stood up and walked over to him. "Someone has to tell me what's going on. It won't be long, will it, Jess?"

He knew she meant far more than the showdown with the rustlers. "No, Lissa, it won't be long. We shouldn't meet here again."

"What am I supposed to do? Spend the rest of my life crocheting and gossiping with Dellia Evers? Jess, you could be shot!" She had tears in her voice as she buried her face against his chest.

He stroked her fiery hair. "That's what I've been trying to tell you, Lissa."

"You could quit. Take me with you back to Texas—or anywhere. Anywhere at all, Jess."

He shook his head and put her gently aside. "We've said it all before, Lissa. I am who I am— a breed, a gunman. Maybe because of my blood, I like the way I earn my living. Hell, I don't know. But I can't change things for you, for anyone."

She watched him as he strapped on his gun. He

could see the anger building in her—and something else. Frustration? Despair? Fear? The sooner this job ended, the better it would be for both of them. Yet he knew that as long as he was here, he could not keep his hands off her.

Just then Jess's ruminations were interrupted. Sligo strode from the line shack, mounted, and rode back toward J Bar. Jess watched until the hoofbeats died away, then rode Blaze quickly down to the cabin to check the note.

A grim smile slashed his face. At last something was going right. Sligo's message was perfect. The rustlers were to hit the herd held in the north basin tomorrow night. That should give him enough time to get Pardee's men in place for a nice little surprise party.

Early the following morning, Lissa had an unexpected visitor. "I do declare, Lissa, you look positively peaked. Here, have one of these cream puffs. They're sinfully delicious. I swear, I'd steal that Germaine away from you if Papa weren't so attached to old Hattie Greeves. She isn't half the cook Germaine is."

She shoved the platter heaped with breakfast pastries at Lissa, who turned her head abruptly. "Lissa, are you ill?"

Lissa had turned even paler, and a fine sweat beaded her forehead, even though the morning air was cool and pleasant, with a soft breeze wafting in the parlor window. "Just a bit of indigestion from last night's rich dinner. Don't be too certain about how wonderful Germaine's cooking would be—everything she fixes is soaked in rich French sauces."

Dellia eyed Lissa's waist, her pop eyes avidly searching for the smallest increment. "Hmm, you do seem to have put on a bit of weight." In fact the weight gain was more in her breasts than her waist, but Dellia, who was matchstick-thin all over, refrained from mentioning that nicety.

"If you'll excuse me, Dellia, I feel a sudden headache coming on." Lissa rose and fled from the sickening aromas of strong coffee and fresh pastry creams, her face taking on a paler hue accented by her mint-green cotton frock.

"Would you be recovered to ride out to Mac-Ferson's tomorrow afternoon?" Dellia called after Lissa. She could barely hear the choked "no" as her companion raced upstairs with unladylike haste.

"Well, whatever's gotten into her?" Dellia huffed, helping herself to another pastry. Then as she chewed, a slow smile spread across her face. The very idea was shocking beyond belief, of course, especially considering who Jesse Robbins was. But having been raised on a ranch, Cridellia Evers knew barnyard facts of life. Lissa must be in a family way!

And if she was declining Laurie MacFerson's invitation to tea, perhaps she had another assignation— such as telling the father-to-be the news? Rising from the sofa, Dellia rang for Germaine to convey her good-byes to the indisposed Lissa, who would not be the only one to miss the MacFerson's tea.

Lissa heard Dellia's carriage wheels grind down the dusty gravel road as she leaned over a basin, waiting for the surges of nausea to abate. It always did after a brutal ten or fifteen minutes, during which she lost all the food she had been foolish enough to consume since arising.

For the past week, she had learned to avoid any breakfast of substance until this accursed meal with Dellia.

"She eats and I throw up. There's justice," she muttered to herself.

But it was justice, inevitable and irrevocable. This past week she had missed her courses for the second time and knew what it meant. She was carrying Jesse Robbins's baby. Her hand slid over her still-flat abdomen protectively. So far Jess had not noticed the slight changes in her body, but it would not be long before her condition became evident.

It won't be long. His words echoed in her mind. He planned to ride as soon as this job was finished, to leave her. Would he still do so, knowing about his child? Lissa was not certain. *How can I tell him?*

She had been the pursuer, the one who teased and tempted until he took what she had offered to no other man. Jess had resented his surrender to their passion; he resented her, the curious white virgin who lusted after an exotic, forbidden man.

Yet she had been as powerless to resist the attraction as he had, and she was going to be the one to pay the ultimate price if he left her. Fear of seeing scathing contempt and condemnation in his silver eyes had kept her silent for the past week.

"I love you, Jess. You must love me." Even as she whispered the words, the sour metallic taste in her mouth told her how bitter and futile it was. He had never said the words. He never would.

Trembling, she splashed her face with cold water and rinsed her mouth, then lay across her bed,

GET YOUR 4 FREE* BOOKS NOW— A $21.96 VALUE!

Mail the Free* Book Certificate Today!

(Tear Here and Mail Your FREE* Book Card Today!)

Get Four Books Totally
F R E E* —
A $21.96 Value!

(Tear Here and Mail Your FREE* Book Card Today!)

PLEASE RUSH
MY FOUR FREE*
BOOKS TO ME
RIGHT AWAY!

Leisure Historical Romance Book Club
P.O. Box 6613
Edison, NJ 08818-6613

AFFIX
STAMP
HERE

trying to think, to plan. She had to tell him before someone else learned.

If Germaine suspected, she would run at once to her father. Lissa had been careful to clean her chamber pot and avoid the hateful housekeeper in the mornings. Of course, since Germaine herself was so often "indisposed" after drinking herself to sleep at night, the woman did not tend to be overly observant early in the day. Still, the thought of Marcus Jacobson's towering wrath made her curl into a ball and lie protectively on her side. She must resolve the dilemma with Jess before her father found out.

Finally, she rolled over and sat up. She was meeting Jess tomorrow afternoon at the pool. Perhaps the time would be right then.

She knew only one thing for certain—time was running out for them both.

Chapter Fourteen

While Lissa and Dellia were having their adversarial breakfast visit, Jess and Tate Shannon were having a tense confrontation of their own with Ringo Pardee in a shabby old bar on the edge of Cheyenne.

Pardee straddled a rickety cane chair and eyed the rotted plank floor strewn with filthy sawdust. His eyes were dark and as colorless as deep water; his thin, angular face was etched in cruel contours. He had a hooked nose and a thin, leering mouth. "This place is a dump. You pick it cause they'd serve yer nigger friend?"

Jess stiffened, but Tate placed a restraining hand on his friend's arm. "We both been called worse, Jess. Let it be—for now," he said, his eyes sending Pardee a clear message.

"You know the job I need done, Pardee. Shannon watches my back. You have a problem with that?"

Pardee raised his big, gnarled hands in mock surrender. "No problem, Robbins. Money's good. I gathered me ten of the best guns between here and the Mexican border."

"I asked for twelve."

Pardee shrugged as the fat, greasy-looking bartender waddled toward them with a grayish towel thrown over his sweat-stained shirt. He set down a glass of whiskey in front of Pardee, then looked at Robbins and Shannon, who had pulled up chairs around the plank table. "Ten of my men are worth twenty of them Wyoming boys," Pardee replied as Jess motioned the barkeep away.

"Since we need to ride this afternoon, I reckon they'd better be," Jess said. "The inside man's left a message for the rustlers. They're going to hit a big herd of beeves in the north basin tonight. We have to be there, hidden and ready to give them a little surprise."

Jess began to outline his plans for the trap, setting up a crude map for Pardee with the used whiskey glasses he commandeered from surrounding tables.

Pardee nodded when the situation was all laid out. "When do we ride?"

"I don't want to draw attention."

"You still think someone with the Association is mixed up in this, Jess?" Shannon asked. "My money's on Brewster."

"You could be right, Tate, but I'm not taking any chances. That's why I picked this place to meet," he said meaningfully to Pardee. "Have the men ride out a few at a time, heading in different directions, then swing northwest until they pick up the railroad tracks to Laramie about five miles from here. We'll be waiting."

Tom Conyers looked up at the thin sliver of new moon and swore beneath his breath. They should have done this job the preceding night when there was no moon. "Damn Sligo's lazy ass for not leaving us word sooner."

The man beside him took a deep drag off his cigarette and flicked it onto the dry ground. "Watch out you don't start a grass fire, you horse's ass!" Conyers hissed. His companion quickly jumped down and ground out the glowing butt with the heel of his boot, then remounted as the rustler boss directed the men to split up and approach the large, scattered herd.

"I don't like this, Tom," Bert Hauser said. "Lookit all them cottonwoods 'n tall grass. Even a bunch of narrow ravines—a whole damn army could be waitin' fer us down there."

"Sligo says there's no one posted here tonight," Conyers replied, but he, too, did not like the lay of the land. "But keep yer eyes peeled."

As the rustlers split up and rode into the basin, Jess, Tate, and Pardee's men watched them from their hidden vantage points around the perimeter. Jess turned to Shannon and said with a sharkish grin, "This shouldn't take long."

Once the thieves had scattered onto the open plain, Jess raised his Winchester and fired rapidly three times, then kneed Blaze into a canter and burst from behind the stand of cottonwoods with Shannon riding behind him. All across the shallow basin, flashes of gunfire erupted. Pardee's men swooped down on the surprised thieves, who were caught in the open.

The dark night air was filled with orange flashes belching from revolvers and rifles. The sound of the solid impact of lead sinking into flesh, the death screams of men, and the bellowing of cattle followed.

More than half the rustlers were knocked from their horses by the opening volley. The rest galloped madly in various directions, looking for an opening through which to escape the withering fire. Cattle were hit as well, and the scattered herd quickly caught the blood scent. They bawled in fright, then began a frenzied stampede.

"Turn 'em!" Jess yelled, aiming his rifle at one of the rustlers, who was riding beside the lead steer, urging it on.

As soon as Robbins's shot knocked the rider from his horse, Jess rode abreast of the steer, reversing its course back toward the tail of the herd. Tate followed suit, turning the cattle behind the leader, and two of Pardee's men who were near enough did likewise. Most of the rustlers were encircled by a bobbing, milling sea of cattle. As if to further seal their doom, the faint clouds that had flitted across the moon were swept clear by a strong summer wind. The rustlers were trapped by the very prize they had sought to steal, easy targets for the cold-eyed gunmen who methodically cut them down.

Tom Conyers had been one of the last to ride into the open. As soon as the killing fire erupted all around his men, he turned his big roan stallion away from the ambush at a dead run, heading toward a narrow ravine that would offer him cover. He had almost made it when the sound of pursuit and a bullet whistling perilously close to his shoulder caused him to lean low over his horse's neck, spurring him on.

Jess recognized the tall man on the roan as the one who had issued orders when the thieves rode into the basin. While Shannon and Pardee cleaned up the last of his men, Robbins pursued the leader, hoping to take him alive. Blaze was gaining on the roan.

Just before the outlaw reached the ravine, he reined in and turned in the saddle, knowing he must deal with his pursuer before he could ride safely down the steep incline. He squeezed off two shots but missed his mark, his aim thrown off by the agitated prancing of his roan.

Jess pulled Blaze to a halt and aimed high on his opponent's right arm. The shot hit with wicked impact, knocking the outlaw off the opposite side of his horse. He hit the ground and rolled to the edge of the ravine, trying to crawl over the side. Jess spurred Blaze forward. When he neared the fallen outlaw, he reined in and leaped from the saddle.

"Lie real still," he said, cocking his Colt with a deadly click.

Conyers swore, breathing hard. "I can't. Musta broke something when I fell." He tried to roll over, with the small Colt house pistol he had pulled from inside his vest with his left hand, but Jess stepped on his right arm, eliciting a harsh gasp of agony and immobilizing him.

"Now, you can bleed or you can talk. Your choice. And while you bleed, I'll keep on massaging that bullet inside your arm." His boot moved again, eliciting another oath. "Who brought you here to take down J Bar?"

"We're just stealin' cattle, that's all," Conyers ground out when he could get his breath. He looked up into the cold, hawkish face of his captor. The breed gunman Jacobson had hired. He swore again as Jess's boot bore down on his arm.

"You didn't just single out Jacobson because you don't like the way he parts his hair. Who hired you? Who's buying the stolen cattle?"

"All right, all right. We was hired . . . got a broken rib. Can't talk," he gasped.

Jess released his arm and watched as Conyers painfully rolled onto his back. "Who is this—" He saw the glint of the small gun in the semidarkness just as Conyers raised it and fired.

The two shots came so close together that they sounded as one. Conyers's shot went wild. Jess hit the outlaw straight in the heart. He knelt and checked for signs of life, then swore as he began to examine the dead man's pockets for any personal effects that might offer clues.

Unlike Billy Argee, Tom Conyers was a seasoned professional who had not so much as a scrap of identification on him, much less a photograph of a woman. But he had admitted he was hired to attack J Bar by someone. Who?

Shrugging, Jess figured he would never know. Although he would inform Jacobson about it, with the demise of this large and well-organized bunch of rustlers, old Marcus's spread would probably be safe enough. If it was some other rancher in the Association or even Yancy Brewster, it was unlikely trouble would start up any time soon. If it did, it was another job of work. He smiled grimly as he retrieved the roan and threw the dead body across its saddle. Let Jacobson hire someone else.

Shirl Henke

*　　*　　*

Dellia Evers was sweating. She rubbed her hand across her forehead and grimaced, then removed the broad-brimmed felt hat that protected her sallow complexion from the sun and daubed at her whole face with a scented handkerchief. This hot and she was well sheltered beneath the thick, draping branches of a willow by the creek. Imagine if she had been watching the J Bar ranch house all this time out on the open plain!

Her tan riding skirt and plain white blouse were chosen for service, not style, cool and suitable for riding on a hot August day. But nothing would have been comfortable for this task. She had been waiting for well over an hour. What if that disgusting little tart Lissa had sneaked off for her lovers' tryst before Dellia had been able to get away from her pa this morning?

Just as she was about to despair, Lissa's gleaming red head appeared on the front porch. She was dressed for riding as she casually sauntered toward the corral with that hateful brute of a dog beside her.

Yancy would be proud of her when she exposed Lissa Jacobson for the whore she truly was! And to think Yancy had once favored the brassy red-head over *her*. "No more, Melissa Jacobson. After today you'll be finished with Yancy and with every decent man in Wyoming Territory."

As Lissa mounted up on Little Bit, she was deeply preoccupied by what she had to tell Jess. Her father was closeted in his office with paperwork and had left Germaine with strict instructions that he was not to be disturbed. Nothing would interrupt her meeting with her lover. She was taking

Cormac out for a run, her excuse for this afternoon's excursion.

The pulse-pounding anticipation that had first made her trysts with Jess so exhilarating was gone now. She was left with only a hollow sense of dread. He had to love her enough to claim her as his wife, to give a name to his own child—but she was trapping him this way. He would resent it.

Jess had ridden in early this morning and reported to her father that the rustling ring had been broken. She had eavesdropped on part of their lengthy conversation, fearing all the while that he would simply collect his pay and ride away. But he had agreed to wait a day or two. The federal marshal was on the way from Cheyenne to claim the dead men and determine if any were wanted.

When he left the ranch house, she had been sitting on the front porch, waiting for him to indicate that he would be at the pool that afternoon. He had been dusty and bloodstained, so exhausted-looking that she had wanted to fling herself into his arms and hold him, just grateful he was alive and that the blood was not his this time. That should have bothered her, but it did not. She was no longer titillated by the forbidden thrill of his dangerous occupation. Now that she loved him, all Lissa wanted was for him to put away his gun and live in peace.

Now I'll find out if he's willing to do it. In her heart of hearts, she feared he would refuse. A man like Jesse Robbins was not easily domesticated. That had been his allure—and her downfall.

So deep was she in thought, Lissa paid no heed to Cormac's antics as he chased after a butterfly, leaping high in the air and gamboling across the open grassland, carefree as a pup. Neither was she aware of the distant figure who followed them as she approached the barren stretch of escarpment and vanished over the horizon.

When she reached the pool, Jess was there, having already bathed his weary, bruised body in the invigorating cold water and stretched out in the shade beneath a spreading cottonwood tree. He was dozing as she approached quietly. She could see the sheen from droplets of water that still clung to his wet hair and upper torso as he lay clad only in denims, bare-chested and bootless. Her eyes drank in the perfect symmetry of his long, bronzed body with its delicious patterns of night-black hair. She felt her heart thrum furiously in her chest and her mouth go dry as she gazed on him like a voyeur, reluctant to awaken him and spoil the perfect enchantment with her news.

"I assumed I'd already passed your inspection, ma'am," he said in a low, amused voice, his eyes still seemingly closed.

Lissa's mouth formed a small "O" of surprise and her face heated as she knelt beside him and placed her hand on his chest. "I was just remembering the first time I saw you wet in that bathtub at the hotel." She moistened her lips provocatively. "And you're right. You passed my inspection early on," she whispered breathlessly as he pulled her down on top of him and kissed her possessively.

From her hiding place, Cridellia Evers adjusted the powerful binoculars she had taken from her father's desk. She had already seen that big evil brute of a blaze-faced stallion the Indian rode, grazing on the opposite side of the pool. The lovers were hidden in the trees, but she could make out the shadowy outlines of two figures, lying prone on the ground. She had already seen Lissa's dog chasing up one end of the narrow little valley and was careful to avoid him lest he alert her quarry to her presence. Turning her horse away, she slipped the binoculars into the saddlebag and rode as fast as she could for the J Bar.

Marcus Jacobson was pleased. The marshal had wasted no time, and now he and Tate Shannon were out examining the remains of the rustlers. Robbins and his men had gotten every damn one of them. The breed was worth every last cent he would pay him. Of course, there was the matter of their leader telling Robbins about working for someone else, but a desperate man, shot and held at gunpoint, would say anything. He dismissed any threat from that quarter as improbable and returned to the tally sheets he had in front of him. This fall, only he would be selling J Bar cattle.

Germaine Channault heard the rapid knocking on the front door and wiped her hands on a towel with irritation. She had croissants rising and Marcus's favorite bearnaise sauce simmering on the stove. Who would come calling in midafternoon? Probably another of that obnoxious vixen's bumbling suitors. If only she would marry one of them and have done with it!

When she reached the front door, the last person she expected to see was a disheveled, dust-coated Cridellia Evers dressed in shabby riding clothes.

"Good afternoon, Mademoiselle Evers. Won't you please come in. I'm afraid Mademoiselle Jacobson is not at home right now."

Dellia hesitated, then answered, red-faced, "I

know. That is . . ." She twisted her riding crop nervously in her hands as she edged past the housekeeper and into the hallway. Following Lissa as Yancy had suggested had been the easy part, but explaining exactly what she had seen was going to prove most humiliating. How could she face Marcus Jacobson's imperious, icy stare?

Germaine studied the nervous girl with shrewd dark eyes. She and Lissa had never been friends, only rivals. And plain little Cridellia always came in second. The chit knew something!

"Come with me into the parlor and have a seat, child. I'll bring you some nice cool lemonade and then you can tell me what's wrong."

Dellia followed her into the large, elegant room and sat on the edge of the elaborately carved Neo-Grecian settee like a bird poised to take flight at the slightest sound. Germaine quickly brought the lemonade. Dellia took a gulp as if tossing back a swig from a jug of forty-rod whiskey for courage.

"Whatever is the matter?" the older woman asked in her most motherly voice.

"I—I don't know if I can go through with this— telling Mr. Jacobson, I mean. It's so awful." Her pop eyes bulged from their sockets as she affixed Germaine with an intent stare.

"Perhaps I could help. Could you tell me first, woman to woman?"

Taking a deep breath for courage, Dellia blurted out her story, ending with the scene she had just left at the hidden pool. "They've been—well, she's given herself to that breed."

Germaine sat very still, taking in the enormity of Dellia's tale. If they were still together at their trysting place, Marcus could catch them! She took

Dellia's thin, bony hand and patted it solemnly.

Marcus was just totaling the last of Moss's tallies when Germaine knocked and asked permission to enter. What now? He muttered for her to come in, still holding the pen in his hand. Her expression was grave and unctuous as she stood to one side of the big walnut door frame and ushered in a very pale Cridellia Evers.

"Monsieur Jacobson, the young lady here has something of great importance to tell you."

Chapter Fifteen

Lissa lay with her head resting in the curve of Jess's arm, gazing up at shifting patterns of shiny green leaves against the brilliant azure sky. She was damp from bathing in the pool, satiated from making love, and frightened to death of what she must tell Jess. When she first arrived at their place, she had held her peace, needing desperately to have him love her, even if it was for the last time. Especially if it was for the last time.

Jess, too, was preoccupied, driven by his own demons, for he knew their idyll had to come to an end. He felt her snuggling against him, soft and warm, fitting so perfectly. Her arm lay draped possessively across his chest, pale against his dark skin. He took her hand in his and held it as he rolled up into a sitting position and looked into her eyes.

"You are so beautiful, Lissa," he began slowly,

238

letting his fingertips trace the delicate contours of her face. She turned her head into his touch and kissed the palm of his hand silently, as if willing him not to speak. Steeling himself, he continued, "I know you overheard me talking with your pa this morning. My job here is over."

"Don't, Jess," she protested. "You don't have to keep on risking your life this way. You could've been killed."

"That's just the point, I could have," he replied flatly. "But I wasn't. And now I have to go."

She had known he would not stay from the first moment she had laid eyes on him. He was a drifter, a loner, a man without allegiances, who could not be tied down. "So it's good-bye, Lissa," she said, "and you ride away without looking back."

Oh, I'll look back, I'll look back plenty. Aloud he said, "You knew it had to end when it began."

"You don't have to ride off to another gunfight. You could quit." Her voice was sharp with desperation.

His face grew shuttered as he nerved himself to destroy her impossible dreams. "Quit and settle down to raising cattle? You still think your pa'd turn J Bar over to me? Wake up, Lissa. He'd see me in hell first."

"I'll go with you—we don't have to stay in Wyoming."

"Where could we go where it wouldn't matter that you're white and I'm not?"

"That doesn't matter to me—I love you, Jesse Robbins! I'll never love another man," she cried out passionately.

"It's no good, Lissa. You've been raised on silk skirts and spun sugar. Your love would turn to

239

hate," he replied in a flat, final tone. He rolled to his feet and extended his hand to her, pulling her up, then walked away from her.

"If you leave me, what am I to do? Marry Yancy Brewster?" She shuddered in revulsion, waiting for him to turn and face her.

Without doing so, he replied, "No. Marry Lemuel Mathis. He seems a decent enough sort."

If he had slapped her, she could not have been more staggered. "After what we've shared, you want me to go to another man. To . . . to let him touch me . . ." Words failed her as she stood hugging herself in desolation, fighting the tears.

"What I want doesn't figure in this, Lissa," he said wearily as he reached for his boots and pulled them on, still refusing to look at her.

"The least you could do is look at me, the woman you're throwing away." She forced back the tears and replaced them with fierce, bright anger.

He turned to her then, calling up a look of contempt. Damn her, she was not making this any easier for either of them! "It was your decision to give me your virginity, Lissa. I sure as hell wasn't the one doing the chasing."

Lissa had been on the verge of blurting out that he had given her a child, but she bit her lip at his cruel words. She would keep silent forever rather than abase herself for this arrogant savage again.

Jess watched the color drain from her face. Her lips compressed into a tight, pinched line. She stood before him, proudly silent with her back straight and her golden eyes glazed with tears. He would curse himself a thousand times for the abominable words he had spoken, yet knew he would say them again if he had to—to end it for her. Better that she should hate him and get on with her life.

Lissa turned and seized her dress, wanting suddenly to be decently covered in front of him, but before she could pull it over her head, Cormac barked, and the sharp metallic scrape of a rifle being levered echoed across the ravine.

Marcus Jacobson, mounted on a big roan, stood silhouetted at the edge of the escarpment. He raised the weapon as he looked in disbelieving horror at his daughter, caught alone with the breed gunman. She had nothing on but her sheer undergarments, and he was bare-chested. Both were damp, no doubt from bathing in the pool. What else they had done he refused even to think about as he drew a bead dead center on Robbins's chest.

Cormac, who had come bounding up to welcome Marcus, stood between him and Lissa, looking from one to the other in confusion.

Lissa dashed in front of Jess, throwing her arms about him. "Papa, no!"

"Get away from him, Melissa, or I swear to God I'll kill you both," he yelled as he rode down the dusty trail to the floor of the ravine.

Jess pulled her arms from his neck and tried to set her aside. "He's got the right, Lissa. Move away before you get hurt," he said gently.

"No! I won't let him kill you," she sobbed, clinging to him.

"Get dressed and get out of here," Marcus snapped with cold fury in his voice.

"Do as he says," Jess reiterated, this time shoving her forcefully away. Cormac, who had remained a silent onlooker, let out a low growl at Jess, then subsided. Jess stood before Jacobson's leveled rifle, understanding the killing rage banked behind those ice-blue eyes. He met the old man's glare calmly, knowing he was going to die. Perhaps it had been inevitable ever since he rode into Cheyenne and first laid eyes on Melissa Jacobson. "Get it done, Jacobson," he said quietly.

"You can't kill him, Papa! I'm carrying his child—your grandchild. You have to let us marry," Lissa said in a breathless rush as she walked toward the father who had adored and cosseted her all her life. Now the hard coldness of his face seemed carved from granite. As her words sank in, she could see him struggle with his rage. He almost fired—at Jess or at her?

Marcus lowered the gun like a beaten man. His tall, elegant body seemed to crumple in on itself. He looked past her as if she did not even exist. "No white man will take your leavings, Robbins. She's got an Injun brat in her belly. You'd better give it a name. I sure as hell don't want it called Jacobson."

Jess stood rooted to the ground, shock radiating through his body as forcefully as if the old man had pulled the trigger. He turned his eyes to Lissa. "You never told me," he accused.

Her chin went up, and he could see her swallow before she spoke. "I was going to before you said what you did. Then . . ." Her words faded away.

He let his breath escape in a hiss, then turned to Jacobson. "I'll take her to Cheyenne tonight and marry her."

Jacobson nodded curtly, then turned away from his only child without so much as a glance, giving a curt command for Cormac to follow as he rode away.

Still confused, the dog looked from Lissa and

Jess to Marcus. When neither of them moved to intercede, he trotted obediently after the old man.

Jess spoke to Lissa, his expression unreadable. "Can you ride to Cheyenne if we take it slow?"

"I'm pregnant, Jess, not crippled," she replied bitterly.

"Get dressed then." He turned away and shrugged on his shirt, then reached for his gun, strapping it on methodically while she quickly slipped on her outer garments.

"You would have just stood there and let him shoot you." There was almost accusation in her voice.

"Like I said, he had the right. I'm not proud of what I've done, but at least I'm willing to pay the price." His voice was as emotionless as his face.

"Even if it means marrying me?" Her hands trembled as she gripped a boot and pulled it on. The task complete, she turned and looked at him. He was gathering the horses and did not answer her. "Would you have preferred to have my father kill you?"

"What I'd prefer has never much figured in my life, Lissa," he said wearily, handing her the reins to Little Bit. His hands circled her waist, and he hoisted her effortlessly into the saddle, then mounted Blaze.

They rode in silence for several hours. The late summer air was redolent with the tang of pine, and the bawls of calves echoed in the distance. Thick, powdery dust rose from the horses' hooves, churned up like a flour cloud when Vinegar mixed biscuits. Lissa fought back her tears and focused on the future. Once they were married, things would work out all right.

Married. She had dreamed of the day ever since she was a girl back in St. Louis, envisioning then a proper courtship followed by an expensive engagement ring and an elaborate wedding at St. Stephens Lutheran Church. She looked down at the dusty riding skirt and boots she wore. Some bridal outfit! But when she surreptitiously turned her eyes on Jess's chiseled profile, she knew that the fancy accoutrements were unimportant. All that mattered was that she would wed the man she loved—and that he would love her in return.

I'll make you love me, Jesse Robbins, see if I won't!

By the time they arrived in Cheyenne, the last pink and gold rays of light were vanishing behind the Medicine Bows.

"We'll have to get hotel rooms for tonight and find a preacher in the morning," Jess said, as raucous noise from an outlying saloon greeted their arrival.

Rooms. Plural. She smiled at his concern for her reputation. "I know where Judge Sprague lives. He's an old family friend. He'll marry us right now," she said quietly.

"Where does he live?" Jess listened to her directions, then turned Blaze down a tree-lined side street. For the past hours he had tortured himself with the insane idea of taking her with him back to Texas. She would be his wife. Only he would ever have the right to touch her, not that vicious Diamond E foreman or that ham-handed Association president. All summer long, thoughts of them putting their hands on Lissa had tortured him. But old Marcus had been right. No white man in Wyoming would take her after the shame

244

of bearing a child with mixed blood.

How he wanted to believe their marriage could survive; he could not. Picturing her in his small, crude one-story ranch house, he knew she would quickly grow to hate it, hate him. Life in Texas was hard on women, even those born to it. For Lissa, raised with every luxury, it would be unendurable. She would end up wrinkled and careworn, old before her time, her bright gold eyes flat with defeat and her fiery hair faded to gray. He had seen so many of those women, dressed in ragged homespun with several small children tugging on their skirts and a baby on their hip. Women with thin, pinched faces, beyond despair, hopeless, dreamless.

Better that Lissa go back East where she had grown up and take their child with her. There the stigma of his blood would not be as bad. Perhaps if the babe resembled her, no one would even suspect. In time, she could have their marriage set aside and remarry. Perhaps he would oblige her sooner by stopping a bullet and leaving her a widow. Either way, he would never see her again—or see the child they had made.

The pain clawed at him as they reined in and dismounted in front of an elegant brick house. When he reached up to help her down, he fought the urge to pull her into his embrace. Instead, he woodenly set her away from him and they walked silently up the steep stairs of the porch. He lifted the heavy brass knocker and let it fall. Its sepulchral sound echoed down the deserted street.

"Good evening," a servant said in equally grave tones as he held the door partially ajar. When his pale eyes lit on Lissa, his demeanor changed immediately. "Miss Jacobson. What brings you to Cheyenne?" he asked with a smile wreathing his wrinkled face. Quickly he opened the heavy oak door to admit her and Jess, eyeing the armed and menacing-looking stranger warily.

"I've come to see the judge, Morton. Is he at home?"

"Right this way. You rest in the parlor while I fetch him," Morton replied, ushering them down a dark, richly appointed hall and into a small room filled with intricately carved oak furniture. English pastoral oils hung from the walls, which were covered with dull maroon paper that soaked up the light from a crystal lamp fixture. Photographs sat on every flat surface in the room.

Lissa picked one up. "That was Mrs. Sprague. She died when I was a child. The judge never remarried," she said wistfully, placing the picture back on a marble-topped table.

He looked at her, standing in this expensive room. "You belong here," he said flatly.

"What do you mean?"

Before he could reply, the door opened and a rotund man with wide brown eyes and close-cropped gray hair stepped into the room. "Morton said you were here, Lissa child. I hope nothing's happened to your father?" He extended two pawlike hands to hers and patted them fondly.

"No, Papa's at the J Bar." She swallowed and took a deep breath for courage. "He sent us here." Turning to Jess, she made introductions. "Judge Sprague, I would like you to meet Jesse Robbins. We want you to marry us."

Jess nodded to the judge, who he noted did not offer to shake his hand. A grim smile slashed his face when the judge held her arm protectively and spluttered.

"Aren't you the gun—the man Marcus hired? Surely, Lissa—"

"I have my father's permission, Judge," Lissa interrupted, moving away from him and taking Jess's arm. Her eyes implored that he question her no further, but it was useless.

His shrewd brown eyes sized up the dangerous-looking breed. Hiram Sprague supposed that a foolish young woman raised back East might think Robbins was handsome, romantic, some such balderdash. "You haven't run away from home, have you? This would break your father's heart, Lissa," he remonstrated.

"I'm afraid I've already done that. You see, Judge, we must marry." She stressed the last words, feeling the heat stealing into her cheeks as the judge paled and looked at Jess.

"She's telling the truth, your honor. If you don't marry us, we'll have to wait until tomorrow and hunt us up a preacher." Jess's voice was level, emotionless.

The old man looked incredulously from the harsh expression on Robbins's face to Lissa, studying them both. God help them, they were telling the truth! "I'm surprised Marcus didn't kill you," he said thickly to the gunman.

The faintest hint of a smile touched Jess's lips. "It wasn't because he didn't want to."

"I'll get my book. Wait here," Sprague said tersely.

Within a few minutes, they were reciting their vows in front of the sternly disapproving judge. When he reached the part that called for a ring,

Lissa was amazed when Jess produced one, a slim gold band, which was obviously very old. He slid it on her finger, saying the words in such a cool, emotionless voice that she wanted to weep.

Judge Sprague pronounced them legally wed and closed his book with an abrupt snap. Jess considered offering the sour old man a fee, then decided against it. He knew Sprague would refuse curtly. He took Lissa's arm, and she quickly drew her hand through the bend of his elbow.

"We'd better try to find a place for the night. Your honor," he said, nodding to the old man who stood with his arms resting around his paunch.

Lissa murmured her good-byes, glad to leave the disapproving presence of a man who had suddenly become a stranger.

When they stepped outside into the cool darkness, she touched the ring, turning it around and around on her finger. It was a perfect fit. "Where did you get the ring, Jess?"

He helped her mount up. "It belonged to my mother."

"Is there no family left?" she asked, realizing that as of now she, too, was completely cut off.

"My parents are both dead. I've got a kid brother." He volunteered nothing else as they rode toward the center of town. *Getting a hotel room is going to be a bitch*, he thought angrily. If that prissy clerk at the Metropolitan had tried to refuse him when he was alone, Jess could only imagine how ugly it would be when he walked in with a white wife. *Wife.* She was his. Just once before he told her good-bye, he could lie with her legally, morally. It was his right. But once he did, how much harder would it be to let her go? Deep in his own tortured thoughts, Jess did not hear her question until she repeated it.

"What's your brother's name?"

"Jonah." A small smile touched his face as he thought about his restless, twenty-year-old brother.

"Does he live in Texas?"

They were nearing a respectable-looking hotel on 17th Street. Jess swung off Blaze. "Let it be, Lissa. I don't want to talk about my family," he said grimly.

She bit her lip but said nothing, just followed him into the lobby. The clerk looked from Jess to Lissa and his eyes narrowed, but before he could voice any protest, Jess shoved the signed register at him along with a sizable amount of cash. "We'll be needing two rooms," he said in a silky, menacing voice that caused the fat clerk to break out in an instant sweat. Without looking at Lissa again, he seized two keys and handed them to Jess.

"Top of the stairs, at the end of the hall."

Jess turned and handed her one key. "Order a bath and whatever food you want sent up to your room. I have to send a wire."

"I'll order for both of us. Don't be long, Jess," she replied in a husky voice. "We have some things to talk about," she added meaningfully.

He sighed. "All right. Let's go up and talk first. I can send the wire later," he said tightly. He glared at the moon-faced clerk, who immediately stopped eavesdropping and bent his head to the account ledgers on which he had been working.

Her room proved to be somewhat spartan compared to the suite at the Metropolitan, but the rates were substantially lower. Jess was lucky to have collected his monthly wage the preceding week, else he would not have been able to afford lodging, meals, and the train ticket he intended to purchase.

Lissa paced to a window overlooking the street and peered out into the darkness, hugging herself, looking very lovely and vulnerable. "Why two rooms, Jess? Isn't it a little late for that?"

"It'll be easier for you to dissolve the marriage later on if there's evidence that it wasn't consummated."

She stiffened. "Then you plan to leave me? Leave your child before it's even born?" She turned to him with furious anger blazing in her eyes, but the naked anguish she saw on his face stopped her rush of heated words.

"Your father will forgive you eventually. Meanwhile, you have other kin back East. It wouldn't be as bad for a child with Indian blood there. . . ." His voice cracked. He swore beneath his breath and turned to the door. "I'm going to buy you a railroad ticket and make arrangements to get you back to J Bar. Marcus can get you at the Squaw Creek station."

She said nothing, just stood silhouetted in the window, a small, solitary figure, until he was gone. He left her key lying on the table beside the door. Slowly she walked over and picked it up. Then a slow smile curved her. lips as she rang for room service.

Jess stabled the horses and made arrangements to get her home the next day, then walked slowly back to their hotel. As he fished his room key from his pocket, he thought of Lissa's lush body lying just across the hall. If he knocked, he knew she would welcome him. Steeling himself, he unlocked his door and stepped into the dark room.

Instantly his instincts, honed by years living on the edge of danger, told him that he was not alone. He froze, gun in hand, peering into the darkness. Then a match flared and Lissa's face appeared, haloed in light.

"You should've saved your money, Jess," Lissa whispered as she lit the lamp.

Chapter Sixteen

She walked toward him like a stalking tigress, clad only in sheer batiste undergarments that were translucent in the soft light. "I am your wife. Can you deny me?" she asked softly. "Can you deny yourself?"

With a snarled oath, he began to strip off his clothes, tearing buttons from his shirt, flinging his gunbelt across a chair, kicking his boots and denims away. "Damn you, Lissa. I'll have to stop a bullet to free you, but tonight you're mine!"

His mouth descended on hers with savage intensity, slanting across it with bruising, possessive force. She melted against him, yielding and sweet and silent. Their bodies fused together, pressing and sliding as their hands caressed, traveling up and down each other's backs.

His fingers caught the lacy straps of her camisole and pulled them off her shoulders, baring her breasts. When his hot, seeking mouth fastened on the aching tip of one pale pink nipple, she arched up, moaning deep in her throat. Her breasts were tender and swollen from her pregnancy, incredibly sensitive. Her fingers glided up into his straight black hair and grabbed thick, shiny fistfuls.

Jess cupped her breasts, hefting their greater size and fullness with wonder. How could he not have seen the changes in her body? Because he was too feverish with lust to take note of anything. No other woman had ever made him crazy the way Lissa did. Then his palms slid over the slight swell of her belly, pulling the tapes of her underwear loose and shoving the sheer cotton over the curve of her hips. She kicked it away as he reached down and scooped her into his arms, carrying her to the bed.

They rolled across the soft coverlet in a tangle of arms and legs, kissing fiercely, raining small licks and bites across each other's shoulders and neck. Lissa could feel the hardness of his sex pressing into her belly and stroked it boldly with one hand. He growled low in his throat and raised himself over her. She spread her thighs and guided him home with a small, whimpering cry.

At first he rode her hard and fast, loving her with the fury and fire of his desperation. Then he stopped and held her tight, realizing that this would be the last night, the last time he lay with her. She seemed to sense the change in him as he resumed stroking her slowly, savoringly.

"Don't ever leave me, Jess, ever . . ." Her voice faded away into breathless gasps. "I . . . love . . . you . . . I . . . love . . . you." Just as she felt the sweeping pull of sweet release swamp her senses, he murmured something in reply, muffled against her throat. Was it "I love you?" She could not be certain.

His staff swelled and shuddered deep within her, and they both fell again into the shimmering world of ecstasy they had so often entered together. This time there was a sense of bittersweet wonder. Time was rushing on, whispering words they did not wish to hear. The beautiful communion was over too soon.

Lissa felt him collapse atop her. His breathing was labored as he cradled her beneath him, struggling to regain control. Her hands glided up his back, tracing the contours of muscle and bone with sweat-slicked fingertips, memorizing every beautiful inch of his body, storing up memories to hold the specter of loss at bay.

Jess, too, seemed to be studying her, holding up a fiery curl and wrapping it about his hand, then rubbing it against his face. "Like silk," he breathed. Warm summer air enveloped them, heavy with the lusty musk of lovemaking and the faint essence of orange blossoms.

They lay, quietly touching, for several moments, more gentle with each other than their passions had ever allowed before. Gradually, the low-burning fires rose once more, hammering in their blood, demanding release. Lissa could feel Jess hardening again, still buried deep within her. She moved against him, tightening her thighs against his hips, urging him on as they resumed their old rhythm.

A sense of frantic desperation seemed to take over as they crested, this time swiftly and hungrily.

They spent the night alternately making love,

then sleeping wrapped in each other's arms, only to reawaken and resume their passion. At last the faint, rosy haze of dawn sent fingers of gold creeping into the room. Jess awakened to feeble light streaming in the open window. He looked down at Lissa in his arms. Her eyes were closed, with deep smudges of fatigue beneath the thick lashes resting on her cheeks. She looked so young and vulnerable that it tore at his heart.

She was his wife, the mother of his child, and he was leaving her. The easiest way would have been to sneak out while she still slept, leaving a note and the railroad ticket, but he could not do it. He propped his head on one hand to better study her sleeping body. A raw wave of possessiveness swept over him. She was his wife, and suddenly all his noble intentions about her remarriage to another man seemed unthinkable.

Another man would raise his child—perhaps treat it hatefully, as he had been treated for what the Anglos considered inferior Indian and Mexican blood. Could he allow that? If the child were a boy, he might return to claim him, but what if it was a girl? He could no more subject a daughter to the hardships of life on his ranch than he could his wife. *Let go the dream, Jess,* he chided himself.

Sensing his perusal, perhaps aware that he was troubled, Lissa awakened, her lashes fluttered open, and their gazes met. "Magic silver eyes," she said softly as her hand traced the raspy whiskers on his jawline. "What are you thinking, Jess?" She held her breath.

"That it's time to say good-bye."

"No!" She sat up and the sheet slid down to her waist. "We're married. You can't just leave me."

255

"We've said it all, Lissa," he replied as he slid from the bed and padded naked across the floor, gathering up his strewn clothing.

"Will it be so easy—just riding away, leaving me surrounded by people who'll scorn me and our child?" She held the sheet protectively clenched over her breasts.

"You know damn well it won't," he snarled savagely. "Get out of Wyoming. Go back East where you'll have the chance to begin again."

"As a divorced woman?" Her tone was scornful and pained.

He paused with his shirt half tucked into his jeans and stared at her. "You came here last night. This is my room, lady. You sealed your chance for an annulment. Or maybe you'd prefer if I hurried up and got careless—"

"Stop it!" She put her hands over her ears to block out his hateful words.

"Get dressed. I'll have breakfast sent up to you," he said, reaching for the door.

As soon as he was gone, she flung back the covers and rushed for the basin in the dry sink. "Forget breakfast!" she yelled at the closed door just before becoming very sick.

Jess sat in the quiet saloon, nursing a cup of ink-black coffee and staring morosely into a plate of greasy fried potatoes he had been unable to finish. A few customers sauntered in to partake of the wretched food, others for a morning jolt of forty-rod whiskey.

Word of his marriage to Lissa Jacobson the preceding evening had already spread like wildfire. Most of the bleary patrons studied him covertly, some with thin-lipped disapproval, others with incredulous curiosity. Old Marcus's fancy Eastern-raised daughter hitching up with a breed killer, imagine that. No one had the nerve to approach the dangerous-looking stranger and ask him about the outlandish tale.

No one, that is, until Camella Alvarez spotted him striding from the saloon and quickly crossed the street on an intercept course.

"Morning, Jess." Her expression was troubled.

He studied her rumpled red dress and the loose, tangled black curls spilling over her shoulders. "You don't usually rise so early, Cammie."

She smiled sadly. "Florie Tyburn almost broke a leg hurrying back to the theater to wake me up with the news. It's true, isn't it?"

He looked up and down the street, which was filling with people on their morning rounds. "This is no place to talk." He had planned to look her up before he left town today. Taking her arm, he steered her into an alley between the saloon and a mercantile. "It's true."

She studied him with shrewd brown eyes. "I can't believe a man like Jacobson would let her marry you, unless . . ."

"Yeah, unless," he echoed bitterly. "No one's ever in a hurry to claim a breed's bastard."

"Are you taking her to the Double R?" Somehow it did not seem likely, knowing Jess as she did.

"Hell, no. That life would kill a girl like Lissa."

"Do you think her life here will be any better now?" she countered.

"She has kin back East," he said defensively, then shut his mouth, angry that he had spoken at all.

257

Shirl Henke

"What does Lissa want to do?" Camella had a pretty good hunch. His expression confirmed it.

Scowling, he said, "She thinks all we need is love to survive. A fancy, spoiled lady like her—what does she know about being a small rancher's wife in a place like West Texas?"

"Maybe you don't give her enough credit. She could learn. Lots of women do. We're an adaptable lot, rich or poor."

He shook his head. "Look, Cammie . . . I'm putting her on a train, sending her back to her pa. I figure she can stay there."

"Maybe he won't let her. He could just throw her out. It wouldn't be the first time," she interjected.

"No matter what, she's his only child. He'll take her back. But he won't want her to keep the baby." He stumbled over the words. *My child*. "If the old man makes trouble, or if . . . if Lissa wants to go East without it . . ."

"I'll help her, Jess," she volunteered before he could ask. "But she won't give it up, *querido*. After all, this baby will be all of you she has left."

In his heart of hearts, Jess did not believe she would do so either, but he had to provide for all exigencies. "I have some money here—and I can wire you more if you need it for her." He took a roll of bills from his vest pocket and handed it to her.

"Keep it, Jess. You'll need it for now. I know where to wire Jonah if Lissa needs your help." She placed the money back in his vest pocket and rose to kiss him.

"You're a good friend, Cammie. Thank you."

She stood in the alleyway with the high plains sun beating down on her back hotly, watching him walk away. *Vaya con Dios, querido*.

A Fire in the Blood

*　　*　　*

When he returned to the hotel, Lissa was dressed and sitting on the edge of the rumpled bed. Her face was pale, but she was dry-eyed and calm. As soon as he entered the room, she shot up, then stood very still with her head high and her back straight, like a queen awaiting execution.

"The train comes in around eleven. We'd better get going," he said quietly. His eyes swept to the tray on the bedside table. "You didn't eat your breakfast."

"I wasn't hungry," she replied woodenly, walking to the door.

He let her pass, then closed it. *Don't think about that bed . . .*

They walked downstairs and through the lobby, silently ignoring the stares of the gathered crowd, both curious and hostile. A low murmuring followed them, but no one spoke up or dared to confront the hard-eyed gunman. Lissa held his arm tightly, looking straight ahead. *Please, God, let me get through this.*

When they approached the train platform, Jess could feel her trembling. "Just a few minutes more, Lissa."

She did not reply. They stood in the shadow of the new Union Pacific building beside the platform, waiting as the train pulled up to the station. A hiss of steam escaped as the engine ground to a stop in front of them.

It was time to say good-bye.

After the train had vanished, Jess turned from his lonely sentinel's post on the rise and kneed

Blaze into a steady canter. He tried to keep his mind blank, not think about Lissa and the baby or what she would do about dissolving the marriage. It did not work.

Deep in rumination, he barely heard the pounding of hooves until the rider had closed with him. Jess whirled in the saddle, rifle drawn from his scabbard. Then he recognized Tate Shannon and reined in.

"A good way to get yourself killed," he said as he replaced the rifle. "What brought you riding hell-bent, Tate?"

The big black man doffed his hat and ran one shirt sleeve across his forehead before replacing his headgear. "Hot today, but not near so hot as it'll be for you if Pardee catches up and blasts you into the next life."

Jess nodded in weary resignation. "Jacobson hired him to kill me."

"Offered him 'n them men who rode with him your cash money for cleaning out the rustlers if they'd finish you and bring Miz Lissa back."

The question remained unasked, but Shannon's liquid brown eyes studied Jess.

"Lissa's on the train. She'll arrive at the Squaw Creek stop-off tonight. I sent word to the old man to collect her."

A look of incredulity filled Shannon's face. "You took her to Cheyenne and spent the night, then left her?"

"I married her, Tate. On Jacobson's orders. He didn't want the baby to have the Jacobson name."

Shannon cursed, then studied his friend. "From the look on your face, Jess, you don't give a damn if you live or die, but I figure on livin' 'n I damn near rode a good horse to death reachin' you 'fore Pardee."

"How far is he behind you?"

"Soon as I overheard him 'n the old man palaverin', I took my own horse outta the cavvy and headed out real quiet. He won't be long. If I found out you rode south this easy, he will too."

Jess scanned the rolling grasslands and the mountains in the distance. "If we swing east and then cut back up north, we might lose them."

Tate shrugged, then studied Jess. "You want him doggin' yer back forever? For five thousand, he'll track you clean to Canady."

"You got a better idea?"

Tate flashed a white grin at Jess. "Ole Ringo was havin' a real busy time of it gettin' his boys to ride along. Seems they ain't real partial to comin' up against you. I figger there won't be more than three of 'em. If we hole up in them rocks over that ridge, we can take 'em."

Jess considered a minute, then nodded to Shannon. "I owe you, Tate."

"You damn betcha, you do. Jacobson never paid me fer backin' you against the rustlers," he said with a chuckle as they rode for cover. They had almost made it when the crack of a rifle echoed across the plains. Ringo Pardee and four men came over the rise at a full gallop, shooting.

"Shit, I figgered he'd only get three men to come with him, tops," Shannon said as he jumped from his horse and returned fire, knocking one of the riders from his mount.

"Never underestimate the power of greed, ole son. Makes brave men out of fools," Jess replied, taking careful aim and firing, then quickly repeating the process until only Pardee and one of his men were left. They circled their horses back out of range.

Robbins and Shannon remounted and gave chase, but the black man's buckskin was played out from the hard ride and quickly fell behind. Jess took out Pardee as the gunman turned to fire his Winchester 73. The lone survivor, Sug Johnson, rode low against the neck of his horse, lashing it with his reins. With Pardee and the others dead, Jess figured Sug would not resume the bounty hunt. He reined in Blaze and rode back to where Tate was cooling his winded mount.

Tate swung up on his buckskin and fell in beside Jess. "I reckon Pardee's dead?"

Jess nodded. "Sug Johnson got away, but he won't come after me."

"You figger on goin' back to Texas?"

Jess shrugged. "Doesn't much matter. I hear they have a dandy range war going on down in New Mexico Territory." He looked at Tate but said nothing.

The black man threw back his head and laughed. "Hell, Jess, I got me no place else to go. I opine ole man Jacobson'll up 'n fire me soon as Sug Johnson reports to him. Let's ride to New Mexico. I ain't seen it in a month of Sundays."

Chapter Seventeen

Spring, 1882

"You must change your will now, *hein?*" Germaine plumped up a pillow behind Marcus's back and watched him lean into it with a grimace as he resettled himself in his big bed.

"No," he replied flatly.

"You will be the laughingstock of the territory, letting that half-breed boy inherit J Bar when you have—"

"I said, let it alone." Marcus's words were sharp and bitten off, causing him to sag in breathless pain as soon as they were spoken. His face was haggard and creased with loose skin that had turned the color of old snow.

Germaine Channault looked down at him, her small, dark eyes glittering with frustration. She said nothing more, only looked at the tray sitting on the bedside table, its contents virtually untouched.

"Take it away. I'm not hungry," he whispered, forestalling any urging to eat that she might have considered.

"Eat anyway," the small, plump man standing in the doorway said cheerfully. "How the hell do you expect to get better if you keep losing weight?"

"Hell, Doc, you and I both know I'm dying. My heart's given out, same as my pa's did."

"No reason to hurry it along by starving yourself," Headly replied gruffly. His pink, hairless scalp gleamed with perspiration when he doffed his bowler hat and laid it carelessly on the table. He approached the bed with a weather-beaten satchel of cracked brown leather.

"I don't need any more of your pills or your platitudes, Doc—just someone to put a stop to the damn rustling."

"I heard you were having trouble again this spring. Thought they were all finished off last summer," Headly said as he took Marcus's veiny hand in his plump fingers and expertly read the pulse. Weak and irregular.

"We have us a whole new crop of thieves, it seems. Territory's going to hell in a hand basket."

Headly looked up at Germaine. "Has he eaten anything this past week?"

"A little *consommé*, some oatmeal." She shrugged. "He asked for *tournedos*, then took only a few bites," she added, looking accusingly at the plate full of juicy pink beef.

"For now, stick with soup," the physician replied, watching her nod and leave with the tray.

"You need to see that specialist in Denver, Marcus."

"We've been over this before, Doc. I'm not leaving J Bar. There's not a damn thing any fancy doctor in Colorado can do for me. Only one thing would make me happy—and that's not likely to happen!"

To punctuate his last, bitter remark, the soft wail of a baby drifted in from the room down the hall where Lissa was nursing her infant son. Both men knew Marcus wanted his daughter to petition for a divorce from her husband and give up the baby to an agency back East. Then Lemuel Mathis would marry her. She steadfastly refused to cooperate.

Headly sighed at the look of intransigence chiseled on Jacobson's face. The stubborn old cuss would die of his own bile before he acknowledged what a fine grandson he had, but there was no use reopening that box of bees again. "I have to get over to the Elkins place. The missus is fixing to have another youngun' any day now. You have Germaine send for me if you feel worse. And keep taking that tonic I gave you. It might strengthen your heart."

When he had finished with Marcus, the doctor walked down the long hall to Lissa's room. Before he could knock, she opened the door. Although she smiled warmly at him, he could see the aching sadness in her eyes. Old Marcus had not been easy on her.

"How's my favorite new mother and that handsome little devil Johnny?" he asked, hearing a gurgle from inside the room.

"Johnny is just splendid," she said with a flash of real happiness shining in her eyes. She turned to the cradle beside her bed and lifted the kicking little bundle for inspection. "He's just been fed and is ready to drift off for his afternoon nap."

Headly inspected the thick cap of inky hair on the baby's head. Still, if he did not know the dark-skinned infant had Indian blood, he would probably not have guessed it. "He is thriving," the doctor said fondly. He had delivered Johnny, ignoring the cruel scandal and gossip that raged in Cheyenne over Marcus Jacobson's fallen daughter. "Wish I could say the same for his mother. You should go back to St. Louis, child. You could build a life for the two of you there."

She laid the sleeping baby in his cradle and walked down the back stairs with the doctor. "I guess it was a mistake, coming home when you wired me that Papa had the heart attack, but I hoped . . ." Her voice faded away in misery.

"You took a terrible risk, traveling through a blizzard eight months pregnant just to reach a man who has refused to acknowledge the existence of his own grandson."

"I couldn't let him die alone. I am his only family since his brother was killed in the Fedderman massacre."

"He's chosen to be alone, Lissa. Who do you have out here?" He wondered about her husband but said nothing.

"Old Vinegar Joe Riland, our chuckwagon cook, has been a loyal friend, but most of the hands, even Moss—well, they'll never forgive me for falling off my pedestal."

The doctor made a snort of disgust. "Durn fool place to put females, especially out here when we haven't got enough to go around as is. I debated about sending that wire. Probably shouldn't have done it, but then I wouldn't have had the chance to bring that youngun' into the world. What are your plans, Lissa? Do you intend to stay on in Wyoming?"

She sighed in perplexity. "I don't know. If Papa . . ." She swallowed painfully. "If Papa dies, then I'll have J Bar to think about. If he leaves it to me," she added in dull misery.

"He's still intent on your getting the divorce and giving up Johnny?" Although it was hard for Headly to believe, he knew Marcus would never change his mind.

"So he says, but so far he hasn't changed his will."

"He's just trying to wear you down. Don't let him." He did not want to say aloud that Marcus did not have much time left. "You 'n Johnny are his only rightful heirs."

Her eyes took on the hardness of polished amber. "I'll hang on, Doc, for my son's sake. Someday J Bar will be his."

"You think of askin' Lemuel for help? Maybe if you agreed to marry him, he'd agree to adopt Johnny." The idea did not sound likely to Headly even as he suggested it.

She shook her head vehemently. "No. I'll never marry again."

He studied her as they stopped in front of his dusty old buggy. "You still love him, don't you, child?" he asked gently.

Her eyes glistened as tears slowly flooded them. She blinked them back. "I was young and foolish then, but I've had to do a lot of growing up fast. He didn't trust me enough to take me with him.

I'm learning to live without him. I have to for Johnny."

"But you still hope he'll come back one day." The elderly physician patted her hand. "You take care of yourself and that boy. He's a fine 'un, Lissa. I'll be by next week to check on your pa. Send word if you need anything."

She smiled. "Thank you, Doc. You've been a true friend."

As he rode away, Doc Headly thought it was a damn sorry day when the only people a spunky young woman like Lissa Robbins could call friends were a broken-down sawbones and a crotchety old coot like Vinegar Riland.

The next morning, Marcus summoned a visitor. When Lemuel Mathis rode up to the ranch house, Lissa was at Vinegar's mess kitchen with Johnny. Germaine showed Mathis upstairs. As soon as she had closed the door, they entered into an earnest discussion.

Unaware of their guest, Lissa returned to the house an hour later and headed upstairs to put Johnny down for his nap. Lemuel stepped into the hall and turned to face her just as she came in the back door.

Eyeing the sleepy-eyed, dark-haired baby with obvious distaste, he nodded stiffly. "Miss Lissa."

"It's Mrs. Robbins, Mr. Mathis," she replied with a dare in her voice, rewarded when he stiffened with shock at her audacity. She smiled wryly. "There's no use pretending a civility neither of us feels, just to spare my father's feelings."

"If you cared at all for him, you would consider his feelings," he shot back.

It was her turn to bristle. "If I did not love my father, I would never have come back here, believe me." She turned and headed into her room, but his words stopped her.

"After he has time to rest up, Marcus will want to talk with you about a matter of grave importance. If you do care for him as you profess, I urge you to consider his proposal very carefully."

Her heart skipped a beat but she did not respond. "Good day, Lemuel."

When Marcus heard her knock several hours later, a bitter smile twisted his lips fleetingly. He had rested since Mathis left, storing up his badly waning energy for this. It would work, he could feel it in his bones. "Come in, Lissa."

"Lemuel said you had something to propose to me," she said tentatively to the cold stranger who had once been her indulgent father. *How haggard and old he looks.* Yet his pale blue eyes were as steely as ever.

"Rather, let's say I have terms for you, terms Lemuel has agreed to, although it took some talking to get him to agree, I don't mind telling you."

She sighed wearily. "We've been over this all before, Papa," she began, but he raised his hand, gesturing for her to be silent.

"You said you came back because you care for me—"

"You know that I do!"

"Then you'll honor my last request. I haven't got much time, Lissa—Doc Headly knows it and you should, too."

She felt tears burn her throat. *Why does it have to end this way, Papa?* "I can't marry Lemuel—I'm already married."

"Lemuel is a close friend of Governor Hale. He's agreed to expedite a quiet divorce."

She shook her head. "I won't do it."

His face broke into a cruel smile. "Forget about your false protestations of love for me. Think of that boy in there." He gestured angrily toward her room where Johnny slept.

"That boy is your only grandchild," she said with growing unease.

He ignored her words. "You'll get the divorce and marry Lemuel—be damn lucky to have him take you with a breed's brat in the bargain."

"I'm going to pack, Papa. Johnny and I will go back to Aunt Edith—"

"I don't think they'll have you once I write them describing how you laid a dirty half-breed killer and got yourself pregnant before he even married you."

She looked at him in dumb amazement, seeing the predatory ruthlessness he had never revealed to her before. "Ever since I was a child, I heard the stories about how you led the vigilantes who hung nesters in front of their wives and children. I never believed my papa could do such things. I see now that I was deceived." Her face was chalky.

"All I care about now is J Bar."

"Maybe it's all you ever cared about," Lissa replied evenly.

"You lost all claim to my love the day you let that trash touch you. Heed my warning, Lissa. You and that boy will have nowhere to go. I'll put you out to starve—or to sell your tarnished wares in Cheyenne to survive. But then you still might starve. Most white men won't take greasers or gut-eater's leavings."

"That speaks well for your paragon, Lemuel Mathis," she replied. Trying desperately to think calmly, she decided to stall until she could have some time to gather her scattered wits. "If I agreed to marry him, what guarantees do I have that he won't turn Johnny out? I certainly won't rely on his word or yours."

"I'll rewrite my will tomorrow, guaranteeing your son a sizable inheritance in trust."

"Half of J Bar," she said coldly and was rewarded when he paled in surprise.

"I won't have that breed claiming this land!" He leaned forward in bed, then fell back, gasping for breath.

Lissa's resolve almost broke. She fought the urge to rush over and help him sit up, to soothe his labored breathing. Sitting still with her nails digging into her palms, she met his icy glare with fathomless, sad eyes.

Finally he countered doggedly. "You sign the divorce petition and I'll give your son half the ranch, provided you agree to sell his share for full market value to Lemuel—your husband."

Lissa did not want J Bar, but it was Johnny's birthright. She could not see him cheated out of it, left impoverished in a hostile white world as his father had been. If Marcus destroyed her reputation in St. Louis, she and her son would be destitute. If only she had some way to reach Jess. But he was gone, perhaps even dead by now. Marcus had tried to have him killed the day he left her in Cheyenne. Perhaps someone else had succeeded where he had failed. How ironic. When Marcus had told her about hiring Pardee, she had packed up and fled to St. Louis in shock and despair. Now there was nowhere left to turn.

"Draw up your papers," she said quietly, walking to the door without a backward glance, unable to bear the look of triumph glittering in his ice-blue eyes.

Just before the door to Marcus's room opened, Germaine sped away from it and down the stairs before Lissa caught her eavesdropping.

Late that night, while everyone on the ranch slept, Germaine Channault slipped from the big house into the shadow of the cottonwood trees at the edge of the backyard. A tall figure with light, wavy hair waited for her.

"You're late," he accused her.

"I had to be certain everyone was asleep."

He made a sound of disgust. "Just so you don't fall asleep from nipping too much at the old man's whiskey."

"How dare you—"

"I dare because I have the right, and you know it," he replied harshly. "Now tell me why you sent for me. I could be out taking down another hundred head off the east range tonight."

"The old fool is forcing her to divorce the breed," she hissed.

He smiled in the darkness. "That could fit right in with our plans . . . if the old man dies as soon as she gets shut of Robbins. You could help him along. A pillow over his face in his sleep. You said he's weak as a newborn colt these days."

"How can you talk so?" she asked, her voice breaking.

"How can you hesitate now? You're the one who sent for me—had me hire Conyers to break J Bar."

"My plan did not include murder."

He laughed, an ugly, rasping sound. "Murder's murder to you only when it's *him,* not that breed or any of the rest of his hands. You listen good. As soon as Lissa gets shut of her husband, you kill the old man. Shit, he's gonna cash in anyway."

He turned to go, but she put a clawlike hand on his arm. "Be careful with that herd."

"I'm not a greedy fool like Tom Conyers was. I'm always careful. Remember what I said. You kill him. You have to do it." He vanished in the darkness.

Judge Sprague had been Marcus's attorney for thirty years, but he did not like this ugly business, not one bit. He shifted nervously, tugging on his tight waistcoat as Lemuel Mathis perused the papers Marcus Jacobson had instructed him to draw up. Lissa Jacobson Robbins sat dwarfed on the big horsehair sofa in his office. The poor thing looked pale as death. No female, no matter what she had done, deserved to be blackmailed, with her own child as a pawn. Sighing, Sprague looked away. If he did not handle the divorce, there were plenty of other lawyers in Cheyenne who would.

Mathis smiled and handed the papers to Lissa. "Sign here." He indicated a blank space with one blunt index finger.

Forgive me, Jess. She signed with trembling hands, realizing that this was exactly what her husband would wish her to do. *I won't let them see me cry,* she vowed, forcing back her tears.

"How long should the divorce take?" Mathis asked the old judge who had married Lissa to the odious killer.

Sprague shrugged his rounded shoulders. "I'll discuss it with Governor Hale first thing tomorrow morning."

Marcus awakened that night from a restless sleep in which he dreamed that Jesse Robbins sat at his desk, in his office, going over tally sheets and making entries in his books.

"No, no, you bastard." He rolled over, doubling into a ball as a searing pain ripped across his chest, setting his lungs on fire. He clawed for the bellpull to summon Germaine but could not reach it because the pain—God, the pain—doubled him up, squeezing every muscle in his body until he lay paralyzed.

Marcus knew that this time he was going to die. "Not yet! No, not yet," he croaked. Not until Lissa had married Lemuel—until he could be assured that Lemuel's issue, not the spawn of that mongrel, inherited J Bar. The vision of Jess at his desk flashed before his eyes again. Sweat beaded on his face as he gritted his teeth and extended his arm to reach for the bellpull a second time. He seized it in one clawing motion, but the force of his lunge threw him from the bed. By the time his body landed on the rug with a muffled thud, Marcus Jacobson was dead.

Across the hall, Germaine Channault slept through the noise, snoring softly, an empty decanter of brandy lying overturned by her bed-side table.

Judge Sprague had just removed his robes and walked over to his desk when Lissa Robbins knocked on his office door, then entered. She was pale but calm as she stood holding her small son in her arms. In fact, he had never seen her look so self-possessed.

"My father died last night," she said emotionlessly. "Tear up that petition for a divorce. I won't be going through with it now." Her eyes leveled on him as the color drained from his face.

Slack-jawed, he sat down, staring at her bright yellow skirt. She certainly was not dressed for mourning, but after the way things had turned out, he supposed it was scarcely surprising. He nodded, then struggled to clear his throat. "I—I'll have to talk to the governor."

"You do that," she replied, then turned and walked from his office.

Word of Marcus Jacobson's death spread through Cheyenne like wildfire. As Lissa walked down the street, people ogled her dark-haired baby and whispered behind their hands. They cast condemning looks at her, the old man's only child, clad in bright clothes, dry-eyed. A hussy who had been forced to marry that gunman and had borne his son. A few shuffled nervously and offered embarrassed condolences, their eyes skittering away from Johnny. She accepted their wishes with terse nods as she made her way determinedly down Eddy Street to Charlotte Durbin's Modiste Shoppe. She had an offer to make to the underpaid, overworked Clare Lang.

Smiling grimly to herself, Lissa prayed the dressmaker's assistant would agree to her terms.

When old Luke Deevers reined in the buckboard at the front yard of the ranch house, Lissa was exhausted. She could still hear Germaine's hysterical screams this morning when she had gone into Marcus's room and found him on the floor, stone cold dead. Lissa had come running to find her father lying doubled up on his side, his face contorted in a grimace of agony. He had died alone, trying to summon help.

The housekeeper had held him, wailing like a banshee while Lissa ran back to her room at the far end of the hall and picked up Johnny, who had heard the uproar and started to cry.

She supposed she should have felt something, some grief, some regret. After all, he was the doting papa who had lavished everything on her—until the first time she had defied him. Then he had turned on her just as ruthlessly as if she were a horse thief or a squatter.

I wonder if anyone besides Germaine will really mourn his passing? she thought as Luke tied the reins to the wagon brake and helped her down while Clare held Johnny.

Taking the boy from her, Lissa smiled at Clare, who was perched, nervous as a sparrow, on the wagon seat. "It'll be all right," she said gently.

The thin girl nodded, and the tassel on her bonnet bobbed in time. "Yes, ma'am." Her hands, red and work-worn, seized hold of the edge of the seat as she carefully climbed down with Deevers's aid.

"Please have one of the hands bring in Miss Lang's trunks, Luke." He nodded and climbed back on the wagon.

"Let's go inside and have some cool lemonade," she said to Clare.

"That would be lovely, Mrs. Robbins," the girl replied with a tremulous smile.

"Don't fret about Madame Channault." *Easy to say*, Lissa thought grimly, wondering if the housekeeper had calmed down yet.

After she had Clare sitting at the kitchen table sipping lemonade and bouncing Johnny on her knee, Lissa set out to confront Germaine. She climbed the stairs and knocked on the housekeeper's door.

Germaine opened it a moment later. Her hair hung in a ratty braid that fell over one shoulder, and her eyes were red-rimmed and swollen into tiny slits from crying. She clutched a half-full decanter to the bodice of her wrinkled dress.

"The men took your father's body to the undertaker in Cheyenne," she said sullenly.

"I know. I talked to Mr. Craig about the funeral while I was there. He's handling it."

"What do you want then? Have you come to gloat now that he's dead?"

"You're drunk again, Germaine," Lissa said levelly, ignoring the older woman's sharp tongue.

"I have the right to grieve."

"Do it on your own time. It should scarcely be any surprise that I'm discharging you. I'll see you have two weeks' extra pay when you leave in the morning. Luke will drive you to town."

The housekeeper's face seemed to narrow even more as she gritted her teeth in outrage, releasing a string of remarkable French profanity. "That old fool Deevers is the only man left who will work for one like you, *hein?* All the rest of the hands will quit. Perhaps that dirty little mess cook will stay— if you'd dare bring him into my kitchen!"

"It's *my* kitchen now, Germaine, and I've already seen to hiring someone to assume your duties. Start packing. You may have had some strange hold over my father, but your power died with him. I want you out of here in the morning, or I'll throw your belongings in a horse trough!"

"You dirty little Indian-loving whore!" Germaine took a step forward, clutching the decanter in her thin, veiny hands. She was wraith-thin but big-boned, taller than Lissa by at least an inch and squirrel-tough.

Lissa did not back down. She had waited too many years and taken too much sly, taunting abuse to let the old hag have the satisfaction. "If you wanted to flatten me, you should've stayed sober, Germaine." Part of her itched to take the bottle away from the drunken old bitch and club her with it. She waited as Germaine seemed to debate her course of action.

The housekeeper finally stepped back, bumping her shoulder against the door frame as a crafty smirk touched her lips. A feral light gleamed in her bloodshot eyes. "I will leave . . . for now."

Lissa turned to retrace her steps, then paused and said, "I don't fear, Germaine. Not anymore." In spite of her brave words, Lissa felt an eerie premonition that made her skin crawl as she walked downstairs. She decided to lock her bedroom door and guard Johnny carefully until Germaine Channault was off J Bar land.

Chapter Eighteen

Pride be damned, she was going to do it. Lissa strode briskly down to the stable with Cormac trotting by her side. Rob Ostler brought Little Bit out and handed her the reins.

"You sure you don't want me comin' along, Miz Lissa?" he asked with a worried frown creasing his youthful face.

"No, Rob. I'll be fine. I have my rifle," she patted the scabbard, "and Cormac for protection. You're needed here. We're too short-handed as is. Moss can't spare a single man."

Moss might even quit himself, she thought dispiritedly. The old foreman had been taciturn, unwilling to engage in the easy camaraderie of earlier years since he learned of her relationship with Jess. After Johnny was born and Marcus's health had failed, Moss's eyes accused her every time they met.

Since her father's death the preceding month, the hands had begun to quit, even refusing to work the vital spring roundup. Moss said they did not want to work for a woman, but Lissa knew he really meant that they did not want to work for a woman who had soiled herself by marrying a man of mixed blood, much less a woman who had carried his child well before their vows had been exchanged.

J Bar was down to forty men, and rustlers were stealing them blind. Lissa wondered if her ranch had again been singled out for the devastating raids. There was no way to be certain because none of her father's old friends would associate with her since her fall from grace. No one would share information with her.

Lissa was abasing her pride enough by riding to Cheyenne to ask Camella Alvarez if she knew how to send a message to Jess. She remembered the conversation between the lovers in that hotel alley the first night after Jess arrived in Cheyenne. They were old friends from Texas. If anyone could help her find her husband, it was the beautiful singer, and if anyone could save Johnny's inheritance, it was his father. She would not ask for herself, only for their son.

What would the "Spanish Songbird" say when Lissa walked into the theater? "She probably thinks we're sisters under the skin, and I guess she's right," Lissa said aloud. Cormac cocked his head as he loped easily alongside her pinto.

When they reached Cheyenne, she rode directly to the Royale Theater. It was nearly noon. Surely even the ladies of the evening had arisen by now.

A Fire in the Blood

The big frame building was three stories high with a false front across the top floor that boasted in two-foot-high red lettering, Royale Palace of Musical Entertainment. Beneath it in smaller print, Beautiful Women, Spirits, Dancing, and Variety Acts were offered. Lissa smiled wryly to herself as she dismounted and bade Cormac to stay. What exactly were variety acts?

Ever since her disgraceful marriage, she had been studiously avoided by the local women when she came to town; only a few men tipped their hats nervously when she passed. Everyone gossiped about her behind her back. Going into a den of scarlet poppies would certainly give them something new to talk about.

She took a deep breath and walked inside the slightly ajar front door. The room was immense, filled with tables and chairs, many overturned. Broken glass glittered dully on the oily plank floor. An ornate bar sporting a painting of a chain of nudes lined one wall. The front half of the place was dominated by the huge elevated stage, now empty. A smell of musty smoke and stale liquor filled the air.

"What kin I do for you, ma'am?" An enormous brute of a man walked around the bar, incongruously clutching a flimsy broom in his hand. His hulking body was slab muscle, and he was nearly seven feet tall, with a bald head that gleamed like a polished gemstone.

Lissa could sense his embarrassment. "I've come to see Miss Alvarez. Is she in?"

His scalp as well as his face pinkened. "Well, ma'am . . ." He shuffled from foot to foot nervously. "Miz Cammie, she had a real busy night last night." Pink turned to crimson. "That is, I don't think she's—"

"It's all right, Eustace. My—er, company, just left." Camella shoved one unruly clump of tangled black curls away from her face, then finished belting her pink silk robe as she descended the stairs opposite the bar. She wrinkled her handsome nose in distaste. "*Dios!* That was some fight last night. Get this sty cleaned up before we have the afternoon trade filtering in for cold beer," she instructed the big man.

She turned shrewd dark eyes on Lissa, studying her dusty riding clothes and long plait of burnished hair. "You are Jess's *gringa*."

"I'm Jess's wife," Lissa corrected firmly.

A look of grudging respect flashed across Camella's face. "I was going to send a note to you one of these days soon. Now you have saved me the trouble. *Bueno*."

Lissa's expression was guarded but curious. "Why would you send me a note?"

A wry smile curved Camella's generous mouth. "Not to check on my competition, *chica*." She tossed her clouds of tangled hair back as she motioned for Lissa to follow her. "Come with me. There is coffee out back in what passes for a kitchen."

Lissa followed the beautiful Mexicana, noting the lush way her figure filled out the thin silken robe. Perhaps this had not been such a good idea after all. What if Camella Alvarez had been in touch with Jess right along? He might have told her what a conniving little hussy Lissa had been, pursuing him with single-minded stubbornness. Maybe he simply preferred women like this one.

"Leave us, Gus, *por favor*," Camella said to the fat cook, who was carrying a huge tin basin of scummy dishwater. He disappeared out the kitchen door as Cammie poured two cups of inky coffee and handed one to Lissa, motioning imperiously for her to have a seat on one of the chairs lining the long table in a corner of the big room.

"I have heard your ranch is in trouble. That is why I was going to send the message."

"Why would you care?" Lissa could not help but ask. "Surely by now Germaine Channault has told everyone who'd listen what a mess I've made of my father's splendid empire, not to mention what a whore I am."

A hearty peal of laughter burst from Cammie. "You are like him, you know? Jess always says things up front, too." She sobered and studied the redhead. "I made him a promise the day he left— to look after you for him."

This was a surprising and unlikely turn of events. "But why would he ask you? You and Jess . . . well, I thought you'd be glad to see me fail."

"He had no one else in Cheyenne he could trust. And he knew if I gave my word, I would keep it," Cammie added with a touch of inbred Spanish pride.

"I stand to lose J Bar if I can't get more hands to work the roundup—and bring in someone to stop the rustlers. I need Jess to save J Bar for Johnny."

"You need Jess to be your husband, I think." She watched as Lissa's face flushed beneath her sun-darkened skin.

"He doesn't want that onerous duty—but his son has the right to his protection. Jess owes me that

283

much. I won't ask anything else," she said defiantly. "Do you know how I can get word to him?"

"*Sí*. His brother Jonah runs his ranch in West Texas."

Lissa almost dropped her cup. "Ranch! He owns a ranch?"

Cammie could imagine the reasons for Lissa's outrage. "It is a small place, nothing like your grand *estancia*. I will send a wire today, but it may take a while to reach Jess, for he is probably off for hire. Jonah will have to track him down."

"Just tell him it's for Johnny or I'd never ask." Lissa was too shocked by Camella's revelations to say anything else. She stood up to leave, but the singer reached across the table and placed a slim brown hand on Lissa's pale wrist.

"You named his son *Juanito*." A sad little smile settled on her lips. "It was his father's name, John."

"I know that," Lissa said tightly. "It also belonged to my maternal grandfather." She paused. "Thank you for everything, Miss Alvarez."

"Camella. Please call me Camella, if you would. After all, we are both outcasts in Cheyenne, no?" She cocked her head and gave Lissa a mischievous grin.

Lissa returned it. "Yes, I guess we are, Camella. At least the men will speak to you. I can't even hire enough men to get me through spring roundup."

Cammie chuckled. "With me it is the men who do the hiring—and the paying. Maybe I can help, though. I know a few grub-line riders who might work for you. Let me see what I can do."

When she emerged from the Royale, Lissa blinked her eyes at the dazzling midday sunlight, then stepped off the plank sidewalk to unhitch Little Bit.

"Well, looks as if you finally found the right kind of place to work. Only I don't think a decent cathouse would take you on." Yancy Brewster slouched against the corner of the building.

Lissa swept him with a contemptuous look. "Oh, I imagine they would, Yancy. After all, they let *you* in. But then, you have to pay them instead of the other way around."

She turned and swung up on Little Bit, but before she could ride away, Brewster had stepped down from the walk and stood in her way. "You dirty whore, pretending to be a fancy lady, 'n all the while spreading your legs for a breed."

Cormac approached, growling low in his throat. Lissa commanded him to stay, then turned her attention to Brewster contemptuously.

"You're drunk. Is that why Cy Evers fired you? Dellia's luckier than she deserves, having her father break her engagement to you."

"I'll get Diamond E yet—'n see you brought low, too." A sly smile wreathed his face. "Just see if I won't."

As Lissa pulled Little Bit's head around, Yancy was too slow to get out of the way. The horse's rump knocked him headlong in the mud while the pinto wheeled and galloped off.

By the end of the week, Lissa had half-a-dozen new hands, all hired through Camella's good offices. Moss still had not quit, for which she thanked what few lucky stars remained in her firmament, and the spring roundup was going as well as could be expected, considering that the rustlers were still on the loose.

The foreman reported another hundred head missing and suspected several thousand would be gone before they had finished the tally. Lissa racked her brains about who could be behind the destructive raids. Jess had wiped out a whole band of the thieves the previous year. Surely there could not be any survivors come back to take revenge on her. But it seemed even less likely that a whole new group of rustlers had settled in northeast Wyoming just to bedevil J Bar Ranch.

Was someone working on the inside again? Jess had caught two men last year who were in league with the thieves. Now, with her men's loyalties so strained, Lissa feared that one or more would not think it amiss to steal from the brand run by a fallen woman. But they would never dare steal from Jesse Robbins. *Jess, where are you?*

The summer wind was scorching, even this far north, Jess thought as he pulled the brim of his hat low over his eyes. Riding stoically beside him, Tate Shannon squinted at the horizon. Soon they would be in Cheyenne.

"We stoppin' in town for the night?" he asked Jess.

"No sense. Might as well ride on through to J Bar," his partner said levelly.

Shannon grunted but said nothing more as he studied Robbins's profile. After spending the past year riding with Jess, Tate knew how bad his friend hurt. Not that Jess had ever spoken of it, but Tate had watched the way his eyes would involuntarily light on women with red hair, and how he covertly watched small children. At first, when Jess was drinking pretty heavily, Tate had tried to get him to talk about his pain. But Jess refused, keeping it locked up inside. Finally Shannon had convinced Jess to go visit his kid brother. When they met up again in New Mexico, it seemed to Tate that seeing Jonah had given Jess a measure of peace. He pulled away from the beguiling oblivion of the bottle after that.

The black man had hoped in time that Jess might return to the wife and son he steadfastly denied, but he did not. They had worked several lucrative jobs in New Mexico. Even though Robbins no longer drank heavily, he took fearful chances with his life, almost as if he were tempting fate to put an end to his misery.

Then the wire had come from Jonah. Lissa's father was dead, and she was in danger of losing J Bar. She asked that he help her for the sake of his son. His son. Tate could still see the look on Jess's shuttered face when he read the words. He had a son. Never once in the past year had he spoken of the baby or speculated about its sex. After the long lonely months of denial, Jesse Robbins had at last been forced to confront his past. Tate Shannon only hoped he would come to his senses when he saw all that he had given up and take his family with him back to Texas.

"What you suppose she named the boy?" Shannon finally said, testing the waters.

"Let it alone, Tate. I don't intend to see him."

"That might not be an easy thing to do," Shannon said genially.

"It's a big ranch," Jess replied, indicating that the conversation was at an end.

They rode into the basin just as the sun was setting. An orange-and-gold haze surrounded the ranch house and lights glowed from inside, as if bidding them welcome. A few hands worked at chores down at the corrals or sat smoking and whittling.

"I'll head down to the bunkhouse," Tate said discreetly as they neared the big house. Without waiting for a reply, he turned his horse away, leaving Jess to greet his wife in private.

Lissa heard the approach of horses in the twilight stillness and laid Johnny in his cradle. She quickly walked down the hall to a window fronting on the road. When she pulled open the crisp yellow curtain and looked out, she dropped it with a sharp intake of breath.

Jess!

He had returned. Over the past two months, she had all but given up hope. But now that he was walking up to the front door, what would she say to him? She watched him stride arrogantly up the walk, graceful and cat-taut as he had always moved. His hat shaded those magic eyes as it had the first time she had seen him, and he still wore the lethal revolver in its well-oiled holster low on his hip.

"Damn, I look a fright," she muttered, peering into the hall mirror. She had spent the afternoon riding with Moss to review how many head had been stolen in recent weeks. Her hair was snarled and dirty, and she had an unbecoming dusting of freckles across the bridge of her nose.

Her heart thudded like a runaway freight train, and her knees were trembling like a yearling at a branding fire. "Get a hold of yourself," she scolded as she heard the front door open and Clare's flustered voice bidding him enter. Lissa finger-combed her hair and brushed off the riding skirt she had not had time to change when she returned from the range.

Jess stood in the front parlor where the shy little maid had left him. She was as timid as Germaine Channault had been outspoken. He smiled to himself, thinking of how much Lissa must have enjoyed discharging the old harridan. Then he heard footfalls on the stairs and stepped into the arched doorway so he could watch her descend. She was as slim as ever, and her glorious mane of fiery hair tumbled over her shoulders. He ached to bury his face and hands in the gleaming curls and press her soft curves against his hungry body. *Get a hold of yourself,* he thought in anguish, schooling his features into an impassive expression as she reached the bottom of the stairs.

Lissa could not keep her eyes from devouring him as he stood in the doorway, looking up at her. His clothes were dusty, and he needed a shave and haircut. How well she remembered the rasp of his whiskers over her sensitive skin. She wanted to touch the hair resting so inky-black against his white shirt collar. His face was guarded, and tension radiated from his body. She walked up to him without speaking, daring to stand close and look up into his silver eyes.

She still smelled of orange blossoms. His nostrils quivered as the old familiar fragrance swamped his senses. "Jonah's message said you were in danger of losing J Bar," he began without preamble.

She gave a shaky laugh. *Well, what did you expect—that he'd fall down and kiss your boots?* "Hello to you, too, Jess." She turned from his molten-silver gaze and walked down the hall to the library. If he wanted it to be all business, she would play by his rules.

"We've been under siege by rustlers since spring. Then after my father died, the hands started quitting."

He followed her into the book-lined room and watched as she opened a ledger and shoved it across the desk. "I'm sorry about your pa," he said quietly.

"You have a good deal to be sorry for, but as to my father—well, don't be sorry about him. I'm not. If he hadn't died when he did—" She stopped herself before she blurted out the rest. What was wrong with her? He obviously had returned strictly out of a sense of duty. Why debase herself any further?

Jess watched the play of emotions cross her face and saw her swallow what she had almost said. Marcus Jacobson had never been an easy man. "I take it he didn't forgive you. You could've left, gone back East."

"I did, but when he had the first heart attack . . . well, it's over and done now. Here are the books. You can see our losses."

He scanned the books and asked a few questions about where and when the cattle had been stolen.

She explained, then added, "I rode out with Moss this afternoon to see how bad it's gotten. I think he wants to quit, too."

An unamused smile crossed his face. "Now that I'm here, he just might do it."

She shook her head. "No, I don't think he will.

He may not like you but he'll respect your orders—so will the rest of the men. They always resent a woman trying to run a ranch."

He looked up sharply and closed the ledger with a snap. "I'm not staying, Lissa, once this is over."

"I know," she replied angrily. "You have your own place in Texas."

"Who told you that?" Already he had a pretty good idea, and he did not like it.

"My friend Camella," she dared him.

His eyes narrowed. "You better be a little more discreet in picking your friends."

"Really? As you well know, discretion was never one of my virtues. In any case, I'm every bit the outcast she is. And after all, Jess, we do have a great deal in common," she couldn't resist adding.

He ignored the innuendo. "You seem to be going out of your way to antagonize the good folks in Cheyenne."

"After marrying you, I didn't have to do anything else."

"I can't change that now, Lissa," he said bitterly. "I can only try to save your ranch."

"It isn't *my* ranch," she replied, willing him to mention Johnny.

"Well, it sure as hell isn't mine!"

"No, it's your son's—or do you even give a damn?"

"If I didn't, I wouldn't have quit a high-paying job and ridden eight hundred miles."

Realizing that a quarrel would solve nothing, Lissa seized control of her blazing temper. She would play a subtler game this time.

"I've had Clare fix a room for you. By the time you take Blaze to the stable, supper will be ready. We eat in the kitchen now, unless you'd prefer the

291

dining room." She held her breath.

He tightened his jaw. "I'll sleep in the bunk-house. Vinegar can get Tate and me something—"

"No!" She took a calming breath and repeated earnestly, "No, Jess. I'm not attempting to seduce you. If you're going to run this ranch, you can't sleep with the hired hands. Even Moss has his own cabin, and he's just the foreman. You are my husband—in name. Everyone would expect you to stay at the house." Her voice was low and hoarse, breaking as she added, "Don't shame me this way, Jess."

He felt as if he had just been poleaxed. How could he refuse? She was probably right. It would be hard enough to whip the J Bar hands in line and deal with that surly old ramrod. He would have to sleep under the same roof with his wife. *But not in the same bed.* "All right, Lissa," he said, expelling his breath on a sigh. "I better go talk to Symington first thing."

"I'll hold supper until you come back," she said and began to fiddle with the papers on the desk as he left the room.

Jess knocked on the door to Moss's cabin and waited as a chair scraped across the planks and footfalls sounded. The old man squinted into the darkness, then swore softly and stepped aside, letting Jess enter the cabin.

"Did Lissa tell you she sent for me?"

"Nope. But it don't surprise me none," Symington said sourly, his eyes moving from Jess up the rise to the big house.

"Yeah. I'm staying there, Symington. Does that put a burr under your blanket?" He was damned if he would explain his sleeping accommodations to anyone.

Moss shrugged disgustedly. "Hell, she married you all legal. It ain't none of my business."

"No. It damn sure isn't," Jess echoed softly. "I hear the rustlers have hit harder than ever this year."

Symington had a bottle of whiskey on the table along with a half-filled glass. He did not offer any to Robbins but gulped down the rest of the tumbler and ran his shirtsleeve across his mouth. "We're down over a thousand head this past month. Reckon some of them fellers you shot up musta come back."

"Only if they're wearing sheets and clanking chains," Jess replied without levity. "How many new hands hired on since I left last year?"

Symington barked a humorless laugh. "Only thing hands was doin' round here was quittin'— til Miz Lissa brung back six er seven new men from town. Over a month 'er so ago."

"I'll need a list of their names. Tomorrow first thing, you show me the places where you've been hit." He turned to go, then paused. "Lissa says you wanted to quit but didn't. You got any problem working for me, say so now. I don't like being crossed."

Cool gray eyes clashed head-on with angry brown ones. "I stayed on 'cause of Marcus Jacobson. I rode fer his brand since I was a slick-ears myself. If he wanted her 'n her boy to have J Bar—well, I reckon that's good enough for me. You bust up them rustlers. I won't cause no trouble."

"Good," Jess flatly, then walked out into the cool night air.

On the way up to the kitchen, he stopped at the pump in the backyard and washed up. As he dried off, he replayed the encounter with Symington in his mind. The old ramrod hated his guts as much as Jacobson had, but he was loyal to the brand. Moss would probably stay on after he left. That was good. Lissa would need the help. Maybe then she could hold on to the place for her boy.

Her boy. That's what Symington called his son. Not Marcus's grandson. Not even *your boy.*

Don't think about him. Jess finished rolling down his sleeves, combed his fingers through his wet hair, and headed toward the amber light of the kitchen and the rich smells of fresh rolls and fried chicken.

The table in the center of the room had two settings on its bright green cloth. Lissa placed a platter of golden chicken in the center of the table and fussed with two big linen napkins.

He observed the nervous little maid, who bobbed a curtsy to Lissa and then left the room, looking for all the world as if he might take a bite out of her instead of the chicken.

"Where'd you get her?"

"Clare used to work for the dressmaker in town, an old tyrant. I offered her a job when I fired Germaine."

He grinned. "No surprise there." As he pulled out her chair, the fragrance of orange blossoms smote him again. When she turned back to look up into his face with luminous gold eyes, his breath caught in his throat.

"Germaine always hated me, and I never understood why. She's in town now, living off the stipend my father left her in his will. It was a lot of money. I don't know why she doesn't go back to Canada."

"Why didn't you go back to St. Louis? Sell the ranch and let someone else deal with the rustlers?"

Her jaw stuck out at that stubborn angle he had learned to recognize. "No one's driving me away. This ranch belongs to our son." She waited for him to ask about his son, but he merely bit into his chicken. The meal continued with little conversation.

Finally he wiped his mouth with the napkin and pushed his plate away. "My compliments to Clare. That was excellent."

"Clare didn't cook it. I did." There was a note of unmistakable pride in her voice. She was pleased with the incredulous expression on his face.

"You couldn't boil water when I left here."

"I've learned a lot of things this past year. While I was living with Aunt Edith, I had her cook teach me. I rather enjoy it."

"You always plan on coming back here to fire Madame Channault?"

"Maybe," she replied enigmatically. "What did Moss say?"

"He'll stay. Said you hired some new men in town."

"That was long after the rustling had started again. I know what you're thinking, but this isn't an inside job unless one of the old-timers is involved."

He studied her. "You think that's possible?"

"Anything's possible."

"Any offers to buy the place?" He had some suspicions but did not voice them aloud for the present.

Shirl Henke

"Not directly." She paused, pleased with the glint of interest she saw in his eyes. "Lemuel Mathis hoped to marry me . . . if I got a divorce from you."

"I take it you turned him down," he said levelly, cursing himself for the flood of relief that she had done so.

"He only wanted the ranch, not us."

Mathis is a fool. "He might be behind the rustling then."

"I doubt it. Pompous old Lemuel, a cow thief?" She dismissed the idea as absurd.

Jess stood up and helped her with her chair. The small courtesy made them seem as intimate as a real husband and wife, used to sharing meals and conversation. Lissa found that she enjoyed the illusion far too much. He could not leave them again. She simply would not let him ride away without a fight.

"I'll show you to your room," she said breathlessly.

He gestured for her to lead the way, then picked up his saddlebags from the kitchen chair and followed her upstairs. When they reached the guest bedroom, the soft sound of a baby whimpering echoed from the other end of the hall.

"Johnny rarely wakes at night. Did I tell you I named him John? It was my maternal grandfather's name as well as your father's. He is John Jesse Robbins." *I'm babbling.*

Jess felt as if he had been kicked by a mule. *John Jesse Robbins. My son.*

Lissa noted his sudden look of vulnerability. "Would you like to see him?" The minute she asked, she cursed herself. *Too soon!* The expres-

296

sionless mask dropped in place again.

"No, Lissa. I don't think so." He closed the door to his bedroom, leaving her standing alone in the empty hall.

Chapter Nineteen

Jess awakened to the smell of frying bacon and freshly made coffee. In spite of being exhausted from the long ride, he had lain awake for hours the preceding night, listening for sounds of Lissa quieting Johnny and visualizing her with the baby. He swung his legs over the side of the bed and rubbed sleep from his eyes. A man could get used to sleeping in beds this soft if he were not careful. But Jesse Robbins was always careful.

"How the hell can I sleep and eat under the same roof with them?" he muttered to himself. There was a bar of soap and fresh water in the basin by the window. Pulling his razor from his saddlebag, along with a change of clothes, he shaved and dressed. Sooner or later he would see his son. Lissa would make certain of that.

Lissa. Just being in the same room with her during dinner last night had nearly driven him crazy.

Vowing to get the trouble at J Bar under control quickly and escape, Jess headed downstairs like a man facing execution.

Lissa was at the stove, deftly forking the last of a hearty rasher of bacon from the iron skillet. She set it on the table beside a platter of fluffy biscuits and a dish of freshly churned butter. Hearing his footsteps, she looked up and smiled. "Good morning."

He could not help but notice the delightful domestic picture she made in the kitchen setting. It was quite different from how he had first envisioned her when they met last year. The spoiled darling in silks now had a smudge of flour on her freckled nose and wore a simple yellow cotton dress covered by a white apron. Her hair was pulled atop her head in a loose bun with wispy tendrils escaping all around, as if she had fastened it hastily.

"How do you like your eggs?" she asked almost shyly.

"Cooked," he replied, "if I'm lucky."

She regarded his saturnine expression, trying to ignore the smell of shaving soap and leather. "You're lucky. Fried over easy all right?"

"Fine." He poured himself a cup of scalding coffee from the big granite pot on the stove and looked out the window.

"Are you always this sociable early in the morning?" she asked as she broke three eggs into the skillet. *How little I really know about him.*

He grunted a nonanswer and watched her with hooded eyes over the rim of his cup. After sipping the steaming brew he said, "Thank God your coffee's better than Vinegar's."

"Thank you, I think, knowing that ink he boils until it'll float a horseshoe."

"No such thing as coffee too strong—"

"Only men too weak," she chimed in, delighted when a genuine smile flashed across his face. She slid the eggs onto a warmed plate and handed it to him. "Help yourself to bacon and biscuits." She gestured to the place setting at the table as she used the back of her hand to push a wayward curl off her forehead.

Standing so close, Jess could see the fine sheen of perspiration on her face. He wanted to touch the damp, springy wisps clinging to her slender neck and run his fingers over the moist skin in the deep vale between her breasts. Instead, he took the plate with thanks and sat down.

Lissa quickly fixed herself an egg and joined him at the table. "What do you think Moss can show you this morning?"

He shrugged and took a swallow of coffee. "I'll see if they're still driving them along the same route as before. Whoever's doing this must be able to ship them from the railhead in Nebraska."

She digested the disquieting idea, then said, "You think it's someone in the Association, don't you? To have that kind of connection."

"Could be. Or it could just be an experienced thief who's worked out a deal with some shady buyer. That's the way it's usually done." He wiped his mouth with the napkin and pushed back his chair. "Thanks for the breakfast, Lissa."

She looked up at him with liquid gold eyes. "Be careful, Jess," she said solemnly.

He nodded and walked out the kitchen door, trying not to think about how Lissa would look in the kitchen of his small home, cooking over the open hearth. He did not own a fancy stove. *You could buy one,* an insidious voice whispered.

When he approached the corrals, they were deserted. Most of the hands had long since ridden out. Symington stood in the stable door, engaged in conversation with a big, burly man whom Jess recognized as the fellow who did the smithing for J Bar, Jethro Bullis. Two other men whose names he did not recall stood back, taking in the discussion. As he approached, their argument carried on the hot dusty breeze.

"I ain't stayin', Moss. Not with her up there spreadin' her legs for that damn breed," the smithy said, unaware of Jess's presence. "Where I come from, his kind don't screw white women."

"Jethro, you better throw a soogan over that mouth of yours—"

"Just where *do* you come from, Jethro?" Jess interrupted Moss in a low deadly voice.

The big man turned to Jess and spat a lob of tobacco juice into the dust near Jess's boots. "What business is it of yourn, ya red nigger?" His pock-marked face mottled with anger.

"I wondered if it was hell. That's where you're headed if your dirty mouth lets out another word about my wife," Jess said quietly.

Jethro threw up his hands with a nasty grin that revealed a mouthful of blackened teeth. "I ain't armed, breed. You wanna take me, you do it in a real man's fight."

"I don't brawl with troublemakers. You're fired. Pack up and get out." Jess watched in disgusted resignation as a few of the remaining hands began to drift toward them.

"You can't fire me. Only Mr. Jacobson's daughter can—"

"I told you not to talk about her," Jess said, wearily unbuckling his holster and handing it to Moss. Damn, if he broke a knuckle on this brute, he would be furious, but he dared not shoot an unarmed man, and he had to establish his authority over the hands at once. The smithy's ugly words about Lissa enraged him, but he forced himself to remain calm. Casting a swift glance around the corral area, he saw no potential tools to aid him in the uneven contest.

Jethro outweighed Jess by a good fifty pounds and was six inches taller. Grinning nastily, he stepped forward and swung. Jess ducked and landed a solid punch to the smithy's paunch as he sidestepped. However, instead of the gasp of expelled breath he expected from Jethro, all he heard was a slight snort. Beneath the fat was a wall of solid muscle.

Jess danced away as Jethro swung again, this time grazing his cheek. The smith was slow and clumsy but strong as a steer and mean as a bull in rut. Jess feinted to the right, then came in for a hard left jab that landed squarely on Jethro's jaw. The pain from that punch radiated all the way up his arm, but the smithy only shook his head and laughed.

By this time, those hands not yet out on the range had gathered and bets were being made with the odds favoring the smithy, who finally caught up with Jess long enough to strike him in the midsection. The force of the blow did expel his breath. Before he could move out of range, Jethro followed up with a second punch to his face that struck dangerously close to his right eye.

He gritted his teeth and sucked in some air to clear his ringing head. As he dodged away with Jethro in pursuit, Jess edged toward the open doors of the stable. If only he could lure the smith inside. He got his wish, but not in the way he wanted. Jethro took a punishing blow to his midsection but kept on coming, enveloping Jess in a deadly bear hug. They fell to the straw-covered ground inside the stable door.

Unfortunately, Jess landed on the bottom, the smithy over him, with a meaty fist raised. When he brought it crashing down to Jess's face, the smaller man twisted away, bucking off his opponent, whose fist connected with bone-jarring force with the hard-packed earthen floor.

As Jethro cursed, Jess rolled up and seized the first weapon that came to hand, a singletree taken off a broken set of harness. Big and clumsy, the wooden post left stinging splinters in his hands as he swung hard at the advancing smithy. Jethro went down to one knee, incredibly not knocked flat by the blow which had hit him squarely across his right shoulder and upper arm.

His damn arm isn't even broken! Jess braced himself and swung again as the smithy reached one huge paw toward the weapon. This time he connected with Jethro's hand and was rewarded by the crack of bones breaking and a sharp, high-pitched squeal of agony. Without pausing for breath, Jess swung again, this time striking the giant across his face. Jethro went down with blood spurting from his broken nose and lacerated mouth. He was out cold.

Jess dropped the singletree with an oath. His right eye was half-closed already, his head and left shoulder were pounding, and both hands felt as if someone had used them for pincushions. He staggered to the door, where the now subdued hands had watched the finale with awe-filled expressions on their faces.

"Show's over." Jess spat blood from a split lip and gestured to Jethro. "Pile him on a wagon and haul him into town. I'll send his wages. Anyone else want to quit, speak up right now." He swept the crowd with a shrewd glance. No one spoke up. "Good. Get back to work."

When they shuffled off, he turned to Moss. "Give me a few minutes to clean up, and I'll meet you back here."

Moss nodded in amazement. "Never seen the beat of it. Nobody's never knocked out Jethro afore."

"I reckon they just never had the right tool," Jess said grimly, then turned and headed to the house.

No one was in the kitchen when he walked in the door, but he could hear the sounds of voices upstairs. Trying to recall where Lissa kept her medical supplies, he began to search the pantry. Quickly locating the basket, he fished through it for what he needed, then carried it over to a small mirror above the sink.

He worked the pump handle until a gush of clean, cold water splashed into the basin, then lowered his bruised, bloodied face and hands into the cool depths.

Hearing the water, Lissa left Johnny with Clare in the sewing room and headed for the kitchen. She found Jess inspecting his injuries over the sink.

"My God, what happened to you?"

"A ton of blacksmith," he muttered.

She took the washcloth away from him and dabbed at his swollen eye. "Jethro?" She shivered in revulsion. "You're lucky he didn't beat you to death."

"He won't be beating up on anyone for quite a while," he replied with satisfaction.

She froze. "You didn't . . ."

He sighed. "No, I didn't kill him, but if I look bad, he looks considerably worse."

She resumed her ministrations. "How could you beat a man his size with your fists?" She took one hand and opened it, examining the abrasions on his knuckles and the red, angry weals on his palms.

"I couldn't. I used a singletree," he replied, wincing as he flexed his right hand.

"A singletree!" The image of Jethro Bullis being flattened by Jess wielding a huge wooden pole seemed ludicrous. A small hiccup of tension-purging laughter escaped her.

"I'm glad you find it amusing," he said testily.

She continued cleaning his wounds. "Well, not exactly amusing, but—" Suddenly it occurred to her that there must have been a reason for the brawl. She sobered. "Why did you and Jethro fight?"

His face grew shuttered. "Moss is waiting. Just let me dig out a few of these big splinters." He reached for a pair of tweezers.

"That cut above your eye should be stitched. Why the fight, Jess?" she repeated as she threaded a needle. When he did not reply, she said softly, "It was about me, wasn't it."

"No. It was about me," he said flatly.

Realizing that she would get no further satisfaction from him, she changed the subject. "I can't reach you standing up. Sit down," she instructed, holding up her needle.

He pulled over a kitchen chair and straddled it, leaning his arms on the back. Lissa stood close beside him and carefully put two tiny stitches into the angry gash over his right eyebrow.

As she worked, she chewed on her lip in concentration, remembering how she had sewn up his injuries last year. The same electric tension crackled between them now, like lightning before a high plains thunderstorm.

Jess, too, was unable to forget the past. His hands gripped the chair back tightly, then quickly let go as pain from the splinters lanced deeply into his palms.

"I'm sorry I hurt you, but I don't think it'll leave much of a scar. Your eyebrow almost hides it," she said breathlessly, unable to meet his eyes.

"It's my hands, not the cut," he replied, also unwilling to look up into her lovely face. But he could see the sweet swell of her breasts. He felt himself growing hard and swore silently as she took one of his hands in hers and turned it palm up.

How small and pale her hands looked, holding his larger bronzed one. How well she remembered the way those long, beautiful fingers felt caressing her. She forced herself to pick up the tweezers, praying she could stop trembling. She set to work, pulling over a dozen jagged bits of wood from his hands. Then she bathed them with alcohol and put a healing ointment over the abraded knuckles and raw sores in his palms.

"I really should bandage them—"

"No. I've got to be able to use my hands or I'll be a dead man."

He started to get up just as she reached over to the sink to set down the ointment jar. His arm brushed her breast as he stood. Her eyes flew up, startled and fathomless, locked with his. They stood frozen that way for a moment, a scant inch apart yet not touching, their breaths melding together in the summer heat.

Lissa reached up tentatively, almost as if she were afraid of frightening him, and caressed his cut lip with her fingertips.

Suddenly Jess grabbed her with both hands and pulled her flush against his body, lowering his mouth to hers. She opened for him, feeling the hot fury of his invasion, tasting the mixture of coffee and blood in his mouth. She cupped his bruised face in her hands and gentled his fierce, angry kiss, then laved at his cut lips delicately with the tip of her tongue. He nearly went mad with the pleasure of her exquisitely feminine touch. A trembling began deep in his gut, radiating outward in undulating waves until it reached his fingertips. He started to pull at the buttons on her bodice.

The low, keening wail of a baby broke the summer stillness and Jess froze. Struggling with every fiber of his being, he set her away. When he released her, his hands left greasy smears on her sheer cotton dress. "I've marked you, Lissa," he said raggedly.

Then he turned and walked quickly out the door.

* * *

Jess and Moss rode over the places where J Bar cattle had been taken recently, confirming his suspicions about the professional nature of the thefts. They spoke little, only exchanging essential information about the rustling and the details of running a large spread.

On the way back toward the ranch house, they saw the vultures circling at a distance. When they rode to investigate, they discovered the source of the trouble at the largest water hole within twenty miles of the main buildings. Over a dozen cattle were dead, some lying half submerged, others nearby.

"How long you think they've been dead?" Jess asked as they examined one steer's swollen belly.

"In this heat . . . hell, hard to say. A day, maybe, but no more. The hands check here often."

"It's poisoned, all right," Jess said, gingerly tasting the tainted water.

Symington threw down his hat and cursed long and colorfully. "Stealin' I can understand, but this is just plain dirt-ornery."

Robbins's eyes narrowed. "Not if they want to force us to drive the cattle to the upper Lodgepole for water."

The ramrod's face was red with fury as he spat in the dust. "Far enough to the east to string 'em out. Easy pickins for rustlers."

"Yeah. Especially since we're so short-handed."

"What you gonna do?" Moss asked as Jess mounted Blaze.

"Tell Lissa I've ridden into town for the night. Don't tell her about the poison. Post a sign and get all the men you can spare to round up the cattle and start moving them nearer safe water. Post a guard on each clean hole, but I doubt they'll poison any others. This one's enough to do the job."

"I ain't got enough men as it is now. How the hell am I gonna do all that?" Frustration reddened the older man's weathered face.

"I'll see who I can hire in Cheyenne. I'll also wire for some guns."

"We'll need a new smithy, too," Moss said wearily, then added, "Jethro always was a ugly troublemaker."

"He got a lot uglier this morning," Jess replied as he turned Blaze toward Cheyenne.

Word of his return to J Bar had preceded him, just as he'd expected. People whispered furiously and watched him with hard, avid eyes, wondering how he had been beaten up and why he was in town. Some were just curious, but many were sullenly hostile. He ignored them as he headed to the Cheyenne Club. Tying Blaze at one of the front hitching posts, he approached the big porch that surrounded the elegant three-story building.

The imposing structure was made of stone with a mansard roof and eight brick chimneys. Several members of the exclusive men's club were standing near the front door, dressed in wool suits and boiled shirts in spite of the blistering summer heat. To say they looked astonished as he approached would have been an understatement.

Jess paused at the top of the steps and sized up the cattlemen, letting his cold gray eyes and the hand resting ever so lightly on his Colt intimidate them for a moment. Then he said, "I'm looking for Lemuel Mathis."

The taller of the two men, an old fellow with thick white hair, returned Jess's hard-eyed inspection. "He's probably in the smoking room." He turned to his companion and said, "Josh, why don't you fetch him for Mr. Robbins?"

The younger man reddened but spun on his heel and vanished inside.

"You know me," Jess said levelly.

"I know of you, yep. Heard you're taking over J Bar."

He waited, but Jess did not answer the implied question. Instead he said curtly, "Tell Mathis I'll be at the Royale. I need to talk to him about poisoned water." He turned and strolled down the steps, leaving the old man staring gape-jawed at his back.

By the time Jess had ordered his second beer, Mathis entered the music hall. Jess observed his approach with satisfaction. One question of his was answered. The arrogant Association president was interested enough in J Bar business to humble himself by meeting with Jesse Robbins. He raised his glass in a mock salute, then downed the beer. "Pull up a chair, Mathis."

The older man stood by the table, hands clenched as if trying to decide which looked less conspicuous, standing alone or sitting at the same table with the gunman. He opted for the latter course of action. Mathis eyed Jess's battered face but made no comment about it. "What's this about poisoned water?"

"The Big Basin water hole. A dozen head dead this morning." Jess watched Mathis's movements as he digested the news. If it was news.

"You sure poison's in the water? Couldn't be something the beeves got a hold of and ate nearby?"

"It's the water. Any ideas where a man could get his hands on enough arsenic to pollute a spring-fed pond that size?"

Mathis's florid complexion seemed to redden subtly, but he betrayed no other emotion. "The Association orders it in quantities. We sell it at cost to members for killing varmints."

"Any member make a sizable purchase lately?" Jess asked as he rolled a cigarette and lit it.

Mathis wrinkled his nose at the aroma. He smoked only the finest Lazo Victoria cigars that the club purchased in New York. "No one I know of. This means you'll have to move the herds farther out."

"You catch on quick." Jess smiled coldly. "I'll be needing more hands. Any idea who in Cheyenne might be willing to work for me? I'll pay top dollar."

"Why the hell did you come back, Robbins?" Mathis asked. "I would've helped Lissa."

"Lissa asked me," Jess replied, watching Mathis's building anger.

"You'll only cause more trouble."

Jess shrugged. "Considering how things stand at J Bar right now, I don't see how. If you run across any hands looking for work, I'd be obliged if you mention J Bar to them." He stubbed out his cigarette and stood up just as Camella Alvarez came walking across the crowded floor.

"Someday Lissa will regret ever laying eyes on you," Mathis snarled.

Shirl Henke

"My wife's already been made aware of her mistake," Jess said softly. Then he walked away from Mathis.

Cammie watched Lemuel Mathis storm out of the place. "I can't believe he actually sat down with you."

"Oh, I can," Jess said darkly. "You look good, Cammie." She was dressed in a skin-tight gown of glittering light blue material. Her breasts swelled above the plunging cleavage. A bright blue plume was perched jauntily in her upswept hair.

"And you look terrible, *querido*. What happened? Someone at J Bar did not welcome you back?" She touched his bruised jaw tenderly, her hand winking with fake sapphire rings.

He winced, then grinned at her, knowing she could read the haunted look in his eyes. "Why in hell did you tell Lissa about my ranch?"

She smiled as he signaled the barkeep for a bottle and tossed a silver piece on the bar to pay for it. "She came to me for help. You asked me to give it."

He poured a stiff drink and belted it down. "You could've sent for me without telling her."

She studied him. "She is planning to move south, yes?"

"She is planning to move south, no," he said tightly, pouring another drink. "It just created . . . another misunderstanding."

She smiled sadly. "Have you seen your son? I would bet he is *muy macho*."

"I wouldn't know. Look, Cammie, I need some information."

"I will do what I can, Jess. I always have, no?" She could feel his anguish but knew it was useless

312

to say anything more. He had come back. For now, that was enough. "What do you need to know?"

She almost suggested going to her room, but quickly realized that would create ugly rumors which would eventually get back to Lissa. Instead, she gestured to a deserted table against the back wall with no view of the stage. He regarded her with a raised eyebrow. "Since when have you become so discreet, Cammie?"

"Since you became married, *querido*," she retorted, pulling up a chair and wriggling her rounded buttocks onto the seat, no mean feat in that narrow skirt, in spite of its daring slit up the side.

Ignoring her remark, he explained about the poison and his suspicions.

"So, you think Mathis may be trying to ruin J Bar?" She drummed her nails on the scarred table, narrowing her big dark eyes in concentration.

Jess shrugged. "He always figured to marry Lissa and inherit the ranch. Once that was out, he might not be above wanting to see her lose it, maybe even buy it cheap when she was forced to sell out."

"But that does not explain the earlier thieves. Then he believed he was going to marry her," she argued.

"It could've been a ploy to get the old man to put pressure on her because he wanted someone capable of rescuing the place from the rustlers. Hell, I don't know." He stared into the amber liquid in the glass. "Just keep your ears open about the arsenic." He drank the whiskey and refilled his glass.

"You will find no answers there, *querido*."

"I'll find oblivion. That's good enough for now."

Shirl Henke

"You should go home to your wife and son, Jess. Lissa wants you back." Her throat ached with tears.

"Then she's an even bigger fool than I am." He polished off the drink and doggedly poured another.

Chapter Twenty

Early the next morning, while Jess was wiring New Mexico for reinforcements and nursing the worst hangover of his life, Lemuel Mathis rode up to the big house at J Bar. He dismounted and had walked as far as the first step when Cormac, out for his morning exercise, came racing around the side of the building. The big hound ground to a halt with a low growl. His raised hackles made him look even more formidable.

Lissa heard the sounds of growling and cajoling from the upstairs window. She ran down the steps, shrieking commands to Cormac, while at the same time trying to smooth her tangled hair and finish buttoning her dress. She arrived at the front door just after the dog had backed Mathis against the wall and was leaning over him with a wolf-sized paw on each side of his prey's head.

"Get this timber wolf in dog's fur off me or I'll

be forced to shoot him, Lissa."

"Cormac, down!" Lissa yelled as she burst out the door.

Perspiration was running down Lemuel's face. Judging by his ashen complexion and the way the dog had immobilized him against the wall, it seemed unlikely that he would be able to free his gun, much less fire it at his intended target.

"Lemuel, I've never understood why Cormac takes such exception to you," she said, realizing that the hound did not plan any immediate mayhem. Actually, it was rather amusing to see the pompous Lemuel Mathis, Cheyenne civic leader, plastered against the wall with his face pressed away from Cormac's fetid breath.

Forcing herself to keep a straight face, she gave another stern command to the great beast. Once convinced that his mistress was serious, he gave up the game and bounded away, leaving Mathis to peel himself from the wall and dust off his jacket. The back of his brown suit coat was liberally smeared with powdery whitewash, but she did not call that detail to his attention.

"A delightful welcome for your friends, Lissa," he said testily as he stalked, red-faced, through the open door.

She had never particularly considered Lemuel Mathis a friend, but decided not to mention that either. "What brings you to J Bar so early in the day?" she asked, ushering him into the parlor.

Johnny let out a loud squeal of delight from the kitchen, where Clare was feeding him a bowl of oatmeal. She noted a look of anger flash across Mathis's face, but he quickly erased it and answered her question.

"I know you've been having trouble with your hands quitting since Marcus died," he began.

"Yes, I've been short-handed for several months, Lemuel," she said, trying to keep the asperity out of her voice. What was he leading up to?

"Well, I certainly don't want you to lose J Bar, with the rustling problem and everything," he said solicitously.

Like hell you wouldn't. "I don't plan to lose it. That's why I sent for Jess." She observed the sly expression that came over his face with unease.

"That is one reason why I'm here, Lissa. I saw your . . . husband in town last night." He said the word 'husband' with obvious distaste.

"Jess went to wire for more help and make inquiries about hands for hire," she replied.

"He also went to become intoxicated at the Royale." With satisfaction, he watched her flinch.

"And you couldn't wait to rush here and tell me," she said stiffly, jumping up from her chair.

"He spent the night with that Mexican harlot, Camella Alvarez."

Lissa blanched. "I don't believe it."

He, too, rose and nodded condescendingly. "Believe it, my dear. His kind will always seek out their own. I felt you should know. Everyone else in Cheyenne does by now. If you don't trust me, you can always make inquiries with some ladies of your acquaintance. Mrs. Wattson, perhaps?" he suggested reasonably, knowing Louella would cut Lissa cold.

With a sinking heart, Lissa realized that Lemuel was not lying. The matter would be too easy for her to verify. All she would have to do was eavesdrop at the Union Mercantile. She faced Mathis's false solicitude, saying, "I thank you for your concern, Lemuel, but what's between Jess and me is for us to settle."

"Divorce him, Lissa," he said intensely. "He isn't worthy of you. It was Marcus's dying wish."

"It was also his dying wish that I abandon my son and turn over J Bar to you. I won't do that, Lemuel," she said bitterly. "This is Johnny's birthright, and I mean to see that he keeps it. You, my father, and Jess can all three go to hell!"

He gave her a look of scathing anger, then walked stiffly to the door. "When you're so far in debt that you'll need a loan to keep J Bar, come see me. Perhaps by then you'll be ready to listen to reason." He walked out and slammed the door.

Lissa wished that Cormac had eaten him for breakfast.

Germaine Channault inspected the selection of ready-made dresses with disdain. "Cheap factory-sewn junk," she murmured beneath her breath. Beside the dresses a display of straw bonnets added a touch of bright color to the otherwise drab emporium, which was cluttered with everything from bolts of fabric to stacks of tinned meats and rolls of the controversial new barbed wire. The smell of tobacco, musty cloth, and stale coffee hung in the dust-filled air.

Pretending to be absorbed in shopping, she watched the flow of traffic through the busy mercantile, searching for the man she had summoned. Finally she spotted him in the section reserved for cook pots and tin dishes. She walked casually over to inspect a heavy iron skillet, then slipped into the cluttered alcove where she could speak with him and not be observed.

"Where have you been? *Merde!* I have been waiting forever," she whispered, feeling a distinct urge to cosh him with the heavy implement.

"In case you haven't noticed, I have a long way to ride. And keep your voice down. I've poisoned the water just as we planned. I figure the J Bar ramrod will move the cattle within the week, and we'll be ready to take them. It'll be real easy."

"You think so, *hein?*" She looked around them, but no one was anywhere near. "I have some news for you. That *bâtard* Robbins has come back." At his muttered curses, she smiled bitterly. "Now things are no longer so simple. He could ruin our plans."

"No. I can handle a dirty Injun. Shit, he's even part greaser. Couldn't be more worthless."

"That is precisely what Conyers and those fools with him thought! They're all dead now. You will do nothing rash, do you understand me?" She placed one reddened bony hand on his forearm with surprising strength.

"I understand," he said irritably.

"*Bien.* I will consider how to handle this Jesse Robbins. For now, be very careful when you take those cattle. He came to town yesterday to wire for more of his kind."

"It'd be easier if we disposed of him before they arrive," he said.

She made a curt dismissive gesture with her hand. "Let me consider it. I will think of a way to dispose of the cur."

He grinned wolfishly. "Then Lissa 'n that boy are ours."

319

* * *

Jess arrived at the ranch house late that afternoon and headed straight to the stables where he encountered Tate grooming his horse.

The big man's smile was blinding in the dim light. "You look like hell," he said cheerfully, noting Jess's bloodshot eyes and exhausted expression. "While you were in town, Miz Lissa had a caller."

Jess pulled his saddle off Blaze and slung it across the wooden rail. "Who was it?"

"None other than Lemuel Mathis. Rooster-crow early this morning, he come ridin' up like his tail feathers was on fire. Now what do you make of that?"

"I saw him yesterday. He left his fancy club and came to the Royale just to talk to me. I wonder what the hell he's up to," Jess mused.

Shannon's expression sobered. "You see Cammie?"

Jess gave him an irritated glance, then began rubbing Blaze down.

"Mathis is still pesterin' her to divorce you and marry him," Tate said when Jess remained silent.

"Maybe she ought to do it. I'll know one way or the other if he's mixed up in the rustling in a few weeks. If he's not . . ." The image of Mathis touching Lissa made his guts knot, but he forced the thought aside.

"You're dumb as dirt, Jess, you know that? That hard-eyed old galoot ain't fit to raise your son. Why, no tellin' what he'd—"

"Lissa will protect the boy," Jess interrupted in a tight voice.

"The boy's got a name. Your daddy's name. He's

entitled to have a daddy just the same as you did, if you ask me."

"Well, I sure as hell didn't ask you, now did I, Tate?" Jess said furiously, throwing down the body brush and walking the big black into his stall.

As he left the stable, Shannon's low mutterings carried after him. "Damn fool's stubborn as a lantern-jawed jackass."

Lissa watched Jess approach the kitchen. Her hurt and anger had simmered until it was scalding. Before he reached the back door, she went to the library, where she knew he would eventually look for her. She sat down with the open ledger and tried again to read the columns of numbers, but her concentration was hopelessly broken just thinking about Lemuel's accusations.

Please let me be wrong, Jess.

The sound of his footfalls was low and quiet when he finally approached the library door. He knocked briefly, then opened the door when she murmured for him to enter.

"You must have had a lot of business in town. It sure couldn't have taken two days just to send a wire. I didn't see any new hands riding with you either," she added, knowing her voice had an accusing edge to it. She was suddenly very glad that Clare had taken Johnny upstairs.

His eyes swept over her bent head, noting the crumpled papers and scratched-out tallies littering the desk. Mathis's gossip must have scraped the bottom of the trough in spite of Cammie's bow to propriety. "I hired two men and sent them out to Moss. I had other things to take care of."

She stood up and looked at him, then walked around the desk. "You need a shave and a bath.

She sniffed haughtily. "You reek of cheap perfume. Camella's fragrance?"

"I was too hung-over this morning to risk shaving," he replied coolly. "As to the perfume . . ." He shrugged. Cammie had hugged him good-bye the night before when she had poured him into a hotel room. "It lingers, I suppose. Old Lemuel Mathis must've broken a leg rushing out here to tattle." *The lying bastard.* He reached for a decanter of whiskey and poured a shot into one of Marcus's fancy cut-crystal tumblers.

She watched him toss down the drink, feeling something wither and die deep inside of her. "You bastard. How could you—and with *her* of all women."

He smiled coldly. "Just exactly how many women do you think a man like me can get in Wyoming?"

She slapped him in pure reflex. The sound was magnified in the evening stillness, like the crack of something breaking. Her heart.

He could see the spitting fury in her amber eyes and grabbed her wrist as her hands curved like claws. The suddenness of the movement threw her off balance and she fell against him, breathing rapidly. Her breasts pressed against his chest as she tried to push away, kicking at him with slippered feet.

"Let go of me, you miserable, whoring—"

When she raised her other hand, he grabbed it too in self-defense. "Calm down, Lissa. This is no time for a tantrum. I thought you were trying to convince me you're all grown up." He felt her go very still in his arms.

Lissa forced her chin up and looked into his eyes. They glowed like silver in the fading light, revealing the intensity of his emotions, emotions he was trying not to reveal.

He could smell orange blossoms and feel the old familiar pressure of those soft, luscious breasts, grown fuller now. Feeling himself losing control, he shoved her back and released her.

"What I do in town—and with whom—is none of your business, Lissa. I told you nothing could ever work out between us. As soon as the ranch is safe, I'll be gone. Next time you're in trouble, you'll have to get someone else to bail you out." He kept his voice level and low, feeling a stroke of anguish for every word he spoke.

His face was set in harsh, forbidding lines, yet she had felt him trembling when he pushed her away. "For a man who just spent the night with a lusty woman like Camella, you don't seem very well satisfied, Jess." She dared him boldly, moving closer. He stepped back. She smiled. He poured himself another drink.

"Like I said, you need a bath. I'll have Clare heat the water." She turned and swished from the room, then paused at the door and added, "Oh, the tub room is at the end of the hall opposite my bedroom."

He nodded curtly, wanting to refuse but too hot, achy, and generally miserable to resist the temptation, which he knew entailed a great deal more than soaking in a bathtub.

Later, when he heard the maid carrying water upstairs, he closed the tally book and walked into the hall. "I'll carry those buckets. They're too heavy for a woman your size," he said to Clare.

She took one look at his battered face and nearly dropped the heavy buckets of steaming water before he could take them from her. "Yes, sir, Mr. Robbins." Bobbing her head, she rushed back toward the kitchen as if her skirts were on fire, calling out, "There's more hot water on the stove."

Once he had filled the big porcelain tub, Jess searched the commodious room's cabinets until he located what must have been Marcus's soap, a plain, unscented bar. Setting a big thirsty towel beside the tub, he walked over to the door and grimly turned the key in the lock. Lissa was the most incredibly determined female he had ever met.

For a while, he had had her believing that he had slept with Cammie, but she was becoming alarmingly perceptive—or he was becoming disgustingly transparent. With a muttered oath, he pulled off his boots, then hung up his guns and shed his clothes. Standing in the middle of the floor, he looked at the filled tub. It was sparkling white and oversized, probably custom-built for Jacobson's long legs. The old boy would be rolling in his grave now if he could see Jess climbing into the clean water, to pollute it with his dirty Indian and Mexican blood.

Blood literally. He winced as the hot water soaked into the cuts and abrasions on his hands. A damn good thing no one in town had started trouble. His gun hand would not be reliable for several days. He laid his head back and soaked, trying to keep his mind on the problem of the rustling and off Lissa and his son.

Finally he lathered up, starting with his head and proceeding down until he was well scrubbed. So busy was he, splashing and washing, that he did not hear a key turn from the other side of the lock. When the door opened, his head jerked up and water flew in every direction. He squinted through eyes burning with soap.

"You forgot to bring up rinse water," Lissa said matter-of-factly as she crossed the floor carrying a big bucket of cool water. She wore a thin, peach-colored robe, belted securely around her waist. The front of it split to her knees when she walked, revealing a delectable length of calf and slim ankle. "Kneel in the tub and I'll pour it over your head."

"How the hell did you—"

"I have a master key to all the locks," she interrupted smugly.

"I'll remember that. Put the water down. I can rinse myself." He looked up at her, as out of sorts as a wet tomcat.

Lissa did not move, but her eyes did, devouring every soap-covered inch of his body, so familiar now. She took in the scar across his side, a neat, narrow ribbon of white against his bronzed skin. "You never did tell me how you got my stitches out," she said in a suddenly thickened voice.

"I cut them out with that." He gestured to the evil-looking Bowie knife attached to his gunbelt. "Will you get out of here before this soap hardens and I crack?" he said testily.

"And here I was going to offer to dry your back," she replied breathlessly. "Oh, well, suit yourself." She bent over and set the big bucket of water on the floor beside the tub. It was filled to the brim and some sloshed over the edge, wetting the front of her robe. The sheer fabric clung to her breasts, revealing that she wore nothing beneath it.

Lissa brushed at the offending droplets. Her nipples hardened beneath the silk. "How clumsy of me." She looked up at him and read the molten desire in his eyes. "Are you certain you wouldn't like me to rinse you off? The water's cool . . ." she added suggestively.

"Get out of here, Lissa," he said through clenched teeth, followed by a string of colorful epithets.

"Whatever you say, Jess." She stood up and walked primly from the room, a slow smile spreading across her face as she called over her shoulder, "Dinner will be ready about seven."

Although Lissa set out splendid beefsteaks to fry and cut up fancy string potatoes, along with a slow-simmered pot of snap beans, Jess did not eat supper at the house that evening. While she was busy in the kitchen, he slipped from the house and rode out as if the devil were chasing him.

Seeing him, Lissa muttered to herself, "You can use the steak for that shiner! Perverse man." She threw down the spoon with which she had been stirring the beans. As if to underscore her ire, Johnny planted one chubby fist in his mashed potatoes, sending them squishing all across the table and over poor Clare who was luckless enough to be holding the squirming boy. She turned a baleful eye on the baby, who gurgled innocently. "I'm sorry, Clare. I'll take him."

"That's all right, Missus, he's such a love. I don't mind, really." She fussed with him, cooing and coaxing until he had eaten most of the remaining soft food.

Ever since the rustling had grown worse and men started quitting, Lissa's increasing anxiety had caused her milk to begin drying up. She could feed him once or twice a day, but that was about all. His diet had to be supplemented with other foods. It was fortunate he'd begun teething quite early. At least one male Robbins was cooperating. She smiled at the messy child as Clare was cleaning him off.

"I'll take him now." She sighed. "Why don't you fix us each a small portion of that steak and potatoes while I change him? No sense waiting for his father," she added tartly.

Jess rode aimlessly for several hours. When it was full dark, he found himself at the cold spring pond that had been their trysting site the preceding summer. He slid off Blaze and walked to the edge of the water. "Just what I need, an ice-cold drink to cool off."

He cursed himself for coming here of all places, as if he needed further reminders of how desperately he wanted her. She was playing with him again, teasing and taunting, just as she had before, and this time there was no Marcus Jacobson to interfere. They were married.

Lissa loved him. Jess accepted that fact with an almost reverent awe, but he could not bear to see that very wondrous love die by inches. And he was sure that if he stayed with her it would slowly die. They would be snubbed, even verbally insulted. Their complete isolation would grow. And the boy, his son, would be just as much a pariah as he. Perhaps Johnny would come to hate his father for the curse of his blood.

If he stayed at J Bar and lived in Marcus's house, Jess knew he would come to despise himself more every time he saw the disgust in other men's eyes. He could not live off a woman's largess. If he had been the kind of man who could, Lissa would not have loved him in the first place. The bleak alternative of taking her and Johnny to his hard-scrabble

327

spread in Texas was an even less inviting option.

"I have to finish this work and get the hell out of here," he snarled, furious with her stubborn determination to use her woman's wiles on him once more. At least she had not tried to force him to see his son. Jess was not certain he could survive that.

"What I need is a good stiff drink."

Remembering that Vinegar kept a stash of bad but potent whiskey in his cookhouse, Jess rode back to the ranch. He was in need of a sleeping potion.

Lissa could not sleep that night, worrying about where Jess had gone. Perhaps she had played her hand too quickly. Surely he would not just ride away. Would he? Her restlessness awakened the baby, who fussed. She went over to the crib and picked him up.

"You're probably hungry, aren't you? Let's see if I can feed you a bit more." She started to unfasten the front of her nightgown, then stopped, deciding to go downstairs and get the book she had been reading. Perhaps if she had her mind occupied by something other than Jess, she would be soothed and able to give Johnny more milk.

She carried the baby downstairs, stopping by the kitchen for a glass of milk for herself, then went to the library and picked up her copy of *Tom Sawyer*. Arranging herself comfortably in the big overstuffed chair by the window, with the lamp burning steadily over her shoulder, she settled in to feed Johnny, who fussed until he was tugging greedily on her nipple. Stroking the soft hair on his dark head, she felt blissfully at peace.

"Still something left for you, little one," she said softly as she opened the book and began to skim for her place.

Jess walked up from the stable and quietly entered the darkened house. Several shots of Vinegar's ghastly swill had done nothing to soothe the ache of desire, but at least everyone appeared to have gone to sleep. Perhaps this was one short-term solution. He could ride out each evening and avoid the house until Lissa and the baby were in bed.

Satisfied with his idea, he pulled off his boots in the kitchen and started off down the hall, then detoured by the study for another drink of decent whiskey to wash the taste of Vinegar's offering from his mouth. The door was ajar, and a light flickered dimly from the kerosene lamp by the window.

He approached the high-backed chair from behind, unaware of its occupants. Lissa, too, thought she was alone in the room as she snuggled Johnny at her breast. Only the sharp intake of breath from behind made her sit up and turn her head.

"Jess!"

He stood mute, looking at the breathtaking picture illuminated in a golden halo of light. Lissa, with her sheer silk robe and gown open. And his dark-haired son nursing contentedly at one pale, heavy breast.

Chapter Twenty-One

His tongue clove to the roof of his mouth as he stared dumbly at the incredible vision. Lissa's angry words jolted him from his stupor quickly enough.

"You're drunk!" She put Johnny up on her shoulder and covered herself as the child fussed.

"I wish I *could* get drunk," he said bleakly.

"Is that the only way you have the nerve to face your own flesh and blood?" She held the boy out to him.

Johnny kicked energetically and squirmed, upset at being disturbed while he was still eating, even though he was well filled by now. "Look at him, Jess. Johnny is your son. Named after your own father—who saw nothing wrong with marrying a woman of mixed blood."

"Leave my father out of this. You don't understand anything about him—or me." He turned away and stalked from the room to the sounds of the baby's rising cries.

The next day dawned as gray and somber as the mood in the house. One of the sudden late-summer storms had rolled by, seeming to miss J Bar with the roiling clouds that often dumped hail and sleeting rains on the hot plains with fierce vengeance.

Jess had already eaten and ridden out by the time Lissa brought Johnny downstairs. After breakfast, the skies cleared and a brilliant yellow sun emerged. Lissa decided it was time for them to settle matters once and for all.

She carefully packed a large hamper with slices of sweet smoked ham, a wedge of hard cheese bought dearly from Union Mercantile in Cheyenne, crisp homemade pickles, and a big loaf of crusty fresh-baked bread.

Jess had ridden out to the herd by the Squaw Creek water hole, she learned from Vinegar. This noon she and Johnny were going to arrive in time to take him for a picnic. As she selected various delicacies, Lissa tried not to think of what she would do if Jess publicly rejected Johnny.

His anguish had been a palpable thing when she caught him watching her feed their son last night. Surely she was not misreading the situation so badly. He had avoided Johnny for the same reason he avoided her, not because he did not care, but because he cared far too much. This was the gamble of her lifetime. She had to convince him that they could be a family if only he was willing to take the chance.

Lissa loaded the feast into the buggy as Cormac stood by, tail wagging eagerly in anticipation of the forthcoming outing. When she climbed the steps to the porch, Clare was standing with Johnny and the rest of their necessaries. "Here's the blanket, Missus, and an extra one for the little tyke," she added with a smile of pure affection for the baby.

Lissa returned the bright smile, wondering what the quiet maid thought of a husband who slept in a separate room and a wife who resorted to following him out onto the open range with their child. "Thank you, Clare. We should be back by suppertime." She looked up at the northern horizon, where more gray clouds were massing. "Unless it really storms. There's a line shack on Squaw Creek where we could spend the night."

"Be careful, ma'am," Clare said, a worried look flashing across her thin little face.

You don't know the half of it, Lissa thought as she climbed into the buggy and reached down for Johnny. She took off at a sedate pace with the dog frolicking ahead. Periodically he would pause and turn to see what was keeping her, cocking his head quizzically as if saying, "Why can't you drive faster?"

Within an hour she heard the bawl of cattle. As she crested the ridge, a thick billow of dust hung in the hot air. The beeves were restless, churning up the parched earth with their feet. Lissa scanned the scattered riders, looking for Jess. He was nowhere in sight. With a sigh, she headed toward Rob Ostler, who had his hands full treating a steer for mange with the standard remedy, kerosene.

Jess reined in at the crest of the ridge and looked down at Lissa, conferring with Ostler. Damn her, she had the baby with her. Just then, she looked up where the young hand pointed and caught sight of him. He kicked Blaze into a canter and rode to meet her.

"What the hell are you doing out here with a norther rolling in?" he asked furiously, angry for many reasons having little to do with a potential storm.

"The sun was shining bright when I left." She looked at the clouds, which had moved considerably closer since she started out.

"For someone who was born on the plains, you sure don't have the sense to know come here from sic 'em."

"I was raised back East," she replied defensively. "Is it really dangerous?"

He studied the sky, which was now darkening by the minute. "Hell yes, it's dangerous."

As if to underscore his remarks, the wind picked up in an eerie keening howl. He looked from Lissa's pale, worried face to the small bundle she held protectively in her arms. With a muttered oath he dismounted, tied Blaze to the buggy, and climbed aboard to drive it.

"Where are you taking us?" she asked, hoping that he was headed toward the line shack.

He did not answer, but asked instead, "Why in the hell did you come out here with the baby?"

It seemed feeble-mindedly stupid to say, "for a picnic," now, with the storm starting to splatter them with fat, cold rain droplets. "We needed to settle some things," she answered vaguely as the wind whipped her words away.

Jess headed toward the line shack on the creek, making no further attempts to communicate with her. Cormac trotted close beside the buggy. By the time they reached the cabin, the storm had soaked them. Jess climbed down and quickly took the baby from Lissa so she could do likewise. "Get inside," he yelled over the crash of thunder. She did so, seizing the hamper and oiled-skin pack from the floor of the rig. He followed her inside and handed Johnny to her as soon as she set down her load. The dog rewarded them with a vigorous shake of his rain-soaked fur.

Jess went back out into the storm to secure the horses under the crude brush lean-to beside the cabin. He unhitched the buggy horse and unsaddled Blaze, then lugged the heavy tack into the interior.

Lissa had laid the fussing baby on the crude bed and was kneeling by the fireplace. Cormac was grooming himself over by the bed, as if guarding Johnny. "There's a fire laid. Papa always insisted the line shacks be kept clean and ready to use in case any of the hands got caught in a blizzard."

"I'll start the fire. You tend to him," Jess replied.

"His name is John," she said softly, brushing off her hands as she stood up.

He ignored her and set about starting the fire. They were both wet; even the baby was damp. She smiled. Perhaps this would work out after all.

Looking around the dusty bare room, Lissa took inventory. A two-tiered bunk bed stood against the far wall. The cornhusk mattresses looked serviceable. She could cover them with the clean blankets Clare had packed. A rickety table and two chairs sat in the center of the room and a crude set of shelves lined the wall opposite the bed. On them sat the usual staples of coffee, corn meal, beans, and rice.

Lissa sat down by Johnny and began stripping off his covers and then his clothes until he wore only his napkin. Talking soft baby talk to him, she elicited a gurgle. Johnny was delighted with the attention. She felt his blanket. "This is damp. I'll put it near the fire to dry. I'm glad Clare packed the other bedding in oilskins." Holding the nearly naked infant in her arms, she approached the fireplace, where bright orange tongues of flame were beginning to illuminate the small bare cabin with a warm glow.

Jess looked up at her. "Other bedding? What the hell were you planning, Lissa? You said something about our needing to settle things." He looked at her suspiciously.

"A picnic," she said with a theatrical sigh. Camella was not the only actress in Wyoming. "If you unfasten that bedroll you'll find the blanket I was going to spread under the big cottonwood down by the creek."

He stood up and did as she suggested, trying not to gaze on the wriggling infant in her arms. "The baby's blanket isn't the only thing we need to dry out," he said with a savage undertone in his voice. "If we stay in these clothes, we'll catch pneumonia." He looked her in the eye accusingly. "You planned this."

"Certainly. I'm such a spoiled little rich girl, even the weather obeys me!" She rolled her eyes. "Actually, I really did set out for a picnic." She pointed to the basket. "Here, hold Johnny and I'll get everything in order." Without giving him a chance to refuse, she thrust his son into his arms.

Jess held the kicking infant as if he were made of china—very slippery china. "I'd forgotten how little they were. . . ." he whispered in an awe-filled voice as he inspected Johnny's fingers and toes, then studied the tiny face with its big bright eyes.

Lissa continued wiping off the table and then set the basket of goodies on it, all the while watching Jess enraptured with his son. Finally, she broke the silence. "You hold him as if you'd had practice." There was so much she did not know about Jesse Robbins.

"I used to watch Jonah for our mama."

"He's at your ranch."

Jess continued studying Johnny. "Yes. He runs it for me while I'm off on jobs."

"What's he like? Jonah." She was pleased that he seemed willing to talk.

"Nothing like me. He's the white Robbins. Yellow hair and light skin. Looks like our pa." Just then Johnny let out a squall and began to gnaw hungrily on one tiny fist. "I think he's worked up an appetite."

He faced her, holding out the baby. As the storm raged outside, they stared into each other's eyes, the crying baby between them. Lissa felt the heat from the fireplace, but knew the fire in her blood roared more fiercely than the flames in the hearth. She took Johnny from him and began to unfasten her blouse with clumsy fingers. The wet cloth made the buttons stick. She could not undo them one-handed.

"Let me help," he said thickly, reaching out and slipping the buttons through the loops with sure, strong fingers.

She looked down at his hands, so slim and graceful. The heat rushed over her in swift, terrible waves, pooling low in her belly. "You said we should

336

remove these clothes before we catch our death."

He pulled a chair near the fire. Lissa sat on it and put Johnny to her breast. Instantly his fussing stopped as he nursed greedily. She felt the flush scalding her cheeks as Jess watched the intimacy. Not daring to meet his eyes, she closed hers, letting the bliss flow over her in waves as the baby's hungry mouth pulled on her nipple, suckling it the same way his father had so many times. The way she wanted him to touch her again. *I'm as greedy as my son.*

When she opened her eyes and looked up, Jess was staring raptly. They communicated silently as rain and wind lashed the small shelter. Slowly, ever so slowly, he reached out and touched the baby's head with one hand, caressing the silky black hair. A tingling shiver ran down Lissa's spine. His other hand lightly brushed her loose blouse away from her other breast, then gently cupped the swollen globe until she emitted a low gasp of startled pleasure.

"So long. It's been so long, Jess." The fury of the storm carried away the sound of her voice, but he understood.

With patient hands he caressed her as she held the nursing infant. Leaning her back against the chair, he unplaited her hair and spread the dark, cherry-red waves over her shoulders, combing the thick, satiny hair with his fingers, gently massaging her scalp.

Still cradling her head in his hands, he leaned over her from behind the chair and kissed her forehead. His lips blazed with the heat of the fire as they moved lower, brushing her thick lashes and caressing her closed eyes, her cheekbones, then nuzzling an ear. His tongue flicked inside the tiny shell, and she shivered with pleasure. He did the same to her other ear and moved to her throat.

She reached up with her free hand and brushed back the lock of straight inky hair that fell over his forehead, then touched his cheek tenderly. When he stepped around and knelt beside the chair, she traced the harsh beauty of his face with her fingertips. He moved near her naked breast, daring to claim what his son had not already taken.

One touch of his tongue circling the nipple led her to cry out his name. As the baby finished his meal and lay back, dozing off contentedly in the heat, Jess continued his attention, teasing and tasting. "Sweet, so sweet, Lissa," she heard him murmur near her heart.

Her hand circled his nape, pulling him closer. His arms now encircled her and the infant with such gentleness that it made tears sting beneath her eyelids. Then he lowered his head to Johnny and kissed his forehead reverently. "Lissa, I love you both," he whispered so softly that she had to strain to hear the agonized confession over the noise of the storm.

Jess stood up on shaky legs and took the dozing baby from her, loosely fitting the dried blanket over him as Lissa rose. "Let me change him so he can go to sleep," she said.

Cormac watched with curiosity as she moved across the small space to the bed, where Jess had laid out the blanket. She placed Johnny on it, then took the pack with clean baby clothes from Jess. In a few moments she had their son ready for bed. Jess placed the carefully wrapped infant on the top bunk and braced the saddle packs around him so he could not roll off the bed. The dog settled himself back in the corner and went to sleep after Johnny quieted.

When he turned to his wife, she stood beside him, holding her blouse and chemise in front of her, her eyes liquid gold, fathomless. "Love me, Jess." She mouthed the words silently, and silently he obeyed, guiding her to sit on the lower bunk. He knelt and pulled off her boots and stockings. Then his hands moved up to her waist, and he unfastened her riding skirts and slid them over her hips, pulling her pantalets with them until she lay naked on the narrow bunk, her skin pale against the dark blanket.

He ran his hands softly across her belly, marveling at its concave flatness, imagining how she must have looked, great with his child. His fingertips grazed the points of her nipples until she arched up from the bed. Her arms reached out, pulling him down over her for a fierce, sealing kiss. As their mouths brushed and devoured hungrily, she ripped frantically at the buttons of his shirt until it was free. Tugging it from his denims, she peeled it down his arms without breaking the rapacious kiss.

Jess threw the shirt away, then left the sweet fire of her lips to stand up. His eyes locked on her face as he stripped away the rest of his clothes. She watched the firelight gild his lean, dark body a marvelous, glistening bronze. Her fingers ached to touch the beautiful symmetrical patterns of black hair that covered his chest and tapered down, only to bloom where his sex stood straining, erect.

When he neared the bed, she sat up and took his staff in her hand and stroked it, feeling him tremble. Her other hand slid down his scarred thigh, then moved back to cup one hard buttock. With a feral growl, he removed her hand and climbed onto the bed, covering her body with his own. Their mouths rejoined greedily.

His hand tangled in her hair, holding her head as his tongue plunged deep into her mouth. He felt her hands pressing against his back, gliding up and down, as she opened her slim, silky thighs and scissored his hips between them.

Her cries were muffled against his mouth as he reached down and touched the wet heat of her. She was as slick as satin and he groaned, anticipating what was to come, forcing himself to roll to his side and wait until his passion came under control. He wanted nothing on earth as much as to plunge deeply within her and find the soaring bliss of release. But it would be no good unless she felt it too. So he held himself teetering on the edge, kissing her breasts, her throat, her face, relearning every curve and hollow of her body. And realized that he had never forgotten a single inch of it.

Lissa could feel the thudding of his heart as he caressed her. Her own heart beat like a mad thing ready to explode within her chest. Where his hands and lips led the way, liquid flame followed, enveloping her whole body in a fire so bright the storm outside could never extinguish it. Her hands clutched at him, clawed at him until he rose and poised himself over her. Then he slid deeply into her, slowly, and held still.

One strong, dark hand held her hip firmly as he seated himself. "Don't move, Lissa," he breathed against her neck.

But she was wild and heedless, so hungry that his impassioned words did not register. Lissa had

waited for the past year, alone and aching for his
touch, for his body to join with hers and fill it,
to make her whole. She arched up against him
and he was lost. They rode, fierce as the storm,
and just as quickly as the rain had begun they
finished together in a white-hot rush of ecstasy.
He collapsed on her, shuddering, and she held him
fast, trembling while they both struggled to regain
their breath.

Finally he raised his head and brushed a damp
curl from her temple, kissing her lips softly and
murmuring, "That was too fast."

"Mmm, I don't know. After waiting so long, I
couldn't have stood another instant . . . but that
doesn't mean we have to stop . . . does it?" She
punctuated her words with tiny nibbling kisses to
his nose, eyes, and lips as she held his face framed
between her hands.

He buried his head against her throat and
whispered, "No, I suppose not . . . but first . . ."
He pulled away with a light kiss and stood up,
reaching his hand out to pull her from the bunk.
"That bed is mighty cramped."

When she stood up, he reached down and pulled
the blanket off the mattress. When he spread it
across the wooden floorboards in front of the fire,
she followed and knelt on it, opening her arms to
him. With the firelight silhouetting them in amber,
they embraced, kissing slowly as they sank onto
the blanket, as oblivious of the hardness of the
floor as they were of the dying of the storm outside.

They made love with slow care this time,
exploring each other, renewing every nuance of
pleasure, communicating with words and with

small inarticulate sounds that transcended speech. When they at last ascended the heights again, they lay still joined, as if unwilling to ever again be separated.

Suddenly, a cold wet nudge against his buttock brought Jess's head up sharply. "What the hell?"

Lissa chuckled as Cormac's long pink tongue scraped along Jess's thigh. "I think he's hungry," she said as she sat up. When her own stomach gave a rumble she added, "So am I."

He watched while she walked to the table and brought the hamper over to their "picnic blanket" in front of the fire. She moved gracefully, utterly unconcerned about her nakedness as she knelt and opened the basket. His stomach growled, and they both laughed.

They feasted on ham, cheese, and sweet-and-sour potato salad, washing it down with mellow white wine. Each took turns feeding the other small bites interspersed with tossing treats to the dog. Cormac finally settled for the remainder of the crockery bowl of potato salad and two large dill pickles.

When the hound had retreated to his corner again and lain down with a resigned sigh, Lissa gathered up their scattered clothes while Jess stoked the fire with more wood.

"My underwear is dry, but your denims and my riding skirt will take until morning, I think," she said with a question unspoken in her voice.

"It's full dark now. We'll have to spend the night," Jess replied. Rising, he walked over to the shelf and blew the dust off a granite coffeepot. "There's coffee and possibles enough to make breakfast."

Before he could say anything else, Johnny fussed in his sleep and Lissa went to check on him. Jess tugged on his damp denims and boots, saying, "I'm going to feed the horses."

When he returned, she had donned her under-garments and blouse and was packing the remain-der of the food in the hamper. She looked up at him expectantly with such hope and fear written across her face that it hit him like the kick of a ten-gauge.

He met her eyes for a moment, then sighed and said, "Hell, Lissa, I guess we could try . . . at least for . . ."

He got no further before she had flung herself into his arms and was kissing him joyously. "You won't be sorry, Jess, I swear you won't."

"I only hope you won't be the one who's sorry, Lissa."

Chapter Twenty-Two

Cammie held the feathered hat up in the light, inspecting the way it was put together, all the while cursing that snotty Charlene Durbin, who wouldn't sell her fancy merchandise to the town's scarlet poppies. Camella Alvarez was forced to purchase her finery from Union Mercantile. Just as she glided silently over to the small, dusty mirror on the counter, two low voices caught her attention.

"I still think it's mighty peculiar, Thad. What's a female doin' with that much arsenic?"

"An' I still think it's none of our business what that hatchet-faced Frenchwoman does as long as she pays her bills. Besides, you'd never even a' knowed what was in that box if the wrapping hadn't got tore off when you unloaded it from the train," the stationmaster's wife admonished him.

They continued their argument as they wandered down an aisle filled with seed grains and hard tack.

Cammie put down the hat and tapped one lacquered nail against her cheek. The Frenchwoman must be Jacobson's former housekeeper, Germaine Channault. And arsenic was used by cattlemen to kill wolves. Could she be mixed up with someone in the Association who had poisoned Jess's water?

Why order more poison from an outside source when Jess said the Association kept a big supply on hand? To throw suspicion off the guilty member? Strolling from Union Mercantile out onto Ferguson Street, she decided to check around. Next week was the big Association gala that kicked off fall roundup. Perhaps she might have some very useful information for Jess and Lissa when they arrived in town.

"We have to go, Jess. If we don't, we'll be cut out of fall roundup. We'll lose a fortune in beef sales," Lissa argued. "The Association would love nothing better than to see us give in this way."

Jess watched her deftly peel potatoes and plop them into a pot of water. He sat at the kitchen table, cleaning his rifle. "I'll ride into town and talk to Mathis about letting our reps ride to Diamond E and Empire Land and Cattle Company roundups."

"Without me," she said flatly. "I'm not made of china, Jess. I won't break if someone snubs me." She wiped her hands on her apron. "I'd love to go to the dance. The real business of roundup takes place around the punch bowl."

He studied the stubborn tilt of her chin. At times she looked disturbingly like her father. "What you really want is to face everyone down by dragging me to their fancy party. It'll just cause trouble, Lissa."

"Since when are you so afraid of trouble?" She walked over and put her arms around his neck, leaning forward to nuzzle his ear. "Admit it, wouldn't you like to see Lemuel Mathis's face when we show up?"

"This isn't a game, Lissa." He stood up and snapped the rifle's lever action closed.

"It's politics, and that is a game—a deadly serious one. Without me, you won't have an entrée to their inner circle. The women may be snobbish, but the men will be too embarrassed not to talk to me. I can wheedle Cy and Jamie into letting our reps on the range."

Sighing, he capitulated. "Just be prepared for some ugly scenes."

In the week since the storm, they had arrived at an uneasy truce. They slept together in the big master suite each night after he sat and watched her feed and change their son. She cooked his favorite foods, and he played with Johnny while she made dinner. Clare went about her chores quietly, giving no indication of how she felt about the new relationship between her employers.

Moss had quickly noted the change yesterday when he came up to the house to go over the tallies with Jess in the office. Lissa had come in with a tray of homemade apple pie and coffee and bustled around, serving the men as they worked. She was the picture of a dutiful young bride. His shrewd gaze had been hard and unreadable, but he thanked her for the pie and returned to business as soon as he consumed it. He told none of the hands that their new boss was there to stay. But was he?

Jess was not at all certain. Sitting behind Marcus Jacobson's big desk, he felt like an intruder. He and

Lissa spent the days being a happy family with little Johnny. Their nights were wildly passionate, obsessive—as if they could not get their fill of each other. Or as if they realized that this idyll could not last. But while she did not acknowledge that, Jess did. He had given his heart and committed his life to Lissa and Johnny. He prayed it would be enough, but feared it would not.

Now after only a few days, they would have to face the outside world. Jess would not mind for himself. He had become hardened since childhood, a childhood he did not want his son to face. And above all, he did not want Lissa hurt any more than she already had been. But she was right about the necessity of going to Cheyenne to make arrangements with Association members about the roundup.

"If only she wasn't so set on this damn dance," he muttered.

They took the best spring wagon to Cheyenne the next day with Clare riding in the back with their luggage while Lissa perched on the high seat beside Jess, holding little Johnny. As soon as they reached the city, Lissa felt the stares. A few men touched the brim of their hats, then looked quickly away. Women swished by, moving their skirts aside as if they would be contaminated by close proximity. A few of the bolder men glared with hard, hostile eyes. All observed the dark child sitting in her lap with various degrees of dislike.

"I told you it'd be like this," Jess said as he watched her clutch Johnny protectively.

Lissa raised her chin. "I don't care. They're nothing but a pack of ignorant jackasses."

As they rounded the corner of 15th Street onto Ferguson and stopped in front of the Metropolitan Hotel, Jess said grimly, "It's only going to get worse." He climbed down from the wagon.

"Then let's give them something to really talk about." Lissa leaned over and gave Jess a kiss on the lips as he lifted her from the wagon seat. When she picked up her skirt and stepped onto the wooden sidewalk, her eyes collided with the cold, twisted face of Yancy Brewster.

Lissa felt Jess stiffen beside her, but he said nothing, just stood taut and still, with his hand resting lightly on his Colt. Brewster stared insolently at her, then at the baby, through bloodshot eyes. His face was unshaven and his skin had an unhealthy pallor beneath his wind-blasted complexion. He looked as if he had slept in his dirty, wrinkled clothes or been up gambling and drinking all night. After a tense moment, he contemptuously spat on the sidewalk and shambled away.

"Cy fired him several months ago—something about heavy gambling debts and drinking on the job. Dellia must have been devastated when Cy broke the engagement. She had her hopes pinned on marrying him." Lissa shivered in revulsion, recalling when he had once courted her.

"Dellia Evers is better off dying a spinster than marrying him," Jess replied. Once he was certain Brewster had gone, he helped Clare from the wagon and escorted the two women into the hotel.

Noah was still manning the front desk. He paled when he saw Jess with Lissa and the baby.

"Wait here," Jess commanded, motioning for the women to be seated in two overstuffed chairs beside a huge potted palm.

A Fire in the Blood

"Afternoon, Noah. I need a couple of rooms. I think the old Jacobson suite would do for Mrs. Robbins and me. We'll need an adjacent room for the maid and our son." His tone of voice was low and silky, but his cold eyes pierced the sweating clerk like silver daggers.

"We're full up," Noah replied, snapping his mouth shut like an irritated turtle.

Jess reached across the desk and grabbed the registry. "Odd. Did all those guests forget to sign their names?" he asked as his eyes swept down the page. He held out his hand for the pen the clerk clutched in a white-knuckled death grip.

"You'll get me fired."

He waited a moment until the red-faced clerk handed him the pen in defeat. Jess signed the register and shoved it back, then waited for the key. Noah fished it out and handed it over.

"There's a spring wagon out front with our luggage. See to it. Then send up hot bathwater for the ladies . . . plenty of it," Jess added with a smile that did not reach his eyes.

Noah rang for the bellman, silently huffing in outrage as the gunman and his womenfolk walked up the stairs.

Once she had settled Clare and Johnny in their room and the luggage had been brought up, Lissa crossed into the bathroom of their suite. "I remember the first time I saw you here." Her eyes danced as she approached him. "All of you."

His face broke into an unwilling smile in spite of his tension. "You didn't stick around to see quite all of me that time. Seems I remember your turning tail and running off when I stepped out of that tub."

349

She eyed the big white porcelain claw-foot tub. "I promise not to run off this time. Let's take a bath together." She appraised the tub critically. "We'd fit."

He raised one eyebrow. "We'll give old Noah a heart attack if we soak his fancy floorboards."

"I dare you."

He walked over to her with a crooked smile on his face and raised one of her hands to his lips. "You dare too much, I'm afraid." He kissed her palm. She caressed his cheek softly and snuggled against him.

A knock sounded on the door. "That's probably the bathwater. Enjoy your soak. I have some business to attend to; then I'll go to Reamy's for a bath and shave."

"What business?" she asked crossly.

"I have to check the telegraph office and some other things. I told you coming along wasn't a good idea." He opened the door and admitted Chris, the brawny bellman, carrying two enormous buckets of steaming water.

While Chris was filling the bathtub, Lissa followed Jess into the suite's parlor. "Will you be back to take me to dinner tonight or should I order a meal sent up?"

"Be ready around seven," he said as he picked up the small satchel containing his clothes.

A secret smile hovered around the corners of her mouth. "Now who's turning tail and running?"

He merely grunted and walked out the door. As soon as he was gone, Lissa knocked on Clare's door. "Do you have it ready?" she asked eagerly.

The little maid scurried over to the large leather traveling case the bellman had set beside her bed.

"It'll need pressing, Missus. I had to fold it up to hide it in here." She pulled out a man's beautifully cut dress suit of dark charcoal wool.

"Oh, Clare, you've done an outstanding job!" Lissa exclaimed as she examined the suit, which had been completed the previous evening. "I'll go see about having it pressed."

Perhaps it was just as well that Jess had left for the afternoon, Lissa thought as she headed down the back stairs carrying the suit. She wanted to avoid the hateful Noah and find Chris's mother, Iris, who was in charge of housekeeping for the big hotel. No one was as meticulous at pressing as Iris Graves.

A few minutes later, Lissa was on her way back upstairs, having left the new suit with the housekeeper. She was just about to round the landing on the second floor when whispered voices stopped her—familiar voices.

"You've been drinking again, Yancy." Cridellia Evers's sharp voice was accusing.

"I only had a few. I been up all night, Dellia, waiting for you to get here. I won us enough cash money to afford that wedding in Laramie. See."

Lissa peeked around the corner at the pair. Brewster was flashing two railroad tickets in front of Dellia's pale face. Should she interfere? Make her presence known? Before she could decide, Dellia threw herself into his arms with a squeal of delight.

"Oh, Yancy, my darling! I knew you'd come for me. We can get married tonight in Laramie and be back here in time for the big dance tomorrow night. I'll be Mrs. Yancy Brewster."

"Shh. Not too loud. We gotta be quiet. You know how your pa feels about me."

Dellia looked into his haggard face. "I know he's been hard on you, dear one, but once we're married, everything will be just fine." She hesitated, sniffing delicately. "Do—do you have any clean clothes? I mean, to wear on the train?"

"No time for gussying up now. Once we're married, I can use yer pa's credit to buy some new duds in Laramie—unless you got some extra money here in your room."

"I have a little." Her voice quavered uncertainly.

"Go get it. Then meet me at the station. The train pulls out in an hour. Here's your ticket."

He grabbed her for a brief, rough kiss, then turned and headed toward the stairs. Lissa picked up her skirts and dashed back downstairs, hiding beneath the open stairwell on the ground floor. Brewster stalked out the side door without seeing her. Breathing a sigh of relief, she began to climb the steps, trying to decide what to do.

Should she attempt to reason with Dellia? That appeared hopeless. The foolish girl had been smitten with Yancy since he had first come to work at Diamond E. His attempts to court Lissa had led to the final breaking of her friendship with Dellia. If she ever could have honestly called it friendship.

But Lissa could not sit by and let Dellia ruin her life, no matter how spiteful the girl had acted. Yancy was a drunk and a brute, and Lissa was positive he would abuse poor besotted Dellia once he married her. Cy Evers would be at the Cheyenne Club. She owed it to the old man to let him know of the elopement. She hurried the rest of the way to her suite to compose a note. Perhaps Cy could prevent their escape with no one in Cheyenne the wiser.

* * *

"We'll take over five hundred head. Easy with the beeves spread out to reach clean water." His face was in the shadows of the railhead building.

"Poisoning the water near the ranch was a good idea, but the time for mere stealing is done now," Germaine replied over the hiss of a train stopping at the depot.

"What do you mean?" the man replied guardedly. "It's too soon. Robbins is—"

"Surely you are not afraid of that half-breed cur, *hein?*"

He bristled angrily. "You know better. I thought you were the one worrying about me."

"Robbins received a wire yesterday which he will no doubt pick up today, telling him his gunmen are prepared to work for him. It is a fortunate thing the clerk in the telegraph office has a special dislike for Indians. He has been most helpful to me." Germaine's eyes glowed malevolently. "We must act at once before help arrives for Robbins and his whore. It is good that he is here in town. When he receives word about the cattle being run off, the timing will work perfectly. Here is what you must do. . . ."

When Lissa awakened early the next morning, Jess was already up, shaving in the bathroom. She slipped a robe on and tiptoed quietly into the doorway to watch the male ritual.

Without missing a strong, sure stroke with the gleaming razor, he said, "Why are you up so early? Thought you'd be tired enough to sleep late."

Her cheeks warmed as she recalled their love-making the previous night. "I'm quite resilient, in case you hadn't noticed," she replied, feeling muscles in her belly tightening as the razor glided along his jaw, shearing away the black stubble with foaming flecks of soap. He wore only a towel tied carelessly at his waist.

She walked into the room and slid one hand up his back, then around his side, tracing the patterns of hair on his chest. "It's very sexy for a woman to watch a man shave," she said huskily.

"It's a damn nuisance for the man," he grunted.

"Did all the men in your family have heavy beards?" He was still not at all forthcoming with information about his past in spite of her efforts to draw him out.

He slowed a stroke and glanced at her with cool silver eyes, then resumed shaving. "I reckon so, although my pa's beard was yellow, like Jonah's. Didn't know my mother's people. They'd all died by the time I was old enough to remember anything."

"You're educated more than most men in Wyoming—"

He laughed mirthlessly. "That wouldn't take much."

"Who taught you—your mother?"

He finished shaving and wiped away the traces of soap from his face. "Nosey, aren't you?" he said, walking past her into the bedroom, where he pulled a clean shirt from his case.

"I've told you all about me. Why won't you tell me about you? Are you afraid if I learn too much I'll have some sort of hold over you—to make you stay even if you still want to go?"

She had hit far too close to the truth. He yanked on his denims and reached for the shirt. "Maybe," he replied grudgingly, then added, "My mother was illiterate, just like most of the impoverished Mexican peasants Richard King brought to Texas. My pa was a book-lover. He taught us the basics." He paused then, as if rediscovering things lost in the mists of the past.

"When I was eight or ten, just a tad, Mr. King found out I could read. He took a shine to me for some reason, maybe because my ma worked at his big house. He let me use his library. It was a whole new world opening up for a poor Mexican breed."

"Why . . . why if you had that opportunity . . . why did you . . ." Her voice was halting, for she was unwilling to break the harmony of his earlier reminiscences.

"The war was hard on my family," he replied with a shuttered look on his face.

He buckled on his gunbelt without saying anything more.

"How old were you when you joined the French Legion?"

"Don't you ever run out of questions?" he asked, obviously wanting to change the subject. "I have to see a man about a roundup."

"Wait, Jess. Let me go with you."

"Do you honestly think Lemuel Mathis will want to see you with me?"

She shook her head. "Not Lemuel. I know he'll refuse. It's Cy Evers and Jamie MacFerson we need to talk with—they'll listen to me."

"Mathis listened to me the last time I had something to say. I can handle him," Jess said firmly.

"Or what—you'll shoot him? Be reasonable, Jess. The Association's too big for you to take on alone. Anyway, Cy owes me a favor." She quickly explained about Dellia's aborted elopement with Yancy Brewster and her part in thwarting it. "I heard him bring her back to her room and post a guard at her door."

"Why didn't you tell me about this last night?" His eyes searched her face, and she knew at once that he was comparing the way Marcus had caught them with the way Cy had caught his daughter.

Lissa met his steady gaze. "I'm learning how you think, Jess. And I guess I just didn't want to give you one more reason to contemplate leaving us again."

He sighed in resignation. "Hell, all right, get dressed. We'll go see Evers."

"It might be best if I—"

"No," he interrupted flatly. "I'm not hiding behind your skirts, Lissa. Either you go with me or you don't go at all."

She gritted her teeth and silently said some uncharitable things about insufferable male pride as she hurried through her morning toilette.

Evers and MacFerson were quartered at the Cheyenne Club. The return note from Cy agreed to meet with them in the Metropolitan's dining room at noon. When they arrived, Cy was already sitting at the private table that Marcus had always reserved. To Lissa it brought back bittersweet memories of happier times with her father.

Evers rose and nodded to Lissa and Jess. He looked grim and uncomfortable as they all sat down together. The serving help had apparently already been instructed not to intrude.

"I owe you for Dellie," Cy said stiffly to Lissa.

"I hope she's all right," she replied.

"Found 'em at the station waitin' on the Laramie night train. I had Brewster beat within an inch of his life 'n threw him on the train with his own ticket," he added with a harsh glance at Jess. "Dellie's cryin' a spell now, but she'll get over it. Your note said you had business with me and Jamie."

"J Bar wants in on the fall roundup," Jess said.

"That's Association business." Cy's shrewd brown eyes studied Jess.

"Next to J Bar, you and Jamie run the largest spreads in southeast Wyoming. If you let J Bar reps participate, everyone else in the Association will follow your lead. Even Mathis."

"Lemuel has a personal reason to refuse me. You understand how that is," Lissa said to Evers.

The old man's face reddened beneath leathery, wind-blasted skin. "I'll talk it over with Jamie. I reckon I owe you that."

"I'd be much obliged, Cy. Jess and I will be at the dance tonight. Perhaps it can all be settled then," Lissa said in a brisk, businesslike manner as they rose from the table.

Chapter Twenty-Three

After Evers had left, Jess turned to Lissa with a shuttered look on his face. "I never said I'd go to that dance. In fact, I don't even own a suit."

"I knew you'd use that as an excuse. Come with me. I have a small surprise for you."

She wended her way from the restaurant back upstairs to their suite with Jess unwillingly in tow. The suit was hanging in the armoire, freshly pressed.

"Clare took the measurements from your clothes. She's really a splendid seamstress. What do you think?" she urged, holding it out with such a look of wistful entreaty on her face that he could not refuse. "I had her make up a new white silk dress shirt as well, and I selected the cravat, but if you don't like the maroon, there's dark blue and—"

"Maroon is fine, Lissa," he said gently as he took the suit from her. It was the handsomest gift he had ever received—at least since the time a wealthy young madam in New Orleans had bought him a solid gold pocket watch. Jess decided it would be politic not to mention that to his wife.

My wife. A rush of emotion overcame him without warning as he touched the rich, dark-gray wool. The lining was of silver brocade, as was the matching vest, and the workmanship was exquisite. These were the clothes of a wealthy stockman, a respectable pillar of the community.

He looked at her gravely, and when he spoke his voice was husky. "Wearing these clothes, going to the Association's big shindig—you're taking me into a world that's closed to me, Lissa. I'm afraid that because of who I am, I'll close it for you, too."

She shook her head and caressed his cheek. "Husband, your nobility is beginning to wear on me. Either they accept us together or I don't want to belong," she said with determination.

He would have argued more, but Johnny's cries from the next room interrupted them.

Jess prepared for the gala like a man facing the gallows. He cared not at all for himself if it turned out to be a disaster. A lifetime as an outsider had inured him to isolation from polite society. But Lissa had grown up as part of this privileged circle, and he knew it was going to be closed to her now too.

Jess stood in the bathroom door looking into the bedroom at Lissa with their son at her breast. Each time he watched, it was as if he were storing up the beautiful memories to last him the rest of his life. Although darker-complected than his fair mother, Johnny could pass for white, especially back East, dressed and educated as a gentleman. The troubling thought had haunted him ever since he had agreed to try living at J Bar.

A feeling of impending disaster gnawed at him. *I'm living on borrowed time with them and only I realize it.*

Early that evening Lissa took the special gown she had selected to Clare's room so the little maid could help her dress. She wanted to surprise Jess. Standing in front of the mirror, she turned this way and that.

"What do you think, Clare?" she asked uncertainly, smoothing one hand over the low-cut neckline. The color was really unusual.

"I think you will be the most beautiful lady there." The maid appraised her handiwork with a critical eye. She had sewn this gown for Miss Lissa while still working at Durbin's over a year ago, but her mistress had never worn the unusual creation of soft, gleaming silk.

"Here, let me." She took the heavy beaten-gold necklace from Lissa and fastened it around her slender throat. Matching gold combs held up elaborately piled coils of burnished curls with a few soft tendrils falling artfully at her ears and on her nape. "Go show your husband."

Nervously Lissa nodded. "First let me kiss Johnny. Are you sure he'll sleep through?" she asked as she knelt by his crib.

"If not, I have plenty of soft food ready for the lamb. Please, don't fret." Clare's eyes were dazzled by how splendid the missus looked. "You'd better not keep the mister waiting."

With a deep breath for courage, Lissa opened

the door and stepped into the suite's parlor. Breath escaped her as she looked at Jess, who was standing by the window, unaware of her entry. His hair gleamed blue-black in the evening light, offset by the snowy white of his shirt collar. The charcoal suit and silver gray brocade vest were tailored to fit his tall, lean figure perfectly. Even in the rarified social circles of St. Louis and Chicago, she had never seen such an elegant man.

He turned, sensing her presence. His appreciative gaze swept from the elaborate hairdo down to the shimmering gown that clung with silky seduction to every lush curve. The color was not quite green, not gold, but a cross between the two, the shade of a new leaf in sunlight. For most women, it was an impossible color, but with Lissa's sun-kissed skin, golden eyes, and burnished hair, it was magic.

She stood poised in the door, her eyes locked on him, acutely aware of his perusal. Striding over to her, he touched the gold necklace and caressed the velvety skin of her throat. "You're incredible," was all he could say as he raised both her hands to his lips and saluted them.

"So are you. The suit fits even better than I could have imagined. You'll have every woman in the place drooling over you." She smiled brilliantly.

His expression was guarded as he replied, "The less attention I attract the better, but I do thank you for the suit—and Clare for her sewing skills."

She ran her hands down his chest, then paused when she felt something foreign. "What—"

He opened the suit jacket to reveal a .38 caliber Colt pocket revolver slung in a shoulder holster. "I know the opera house doesn't approve of guns, but I never go unarmed, Lissa."

"I'm certain there'll be no need for it," she said, trying to assure herself more than him. One look into those cool gray eyes made her realize that protest would be useless. He would always be a man who lived in the shadow of the gun.

When they arrived at the corner of 17th and Hill streets, they saw a press of elegant carriages with passengers disembarking, ladies bedecked in brilliant silks, and gentlemen in handsomely cut dark suits. Jess had hired a small buggy for the short ride from the Metropolitan. He assisted Lissa down, and they approached the three-story brick monstrosity that had opened amid great hoopla the past May.

The opera house proper boasted seating for one thousand patrons, but the elite Association gala was being held in a posh ballroom on the second floor called the Library Hall. They had no more than walked through the main entrance on 17th Street when the subtle whispers and insulting silences began. Gushed greetings were being exchanged between expensively jeweled ladies, while hard-eyed stockmen clasped one another's callused hands, but no one approached Jess and Lissa. Everyone knew who they were. Some averted their eyes or turned their backs. Many stared openly as the couple ascended the fanning stairs to the ballroom.

"Are you sure you want to go through with this?" he asked her, sotto voce.

"Leave—and give those vipers the satisfaction?" She snorted indignantly, then smiled up at him.

He scowled as one matron in a garish silk paisley gown stared at him through a lorgnette. The old harridan was scalded by eyes the color of boiling mercury and almost dropped her pretentious glasses.

The orchestra was playing a sweeping waltz when they entered the crowded room. "Quite a bit more elegant than the fiddles and guitars at J Bar shindigs, isn't it?" Lissa asked, seemingly unconcerned by the thinly veiled hostility surrounding them.

"There's Evers," Jess said after scanning the room quickly. As they crossed the polished maple floor, men and women stood aside as if reenacting the parting of the Red Sea.

He nodded to Cy Evers and Jamie MacFerson. A third man, Noble Winthrop, stood with them. All three acknowledged Jess and made self-conscious bows to Lissa. If not friendly, they were at least polite. Then the dour Scot cut through the preliminary courtesies, addressing Jess.

"Cy tells me you want to send reps to the fall roundups."

"Yes. And we'll expect all the other district reps to attend J Bar's as well," Jess replied. "Any problems with that?"

MacFerson shrugged. "One to ask is Lem Mathis."

"Mathis'll do what the big cattlemen tell him to," Jess said flatly.

MacFerson tugged at the tight neckband of his starched shirt where the reddish flesh was puddling over. "Empire Land and Cattle will go along."

Jess's eyes moved to Cy.

"You're in with Diamond E." Evers turned to Winthrop. "Noble here runs the Circle W down on the territorial line."

"I'll agree to go along," Winthrop said to Jess.

A crafty look passed over Evers's weathered face. "I reckon you can pass that along to Lem 'n see what he says."

Jess nodded. "I'll do that. Obliged."

Cy Evers raised the glass in his hand and gestured toward the elaborately festooned tables along the far wall where drinks were being served. "Last I seen of Lem, he was greasin' his elbow over thataway."

The Robbinses bade the trio good evening and headed toward Mathis, who was engaged in conversation with a group of men and women.

"Poor Dellia. I imagine she's beside herself missing the ball," Lissa whispered to Jess.

"She's lucky her pa caught her when he did," was all Jess felt like saying on that subject. "It might be better if I went to see Mathis in the morning, now that the roundup is settled."

"Quit trying to protect me, Jess. I had to face down Lemuel Mathis alone before Papa died." She remembered Mathis's gloating face when she had been forced to sign the hateful divorce petition.

He felt her tremble. "Then there's no—"

"Yes, there is. I *want* to tell him, Jess." Her voice was tinged with iron and her chin was pugnaciously out.

As they neared the small group, Mathis caught sight of them and gave a false smile that more closely resembled a sneer. "Well, the new owner of J Bar and his lady."

"Married women hold their own property in Wyoming, Mathis. J Bar is still Lissa's," Jess replied.

"Of course, of course." He looked expansively around the assemblage as if they were all sharing a private dirty joke. "Horace Wattson and Mrs. Wattson, their daughter Miss Emmaline, Jake Moorhead and Mrs. Moorhead, you all know Miss—" He corrected himself a little too pointedly, "Mrs. Robbins and her husband Jesse."

The men nodded politely enough, but Louella Wattson drew herself up as if a muddy pup had just shaken himself on her taffeta gown. Emmaline looked about ready to faint. "I think we need some fresh air," Louella huffed.

Lucy Moorhead stared at Jess in amazement, unable to keep the frank sexual interest from her eyes. "Yes, air, that's just the thing."

"Come along, Emmaline," Louella added, fairly dragging the fluttering little wren by one matchstick arm.

The men quickly excused themselves and escorted the ladies away. Tension between Mathis and Robbins crackled.

"I saw you talking to Cy and Jamie."

Jess smiled. "With you being the president of the Association, as a courtesy I wanted to let you know J Bar will participate in the district roundup."

A frown creased his broad forehead, but Mathis quickly erased it and smiled glibly. "Really, I understood you were so short-handed you wouldn't be able to send any reps."

"That's all changed since Jess is back," Lissa interjected. "J Bar will be well represented."

Mathis's expression changed subtly as he looked from Lissa's defiant face to the unreadable mask of his dark rival. "You planning to stay around this time, Robbins?"

Jess felt Lissa stiffen, but before she could say anything, he exerted a bit of pressure on her arm and replied, "That's for me to settle with my wife." Without another word he turned, guiding Lissa along with him, his hand possessively against the small of her back.

They walked toward the opposite end of the refreshment tables that groaned with champagne punch and an assortment of delicacies, including the cattlemen's perennial favorite, fresh oysters. When they reached the huge punch bowl, the other revelers stepped away. Jess looked at the black man serving the drinks, indicating that he and his lady wished a libation. With a broad smile lighting his face, the man filled two crystal cups to the brim and handed them over.

"Our business here is over, Lissa. We should leave," he said, swallowing the bubbly sweet liquid with a grimace of distaste.

"What, and deprive Lucy Moorhead of her fantasies?" she whispered. "She's been devouring you with her eyes ever since we stepped into the room."

He chuckled mirthlessly. In fact, any number of the women, some quite handsome younger matrons and a bevy of unmarried girls, had been covertly casting admiring glances his way. He was used to sly lust from proper white ladies. "It's only the thrill of the forbidden. If I were to approach any one of them, they'd drop through the floor in outraged indignity."

She could see the way his jaw hardened and his eyes narrowed, subtle signs of agitation. Lissa now realized that social rejection hurt him a great deal more than he let on. That was why he felt he was harming her by staying. *I'm learning to read him.* She set her half-empty cup down on a table and said, "The least we can do is show them how well we can dance. . . ."

A bitter smile touched his lips. "You mean show them that a breed gunman can dance at all."

"I already know how well you dance. Remember our moonlight waltzing at the ranch? Now I want to dance with you in public—to show everyone how proud I am to be your wife."

She looked so desirable and stubborn, standing expectantly with her upraised palms open to him, that he could not resist.

"I think this is a big mistake, Lissa." Setting down his cup, he took her in his arms just as the orchestra struck up another waltz.

As they swept around the floor in perfect rhythm, every eye in the crowded room seemed to be fastened on them.

"I'm the envy of every woman in the place," she breathed against his shoulder.

"Only in the night, Lissa. None of them would be caught dead with me in daylight—least of all right here, dancing."

"You just might be surprised—but don't put it to the test. I'm a very jealous woman." He tightened his possessive hold on her a fraction, and she smiled to herself.

Across the room, Emmaline Wattson fanned herself in extreme agitation as she watched the striking couple dance. "I cannot believe Mr. Mathis and the other gentlemen in the Association countenance this," she said in a quavering voice to her mother, Louella.

Geraldine Cameron, a young rancher's wife from Albany County, overheard them and chuckled. "J Bar is the biggest spread around. The Association can't keep him out even if he is a Mex-Injun. Anyway, he sure cleans up real purty."

Mrs. Wattson took in a hissed breath. "For shame, Geraldine. Better not let your husband hear any such thing!"

Geraldine just smiled and rolled her eyes. "I can look without my man bein' any the wiser."

Louella squinted at the pair gliding across the polished maple floor with such grace and flair. Everyone was watching the disgraceful spectacle. "Come along, Emmaline. This time I *do* feel a need for fresh air."

As the mother and daughter wended their way through the arched doorway into the less crowded hall, Julia Creed joined them.

When the music stopped, Jess bowed to Lissa and escorted her from the floor. "Satisfied?" he asked her, noting the hostile expressions around the room. He did not want an open confrontation that would humiliate Lissa.

She smiled rather wistfully, wanting to dance all night with her handsome husband, but realizing that he was right. "I suppose it would be wise for us to leave," she said in a subdued voice.

They walked through one of the smaller side doors and began to cross the long hall toward the front stairway. "Wait here, Lissa. I'll get your wrap from the clerk," Jess said, walking quickly across the hall to where he had deposited her silk shawl when they entered the building.

She began to stroll slowly toward the turn in the hall. Around the corner, voices drifted above the low murmur of noise from inside the ballroom.

Julia Creed, the town's worst gossip, was speaking. "I tell you it was some scandal. Cy Evers is hushing it up, but everyone knows."

"Or will when you're through," her husband said drily.

Undeterred, she continued, "That foolish Cridellia was actually eloping with that drunken Yancy Brewster. Cy caught them just in time at the train station. Dragged her away in tears."

"Imagine the upstart, him without a cent to his name, no social position, trying to marry that girl just so he could get his worthless hands on Diamond E," Horace Wattson said indignantly.

"Well, if you ask me, it wasn't half so bad as the spectacle we've all been subjected to this evening—that Jacobson hussy parading her savage around dressed up like a respectable rancher," Louella Wattson said snidely.

"Yes," Julia chimed in quickly, "whatever else his faults, Brewster is white!"

"Not to mention that mongrel brat Lissa Jacobson dropped—as if everyone can't count the months! Dellia may be foolish, but she is a decent, God-fearing woman with morals," Louella added righteously.

"White or whatever, I don't cotton to a no-account takin' advantage of a female just to get his hands on her daddy's land." This from the stentorian voice of Judge Sprague.

Jess, who had returned with Lissa's wrap, stood silently behind his wife, overhearing the vicious conversation that had frozen her against the wall. Wordlessly, he enveloped her in the folds of soft silk and held her as if he could protect her from the cruelty. But he could not.

Guns and the violent men who used them he understood, but how could he deal with acid-tongued harridans and puffed-up old men? "Respectable society is an enemy I never could fight, Lissa. Not for me, not even for you," he murmured against her neck.

She swallowed and held her head up high. "Give me your arm, Jess. Let's show those nasty old hypocrites the stuff we're made of and snub them cold." *Please don't let them drive you away from me.*

He did as she asked, and they rounded the corner. The small group of gossipmongers were dispersing as others entered the hall. A few revelers, like the Robbinses, were preparing to depart. Lissa let her contemptuous glance sweep from the Wattsons to the Creeds and then to old Judge Sprague, whose face mottled red with embarrassment. Horace Wattson looked decidedly nervous as the gunman with the glittering silver eyes neared him, but Jess gave him scarcely a glance as he steered Lissa toward the wide staircase.

Just then the figure of a tall man crested the stairs with two of the opera house ushers racing behind him. Several of the women gasped in shock at Yancy Brewster's appearance. His clothes were torn and filthy, and his face was swollen and discolored, evidence of the beating Cy's men had given him.

"Looks like Evers's hands didn't do as good a job as he thought," Jess said, instinctively knowing who the enraged man would fasten upon. As Brewster shook off one of the ushers and headed toward Robbins, Jess set Lissa behind him.

"Well, well. Look at the fancy-ass gut-eater all dressed up like he was a white man," Brewster sneered.

Jess could smell whiskey on him from ten feet

away. "You should've stayed on that train, Yancy." He watched Brewster's hand near the Army Colt he wore on his hip.

"'N leave behind everything I worked for? Let you get away with dirtyin' her so no white man'd touch her? Shit, I had to settle for that bug-eyed little Evers bitch."

"Shut up, Brewster, you always were a foul-mouthed cur," Jess said, trying to get close enough to the drunk to disarm him before someone in the crowd was hurt by accident.

"Didn't want Dellia but, hell, Diamond E's almost as good as J Bar." He turned venomously to Lissa, "Then you, you greaser lover—you had to tell old man Evers and spoil that too. Not bad enough you're screwin' a—"

"That's enough, Brewster!" Jess's voice crackled like shards of glass. He had moved close enough to the enraged man now, and the rest of the crowd, which had been drawn by the outburst, hastily drew back.

"Robbins ain't armed," one voice said above the low hum of whispers.

"His kind can always take care of themselves," another replied.

Cy Evers, who had been at the far end of the ballroom when the altercation erupted, shouldered his way through the press of people, yelling at Brewster. "Yancy, you son-of-a-bitch, I'll kill you for this!"

But Brewster was fixated on Jesse Robbins with the single-minded determination of a drunk with a longtime grudge.

"Stay out of this, Evers," Jess said as the older man finally emerged in the open hallway.

Brewster shouted a vile epithet and drew his gun, but before he could raise it to fire, Jess's pocket revolver barked twice, hitting the big man at close range with two .38 caliber slugs. The Colt dropped from Yancy's lax fingers, and his lanky body crumpled, tumbling backward and rolling down the shallow circular stairs until he lay sprawled grotesquely midway to the bottom.

Women screamed and fainted, and men rushed forward to see the body. Jess replaced the revolver in his shoulder holster, then turned back to Lissa, who rushed into his arms.

She clung to him, trembling as Lemuel Mathis and Cy Evers approached.

"I'm obliged to you, Robbins," Cy said grimly.

"I've sent for the marshal," Mathis added with a self-satisfied air.

"Well, you tell him what happened when he arrives. I've got to get my wife out of here." With his arm around Lissa, Jess headed toward the side stairs leading to Hill Street.

Chapter Twenty-Four

They rode back to their hotel suite in silence. Lissa held tightly to Jess's arm, still seeing the crazed hatred in Yancy Brewster's eyes. What if she had been able to talk Jess out of carrying the hidden weapon? He would be the one now lying dead on the opera house floor. She shivered just thinking about it.

Jess felt her mute misery and her trembling. Damn, he had known it was a mistake to return to her bed and give her hope for a future together. If the whole awful debacle of being cut at the dance and subjected to such vicious gossip was not bad enough, he had to kill a gun-crazy drunk. Brewster could have shot Lissa in the fracas. Just thinking about it made his blood run cold.

Given how the town in general and Lemuel Mathis in particular felt about him, he still stood a good chance of being arrested on some technicality.

Cy Evers was probably decent enough to see that it did not stick, but the scandal would further wound Lissa and leave her and Johnny completely isolated.

When they arrived at the hotel, Jess escorted her upstairs. Once she was safely ensconced with their son, he would take care of his business with the sheriff and indulge his need for a drink at the saloon.

A small wail carried through the door, and Lissa smiled tremulously, her eyes luminous with love as she entered the suite. "He's woken up hungry." She started toward Clare's room, then turned back to Jess. "I'll bring him to our room to feed him," she said softly, knowing how he liked to watch.

Jess felt defiled and unworthy. He had just killed a man, one of so many, and not all of them as justly in need of a bullet as Yancy Brewster. "I have a lifetime of blood on my hands, Lissa. Scarcely the legacy I want to pass along to my son. Take care of Johnny and go to sleep. I need to be alone for a while."

"You've been alone too long, Jess. That's the trouble—"

"No, the trouble is my dragging you and Johnny down with me."

"Stop it, Jess," she said in a choked voice, reaching out to him.

He put her hands aside and stepped determinedly away. "If you won't think of yourself, at least think of your son. You heard those old harridans tonight—and their menfolk. They'll never let you forget Johnny was conceived outside wedlock. They won't let him forget it either when he gets old enough to understand—not bad enough that he's got Mexican and Indian blood, but as far as they're concerned, he's a bastard to boot."

She blanched white and stood frozen. "Why are you saying such horrible things?"

"Just think of Johnny, Lissa, not us. Take a good look at your son. He's only an eighth Indian. Back East, no one would have to know the circumstances of his birth or who his father was. You could be a widow lady. Hell, say your husband was some dead Spanish nobleman. Nobody would know. They'd think it was romantic. Just . . . just think about it, Lissa. I have to go out now. I'll be back late."

He turned quickly and left. Her cry echoed in his ears, "Where are you going, Jess?"

She might think he was headed straight to the Royale to see Cammie. That would suit his plans well. Better to hurt her quickly and have it over with than let her keep holding on until they destroyed not only each other but their child as well.

After he was gone, Lissa changed out of her finery and slipped on a nightgown and robe, then took her fussing son from Clare.

"He must've heard you come upstairs, for he didn't make a peep all night until you returned," the maid said, embarrassed to have overheard the argument between the missus and her husband.

Smiling distractedly at Clare, Lissa took Johnny to her room and sat on the bed to nurse him. As she watched his small mouth tug eagerly at her tender nipple, she caressed his silky hair with adoration.

"How beautiful you are. Your father's son for certain," she whispered, trying not to think about Jess's words.

In spite of her resolve, she studied Johnny's face and features. Jess was right about the prejudices that would follow him if he grew up in Wyoming. Could Johnny pass for white in a new place? Her aunt and uncle in St. Louis knew little about the man she had married or the circumstances of Johnny's birth. She could go back and pick up the threads of her life as a respectable widow with a son who would be admitted to the highest ranks of society.

The baby finished his meal and nuzzled against her breast, a milk bubble on his rosebud lips. A wave of love washed over her as she held him. "No, little one, I won't betray your birthright with lies. You should be proud of who you are and who your father is." Sneaking away to build a life on a lie would not guarantee her son a better future— only one without a father's love.

Lissa had never been certain that Jess loved her with the same unconditional desperation with which she loved him, but she did know for a certainty that he loved his son. She would never see John Jesse Robbins cheated of that as long as she drew breath.

Jess's destination was not the theater but the sheriff's office in the courthouse. He would have taken bets that Lemuel Mathis had beaten a trail to the law before Brewster's corpse got cold—and won the wager. Mathis had visited the sheriff and sworn out a complaint. There were ordinances against carrying guns within the city limits, laws observed far more in the breach than by their enforcement. The nicety that he would have been killed by Yancy if he had gone unarmed was beside the point to Mathis.

Fortunately, the sheriff, a shrewd Irish politician named Sean Feeney, was inclined to take Jess's point of view. This more likely happened because Cy Evers and several other witnesses corroborated the facts, or perhaps because the fat old sheriff was nervous in the presence of a famous gunman. In any case, Jess left the thick brick walls of the impressive courthouse behind, relieved when the issue of Brewster's death was finally settled.

After walking around for the better part of an hour, he realized that he was postponing the inevitable. He began to retrace his steps to the Metropolitan. Crossing Eddy Street, he decided to stop in a saloon for a fortifying drink, which quickly turned into several. The bartender was corpulent and sweated nervously as he served Jess. Cammie found him two drinks later. She had just finished her late show when word of the shooting fracas reached her at the Royale. She had quickly changed and went searching for Jess.

"It took me long enough to find you. I expected you would be cooling your heels in one of Feeney's new cells," she said, sitting down at the battered table beside him. "Buy me a drink?"

He looked at her morosely, then motioned to the fat barkeep for another glass. "What the hell do you want, Cammie?"

"I am not certain this has anything to do with Brewster coming after you tonight . . . but I learned something very strange the other day. I planned to tell you about it before you left town."

Jess rubbed his aching head. "What, Cammie?"

She proceeded to explain about overhearing the conversation concerning Germaine Channault's bizzare purchase of arsenic.

If Jess felt any effect from the whiskey he had consumed, it quickly evaporated. "What the hell would that old crone want with arsenic if it wasn't the stuff that poisoned our water?"

Her eyes narrowed. "That is the conclusion I also reached, *querido*. I have been asking around town to see if anyone from the Association has been seen with the Frenchwoman."

He looked at her with silent expectation.

She shrugged. "So far, I have learned nothing."

He pushed back his chair and rose. "I'd appreciate it if you'd pass on anything you hear. Maybe I'll just dust off my rusty French tomorrow and have a little talk with the old biddy."

By the time he slid the key in the lock to suite 12, it was three a.m. He expected everything to be quiet and dark—at least, he hoped it would be. But a dim light sent a dull golden shaft from beneath their bedroom door. He opened it and found Lissa standing with her arms around herself, looking frail and delicate, silhouetted against the dark window.

She turned as he entered. Her face was pale, and her amber eyes had big, dark smudges beneath them. She flew into his arms. "Jess, I've been so worried." Her head came up and she looked him in the eye. "You've been drinking."

He smiled wearily. "Didn't pass the sniff test?" At her look of pain, he cursed himself silently. "I'm sorry, Lissa. That was uncalled for. I went to the sheriff's office." He outlined what had happened as he stripped off his dress clothes and turned down the lamp.

"Do you still think Lemuel is involved with the rustlers trying to break us?" she asked, shedding her robe and slipping into bed.

"Could be. God knows he has enough bile in his system to poison half of Cheyenne." He voiced aloud the idea Cammie had given him. "Germaine could be working for Mathis."

"I've been thinking about the poisoned cattle, too," Lissa replied. "If we could find out if Lemuel has been seen talking to Germaine, we'd know he was guilty."

"Forget about Mathis's spleen and get some sleep, Lissa. This has been a hellacious night for you."

"Oh, I don't know. I got to dance with my husband in public. That part of the evening was grand."

He scowled in the dark. "Not so grand when everyone was whispering about us and giving us looks that could wither a thistle bush," he replied grimly.

Her heart tightened in her chest. She could feel him withdrawing from her even though they lay in the same bed. Before he could say anything about what was best for Johnny and provoke another argument, she rolled over against him and lay partially across his body. Only the sheer silk of her nightgown separated their flesh.

"You're right. Let's forget Lemuel and all the good folks of Cheyenne. . . ." She lowered her head to his, covering his face with her long hair as her lips brushed and teased his.

If this was going to be his last night with her, Jess wanted it to be a glorious one, filled with life and love, not death and bigotry. He pulled her atop him and enfolded her in his embrace, kicking the rustling sheets to the bottom of the big bed.

Lissa's body wriggled against him as she pressed her breasts against his chest and tangled her legs with his. Her mouth opened for his kiss, and hot darts of pleasure tingled on their dueling tongues, radiating through her breasts and belly, all the way to her toes. She could taste the faint tang of whiskey and tobacco in his mouth as she pursued the kiss with as much zeal as he, biting his lower lip, then running the tip of her tongue inside, along his teeth, until he nipped softly at the velvety tip of it, then sucked it.

His hands ran over her sleek little buttocks, then embraced the slender curves of her waist. He raised her, holding her above him so her breasts hung suspended like plump melons, tempting him to taste. When he took one pebbly nipple into his mouth, the sweet richness that nourished his son trickled onto his tongue and he trembled with love for her.

Lissa threw back her head as the ripples of pleasure coursed through her. Jess turned his seeking hot mouth from one breast to the other, tasting and caressing until she was frenzied with desire. Her legs scissored over him, trapping his rigid phallus between her thighs. She squeezed until he groaned in pleasure. Then he lifted her higher and pulled her up into a kneeling position with her legs straddling his shoulders.

"Hold onto the headboard, Lissa," he commanded hoarsely.

Blindly she obeyed, her small hands clutching it with whitened knuckles as his hot mouth fastened on her sleek, velvety petals, parting them with his tongue as delicately as a bee seeking nectar from a wildflower. When he touched that small tight bud at the center of her being, coaxing it with deft circling motions, she almost screamed with the incredible ecstasy. What wild, forbidden magic was this? Surely men and women could not love this way.

Surely they could! His hands cupped her buttocks, holding her as his tongue and lips worked so exquisitely that she thought the pleasure would drive her over the abyss into madness.

Jess could feel her arching her back as her climax neared. He slowed and gentled the caresses, prolonging the delicious sensations for her, and for himself. He loved the taste of her, loved feeling her quiver in the throes of this new passion. Her head fell back, and her long fiery hair fell onto his belly, brushing lower, tickling and tantalizing his hard staff as it strained for more of the silky stimulation.

Lissa did go over the abyss—not to madness but rather to a fierce, shattering release that sent tremors racing from her head to her toes.

Jess held her until the spasms finally slowed and ebbed. Then he slid up between her legs. Her hands still clung to the headboard. He pried them loose, and she slid bonelessly into his arms.

"Wha—what did you do to me?" she whispered, when she could breathe again. She still was not certain if her heart had resumed beating or was pumping so fast that it had gone numb in her chest.

He kissed her throat and pressed her against him, holding her possessively. He must leave her and their son, but after this night, she would always be his. "Did you enjoy it?" Foolish question.

"Yes," she said so softly he could barely hear. Then she settled back on his legs and felt his rigidly straining erection. "But you . . . you didn't . . ."

"Yes, I enjoyed it—enjoyed giving it to you, but no, I didn't come with you," he whispered, tucking a wayward curl behind her ear. His breath was expelled in a gasp as she wriggled her bottom against his staff.

A bemused look came over her face in the dim predawn light, and she chewed her lip as she pondered. "Jess . . ." she began very low, almost afraid to ask such a bold question. "If you could make love to me that way . . ."

"Mmm," he murmured against her ear, knowing what she would do.

She knelt, then moved back and bent down, taking his phallus in her hands experimentally, almost as if awaiting instruction. She looked up at his face, which was taut with sexual tension.

"You're a bright woman, Liss. You figure it out," he said in a raspy harsh voice.

She chuckled boldly then and bent over to taste of him as he had of her. How hot and hard it was! A thrill of excitement rippled over her as she experimented with the velvety tip, flicking her tongue around it until he arched his hips and let out a guttural cry. "Like you said, I am a bright woman," she murmured, just before she drew him deeply into her mouth.

He trembled and cried out, then gave in to the blinding pleasure. His hands tangled in her hair, guiding her movements as she caught the rhythm that swiftly brought him to the edge of the abyss.

Lissa felt him trembling and swelling, then the hot, sweet seed came spilling out, and she tasted of him as fully as he had of her. She gloried in it. His hands clenched into fists and his long, hard body bucked. He was as completely in her power as she had been in his.

Raising herself up, she watched him with a possessive smile curving her lips. When she lay over him and snuggled against his chest, he came to his senses enough to embrace her tightly.

"Lissa, Lissa," he whispered, kissing the top of her head. She lifted it and looked into his eyes.

Then she raised her mouth to his slowly and they kissed, a tender, deep caress that went on and on until the fire in their blood rose once more, scorching them with its all-consuming intensity. They rolled back and forth across the big bed, arms and legs entwined, hands rubbing and gliding, mouths tasting. Their desperation was fueled by the unspoken specter of final separation.

She arched her pelvis against the hardness of his staff, then opened her thighs to his entering thrust with a small, mewling cry. He rolled her atop him and held her hips, arching his strongly muscled back to penetrate her most deeply. She leaned over him and his hands slid up to hold her breasts, cupping and teasing them with an exquisite tenderness at odds with the harsh, hungry rhythm with which they had mated.

They were like two passengers on a runaway train, madly craving the fierce, swift ascent on their journey, yet never wanting the thrill to end, for when it did a terrible reckoning would follow. When the blinding glory of surcease washed over Lissa, Jess followed her to the conclusion of their breathtaking ride.

The morning air was chill on their sweat-sheened bodies as they collapsed, still entwined. Cradling her in his arms, he pulled the sheet over them and they fell quickly into an exhausted, dreamless slumber.

A sharp rapping on the front door of the suite finally awakened them. Jess could hear Clare speaking to someone as Johnny's fretful cries drifted faintly from the other room. Lissa felt Jess untangling his arms and legs from hers. She sat up as he slipped from the side of the bed and reached for a pair of denims he had tossed across a chair yesterday.

Her breasts were tight and painful, and Johnny's cries reminded her that it must be late in the morning. She looked down with a blush at the telltale abrasions and love bites covering her body. She was sore for more than one reason!

"That's Tate," Jess said as he reached for the door. "There must be trouble to bring him to town." Carefully shielding her, he cracked open the door and stepped through it as Lissa rose with the sheet draped around her body.

"Send Clare in with Johnny," she called after him. In a moment, the maid entered with the fussing baby. Unable to meet Clare's red-faced embarrassment, Lissa seized her son with a murmured thanks and dismissed the girl, then carried Johnny over to a big chair by the window and sat down to attend to both their needs.

In the next room, Jess greeted Shannon with a troubled nod. "What's brought you to town, Tate?"

"Damn rustlers run off near a thousand head at the upper Lodgepole last night."

"A thousand head!" Jess echoed incredulously. "They can't drive that many beeves all the way to Nebraska—a herd that size would slow them down. And it's too damn big for quick illegal sales to smaller ranches or nesters along the way."

"I figger they just plan to run their legs off and scatter 'em," Tate said grimly. "Mebbee kill 'em. Someone's out to ruin J Bar. No more doubt about it."

Jess swore. "How many of the J Bar men you think would back us?"

"Moss was real pissed about them sons-of-bitches killin' beeves this way. He might convince the long-time hands into ridin' for the brand."

"There's something funny going on, Tate," Jess said, wishing he had had more sleep last night. If only he could think straight. "I found out that crazy old housekeeper bought some arsenic last month."

"That Frenchie?" Tate asked, scratching his head. "What the hell would she have to do with the rustling?"

"That's what I mean to find out. You take Lissa and Johnny home. I want her safe at the ranch—away from Germaine Channault. I'm going to go have a little talk with Madame Channault—and see if I can drum up some more men here in town to ride with us."

"No one would before," Shannon said disgustedly.

"That was before Cy Evers owed Lissa and me each a favor," Jess replied enigmatically.

"When you get to J Bar, have Moss and whoever he can muster start rounding up all the steers they can save." He returned to the bedroom and closed the door behind him.

Lissa, who had hastily donned her robe, sat nursing Johnny. She looked up with a worried expression on her face. "What's happened?"

"Another raid on J Bar cattle. Tate's going to take you back to the ranch. I have some business here in town." He debated telling her he was going to confront Germaine.

"What business, Jess?"

Reluctantly he admitted, "I'm going to have a little talk with Germaine before I leave Cheyenne. Can you think of any reason she'd be involved in this mess?"

She shrugged helplessly. "She always hated me—ever since I was a child. I never understood how much until after she learned about us. I think she's dangerous, Jess."

He quickly donned the rest of his clothes and strapped on his gun. Looking up grimly, he replied, "I doubt I'll have to shoot her, Lissa." He bent over and kissed her lightly. "Tate will be waiting outside for you and Clare as soon as you're ready."

"We'll only be a few minutes," she replied. "Be careful . . . I love you," she added softly as he slipped through the door.

When Jess was gone, a trembling Lissa sat down to calm her fretful son and finish feeding him. She called out for Clare to begin packing. Within half an hour they were on their way back to J Bar with Tate Shannon.

Jess went to Abney's Livery to get Blaze, then rode over to the Cheyenne Club for a talk with Cy Evers. As luck would have it, the old man was just walking to the club's private livery to get his horse. He turned as Robbins dismounted near the path.

"You're out early after a late night, Robbins," Cy said shrewdly, waiting for Jess to explain his reason for the unexpected visit.

"I just received some bad news." He quickly explained about the scattered herd and the need for haste rounding them up. "J Bar stands to lose over a thousand head if I can't get Moss Symington some help."

"Someone seems to have it in for the brand," Cy said, scratching his head. "I'd opine they just had it in for you, 'cause of Lissa and all, but hell, this started afore Marcus ever sent for you."

"That's what I figure, too." Jess related the information Cammie had given him, then added, "I thought someone from the Association might be involved."

Evers's keen brown eyes studied Jess. "You mean Lem Mathis, I reckon. Damned if I kin believe that. Even though he did have a rightful grudge agin you."

"I'm not accusing him yet—but I need help to save those beeves while I do some more investigating." Jess's eyes met Evers's levelly.

The old man sighed. "You know I owe you for last night—Lissa, too, for saving Dellie. I'll send a couple dozen Diamond E hands to give Moss some help."

"I'm obliged, Evers." Robbins nodded and mounted up as the old man vanished inside the immaculate livery stable.

Jess headed across 17th Street up to 16th, where the Inter Ocean Hotel was located. Germaine had been staying there since she had been discharged from J Bar. The hotel lobby was surprisingly well appointed. At first Jess was taken aback, but remembering what Lissa had told him about the generous bequest Marcus had left the old harridan, he imagined she was enjoying being waited upon.

The clerk eyed his gun nervously. "Mornin'. You lookin' for a room?" he asked suspiciously.

"No. A roomer. I understand Madame Channault lives here." He waited for a reaction.

The clerk hesitated a moment, then shrugged. "Room 17—at the back end of the hall next to the fire door."

Jess quickly made his way upstairs and knocked on the door. No answer. He tried the lock with no success. Looking up and down the hallway, he pulled an eagle feather from his hatband and used the stiff quill to poke inside the lock. After a moment's experimentation, it clicked open and he slipped inside.

With mixed emotions, Lissa watched the big white ranch house come into sight. It was her home and her prison, a beautiful gilded cage that symbolized everything tearing her and Jess apart.

If I were an impoverished seamstress like Clare Lang, he'd take me to Texas with him in a trice.

But she was the heiress to her father's empire. Most successful cattlemen scorned the label of "cattle baron," yet that was exactly what they were—absolute rulers commanding hundreds of thousands of acres. J Bar with all its holdings was larger than some European nations and even a few eastern states. And Lissa Robbins wanted no part of it because she and Johnny would hold it at the cost of Jess.

She could see Cormac break away from the men at the corral and bound toward their wagon, barking a joyous welcome.

Shannon stopped the spring wagon in front of the big house and helped her and Clare down, saying, "I'll unload the wagon."

"No, Tate. I know how badly you need to get every man out after those beeves. We can always get the trunks unpacked," Lissa replied as she greeted the hound's exuberant welcome. "You go ahead." Once Cormac had calmed, she turned to Clare and took Johnny from her.

Tate tipped his hat at her and Clare, then untied his horse from the rear of the wagon, mounted, and rode toward the far corral where the men had gathered, awaiting instructions.

Lissa walked to the porch, holding the baby. She watched with a worried frown as the men listened to Shannon and Symington issue orders. Then they all mounted and headed north.

"I pray Jess can bring some Diamond E boys to help," she said to Clare. As they entered the front door, the dog let out a whine, tail wagging. "No, you rascal. Come around to the back and I'll let you in the kitchen—where you can do the least damage," she added with a grin.

The dog bounded from the porch and headed toward the back door at a swift trot.

"I do believe he understands every word you say," Clare said in amazement as they stepped into the dim hall.

Suddenly Cormac started barking at the back door. Lissa blinked, letting her eyes grow accustomed to the interior after hours of riding in the brilliant sunlight. "That devil certainly is impatient." She handed Johnny to the maid. "I'd better go let him in."

She had taken only a few steps when a dark figure materialized from behind the draperies in the parlor and stepped into the hallway, blocking her path. "You will remain inside and make not a sound if you wish that mongrel bastard to live," Germaine Channault said in her heavily accented English. A .36 caliber Colt Brevité gleamed in the dim light as she leveled it on the terrified maid holding Johnny.

Chapter Twenty-Five

Lissa stepped back, placing herself between Germaine's gun and Johnny. "We know you're involved with the rustling. What are you doing here?" She struggled to keep her voice level.

The glow from the old woman's black eyes blazed with mad triumph. "I am taking what should rightfully have been mine twenty-five years ago."

"What she means, dear sister, is that I'm claiming my birthright now that I have the guns to break J Bar." Lissa whirled around with a gasp and faced a tall, broad-shouldered man descending the stairs from the darkened landing. He had tan hair, light hazel eyes, and a cruel smile twisting his well-formed lips.

"Sister?" she echoed, backing away from him toward Clare and the baby.

"Your father was my lover in St. Louis, long before he married Mellisande Busch. I bore him a son, an heir—something that pale little nothing could never do. All she ever gave him was you." Germaine's gun hand shook as she spilled out her venom.

Lissa tore her eyes away from the twisted visage of the old woman to look at the man who was supposed to be her half-brother. His features were regular and strong, but bore no particular resemblance to Marcus's, nor did his coloring. Before it grayed, her father's hair had been quite dark, as was Germaine's. Some man had given her son much fairer coloring.

"I don't believe you. Why would my father refuse to claim a son when he wanted one for J Bar so desperately?"

"He was blinded by the pedigree of that society bitch he married. I was only a poor serving girl who came from Quebec, looking for honest work. I met your father when he came to St. Louis on business." Germaine could see the look of contemptuous disbelief in Lissa's wide gold eyes—her mother's eyes. "I was not always old and haggard. Life has been harsh for me and I have suffered, but once I was comely enough to catch Marcus's eye, even if he was faithless. He tired of me when I was heavy with his son. He'd met your rich mother by then," she said spitefully.

"He would have acknowledged his own child," Lissa replied, "certainly after my mother died if not before—"

Germaine cut her off with a coarse French oath. "He claimed I had other lovers—that Marc did not resemble him. He was a fool to hope your mother would give him sons."

"After I was born," Marc said, "my mother followed the old man to Wyoming. He wouldn't accept her bastard. Afraid your fancy mother might suspect. He agreed to hire her as housekeeper—but only if she sent me to live with relatives in Quebec. I've been on my own since I left them when I was fourteen," he said with an accusing look at his mother.

"I did what I could—sent money when you wrote me from Nebraska. I had to do as Marcus wished or we would have lost our chance for everything—the ranch—"

"My father made you a generous bequest. Now I see why. But he left the ranch to me. There's no way you'll ever get it." Good Lord, did they plan to kill her and Johnny in some insane scheme to inherit?

Marc Channault laughed, a harsh rasp that made Lissa flinch. A terrified Clare tried to quiet the fretting baby.

"Oh, we'll get it, all right, little sister. And we have just the ticket right here to guarantee everything." He reached out and rubbed Johnny's dark hair with a callused hand.

Lissa's heart froze. Forcing down the terror that clawed at her, she said, "If you harm him—"

"Oh, wouldn't dream of it, Sis. Wouldn't dream of disturbing a hair on his head." Marc chuckled.

"That filthy mongrel—the son of a savage, and still your father would not disinherit him for his own white son," Germaine spat in a choked voice.

"Now calm down, *Maman*, dear. You're frightening my little sis here. All we're going to do is keep the boy here at the ranch, as a sort of guarantee that you'll behave when you and your long-lost brother go to town and meet with your lawyer.

You're going to sign over half the ranch to me. After all," he shrugged, "it's only fair."

"You're mad!" The minute the words escaped her lips, Lissa regretted them. His light eyes had the same eerily feral gleam to them as Germaine's black ones. "I—I mean no one would believe it, least of all Judge Sprague." *And Jess won't let you do this!*

"If you wish your son to live, you will convince the judge and everyone in town that Marc is your half brother." Germaine's voice was lethal.

Marc put one big hand around Clare's thin arm and shoved her firmly into the parlor. "Let's all get comfortable. Might as well, seein' as we're all going to be living in the same house from now on."

"You can't just hold us prisoner here," Lissa protested as Germaine approached her with the pistol aimed at her chest.

"We will wait in the parlor," the old woman purred, her mercurial mood shifting again.

"Wait for what?" Lissa asked with dread as she sank onto the sofa beside Clare and the baby.

"Why, for my men to report to me that you have become a widow," Marc replied genially as he walked over to the parlor window and looked out at the road.

"You can't kill Jess! Better men than you have tried and failed," she said with far more bravado than she felt.

"My men are good—and greedy. I promised a five-thousand-dollar bounty to the man who brings me that fancy .41 caliber Colt Lightning of his. See, I had my men run those cattle as a sort of decoy to flush Robbins out and separate him from you.

It worked perfectly. *Maman* and I waited in town until we saw you leave. Then we rode ahead to be your welcoming committee here."

"You were the one all along trying to break J Bar—to run my father out of business." Lissa was terrified and baffled at the same time. *Jess, you've always beaten the odds. Oh, please!*

"If he would not give me the ranch, it was only just that I deprive you of it." Germaine said. "Always I kept searching for a way to reclaim Marc's birthright. Then when Marcus died, it occurred to me that you would do anything for that half-breed's brat—even give my son what is rightfully his."

"The rustling provided me with some pretty easy cash money before that," Marc added cheerfully. His grin turned to a scowl. "Before Robbins shot up Conyers and his gang. It's taken me a while to find more good men."

"But now our plans will finally come to fruition." Germaine's malevolent eyes narrowed on Johnny. "Once that half-breed trash is dead."

Lissa shivered and fought the urge to take her son in her arms. She must stay unencumbered so she could act when an opportunity presented itself.

"It doesn't matter now, *Maman.* Robbins'll be pushin' up daisies real soon," Marc said nonchalantly.

"Don't count on it," Lissa replied quietly as Johnny began to whimper. "He's hungry. I need to feed him."

Marc's crafty yellow eyes went to her breasts with a lascivious leer.

"He's weaned," she said coldly. "I have to fix some solid food—in the kitchen."

"I'm a mite hungry myself. Why don't you see what's out there, *Maman?*" he replied as he walked into the hallway with an expansive gesture toward the kitchen.

Lissa and Clare rose and preceded Marc down the hall. Outside Lissa could still hear Cormac's low growls. If only there were some way to loose him into the house. But both Germaine and her son were armed. Her mind raced. The gun case was in the library, but there was no way to reach it.

"As soon as your men come to report on the Indian, have them shoot that brute," Germaine said to Marc.

He laughed. "You always did hate that dog. I'll finish him after I eat."

Not for a moment did Lissa deceive herself into believing that once they had half the ranch they would not kill Johnny and her for the rest. She had seen the venom in Germaine's eyes when the old woman glared at Jess's son. *Oh, Jess! Think, Lissa, think.* He could be lying somewhere out on the deserted plains, shot, dying. She had to act now.

They entered the kitchen, and Germaine inspected it with as much disdain as Queen Victoria viewing a minstrel show. "I will hire my own cook." She walked over to the cabinet beside the pump and reached for the bottle of whiskey inside.

"Put it back, *Maman.* You need all your wits about you now," Marc commanded.

Lissa looked at him, momentarily stunned. The tone of his voice, the imperious command reminded her of her father. *Could* this monster actually be her brother?

Germaine pursed her lips angrily but did as he told her.

Lissa fired up the stove and put a pot of water on to boil, then opened the cannister filled with rolled oats. "Just a little while, Johnny," she said softly, motioning for Clare to sit down with him on a chair near the wall, out of the way. She searched the cabinet and pulled out a small bottle of tonic. "For his teething," she explained and leaned over to rub a bit on his gums. As she did so, she whispered to the maid, "Get ready to duck into the pantry—fast."

Germaine had pulled out a slab of bacon from the pantry, conveniently leaving the door ajar as she brushed past Clare. She took the meat to the table and selected a knife, then began slicing it. Carrying the knife with her, she approached the stove with a skillet filled with bacon and placed it on the front plate.

Soon it was sizzling, and the water had come to a full rolling boil. "Come fix your oatmeal for that brat. I cannot abide his whining," Germaine said to Lissa.

Lissa considered trying for the knife but decided against it. *I can't match strength with a madwoman.* She picked up the open cannister and approached the stove, then suddenly flung it in Germaine's face and seized the pot of boiling water and flung it into Marc's face as he tried to grab her.

While his mother was temporarily blinded by the dry, powdery meal and he was screaming with his burned face, she raced to the kitchen door and opened it for Cormac.

The hound was across the porch and through the door before Clare and Johnny had the pantry door between them and the chaos erupting in the kitchen. Cormac leaped on Marc, knocking him to the floor before he could discharge his rim-fire Colt. Germaine, who had slid her pistol into the pocket of her skirt, was blinking, teary-eyed, as she extracted the weapon.

Spying the butcher knife she had dropped on the floor, Lissa ran to seize it, only to have the older woman shove the gun into her side before she could reach it. "Call him off or I'll kill you," she shrieked above her son's screams as he wrestled with the huge hound who was tearing at his gun arm, trying to reach his throat.

Rather than give up her only chance at freedom, Lissa gambled. She knocked Germaine's gun away from her side and reached up for the skillet handle on the stove. The gun went off, grazing Lissa's arm, but she brought the sizzling skillet tumbling down onto the Frenchwoman's head.

Cormac, hearing Lissa's involuntary cry when she was shot, abandoned Marc and turned on his mother. Stunned by the skillet and burned by the spattering grease, Germaine dropped her gun, which skidded across the floor. Ignoring her injuries, she lunged at Lissa with a screech of rage. The dog leaped between them.

Marc Channault seized his Colt and cocked it as he rolled up, heading for the pantry and Johnny. Just as he yanked the door open, a deadly voice from behind him yelled, "I'm here, Channault." Jess stood outlined in the kitchen door.

Marc Channault whirled and fired, but his shot went wild, blasting into the ceiling. Jess's bullet hit him squarely in the chest. He fell backward into the hallway.

Germaine screamed his name as she struggled with Cormac. Lissa called the dog off, but as soon as he released the crazed old woman, she seized the knife from the floor.

"You've killed him," she shrieked, trying to leap up and go for Jess with the knife. The big dog's jaws snapped, closing on her billowing skirt. She fell, twisting her arm and landing on the knife, which imbedded itself to the hilt in her chest.

Lissa slid away from the bloody corpse and jumped up, running into Jess's arms. "They said they sent men to kill you!" She buried her face against his chest and held on to him, trembling. "How did you know they'd be here?"

"I went to her hotel room in town this morning. She was a real doting mama. Kept all sonny boy's letters and reports on the cattle he'd stolen. It didn't take a Napoleon to figure out running off the cattle was a diversion. Once I knew she believed her son had a legal claim on J Bar, then I knew you and Johnny were in trouble, left here alone."

"No one tried to ambush you?"

"Probably would've if I'd caught up with Tate and the Diamond E men."

"They came?"

"Cy agreed to send them. They'll round up the scattered herd. Once I take the Channaults' bodies to the sheriff in Cheyenne, their gang will head out. J Bar's seen the last of rustler troubles. The inheritance is safe for Johnny now."

Lissa's chest tightened as a feeling of foreboding squeezed her heart. "Jess—"

Just then Johnny let out a loud wail. Clare held him in a death grip as she huddled against the far wall of the pantry. Lissa released Jess and walked into the storage room for her son. "It's all right, Clare. Come out now. Everything's over. They can't hurt you," she said soothingly to the maid as she took her son and looked questioningly at her husband.

The white-faced maid shuddered and looked away from the two bodies, then made a run for the back door and was sick over the side of the porch. Lissa held Johnny, kissing his head as he cried furiously. Looking up at Jess, she said, "I'd better feed him. He's really starving now."

Jess examined the oozing wound on her arm and noticed the red weals on her hands from the hot pots. "I think you need some attention first."

"It's just a scratch, and the burns aren't bad. I'll feed Johnny before I tend them."

"Will you be all right here? I have to take these bodies to the sheriff and do some things in town. I expect Tate and Moss will ride in by dark."

He touched her cheek tenderly, then ran his hand across Johnny's dark hair. They stared into each other's eyes silently for a moment. No words were spoken, but she understood and he knew that she did. The baby continued to cry.

"I have to . . ." Her voice failed her. Finally she worked up her courage and said, "You aren't coming back, are you, Jess?"

"The ranch is safe. Moss is loyal to the brand. He'll handle things for you."

For me. For Johnny. But never for you. "J Bar will always stand between us, won't it, Jess." It wasn't really a question.

"It's for him, Lissa." He looked at his son, who had subsided into red-faced whimpers. "Take him

East with the income you'll have from the ranch. Start a new life."

"Where no one will call him a breed or a bastard." She nodded in resignation, then rose on her tiptoes, with the crying baby between them, and kissed him tenderly on the lips. "Keep safe, Jess—or if you can't do that, be careful." Lest she break down again, Lissa turned and fled past Marc Channault's body, through the hallway and up the stairs to her room, not caring at all if the dead man had really been her half-brother or not.

As Johnny's wails subsided, Jess carried the two bodies out to the spring wagon, tied Blaze to its back, and began the long ride into Cheyenne.

Just as Jess had predicted, Tate, Moss and most of the hands returned that night. The rustlers, seeing the Diamond E men arrive along with so many J Bar men, gave up and scattered. Without the enticement of the bounty on Jesse Robbins, they had no reason to stand and fight.

Early the next morning Cy Evers rode up to the front door, hat in hand, red-faced and nervous. Lissa ushered him into the kitchen and fed him a hearty breakfast to put him at ease.

"I know why you're here, Cy, and I'm grateful." She hesitated. "I—I'd like to think my father would be, too." She did not really believe it, but it might make Cy feel better.

He surprised her by saying, "Marcus was my friend, but he was a fool." Cy studied her over the rim of his coffee cup with shrewd blue eyes. "I owe you a lot for savin' my Dellie from that skunk, Brewster. . . . Time was I thought Jesse Robbins

was just like him, mebbe worse," he added in cha-
grined honesty. "But I was wrong. He came to
me last night. Told me he had no right to what
Marcus built. Never wanted it, but he loved you
and couldn't help that, even if he was sorry for
the hurt he put on you 'n on his boy. I told him
Marcus 'n me and all them good folks in Cheyenne
had a lot to do with that hurt. Told him I was
sorry."

"He asked you to handle our fall roundup and
hire me a professional manager, like the foreign
stock companies have, didn't he?"

He could see the quiet acceptance in her and
the pain she hid beneath it. Marcus Jacobson's
headstrong, spoiled little girl had grown up. He
only prayed his own daughter showed half her grit
and maturity someday. "Yep, 'n I said I'd be proud
to do it."

She reached her hand toward him, hesitantly.
Then he too reached out, clasping her small,
smooth hand in his veined, gnarled one.

"Thank you, Cy."

Roundup went smoothly, and the profits from
sales were the best ever. Her new manager, Jack
Eckert, was efficient enough to run J Bar without
any help from her.

Winter arrived, leaving Lissa snowbound with
only Johnny and Clare for company at the big
house, although they did hire several youths
from town to do the heavier cold-weather chores
such as chopping firewood. Cormac was allowed
to sleep in the kitchen and frequently accom-
panied her down to the bunkhouse to visit Vinegar.

Cy was an occasional visitor when the storms blew over. He had sent the embittered and humiliated Cridellia East to some distant kin in Knoxville. In March he was delighted to share the news with Lissa that Dellia had become engaged to a prosperous older merchant. His family assured him that the man was of fine character and doted on his young fiancée.

Doc Headly made several calls, checking on their health during the bitter winter season and keeping Lissa abreast of the goings-on in Cheyenne. Lemuel Mathis married Emmaline Wattson and bought up the small Circle Q spread to the west of J Bar. Quite a comedown from his ambitions of owning the biggest outfit in the territory.

Spring slowly began to whisper across the sear brown grasslands of the basin with its soft, warm winds and sweet green breath. Lissa smiled to herself. She had a proposal for Lemuel Mathis, one that just might give them each their heart's desire.

Chapter Twenty-Six

Camella Alvarez dropped the spoon against her saucer with a clatter, then glanced around the almost deserted dining room at Esselborn's. It was not the best restaurant in Cheyenne, but the food was good and the owner would serve fallen women such as Cammie and Lissa. "What do you mean you've sold J Bar to Lem Mathis?"

"He received good terms on a loan from his father-in-law's bank. Horace Wattson is thrilled to see the J Bar brand owned by his son-in-law. I've put the money in trust for Johnny. My Uncle Phineas is investing it for me in St. Louis," Lissa said with a sly smile.

Cammie returned the smile. "Let me guess—you do not plan to return East with your *niño*."

Lissa fished around her plate of dried-apple pie and took a bite. "Well, I was sort of thinking that some traveling might do us a world of good after being cooped up all winter. Johnny's a year old now and weaned . . ."

"And you think Texas would suit you, no?"

"I think Texas would suit us, yes."

"Jess will be *muy furioso*," Camella replied, brushing a pastry flake from her chin with a gamine grin.

"I figure once we're there and J Bar's gone . . . he'll be stuck with us," Lissa said nervously. "After all, he did keep telling me it was my ranch to do with as I saw fit for Johnny's benefit. I just happen to think having a father will be of more benefit to my son than having a cattle empire."

"And you have come to me for directions to the Double R," Cammie said, seeing the determined gleam in her friend's eyes. "Things will be very dull in Cheyenne when you are gone. I shall miss you."

She began to draw a map.

The summer sun had always been merciless on the high plains of Wyoming, but the farther south they journeyed, the more grueling it felt. The air was damp and heavy as well as stiflingly hot. Johnny, teething and fretful, dozed restlessly in his mother's lap as they bounced along what passed in the Big Bend country of West Texas as a road. Cormac slept on the floor, cramped between the hard-backed seats of the small vehicle. Outside the coach, Tate Shannon rode with a small cavvy of Lissa's best horses, which she was bringing as a dowry of sorts to the Double R.

The stagecoach ran once a week from Persimmon Gap to the sleepy little village of Terlingua, which she understood was mostly Mexican. Although not as fluent in Spanish as she was in French, Lissa had learned a smattering of the language in her school days. For the past five-hundred miles she had been forced to become increasingly more proficient, although Tate's border Spanish served them adequately when she became stumped.

She was everlastingly grateful that Jess's old friend had agreed to accompany her to the ranch. She gazed across the shabby coach, which carried one snoring drummer besides her and Johnny. Clare had not come with them. In truth, she had always remained a little afraid of Jess, and the idea of living near the border, hundreds of miles from anything but cows, Mexicans, and Indians, terrified her witless, not to mention traveling in the company of a black gunman. Lissa had made her a generous loan with which she opened a dress shop in direct competition with her former employer, Charlotte Durbin.

Lissa had bidden farewell to her unlikely assortment of friends—Cy Evers and Doc Headly, Vinegar and Moss, even Cammie. Much as she would miss them, she knew her life in Wyoming could never be the same as it had been before Jesse Robbins had ridden into it. None of the respectable women in town would ever allow her within their society again. Jess had certainly been right about that, but he was wrong, desperately wrong, about her moving East with their son and hiding Johnny's paternity.

The farther into Texas they traveled, the more Mexican the population became, and the more mixed bloodlines became evident. Most of the Spanish-speaking people of this region had some degree of Indian blood. Her son could live and grow here without the stigma he would experience in the Anglo north. If the ranch was poor and small—well, she had brought along a small nest egg of cash and the willingness to work hard.

The flat, desolate desert country they had traveled through gave way to increasingly lush vegetation, sparkling creeks, and awe-inspiring mountains as they entered the Big Bend country. It was incredibly isolated and wild, and Tate had warned her it was filled with outlaws and all sorts of desperate men and dangerous animals, but it was also breathtakingly beautiful.

She guessed that Jess had selected the land for its very remoteness from the civilization that had dealt so cruelly with him and his family. "I will make this my home. I don't care if the Double R ranch house is a *paisano*'s *jacal*," she murmured, gazing out the window at the passing scenery.

When they reached Terlingua, Tate purchased a rickety old wagon and a team from the small livery. Everyone stared at the fire-haired *gringa* who carried a mixed-blood baby and traveled with a black Americano, yet their curiosity seemed more awe-filled and friendly than hostile. The ranch of the Robbins brothers was only a few hours away. They should arrive well before dark—a good thing since Terlingua's only accommodations were the rooms the *putas* used above the dirty cantina on the square.

When Lissa finally pulled the rented wagon up in front of Jess's house, she had a fleeting second thought. Tate put the cavvy in the small corral while she climbed down from the seat with a squirming Johnny in her arms and inspected her new home. The land was excellent graze, with a fresh-running stream and thick grass, hidden away in an isolated mountain valley. The cattle they had seen along the way were plentiful and fat, not the scrawny longhorns of the panhandle country, but meaty Herefords, obviously expensive breeding stock.

She scanned the scene, then returned her attention to the house. It was little more than a log cabin, flat and squat, with only two small windows visible from the front. The area around it, with the exception of one live oak, was starkly denuded of anything resembling vegetation. Dust blew across the front yard and piled in a fine silt against the heavy door, which was inhospitably closed.

"Sure does look deserted," Tate said uncertainly when he walked up from the corral. He had never been to Jess's place before, but had feared the worst from what his friend had told him.

Lissa set Johnny down on the bare brown dirt and commanded Cormac to watch the toddling boy, a duty the hound took very seriously. She walked around the side of the building, which was about twenty feet across. "I imagine his brother is off somewhere working stock for the day," she said to Tate as she inspected the bleak little single-story cubicle.

"Well, it is . . . sturdy," she said as she completed her circle of the building. Tate merely grunted.

The back had two additional windows, and each side had one, all covered with oiled paper in lieu of window glass. The front and back doors were made of heavy pine planks. She eyed the creek that curved within a stone's throw of the house. "Why in heaven's name, with such a good water supply, didn't they at least plant a vegetable garden . . .or something?"

Tate shuffled uncomfortably. "Most men livin' alone, they don't think much about vegetables."

She could have sworn he was blushing beneath his ebony skin. She harumphed in disgust. "They must've cut down every tree around to build the damn cabin. Well, let's see what the inside is like. I have a feeling I'll need to set to work right off." She scooped up the baby and dismissed Cormac, who trotted down to the stream for a drink.

She lifted the heavy iron latch on the front door, and it creaked in protest as it opened. Blinking her eyes, Lissa adjusted to the dim light inside. The main room was a combination of kitchen and living quarters, with a big stone fireplace on the east wall. The floor was planked, not dirt, thank heaven, but it was splintery and bare, coated liberally with the fine yellow dust that blew outside.

Furniture was rudimentary—a serviceable table with four chairs, an old and somewhat better-crafted pie pantry, which she suspected had been in the family for a while, and a washstand with a chipped pitcher and basin atop it.

Two doors led off the main room. She glanced in each. They were similar, both possessing large beds and a single chair. One bed was rumpled, with dirty clothes strewn about it. Several pictures sat on a small chest. The other was austerely bare, the covers smoothed carelessly across the rough mattress. *Jess's room.* He had obviously not been home to sleep in it for some time.

Lissa walked into Jonah's room and picked up an old photograph. The faded picture was of a tall, fair-haired man standing proudly beside a diminutive dark young woman. In front of them were two boys, the taller perhaps seven or eight years old and the small one little older than Johnny. Jess's fierce eyes stared at the camera from a hostile, closed face. His coloring was obviously inherited from his mother, even though the beautifully chiseled features bore a decided resemblance to the handsome man. Little Jonah was blond and fair-complected. *He's the white Robbins.*

Trembling, she replaced the picture just as the sound of a gun being cocked was followed by a deadly command.

"Drop your gun on the floor, stranger. Real slow."

Tate did as he was bidden by the yellow-haired youth with the 44-40 Winchester leveled at his gut. "You must be Jonah. Jess said you was the spittin' image of yer pa."

"Please, we didn't mean to intrude." Lissa stood in the doorway, embarrassed to be caught going through her young brother-in-law's bedroom. "But no one was home, and we've come such a long way."

Jonah Robbins quickly uncocked the rifle and set it against the wall, his face a study in youthful amazement as his gray eyes moved guilelessly from her to the dark child in her arms. "You . . . you must be my brother's wife and son."

He stared at Johnny with such awe that Lissa smiled.

"I never thought I'd be an uncle one day—and then—" His face reddened, and he cleared his throat. "Well, I never thought I'd ever get to see him."

"His name is John Jesse Robbins. Johnny," Lissa replied, carrying her son over to where Jonah stood. "You're his only uncle, Jonah."

"You're Lissa," he said, as if he could not believe it.

"And this is Tate Shannon, an old friend and partner of Jess's, who was kind enough to come with us."

Jonah offered his hand to the gunman. "I've heard Jess speak of you. Welcome to the Double R." He looked from Tate back to Lissa, uncertain of what to do next.

"I'll unload everything, then take the horses and wagon down to your stable and unhitch 'em. You folks got family things to talk about," Tate said and quickly left the cabin.

The youth's bright yellow hair and lighter skin were in decided contrast to Jess, but both brothers had obviously inherited their features from John Robbins. She handed the boy to him, and he took Johnny awkwardly.

"I never held a youngun' before," he said nervously. "Howdy, Johnny."

"He's become quite a good traveler since we left Wyoming," Lissa said, waiting for Jonah's reaction.

He looked at her uncertainly. "Jess never talked much about gettin' married, but I kind of read between the lines about what he didn't say." His face colored with a red flush.

"He didn't want to marry me—wouldn't have except for Johnny," she replied softly. "Then he left us . . . for our own good. People in Wyoming didn't approve of my marrying a man with Jess's reputation," she added bitterly.

"Yeh, a hired killer with a big reputation. But more than that, he's a breed and a greaser to boot." Jonah's youthful face suddenly looked harsh and old beyond his years. "I reckon you're right. He just wanted to protect you."

"I had more than a little part in my own downfall. No one could blame it all on Jess," she said candidly, meeting his troubled gray eyes. "He wanted me to go East, where I could pose as a respectable widow and pass Johnny for white."

"But you decided to come here instead," he said, a slow smile beginning to creep across his face.

Relief washed over her. She had an ally. "Yes, I did. I love your brother, and I don't want his son to grow up without him. Have you heard from him lately?" she asked worriedly.

"Not for several months—but that's not unusual," he hastened to add. "He's up in Indian Territory, chasing some pack of outlaws with big bounties on them. We need the money. We've been working real hard on improving our breeding stock, even selling some horses to the Army up at Fort Seaton."

"You must've noticed the cavvy we brought. When I sold J Bar, I kept a few of the best saddle horses."

"Yes, real beauties," Jonah said excitedly. Then her words registered. "You *sold* that huge ranch?"

She faced him determinedly. "It would always have stood between Jess and me. I put the money in trust for Johnny when he grows up, and no one can touch it until then." She smiled nervously and shrugged. "So I guess you and Jess are sort of stuck with us."

He looked at her in amazement, then threw back his head and laughed. "Lissa, you are something!" His eyes danced. "Really burned your bridges good. Jess'll have a real Injun fit."

"Yes, I imagine he will."

Johnny began to squirm, wanting to get down to explore. Lissa took him from Jonah and set him on the floor. Immediately he raised a chubby hand from the dusty plank. It was blackened with dirt.

"I think a woman's touch is long overdue here. Do you have a scrub bucket or rag mop?" she asked, once more eyeing the bleak little cabin.

He reddened. "Got a bucket, but no mop. I reckon I kind of let the house go, there's so much outdoor work to do."

"Tate will help you with that, if you'd be willing to take him on. He's done with guns." *If only Jess will do the same now.*

"I'd be real glad of the help, but we can't pay much now . . ."

"He'll work for food and shelter until the place starts showing a profit." At Jonah's relieved look, she smiled. "Why don't you go take a closer look at those horses while I unpack our things and see about a bit of straightening up before I start dinner."

"You can cook?" The joyous expression on his face was amusing, but at the same time touching. Had Jess ever been this open and guileless? Somehow she doubted it.

Just as Jonah stepped out the door, Cormac picked that moment to return from his foray down at the creek. "Jeezus! I knew you brought horses, but I never saw one built like this!"

413

The wolfhound cocked his head to one side, sniffing undecidedly as Jonah stood frozen against the door sash.

Lissa chuckled. "This is Cormac. He's an Irish wolfhound. They use them to kill timber wolves and coyotes up in Wyoming."

"I believe it," Jonah replied, still plastered to the door. "I'd bet on him against a pair of grizzlies!"

Cormac gave another sniff and then, to Jonah's horror, rose on his hind legs and planted his enormous forepaws on the young man's broad shoulders, giving him a generous slurp across the face.

"He likes you. It took him a moment to recognize the scent, but you must smell like Jess to him. Odd, he usually doesn't take to strangers at all, but he acted the same way the first time he met your brother. And Jess reacted just like you have," she added, laughing.

When Cormac dropped his front paws back to the porch, Jonah began to relax and gingerly stroked the dog's ears. The wolfhound's tail wagged so hard the floorboards vibrated. "He really could be a help with varmint control around here."

"He's also a good nanny," she said, as she picked up her filthy little boy. Until she did some work around here, Johnny would stay cleaner if he played outside in the dirt!

The following months saw some dramatic changes at the Double R ranch. Lissa quickly scrubbed up the small cabin and unpacked such amenities as table linens, a variety of cook pots, a set of crockery dishes, most of which had miraculously survived the bouncy ride from

Wyoming, and a bolt of brightly checked yellow cotton, which she stitched into window curtains. She had Tate and Jonah build doors for the two bedrooms, and once the latest bunch of horses was sold at the fort, they promised to begin felling timber to build an addition onto the cabin. The flowers she had planted around the house and the vegetable garden in the back were coming up nicely.

Getting used to the far more humid heat of West Texas was Lissa's biggest adaptation, but as the weeks sped by, even that paled in comparison to her fears for Jess, who had not written Jonah since riding into the deadly no-man's-land known as the Nations.

Her fears were kept at bay by her young brother-in-law, who had been forced to accept Jess's dangerous occupation over the years. She and Jonah grew as close as sister and brother during that long summer.

"You're nothing like Jess led me to expect," Jonah said easily one evening as Lissa was rolling out biscuit dough on an immaculate new table Tate had made for her baking.

She rubbed a smudge of flour from her nose with the back of her forearm. "Let me guess—he said I was a fineborn lady who was used to being waited on hand and foot. A princess."

"Something like that. He sure never said you could fry the crispest catfish in the whole blame state or fix up a dingy old place like this." He gestured to the brightly curtained windows, which now had shiny glass in them, courtesy of their last trip to Terlingua. A pot of fresh daisies decorated the kitchen table, and a pretty braided rug lay in front of the hearth. The floors had been sanded, scrubbed, and then waxed to a decent shine and the walls whitewashed.

Lissa finished arranging the biscuits in a tin pan and set them aside to rise, then went to the fireplace to check on the fat she was rendering in a big iron skillet on the grate. "Cooking over an open fire took some mastering. I'm still far from perfect."

"Aw, you're great, Liss, and besides, next time we go into town that cookstove we ordered should be there. Don't know why Jess never thought to buy one before."

"I imagine he never figured there'd be a woman here to use it," she said sadly.

The specter of her husband was always present. Every day that passed without word from him made them grow more worried. No one ever voiced aloud the possibility that he had died up in the Nations, but each secretly feared that Jesse Robbins might never come home.

Jonah had shared a great deal of their past with her, explaining things that enabled her to understand her husband better. One evening she had found a set of discharge papers from the Union Army for John Jeremiah Robbins, dated 1863, hidden away in the family Bible.

"Pa was shot up pretty bad at Gettysburg and sent home," Jonah said, looking at the yellowed papers that mutely bore testimony to his father's suffering.

"It must've been hard being Federal sympathizers in Texas," Lissa said.

Jonah gave a sharp bark of mirthless laughter. "I was just a baby when it all happened. We lived down near Brownsville then. Our ma's folks worked for the Running W."

"Richard King's ranch. I know," Lissa said. "Jess told me Mr. King was kind to him."

"He was a dyed-in-the-wool Reb, but he honored our pa's convictions. We had a pretty nice spread back then. House was a lot fancier than this one." His face hardened. "Night riders burned it to the ground back in '69. We lost everything. Pa was too crippled up to start over again. He died a month later. If they'd put a bullet in his heart, it would have been easier on him. Jess was barely fifteen, but he became the man of the family then. He got help from Mr. King for ma and me. Once a *Kineño*, always a *Kineño*. She went back to work as a housekeeper for Mrs. King.

"Funny, everywhere else the Rebs lost their homes because they couldn't pay the back taxes. Here my pa fought for the Federals, and we lost out just the same," he said bitterly. "That was when Jess had a price put on his head. He found out who done the burning. Couple of fellows from Brownsville were the ringleaders. Called themselves the White Knights," Jonah scoffed. "Some knights, dressed in bedsheets to hide their ugly faces."

"So he killed them."

"He shot them in a fair fight—hell, one sixteen-year-old boy with a cap-and-ball pistol against two grown men with fancy Colt revolvers. But they had friends—powerful Anglo friends—who were Rebs. They put a price on his head for murder. That's when Jess went to New Orleans."

"And took a ship to North Africa where he joined the French Legion?"

"We didn't hear from him for over a year. Ma was plenty worried, but then he started sending money." Jonah shrugged. "I don't know how he earned it if they pay anything like our army does. Maybe cards—or maybe he started taking jobs like he does now. Ma died before he came back. When he did, Mr. King had gotten the murder charges dropped, but we had to start over. Then there was just Jess and me. Been that way ever since."

"He's never talked about his time in North Africa, has he?" Somehow she knew this was true.

"It changed him, even more than what happened here, I think. But, no, he wouldn't talk about it."

How many secret hurts did Jesse Robbins hold behind those cool silver eyes? Lissa only prayed that one day soon she would be able to unlock his heart and free all that pain once and forever.

Chapter Twenty-Seven

The searing heat of summer at last gave way to cooler days. Roundup was done, with a tidy profit realized from the sale of their four-year-old steers. The three-room cabin had now been substantially enlarged with the sprawling addition of a large new bedroom with a smaller nursery adjacent to it. Jonah and Tate had even built two sturdy new corrals beside the stable. If the Double R was not an imposing kingdom such as J Bar, it did have the look of a prosperous small ranch.

As she watched her young brother-in-law bring up the wagon from the stable, Lissa looked at her home. "All it needs is Jess to return and run it."

At last they had received word that he was still alive. A bank draft for three thousand dollars had arrived the preceding week from the Nations. Jess had collected his bounty money. If the job there was done, why did he not come home? Or at least

419

write to his brother, telling him about his plans?

"Penny for your thoughts," Jonah said, then chuckled. "Maybe I should say a dollar, now that we're becoming so prosperous we can afford a maid."

Not wanting to discuss her fears about Jess, Lissa responded to his mention of Lucita. "We're lucky to have hired her from the Valasquez family. They were really gracious in offering us such an experienced worker."

Jonah shrugged. "They're the biggest *hacendados* in Coahuila. What's one more maid to them, more or less."

"Still, you're looking forward to the trip over there to pick her up." She eyed his new shirt and cleanly shaven face. "Couldn't have anything to do with Don Hernan's pretty youngest daughter, Ursula, could it?" She knew he was smitten with the girl.

His face reddened. "She's a fancy lady. They'll arrange a marriage for her with some rich *criollo*. I don't stand a chance. What have I got to offer her?"

"Honestly, Jonah, what is it about you Robbins men? You sound just like your brother. It seems life here has agreed tolerably well with me—or don't you consider me the lady Doña Ursula is?" She could not resist teasing.

"You know better than—" Jonah stopped in midsentence as he caught sight of the rider on the ridge.

Lissa immediately turned and looked across the valley to the big black stallion with the blaze face. His rider sat motionless, looking down with burning silver eyes at the transformed ranch.

Jess could scarcely believe the changes. Their cabin was double its original size and sparkled with whitewash. Window boxes filled with bright fall flowers graced every glass-paned window. The yard was green with grass, and several saplings had been transplanted around the building. Two corrals filled with prime horseflesh had been added to the stable.

Then the breath was squeezed from his lungs when he saw her. At first she had been hidden by the wagon Jonah had pulled up beside the house. Now he could see her hair gleaming like cherry flame in the sunlight. *Lissa. Here in Texas!* His heart slammed against his ribs as he rode to meet his wife.

Lissa felt her knees turn to water. At last, after nearly six months of waiting, he had returned. She was scared to death. "Please, do me a favor, Jonah. You and Tate take Johnny along with you to the Valesquez ranch."

"They love to spoil him. Be my pleasure," Jonah replied easily. "Of course, he'll insist Doggie-Dog come along, too."

Lissa smiled in spite of the nerves twisting her insides. "By all means, take Cormac along. He's down at the stable with Johnny now."

Jonah jumped back on the wagon and headed to the stable, where the lively little boy was "helping" Tate with chores. He gave his brother a salute and a grin as he swung the team around and headed off. "We'll be back tomorrow," he called out to Lissa.

She nodded but could not speak. Her heart was caught in her throat. More than anything, she longed to run across the distance separating her from Jess and fling herself into his arms. Instead, she stood in front of the house, waiting as he slowly rode toward her. *Don't lose your nerve now*, she admonished herself.

"Welcome home, Jess." Damn, her voice cracked!

Jess looked down at her, sun-gilded, even more golden than she had been in the north. Her hair was plaited in a fat braid that hung over one bare shoulder. She wore a low-cut Mexican *camisa*, a sheer white cotton drawstring blouse. A full, dark-green skirt of lightweight cotton came barely to her slim ankles. On her feet she wore *huaraches*. The simple peasant woman's clothes looked oddly right on her slender, golden body.

As he swung down from Blaze, he winced, then quickly straightened up, but she could tell he was hiding something.

"All this your doing?" He gestured around to the flower boxes and saplings.

"Yes, and there's a big vegetable garden out back, too. Your brother's partial to my snap beans." *What an idiotic thing to say!* She approached him, noting the way he favored his left arm. "You're hurt," she said, almost accusingly.

"Just a scratch. It's healing." He ignored her protest and went on the attack before the joy of seeing her permeated his reeling senses. "How the hell did you find this place? Cammie?"

She nodded. "She gave us good directions."

"You endangered not only yourself but Johnny, too."

"Tate came with us. We were safe enough. He's still here, working with Jonah."

"I can see they've been busy. I told you I wouldn't live off your money, Lissa."

She drew herself up angrily, then stopped short and made herself calm down. "We didn't use my money. Profits from Double R's fall roundup were pretty good. With Tate helping Jonah, they did really well. All I brought were my personal belongings and half a dozen horses to add to your breeding stock. Call it a dowry."

She studied him, the stubborn set of his jaw, the way he hooked his thumbs arrogantly in his gunbelt. He needed a shave. Were there a few gray hairs sprinkled in his sideburns and temples? She ached to reach up and touch his cheek.

"You shouldn't have come, Lissa. This place will destroy you," he said in a low, intense voice.

"It hasn't yet. I've been here six months, and I love it."

"I'm talking about six years—sixteen years—not a few months." He stepped forward angrily, as if he were going to reach out and shake her, then dropped his hands with a grimace.

"You *are* hurt. We can argue just as well inside while I'm tending that 'scratch'." She turned and walked into the house.

He followed. "Isn't this where we started?"

"No. It started when I interrupted your bath. Speaking of which . . ." She turned around and sniffed him, then added, "You could certainly use one."

"I'll go down to the creek after a while."

"We have a tub now, and the pump out back's been fixed." She watched him from the corner of her eye as he looked around the room. Then he took a seat at the table, appearing haggard and weary.

She turned and reached for the simple medical supplies sitting in a basket on the hutch. "Take off your shirt and let me see what new scars you've collected."

"Who's running J Bar for you? Cy Evers?"

She almost dropped the basket. "No, I sold it to Lemuel Mathis. I made quite a good deal with Cy's help. Cy told me he was wrong about you." She faced his wary expression hopefully.

He brushed the remark aside. "What did you do with the money? There must've been quite a bit of it."

"It's in a trust fund, in St. Louis. My uncle has invested it for Johnny's future."

"And you came here with nothing but a wagon-load of pretties and high hopes," he said harshly. "I could've been killed. Left you stranded here all alone."

"The thought did cross my mind from time to time over this summer. Jonah and I were both relieved when you wired the money. At least we knew you were alive." She looked at the tender red skin healing over the bullet hole in his left bicep. "Too bad it wasn't your right arm."

"I can shoot almost as good with my left hand," he said as she examined the wound. The instant her cool, soft fingers touched him, he felt a jolt that made him flinch.

"I'm sorry. I didn't mean to hurt you." She reveled in the heat of his body, the rough, familiar texture of his skin. And she began to tremble.

"It's all right," he replied, trying not to smell her orange blossom essence.

"We made a good living this year. With the new Army contract Jonah just signed, it should be even better next year. You don't need to risk your life anymore, Jess. Hang up the gun and become a rancher."

"It's not that easy. There are always things that can go wrong. Drought, disease, Indian raids from Mexico."

"Life's always a risk—anywhere. There are no guarantees, Jess. I'm not asking you for one," she said quietly as she cleansed the wound, probing to make certain it was not healing over putrefaction.

"You and Johnny could've been safe back East. No one there would've known about his background."

"Including him? Was I going to lie to him? He has a great deal to be proud of. Jonah's told me about your parents. Your father was a war hero, and your mother was a woman of rare courage, too. They had principles, integrity—a heritage I don't plan to cheat my son of, especially considering how selfish and ruthless his other grandfather turned out to be."

"You can't eat principles, Lissa. I watched my mother die by inches after we were burned out and lost the ranch. Pa may have been a *federal* hero, but Texas is reb country. My parents lost everything. Then when Pa died, Mama just gave up."

"You mean after you took your vengeance on his killers and then ran off?" Hot anger had been building to the boiling point in her as they argued. Her voice was sharp, and she saw that her question had taken him aback.

"I did what I had to," he said defensively, reaching for his shirt.

"You left her alone with a baby to care for while she was still grieving for her husband. That seems to be your long suit, Jesse Robbins—running away from people you love. Trying to solve all your problems with a gun." She set down the disinfectant bottle with a sharp thud. "You're a fool, Jess! You have so much bitterness welled up inside you that you've lost all judgment. I've traveled nearly a thousand miles, waited for two years, and made a home here for us to share as a family, but it's still not enough to convince you. Nothing I can ever do will change you. I've abased myself for the last time!"

Tears stung her eyes as she whirled away from him and ran for the front door.

Jess reached out with his injured arm, but she slipped free of his grasp. "Lissa, wait!" He swore as a sharp surge of agony lanced through his wounded bicep; then he followed her outside.

She raced heedlessly down toward the creek, where a dense stand of redbud trees grew. Not watching where she was going, Lissa only wanted to escape the pain clawing at her with its terrible promise of life without Jess, of her son growing up without his father.

He chased her, calling out her name, but Lissa was beyond reason. After all the endless waiting and hoping, something deep inside her had finally snapped. She dodged stickers and ducked branches as she ran alongside the sluggish path of the creek, splashing through the water. Finally, when the stitch in her side robbed her of breath, she crumpled onto the stone-strewn ground, gasping and sobbing alternately. Jess's voice echoed somewhere to the left through a thick stand of mountain laurel.

Jess searched the dense undergrowth with mounting apprehension, calling out Lissa's name.

Her words haunted him, hammering in his head over and over. Had he really been running away all of his life? The truth hit him, like scales falling from his eyes. His wife had never been one to sugarcoat the medicine. *His wife.* Had he finally driven her away for good?

Cursing his own stubborn blindness, he called her name again. The Texas brush was alive with poisonous snakes, wild animals—even rabid ones. She could be in danger. Then he saw her, crumpled beside the stream, a small, forlorn figure with her hands covering her face, racked with silent weeping. Every shudder of her slender body ripped through his gut. Jess stood frozen, trembling so badly he could scarcely breathe. *If I lose her now. . . .* Finally he said her name, low and hoarse.

"Lissa."

She raised her head and saw him standing there. Lissa could sense his fear, and his need. Scrambling to her feet, she flew into his waiting arms.

Jess held her so tightly that she could not breathe. Lissa could feel his whole body shaking so badly, she marveled that he could stand. She whispered his name softly, unable to caress him as she wished because he had imprisoned her arms at her sides. Instead she brushed her face against his and felt the wetness of his tears.

"Lissa, Lissa. I could have lost you—I drove you away."

The anguish in his voice made his words difficult to decipher, but she felt them in her heart. Finally, he loosened his hold enough that she could reach up and touch him. With wonder, she let her fingertips glide along his beard-stubbled cheek to touch the wetness of tears. His gray eyes glistened like the purest silver as he gazed into her face.

Her throat tightened as she looked up at the hard loner whom she had loved so long. Killer, renegade, outsider. All meaningless words. He stood before her now with his very soul bared as she knew he had never revealed it to anyone before in his life. Or ever would again.

"Can you ever forgive me?" he whispered.

"How could I not? I love you more than life." She cupped his face between her hands and looked deeply into his eyes.

"I love you so much it's always frightened me—almost driven me crazy at times. It's like an obsession, a fire in the blood. Only having you with me can quench the flames," he whispered as he lowered his mouth to hers.

His kiss was worshipful at first, gentle and reverent, a poem to the love and life they had almost lost. Then gradually, it grew fierce and passionate as the old familiar fires raged between them. She held him tightly, pressing her body against his, running her hands up and down his arms. Then she squeezed the bullet hole in his left arm and felt him flinch with pain.

"I'm sorry, darling." She pulled back. "You're hurt."

"Mostly just filthy," he replied with a laugh. God, how good it felt to laugh, to be free to accept Lissa's love. "We have the rest of our lives for passion . . . and the rest of our lives to be a family," he added as he put his good arm around her waist and began walking back toward the house.

When they reached the cabin, Lissa heated water and showed Jess the big tin tub sitting in the center of their bedroom. Soon she had it filled and ready for him.

He glanced around the new addition with its neatly whitewashed walls, bright curtains, even a braided rug on the floor. "Sure is a lot bigger than my old bedroom."

She smiled as she set several fat towels beside the tub. "That was only for sleeping. I figure we'll do a lot more than just sleep in here."

"You do, do you?" he replied with a grin as he pulled off his shirt and began to unfasten his pants.

"Hardly took Jonah and Tate any time at all to build it. I also figure, with you helping, adding on the next room will go even faster."

He kicked his boots into the corner and stepped out of his denims. "How many rooms do you 'figure' we'll need?"

She shrugged casually as her skirt joined her *camisa* on the floor. "Depends on how many babies we can make in the next ten or twenty years. Johnny'll be two in the spring. Past time he had a little brother or sister, don't you think?"

Looking at her silken curves revealed through her sheer cotton undergarments, he could not think very well at all. All the blood had rushed from his brain and traveled to another part of his anatomy. "You're so beautiful, Lissa."

She slowly slid off her camisole. "Life on a Texas ranch must agree with me."

His breath caught as the milky paleness of her breasts contrasted with the golden skin above them where her low-cut Mexican peasant blouses had left the sun free to touch her. He watched, enthralled, as she untied the tapes of her underdrawers and let them fall.

"I figure I'm pretty sweaty, too. And there's room enough in that tub for the two of us," she said, her eyes boldly raking his lean, naked body, pausing to stare hungrily at his pulsing erection.

"I like the way you figure," he whispered hoarsely as he approached her. "You must've bought that oversized tub on purpose."

She chuckled. "As soon as I saw it in the catalogue, I had to have it. It's not as fancy as the one at the Metropolitan Hotel, but I'll never forget you sitting there, all covered with soapsuds."

"Brazen hussy," he murmured as he took a pale breast in each hand, teasing the hard little nipples. She arched against him, following him toward the tub.

They climbed in together and knelt facing each other. He picked up the soap and began to work up a thick lather across his chest. "This bring back any fond memories?" he asked with a wicked smile.

She rubbed the tips of her breasts in small circles on his chest until his flat male nipples hardened. She looked down at the bubbles. "This might be a unique way of sudsing up."

He agreed with a sharp gasp when she took the soap from him and began to work the lather lower, down his belly, until she had slicked his rigid staff, then pressed herself close against him, trapping his phallus between her thighs. "See . . . washes everywhere," she whispered thickly.

They spread the silky suds from head to toe over each other, letting their hungry hands glide and caress, explore and remember every curve, muscle, nuance. Murmuring wordlessly, crying out with small gasps of pleasured surprise and amazement, they lost themselves in one another.

"Enough. We're clean," he finally gasped, seizing one of the pitchers of water from beside the tub and dumping it over their heads. Drops splashed everywhere as he shook his shaggy shoulder-length hair and she wrung out her waist-length mane of dark curls.

He stood up and grabbed a towel, then reached for her hand and pulled her up. After helping her dry the excess water from her masses of fiery hair, he took another towel and rubbed her body, then helped her step from the tub. Lissa returned the favor, drying his body with loving care, noting a few new scars, kissing them and the old ones until he tugged away the linens with an impatient growl and picked her up in his arms.

"Jess, your injured arm."

"The hell with it. I can't even feel it." He laid her on the big bed and covered her with his body.

Lissa's arms reached up to pull him close as her thighs opened and locked around his hips. "Now, Jess, now," she urged as he plunged deeply into her. She arched and dug her heels into the backs of his thighs, undulating as he thrust.

"At last. Home. I'm home," he whispered against her throat as her silky sheath squeezed his staff.

They both spiraled off in blinding bliss, as fierce as it was swift. He collapsed atop her for a moment, then began to move again, far more slowly, more gently than before, worshipping her with his body, kissing her face and throat, nuzzling and suckling her breasts.

Lissa ran her fingers through his straight, night-dark hair and pulled his head up to hers for a deep kiss, tasting him as she rimmed his beautiful mouth with the tip of her tongue, then danced inside. He slanted his lips across hers and let their tongues collide, duel and twine, drinking in the essence of his wife.

They moved in perfect rhythm, giving those tiny involuntary, unconscious signals to each other that only longtime lovers knew, telling each other whenever the crest grew near, backing away from the precipice, prolonging the perfection of union. Then, finally, it came, softly whispering over them like a spring wind on the plains, hot yet sweet with a promise that built and built to a culmination so powerful it left them utterly at peace. Whole.

"Did you mean it?" she finally whispered, her hand resting against the steady thrum of his heartbeat as she lay nestled against his side. "About being home at last—for good?"

"I meant it. I'm not saying I'll never strap on a gun again, Lissa. This is dangerous country. But I won't hire out anymore. The three thousand I sent was only part of the bounty. There's another eight thousand coming. I reckon it'll buy you a few more pretties to hold you until we start getting a real income from that Army contract."

She shuddered, thinking of the danger he had been in to earn that kind of money. "Just so you stay here with us. I don't care about anything else."

He looked down at her and took her hand in his, examining it critically. Her nails were shorter, but otherwise the skin was not reddened or workworn. "It's remarkable. You seem to bloom where other women fade, but I don't want you working yourself to death. We'll hire more servants."

"I don't need to be waited on, Jess. I love the work here. I never really belonged at J Bar. You're not the only one who's come home."

Her simple declaration stirred emotions he had buried for years. "You always wondered about my stubbornness . . . my insistence that you couldn't fit in my life or me in yours . . ."

When he hesitated, she caressed his cheek and prompted, "It happened in North Africa, didn't it?"

He took a deep breath and began. "Her name was Monique Dupres, and she was my commanding officer's daughter. They were some sort of land-poor minor French nobility. She was blonde and pretty—at least as much as I can remember now. It was so long ago. I was barely eighteen, but I'd been in the desert campaigns against the Tuaregs for over a year when I met her."

"You were dark and dangerous, exotic to her, and she was fascinated with you." She began to understand.

"Yes. Until Monique, all I'd ever sampled were a few Mexican and Indian girls here and some Algerian whores. She seemed like a goddess to me." He chuckled mirthlessly, but he could feel that the bite of old bitterness was gone. "As I look back on it now, I realize she seduced me."

He raised one eyebrow at Lissa, who blushed but met his gaze. "I may have teased a little . . ."

"A little? Anyway, we became lovers. She said I was her first. Now knowing what I've learned about fine white virgins, I know she lied," he said, gently tracing his fingertip along the curve of her cheek as she blushed. "But I believed her then and spun a lot of foolish daydreams. Saved all my pay to buy a fancy engagement ring. The night I was going to give it to her, the fort was approached by the rebel chieftains under a flag of truce.

"I was telling Monique about my grand plans for returning to Texas when her father interrupted us. He'd come to make certain she was hidden while the Tuaregs were inside the fort. He picked a bad time, since we'd just finished making love. He caught us in her bed. She jumped away from me and began screaming and crying that I'd forced her. I grabbed the ring from the bedside and told him I intended to do the honorable thing and marry his daughter.

"He laughed. Said he'd already made the arrangements for her to marry some fellow officer—a white man with a fancy title and lots of money. She knew all about it. In fact, she was leaving for Algiers the very next month to prepare for the wedding. I was just a diversion for her while she was bored, stuck in the desert."

For a man of his pride, Lissa could well imagine how devastating that must have been. She held him tightly as he continued.

"He would've had me quietly executed on some trumped-up charge just to keep her involvement with a 'sauvage' quiet. I was no more to the colonel or his daughter than any despised desert tribesman. But the Tuaregs had played Dupres for a fool. Their truce flag was a ruse to get inside the fort. They picked that time to blow the arsenal. Things happened pretty fast after that. Dupres lost over half his command and his own life before it was over."

"Whatever happened to Monique?" Lissa asked.

"She survived the massacre. The next week, when reinforcements came, she rode off to Algiers to marry her betrothed. I sold he ring and sent the money to my mother. The next time we had a liberty in Algiers, I deserted. Took a ship to Majorca and from there to New Orleans and home."

"And so you became a gunman," she said, understanding it all now, hurting for the body whose dreams had died so young.

He looked down at Lissa with a wistful smile on his face. "For years I replayed that scene in Monique's bedroom, remembering her lies to her father, the way she called me a *sauvage americaine*, a boy she would never marry. I heard the colonel's disgusted laughter. I knew the gulf that separated people like me from white society, and it ate at me."

"And now?"

"And now it's over at last. What you said about my running away from those I loved—it was true. I'd spent my whole life running one way or the other. But no more, Lissa. I don't have to live by my gun. I don't have to prove anything. I won't ever run away again."

"At last, home," she whispered as she kissed him, content and secure in his love. The specters of the past were vanquished forever. "Tomorrow we'll have to go and collect Johnny and Cormac and Tate and Jonah."

"That's tomorrow. Now, about those brothers and sisters for Johnny . . ." he whispered low.

She rolled into his arms, eager to begin the new project.

Author's Note

When Carol and I decided to do this unusual Western love story, we only knew that the heroine was a reckless and spoiled cattle baron's daughter and the hero a dangerous half-breed gunman hired by her father. Beyond the tempestuous pairing of Jess and Lissa, we had no idea what course *A Fire in the Blood* would take. As usual, our research provided the framework on which to weave a plot and develop our characters.

When I dug into the background reading, I found an embarrassment of riches. More has probably been written about the cattle barons and cowboys than any subject in history. For the flavor of their colorful vocabulary, I owe Ramon Adams a great debt. His study of their idiom, *The Cowboy Says It Salty*, was a delight to read. Mark Brown's *Before Barbed Wire* was a poignant and beautiful photographic essay. However, of all the background materials dealing with the way cowboys talked, worked, played, and thought, Teddy Blue Abbott's *We Pointed Them North* is the primary source par excellence. Teddy Blue's anecdotal reminiscences are earthy, vivid, and so hilarious I found myself laughing out loud as I read.

As always, the Time-Life Old West Series was a superb source of pictorials and history as well as bibliography. I especially recommend *The Townsmen*, text by Keith Wheeler, *The Gunfighters*, text by Paul Trachtman, *The Cowboys*, text by William H. Forbis, and *The Ranchers*, text by Ogden Tanner. These gentlemen are scholars who know how to entertain a writer as she researches.

For more detailed information on the Wyoming range wars, the politics involved in the Wyoming Stock Growers Association, and the exploits of such famous range detectives as Tom Horn, I relied on Harry Sinclair Drago's *The Great Range Wars*. A caveat about the infamous Tom Horn: Although my story is set in the 1880's, he did not become a household word until approximately a decade later. For referring to him in *Fire*, I plead literary license. No other actual historical figure would have served half so well.

Carol and I hope you have enjoyed our old-fashioned, shoot-em-up variety of romance. Jess was one of our more vulnerable heroes, and Lissa certainly turned out to be as bold and unconventional as any frontier woman. We like to think of our protagonists as actually having lived and hope you do too. Please write and let us know. A stamped, self-addressed envelope would be greatly appreciated for replies. Happy reading!

Shirl Henke
P. O. Box 72
Adrian, MI 49221

TERMS OF LOVE

SHIRL HENKE

Cassandra Clayton can wield a blacksnake whip as well as
any mule skinner and cuss as well as any Denver saloon girl.
There is one thing, though, that she can't do alone—produce
a male child who will inherit her freighting empire. Steve
Loring, wrongly accused of murder and rescued from the
hangman's noose, is just what Cass needs and with him she
will produce an heir. But Steve makes it clear that silver
dollars will never be enough—he wants Cass's heart and soul
in the bargain.

_4201-0 $5.99 US/$6.99 CAN

Dorchester Publishing Co., Inc.
P.O. Box 6640
Wayne, PA 19087-8640

Please add $1.75 for shipping and handling for the first book and
$.50 for each book thereafter. NY, NYC, and PA residents,
please add appropriate sales tax. No cash, stamps, or C.O.D.s. All
orders shipped within 6 weeks via postal service book rate.
Canadian orders require $2.00 extra postage and must be paid in
U.S. dollars through a U.S. banking facility.

Name_____
Address_____
City_____State_____Zip_____
I have enclosed $_____ in payment for the checked book(s).
Payment <u>must</u> accompany all orders. ❏ Please send a free catalog.

NIGHT WIND'S WOMAN

SHIRL HENKE

"Theirs will not be an easy path to travel, but they are fated to love." So speaks the Indian medicine woman when Night Wind leads his beautiful Spanish captive into the remote Apache stronghold. Proud and untamable as a lioness, Orlena vows she will never submit to the renegade who nightly teases her body into a frenzy of longing. For though his searing touch promises ecstasy, his heart is filled with hatred. A long-ago betrayal has made this man her enemy, but a bond even stronger than love will make her Night Wind's woman.

___4507-9 $5.99 US/$6.99 CAN

Dorchester Publishing Co., Inc.
P.O. Box 6640
Wayne, PA 19087-8640

Return To Paradise

SHIRL HENKE

Dazzlingly handsome, aristocratic and cultured, Benjamin Torres is everything Miriam wants in a husband. Yet the moment she sets eyes on Benjamin's half-caste brother, it is Rigo's bronzed, naked body she sees in her fantasies, Rigo's sardonic black eyes that seem to tempt her to indescribable transgressions. Those brief hours of ecstasy and betrayal will set brother against brother and ignite a firestorm of passion that only love can quench.

___4431-5 $5.99 US/$6.99 CAN

Dorchester Publishing Co., Inc.
P.O. Box 6640
Wayne, PA 19087-8640

Please add $1.75 for shipping and handling for the first book and $.50 for each book thereafter. NY, NYC, and PA residents, please add appropriate sales tax. No cash, stamps, or C.O.D.s. All orders shipped within 6 weeks via postal service book rate. Canadian orders require $2.00 extra postage and must be paid in U.S. dollars through a U.S. banking facility.

Name_____
Address_____
City_____State_____Zip_____
I have enclosed $_____ in payment for the checked book(s).
Payment <u>must</u> accompany all orders. ❑ Please send a free catalog.
CHECK OUT OUR WEBSITE! www.dorchesterpub.com

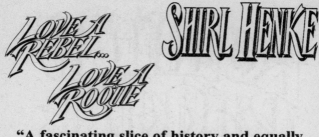

"A fascinating slice of history and equally fascinating characters! Enjoy!"
—Catherine Coulter

Quintin Blackthorne will bow before no man. He dares to despise his father and defy his king, but a mutinous beauty overwhelms the American patriot with a rapturous desire he cannot deny.

Part Indian, part white, and all trouble, Devon Blackthorne will belong to no woman—until a silky seductress tempts him with a passion both reckless and irresistible.

The Blackthorne men—one highborn, one half-caste—are bound by blood, but torn apart by choice. Caught between them, two sensuous women long for more than stolen moments of wondrous splendor. But as the lovers are swept from Savannah's ballrooms to Revolutionary War battlefields, they learn that the faithful heart can overcome even the fortunes of war.

___4406-4 $5.99 US/$6.99 CAN

Dorchester Publishing Co., Inc.
P.O. Box 6640
Wayne, PA 19087-8640

Please add $1.75 for shipping and handling for the first book and $.50 for each book thereafter. NY, NYC, and PA residents, please add appropriate sales tax. No cash, stamps, or C.O.D.s. All orders shipped within 6 weeks via postal service book rate. Canadian orders require $2.00 extra postage and must be paid in U.S. dollars through a U.S. banking facility.

Name_____
Address_____
City_____State_____Zip_____
I have enclosed $_____ in payment for the checked book(s).
Payment <u>must</u> accompany all orders. ☐ Please send a free catalog.
CHECK OUT OUR WEBSITE! www.dorchesterpub.com

TERMS OF SURRENDER

SHIRL HENKE

"Historical romance at its best!"
—*Romantic Times*

Devilishly handsome Rhys Davies owns half of Starlight, Colorado, within weeks of riding into town. But there is one "property" he'll give all the rest to possess, because Victoria Laughton—the glacially beautiful daughter of Starlight's first family—detests Rhys's flamboyant arrogance. And she hates her own unladylike response to his compelling masculinity even more. To win the lady, Rhys will have to wager his very life, hoping that the devil does, indeed, look after his own.

__3424-7 $4.99 US/$5.99 CAN

IMAGES IN SCARLET

SAMANTHA LEE

Allison Caine hardly imagined the road to Santa Fe to be picture perfect, but the headstrong photographer has to admit that she never expected a man sleeping in the middle of the road to bar her path. And for a man with no memories, the virile "Jake" sure seems built to make a few worth remembering. Snatches of his life are all Jake can summon of his fragmented past: swirling images of sheets of scarlet and a woman beneath. But now—a beauty that consorts with outlaws and whose lips promise passion untold—Allie makes him ache for the truth which is just beyond reach. Deep in his heart he knows that he is the man of her dreams and not the killer his flashbacks suggest. All he has to do is prove it.

___4578-8 $4.99 US/$5.99 CAN

The Cowboys
PETE

LEIGH GREENWOOD

Pete rides up to the Winged T cattle ranch with one purpose: to retrieve his stolen money. A self-proclaimed drifter, he is not a man to get roped into anything. But within moments of his arrival he finds himself owner of a cattle ranch and husband to a charming woman. His new wife looks at him as if he were a cross between Paul Bunyan and Wild Bill Hickok—a lot of pressure for a confirmed wanderer. But when he takes the petite beauty in his arms, he wonders what it would be like to be tied to one place, to one woman. For though he came in search of his fortune, he finds something far more precious: the love of a lifetime.

___4562-1 $5.99 US/$6.99 CAN

BY ANY OTHER NAME

LORI HANDELAND

From birth, Julia Colton's father taught her that the Jayhawkers of Kansas were the enemy—especially the Murphys, who took the Colton's rightful land. But when Ryan Murphy saves her from a group of Jayhawkers, she begins to question her alliances. For when he steps in like a hero from a fairy tale, Julia sees a tenderness in his blue eyes she has never seen in any man. Soon the star-crossed lovers will forsake their families and risk all they have ever known for a love stronger than bullets and deeper than blood, a love that is just as true by any other name.

___52252-7 $5.50 US/$6.50 CAN

Wild Fire

NORAH HESS

The Yankees killed her sweetheart, imprisoned her brother, and drove her from her home, but beautiful golden-haired Serena Bain faces the future boldly as the wagon trains roll out. But all the peril in the world won't change her bitter resentment of the darkly handsome Yankee wagon master Josh Quade. Soon, however, her heart betrays her will. His strong, rippling, buckskin-clad body sets her senses on fire. But pride and fate continue to tear them apart as the wagon trains roll west—until one night, in the soft, secret darkness of a bordello, Serena and Josh unleash their wildest passion and open their souls to the sweetest raptures of love.

___52331-0 $5.50 US/$6.50 CAN